DREAM BOAT

The Claudia Series by Marilyn Todd

I, CLAUDIA
VIRGIN TERRITORY
MAN EATER
WOLF WHISTLE
JAIL BAIT
BLACK SALAMANDER

DREAM BOAT

Marilyn Todd

This first world edition published in Great Britain 2002 by
SEVERN HOUSE PUBLISHERS LTD of
9–15 High Street, Sutton, Surrey SM1 1DF.
This first world edition published in the USA 2002 by
SEVERN HOUSE PUBLISHERS INC of
595 Madison Avenue, New York, N.Y. 10022.

British Library Cataloguing in Publication Data

Todd, Marilyn
Dream boat
1. Claudia Seferius (Fictitious character) – Fiction
2. Rome – History – Empire, 30 B.C.–284 A.D. – Fiction
3. Detective and mystery stories
I. Title
823.9′14 [F]

ISBN 0-7278-5818-1

Typeset by Palimpsest Book Production Ltd.,
Polmont, Stirlingshire, Scotland.
Printed and bound in Great Britain by
MPG Books Ltd., Bodmin, Cornwall.

This is for Mike Ashley, with thanks

Chapter One

'Kidnapped?' Claudia spun round. 'What do you mean, the silly cow's been kidnapped?'

Jupiter, Juno and Mars, give me a break. I've hardly caught my breath from Gaul, avoiding that final ferry ride across the River Styx by so narrow a squeak I do believe Hades' brimstone still prickles in my nostrils. You don't seriously expect me to believe a major crime has been committed the instant I return?

'Read this, then, if you don't believe me.' Julia thrust a scruffy piece of papyrus at her sister-in-law and rejoiced in yet another exquisite reason to hate her.

Not enough that this long-legged, money-grubbing trollop had lured her dear brother into matrimony. Oh, no. The bitch had wheedled her way to inheriting the whole of Gaius's estate! Julia sniffed loudly. They should be mine, she thought. Mine. His prestigious wine business, his investments, the country villa, this . . . her hooded glance took in the rare woods and opulent marbles, the eye-watering dazzle of bronze, gold and silver, yes, this should be mine, too, this magnificent town house. Not that – that – that *unspeakable* creature, perusing the ransom note in her high-backed padded chair!

Julia folded her arms across her chest and scrutinised the little office with its fine peacock mosaic, its maple wood desk encrusted with ivory, its wide double doors opening on to a peristyle alive with birdsong and the scent of white lilies. Under the laurels, that vicious, cross-eyed feline of Claudia's stretched and yawned beside a half-eaten mouse. Julia imagined it clawed the furniture indoors, given half a chance.

To the west, the sun began to sink below the rooftops, turning the sky a violent ragged-robin pink and now, listening to the gentle splash of the fountain in the garden, she acknowledged bitterly that hers were stale grievances, raked over so many times in the past ten months since Gaius had died that the repetition had begun to pall, even on her.

Until today.

Today, in *his* house, in *his* office (which this little cat had already had the temerity to redecorate), Julia was fully justified in adding another vitriolic string to her lyre. '*Now* will you treat this seriously?' she snapped. 'My niece, who – may I remind you – is also your stepdaughter, has, as that demand makes clear, been abducted.'

Actually, what rankled was not so much that Claudia had found the concept of Flavia's kidnap incredible – indeed, Julia herself had had to read the letter twice – it was sweeping in here unannounced in the middle of a heatwave to find nothing going on which really got her goat. Talk about insult to injury. After all, you'd expect, wouldn't you, to catch the baggage out? Find her cavorting with some fancy man, whereupon they could have denounced her and got the will reversed before she spent the sodding lot. Alas. Julia snorted. No man. Worse, no *sign* of a masculine presence . . . and she hadn't caught her sister-in-law disporting herself with gaiety, dancing or enjoying any other entertainment unsuited to the state of widowhood. Damn! Julia's fingernail snapped in her teeth. The last thing she'd expected (or indeed had hoped) was to barge in and find Claudia Seferius poring serenely over the estate ledgers!

What made the whole thing truly unbearable, however, was seeing Claudia's glossy locks, coiled and immaculate, and her robe crisp and fresh in the late afternoon. Absently, Julia's fingertips pushed away the straggles of hair which plastered themselves to her forehead and too late remembered the sweat patches under her arms.

By Hermes, did the gods have *no* pity?

'When did it arrive, this demand?' Claudia turned over the tatty sheet to examine the underside.

'Just now, of course!' Julia cried. 'It was the first thing we thought of, to come to you.'

And we all know why, don't we! 'Oh?' Claudia leaned back in her chair and threw one casual leg over the other. 'Why's that, then?'

'Well . . .' The older woman made a vague gesture with her hand. 'It's obvious, isn't it?'

'Because Flavia is just fifteen years old, you mean? The product of my late husband's loins, dear little child that she is?' Claudia flipped the counters to the end of the abacus. 'Sorry, sentiment won't wash. Gaius wanted nothing to do with his daughter, she was fostered to you from birth.' Foisted would have been a better word. 'So I ask again, why, if the ransom note was delivered to you, have you brought it to me? Incidentally, I suppose it's too much to ask whether you thought to question the messenger?'

The flush which rose to Julia's thin cheeks spoke for itself. 'We – that is, *Marcellus* didn't . . .' Recovery was swift. 'My husband is a prominent architect,' she reminded her sister-in-law, plumping herself down in a chair. Azure blue, indeed. Gaius would never have stood for such a gaudy shade of upholstery! 'He receives a score of letters every day.'

'They all look like this, do they?' Claudia waved the greasy scrap of parchment and the thought flashed through her mind that, yes, in all probability, a number of them would. Marcellus might be an architect, but he was by no means a prominent one. In fact, he wasn't even a very *good* one. Over the past few months his practice had dwindled to virtually nothing, and this was no mean feat when virtually the whole of Rome was in the throes of rebuilding – marble for brick, bronze for wood, pavements for mud! 'How much does he owe?' she asked.

'How dare you!' With a puff of indignation, Julia shot out of her chair. 'How dare you insinuate—'

As an actress, Claudia thought, she wouldn't be given a job in a crowd scene. 'Come, come, Julia, we both know the score. Sit down and take a goblet of wine.'

Claudia inhaled the fragrance of the rich vintage, admired

its ruby tints as it trickled through the fingers of the dying sunlight into the frosted green glass. She pushed the goblet across the desk, only for it to stand ignored. Very well. Play it your way.

'You imagine I don't know why you're here instead of Marcellus?' she asked, gently sipping Julia's wine. Typical slimy move, sending his wife to do his dirty work. 'Money, Julia.' Bushes were for idle cats to snooze beneath, not for beating round. 'Not out of concern for my late husband's daughter. You're here because you want me to stump up the ransom.'

The older woman subsided into her chair and scowled at the newly painted floral frescoes, the damask roses, the acacias and the heathers turning scarlet in the sunset. 'You can afford it,' she muttered. 'We can't.'

How true. Marcellus had been siphoning off Flavia's annuity for months – at least he had been, until Claudia severed the allowance. It stood to reason that, with his business in trouble and his income cut short, the next step would be to borrow and moneylenders (as Claudia knew from painful experience) bled their victims down to the bone.

Not that she'd been under any legal obligation to underwrite her wretched stepchild in the first place. Gaius' will was unequivocal. The widow inherited everything, the relatives not a copper quadran. Nevertheless, a – shall we call it goodwill? – gesture was enough to prevent either Flavia or her grasping foster parents digging for dirt, because the last thing that bunch of spongers wanted was to see their clover supply drying up.

Some charities, Claudia reflected, were well worth the sacrifice. Which was not to say she was prepared to indulge Marcellus's recklessness indefinitely! Idiot. Why couldn't he content himself with what every other person in his situation did? Cream a bit off the top and be happy? Claudia stared at her thin-nosed sister-in-law from under lowered lashes, saw the deep lines of dissatisfaction around the mouth, the permanent frown on her forehead and understood why Marcellus slept in a separate bedroom.

Pursing her cherry-tinted lips, Claudia studied the limp piece of parchment in her hand. Badly written, poorly spelt, there was no mistaking the message, though! Flavia had been kidnapped, they were to await further instructions. The consequences were unambiguous, too. Call in the army and Flavia dies.

Shit.

Under the laurels, Drusilla, her blue-eyed, cross-eyed, dark Egyptian cat, began to lick a languid paw in preparation for the evening hunt of moths and mice and crunchy creepy-crawlies.

'I presume you've checked that Flavia isn't staying with friends?' Claudia asked. The Games of Apollo kicked off in two days when there would be eight days of races and feasting and plays. Could this be some teenage prank related to the festivities?

'The girl has no friends,' Julia retorted, and Claudia could well believe it. A sulkier, more self-centred little madam was impossible to find. 'She simply went out last night and never returned.'

Something slithered around in Claudia's stomach. 'What time did you notice she hadn't come home?' she asked, instinctively knowing the answer. The poor little cow hadn't been missed until that note arrived!

'I've been busy,' Julia snapped. 'To make ends meet, we've had to sell some of our slaves, which loads extra work on me – and besides, the girl's old enough to come and go as she pleases.'

'In other words,' Claudia drained the goblet in one swallow, 'you can't actually pinpoint when she was snatched.'

'Now that's where you're wrong.' A smug expression settled on Julia's features. 'I've narrowed it down to last night, because the only things missing from her bedroom are the clothes and jewels she went out in.'

'Which were . . . ?' No wonder Gaius had had little truck with his doltish sister. She was as slow as he'd been sharp, as dull as he'd been shrewd, self-centred as he'd been focussed. In fact, Claudia did not recall Julia ever once tipping back her head and roaring with laughter, as her brother had used to do.

'She was wearing her best rose-red tunic shot with gold. A ring set with jade, another with agates, two matching silver armbands, her favourite faience pendant, gold ear studs and,' Julia finished on a note of triumph, 'the emerald pin I'd given her for Saturnalia.'

Good grief. The surprise is not that Flavia was kidnapped, more that she wasn't robbed! 'Is it usual for Flavia to leave the house dressed like a dog's dinner?' For a girl with no friends and with the Games not kicking off for two days, surely Julia thought it odd, as Claudia certainly did, that Flavia had gone out in her finery?

'Oh, didn't she tell you?' Julia's smile was pure reptile. 'That's why she's been all Apollo-this, Apollo-that, of late. You must have noticed her preoccupation?'

'Teenage girls fall in love with gods and heroes all the time,' Claudia said. One minute it's dolls and skipping ropes and dressing up. Next, it's spots, cosmetics and infatuation with either ruff-tuff, he-men types such as Hercules, whose bulging pecs and oozing masculinity sends them swooning in their pillows, or else they fall for the dreamy poet-cum-musician types. 'Long-haired Apollo with his lyre and romantic verses is always a hot favourite,' she pointed out. And – like every teenage crush – gloriously out of reach!

'That's as maybe,' Julia said, 'but it's been driving me demented. Her bedroom walls are covered with ghastly yellow sun discs, which she's painted herself, hundreds of the blessed things, and all because she's been invited to take the lead role in Friday's production of *The Serving Women*. That's when—'

'Yes, yes, I know what it is.' Everyone in Rome knows, you stupid cow! Claudia got up and began to pace the office. How many generations had turned to dust since that fateful day when Rome had been besieged by an enemy who took to demanding high-born female hostages? Quite for what purpose Claudia shuddered to imagine, but out of hardship, heroism is born. A humble serving wench gathered together a group of equally spirited young women who, disguised in their noble counterparts' finery, employed strength, cunning and resilience to turn the tables on their assailants and save the day. In return, Rome honoured their courage every year by re-enacting the drama.

'Exactly what connection does this have with Flavia's abduction?'

'No need to get prickly.' Julia bridled. 'I just wanted you to be aware that the Prefect organising the show felt our little Flavia was perfect for the lead. Not everyone gets selected, it's a tremendous honour for us—' Claudia's sizzle of a glare cut her short. 'Anyway,' Julia finished stiffly, 'the point is, she didn't return from rehearsals.'

Out in the garden, the trunk of the sour apple tree glowed like a dying ember in the last vestiges of twilight. In the distance, a trumpet blasted, a signal to heave open the great city gates. Would that a second blast could spirit away this carping hag!

'What about the authorities?' Claudia asked, returning to her desk. 'Has Marcellus notified any of the officials?'

There's a clue here, she thought. Something Julia had said . . . something which didn't add up.

'Are you mad?' Julia squeaked. 'You've seen what it says in the letter, they'll kill her!'

Claudia moistened a fingertip and ran it lightly over her eyebrow. 'I doubt whether anyone who spells authority with an "O" is in an intellectual position to find out,' she said dryly. 'I advise you to seek official help.'

'I will not,' Julia snarled, 'compromise this girl's life for a measly sesterces or two.'

Claudia heard her chair scrape across the mosaic floor. Then again, it could have been the grinding of her teeth. 'This is not a question of compromising Flavia's life,' she hissed back, 'it's a matter of basic common sense.'

The kidnappers *might* settle for a single payment. Then again, they might not. Greed is an unpredictable commodity. Moreover, they *might* return the girl alive, but in all probability they would not. No witnesses. No loose ends. Without doubt, this was a job for the professionals.

'So what are you saying?' Julia tried to shrug free the clammy tunic which was sticking to her back. 'I'm to return to Marcellus and inform him you won't help?'

Well done, Julia, you're catching on at last!

A mental picture formed in Claudia's mind. Her brother-in-law's lizard smile. Complexion like an unripe mulberry. How often over the past ten months had he 'just happened' to be passing, or (surprise, surprise) found himself seated beside her in the theatre? Of course, if she could just see her way clear to advancing a couple of hundred to tide him over until the next contract. Handing Marcellus money was akin to tipping water over sand, you never saw a drop of it again.

Claudia poured herself another glass of wine and drummed her fingers lightly on the table.

Except that was only half the story. Dammit, every time they met, his palm would contrive to alight on some curvaceous part of her anatomy and despite swatting him off like a gadfly, that sticky imprint seemed to linger for hours! Marcellus, you lecherous warthog, you can bloody whistle for your money and, Croesus, it would need a sturdier abacus than the one on her desk to reckon up the number of times Julia had cut her in the Forum or slandered her reputation!

And Flavia was turning into a right little chip off the sour old block.

Little? Claudia picked up a quill and ran the feather lightly down her cheek. Ho, ho, did I say, *little?* In the five years since Claudia had married into this family of misfits, Flavia had evolved from an awkward, lumpy, difficult child into an awkward, lumpy, difficult teenager. The only girl with less sex appeal than a plucked goose! Numerous attempts to get her married off had fallen flat, thanks to Flavia's outrageous sullenness, until it had almost reached the stage where they'd run out of decent families to approach. What prospects then? Unless the silly cow came to her senses, and quickly dammit, she'd be stuck for life with some dim-witted dolt of a husband – or worse, with an ageing roué who'd view her as nothing more than his personal prostitute to use how and when he wanted! Young women, as Claudia knew to her cost, were not in a position where they could pick and choose.

'That's it, then?' Julia blinked down her long, skinny nose. 'We're on our own in this, Marcellus and I?'

As the last trace of light faded from the room, Claudia traced a circle with her finger round the rim of the goblet. A smarmy spendthrift brother-in-law. A stepdaughter who's moody, rude and ungrateful. The sister-in-law from hell. I'd rather roll naked in a bed of stinging nettles before lending these deadbeats a hand!

Julia's narrow jaw was rigid. 'You're leaving us to cope alone?'

'Definitely –' Claudia tossed back the last of her wine – 'not. Count me in.'

Chapter Two

'I don't believe this.' Claudia paced her bedroom like a leopard in a cage. 'I don't believe I could be so bloody stupid!'

'Mrr?' Drusilla, draped lengthways over her mistress's pillow, twizzled one ear around.

'I need a doctor. I'm ill.'

She felt her forehead. It did not feel like a forehead sickening for a fever, but what else could explain the aberration?

'Hrr.'

'Oh, fine for you to say, my girl! You haven't landed yourself the job of tracking down a gang of kidnappers for a family you can't stand and who, in turn, hate your very guts.' She poked around in search of tell-tale swellings in her throat. 'I ask you, what do I know about criminal behaviour?'

'Brrp-brrp.'

'Other than my own, I meant.' Claudia stuck out her tongue and studied it by lamplight in the mirror. 'I ought to send for a physician,' she told the reflection. 'I have a terminal disease.'

What other explanation could there be, for not only shouldering the role of gumshoe, but – and this is what hurt – agreeing to settle the bloody ransom? Was she absolutely barking loony?

'You do realise, don't you,' she addressed the cat accusingly, 'that the coins in my coffers are gasping like fish in a drained pool?' She checked her skin for signs of plague or jaundice. 'The family don't know, of course,' nor did anybody else, 'but Claudia Seferius is broke. Skint. Borassic. Cleaned out. Bust, and on her uppers.'

Good grief, why else would she have been stuck inside her dreary office yesterday when she could have been out dancing, hurling dice or eyeing up the hunky gladiators as they trained? Someone had to stretch those stubborn bills!

'Bloody merchants.' She prodded her appendix. 'This is their fault.'

It's all very well having your husband pop off when he did, him in late middle age and the widow not yet twenty-five when she inherited his thriving enterprise, but what provisions were there for fellow merchants refusing to deal with a woman? Claudia pulled down her eyelids and checked the colour of her eyeballs. Poor old Gaius. Not such a bad old duffer, really. She thought of his bronze bust, dulling in the cellar and his ashes which lay crumbling beneath a marble tomb along the Appian Way. She supposed she ought to visit it some time.

She held out both hands to test for tremors and thought, if she didn't have the shakes before, the merest mention of her fellow guildsmen should surely bring them on! Her husband's ashes were still warm when the rotten sods had banded together in an effort to freeze the young widow out of trade. Their aim? To have her assets stripped from under her, her business torn apart, the proceeds divvied up among themselves. Well. Claudia Seferius, as they would find out eventually, was not the type of girl who could be bullied out of business. In the meantime, however, survival demanded drastic steps be taken: hefty bribes, for one thing; selling her dry, fruity red wine at a loss for another. And temporary though these measures were, right now her piggybank was emaciated to the point of collapse.

Claudia explored for tumours, listened for the first manifestations of pleurisy, pneumonia, bronchitis and wondered, what *were* the symptoms of dropsy?

'Dammit, Drusilla, the Games of Apollo start in two days!' Festivals and frolics, feasting and tomfoolery. Chariot races, processions, athletic events, theatres. Oh, and did I mention processions? So how does Claudia Seferius choose to spend her time? Playing 'tag' with a gang of kidnappers!

She hurled the mirror out of the window. Useless bloody thing. Doesn't even show up deadly rashes.

'Of course, I'd have a better chance at catching them, if they followed up with the ransom note they threatened.' Await further instructions, the original letter said. But for how long?

Is Flavia alive?

Resting her elbows on her red-painted balcony rail, the heatwave – what else? – pressed like an anchorstone upon her chest. Claudia let her gaze fall on the seething tide below. Dogs, oxen, wagons, carts and barrows surged and staggered, cranked and rumbled their way along the street by the light of dimly flickering torches mounted on the walls. Since Caesar's time, wheeled traffic had been banned during daylight hours (the streets were clogged enough), leaving only night-time free for deliveries too cumbersome to be transported in simple panniers on the backs of donkeys and mules. But short nights squeezed tempers as well as consignment times.

'Oi, you!' Red in the face, a wagoner transporting slim-necked amphorae of olive oil cracked his bullwhip. He was late, as usual, and the delay was always someone else's fault and never his. 'You're blocking half the bloody road, move over.'

'Sorry, mate, this here's my drop-off point.' The carter, his arms full of new roofing tiles for the house three doors down, staggered under the weight. 'You'll have to back up and go round the block.'

'The hell I will! Now you move that cart or I'll bloody move it for you!'

Traffic began to jam in both directions, and when the sweaty wagoner took it upon himself to lead the carter's mule down the nearest side street, sending a score of terracotta tiles crashing into splinters as they slid off the open back end, punches needed no encouragement. Gradually more and more drivers became embroiled in the brawl, pitching in with either verbal or physical abuse, until the rumpus had attracted half the population of the city, or so it seemed. Swarms of beggars gushed from the twisting narrow alleys. Pie sellers, cutpurses, whores, wine vendors – out they came, ever hopeful of cashing in on the occasion, and suddenly everybody was shouting over everybody else in an effort to be heard. No wonder they called Rome the city which never sleeps!

'Mrrr!'

'No one's locking you in,' Claudia told Drusilla, 'but I can't hear myself think with that racket.' Heatwave or not, she slammed the shutters and instantly the tumult dimmed to a throb. In her bedroom, a single lamp burned with aromatic lavender oil.

Where are you, Flavia?

'Frrr.' Drusilla uncoiled herself from Claudia's pillow and scratched at her ear.

'Yes, poppet, I know she's a horrid little beast and we'll all be glad to see the back of her.' Claudia considered her supper tray and selected a fat, pink prawn for the cat. 'But that doesn't make kidnapping right.'

Have they hurt you? Mistreated you? Are you frightened, crying and alone?

She picked up a still-warm roll, inhaling the smell of garlic, thyme and rosemary and found the aromas made her stomach heave.

Have they treated you civilly?

Pictures formed and dissolved in Claudia's mind and she squeezed her eyes shut. The possibility of Flavia being snuffed out like an old tallow candle sent a vicious pain through her head. She's too young, she thought. Too naïve. She'll be terrified.

When Flavia's mother died giving life to the girl, she left behind a daughter who Gaius didn't want and three sons who he did, with the result that Gaius used his famous bullyboy tactics to dump Flavia with his youngest sister, taking care to oil the path, however, with sufficient funds to silence any squawks of protest. No one could ever say for sure whether Flavia was miserable by constitution or whether being unwanted had rubbed off on her somehow, but by all accounts, she'd adopted an unlovable nature with uncharacteristic alacrity – scowling when she should have chortled, sulking when it came to playing games – so that when Claudia entered the scene, a scant five years back, the pattern was set like cement.

Flavia was miserable. This made Marcellus miserable. Which in turn made Julia even more miserable than she already had been.

Oh, Flavia, couldn't you have just *tried?* Met them, if not in the middle, then at least one third of the way? Recently, Claudia thought she'd actually seen a chink in the girl's armour. Admittedly, the visit had not been a social one – Flavia had come to whinge about her allowance being severed – but, like most teenage girls, she had become obsessed with her appearance of late and in one candid moment blurted out, 'I *hate* the way I look!'

'Did I tell her to stop looking? Drusilla, I did not.' Neither did Claudia tell the girl that the only person who could help her appearance was herself. 'With commendable patience, I pointed out that spots clear naturally, excess weight can be shed and that a good seamstress could work miracles on those rounded shoulders.'

However, before she'd even broached the miracles of cosmetics, Flavia had snorted, 'You just don't understand!' and flounced out, slamming the door in her wake.

'Mrrow.'

'Some of her behaviour is understandable, I grant you.' Claudia stripped the flesh off a quail for the cat. 'Gaius never made a secret of his irritation with his daughter.' Which would leave deep scars on even the hardest little nut! 'But you'd have thought Julia and Marcellus, being childless, might have been more receptive to the love of a toddler.'

Instead, Flavia had been given free rein to hone the only skill she possessed, namely being as perverse as she was able, and dear lord, was that girl able! Julia had grown more sour and more frigid with every year that passed, the family's only salvation lay in marrying Flavia off. Only here she had proved her claim to title of The Most Contrary Little

Madam in the Universe. She had categorically refused all suitors!

'No, let's be fair, poppet. More often than not, she repelled them.' Which wasn't the same thing at all!

For a brief, glorious moment, standing in the stillness of her shuttered bedroom, Claudia pictured the final denouement in the kidnappers' plan. That exquisite moment when the gang collected the ransom. They would gather round and slowly lift the lid of the money box. *Shock!* In place of a pile of shiny gold coins, they'd see only air. And at the bottom, a note which read 'Keep the bitch. We've had enough.'

Ah, well. A girl can dream . . .

Since the altercation in the street had now been resolved, dispersing with it the hucksters, whores and pickpockets, Claudia flung open the shutters again and stepped out on to her balcony. Shit. In the half hour since she'd retreated, a breeze had sprung up from the coast, thick and gummy, the sort which carries with it flies and biting insects, malaria and plague. Terrific! Any more surprises?

Below, black-clad undertakers moving, for delicacy's sake, under cover of darkness carried away a corpse on a stretcher. In the flickering light of the torch-bearers, she recognised the baker's mother, who must have been ninety if she was a day, and from her balcony Claudia saluted a final farewell. That's the way to go, she thought. Strong of body, clear of mind and knocking on a hundred. Not fifteen, trussed up like a chicken to be bought and sold as cheaply as a sack of sorrel leaves.

Long after the undertakers had wound their way down the hill, Claudia stared after them, and when the herald called out the hour, she could not be sure whether it was two or three that he called. Maybe both.

What greedy, twisted mind was so callous that it would put a young girl through torment? Why target Flavia? Heaven knows, Marcellus wasn't wealthy! Why not pick on the daughter of a rich merchant or (better still) an aristocrat?

The word aristocrat made something prick inside and – quite unbidden – a tall, familiar figure towered over Claudia's subconscious. Clad in trademark long patrician tunic and high boots, he speared his fingers through the thick, dark waves of hair which fell carelessly across his forehead and, with a twinkle in his eye, proceeded to reply to her question by reminding Claudia that the higher one's financial status rose, the more protected one becomes. Which, by his reckoning, left her as vulnerable as a new-born fawn.

'Sod off,' she told the laughing vision, but goddammit, the vision wouldn't budge. Tartly she reminded it that it was Marcellus who had been targeted, not her, she was only helping out here as a favour. She thought she heard the vision laugh and say, 'Like hell you are,' before it faded.

Damn you, Orbilio. Damn you to hell. She scrubbed her eyes with her knuckles. Wherever I go you're dogging my footsteps, intruding into my thoughts. She sighed. Any other man, of course, and she'd suspect he fancied her. Not Supersnoop. He was too damned businesslike for that! That aristocratic ferret knew trouble was attracted to Claudia like fleas were to a mongrel – he simply saw her as his personal stepping stone to the Senate. Fine. She didn't give a hoot for broad, bronzed shoulders and strong white even teeth. Who cared that he smelt of sandalwood, with just a faint hint of the rosemary over which his clothes were aired? And it didn't matter to her the way dark hairs curled over the back of his wrist, or whether a little pulse throbbed at the base of his throat.

Nevertheless, something tingled deep inside her. Indigestion, probably. She'd had nothing to eat since lunchtime.

All right, she thought, kicking her mind back on track. We've established that the gang targeted Marcellus because he's an easy hit and gives the impression (who doesn't) of being moderately well off. Does it therefore follow that he knows the kidnappers? Could this be personal? A grudge? It would explain the run-around, the wait, the deliberate drawing out of tension.

How much will the kidnappers ask for? How much is Flavia worth?

A faint greyness began to show in the sky over the

Esquiline Hill and, far in the distance, the first trumpet sounded, reminding delivery men that the gates would close shortly. Claudia rubbed at gritty eyes.

'Call in the army and the girl dies.' The note was explicit. She could not afford to risk it.

She would have to – her nails made gouges in the woodwork of the rail – she would have to go it alone and trust to heaven her skills were adequate. Or else the next bier being carried by the undertakers would be Flavia's . . .

Empty at last, the street reeked of horse manure and pitch, stale sweat and axle grease, the air cloudy with dust churned up by hooves. A latecomer clattered over the cobbles, racing for the exit with two dogs yapping at the cartwheels. Apprentices skulked back to their garrets, blowing kisses on the sticky air to lovers; there was just time for a quick wash and change before setting off for work. From the bakery, yeasty smells began to filter out, a harsh reminder that, despite death in the family, the wheels of commerce must still turn.

Why don't they come? Claudia wondered. Why doesn't the gang follow up on their note? Why this ghastly, interminable wait?

'Mrrrp.' Drusilla jumped down from the bed, arched her back in a sinuous stretch then poured herself through the balcony rail.

Goddammit, why don't they just get in touch!

Silent as a ghost, four paws landed on the porch roof below, padding softly over the tiles before being devoured by the shadows.

Merciful Minerva, Drusilla had given her the answer! The kidnappers were toying with the girl's family the way a cat toys with a vole. They want Julia and Marcellus to know who's running the show. They need to show them who's in charge!

Well, well, well. This put a different slant on things. 'To win the game,' she told her invisible opponents, 'one has to be pitted against a weaker rival. You're just to be pitied.' With one happy puff, Claudia extinguished the lamp and let the sticky breeze carry the lavender vapours into the night. 'Make no mistake, suckers! Your scalps are *mine*!'

Nevertheless, despite her upturn in mood, there was no denying who had the upper hand right now! They knew damn well they could pull Julia and Marcellus about like marionettes on a string and that, with a fifteen-year-old's life at stake, the pair were powerless to protest. Flavia was not the only victim here! The bastards intended that Julia and Marcellus should suffer too, until eventually they became weak and vulnerable, their spirit sucked dry by the kidnappers' vampire-like need to dominate and control.

What the gang hadn't reckoned on, however, was a third party becoming involved.

Blackmail Claudia Seferius? I don't think so.

She lay down on the bed and closed her eyes. You need to show who's in charge? Be my guest. If the need to dominate's so strong, it means Flavia's alive, otherwise you'd have nothing to bargain with.

Oh, Flavia. Where are they holding you?

Was she tied up in some dingy attic, gagged and blindfolded? Locked in a windowless shepherd's hut high in the hills? Was she too scared to cry? Or had she tried to call for help and been whipped for her pains? Was she sobbing into a dirty pillow, or convulsing with fear on a floor of tamped earth? Was she bloodied, bruised and beaten? Had the bastards raped her? She could be imprisoned in a ghetto on the Aventine, where one more scream passes without comment. Or held in a disused warehouse across the Tiber, where screams go quite unheard . . .

Dammit, Flavia could be anywhere!

And when you're fifteen, alone and terrified, that is no place to be.

Chapter Three

As the sun climbed slowly above the Mount of Osiris, bathing the valley in its honey rays and turning the ceremonial pool to molten silver, the girl called Donata could hardly breathe for the excitement. Everyone else would already be clustered in the temple forecourt, but since today was to be the most important day of her life, preparation was paramount and she paused to check her appearance in a disc of copper polished so finely that she could see every lash of her kohl-rimmed eyes, every carved line on her glazed blue scarab amulet. Satisfied that no pleat was ever sharper, no fingernails better hennaed, she dabbed a little musky perfume behind her earlobes. Outside, the rattle of sistrums, light and melodious, filled the still warm morning air and, as she ran across the grass towards the forecourt, she inhaled the fragrance of sweet gum burning in the brazier.

'You're late,' snarled a temple assistant, but Donata didn't hear. The sun was rising ever higher over the top of the mountain, and she closed her eyes in ecstasy. I am ready, Lord. I am ready.

Her eyes were still squeezed tight in piety when the High Priest mounted the steps, his shaven head showing clearly the strong, broad ridge of his skull which arced high above his ear down to his shaven brow.

The power of his voice reached out across the congregation. 'Hail to thee, Ra, in thy rising!'

Donata gripped her hands together and joined the chorus: 'Mine eyes adore thee.'

The High Priest spread his bare arms wide. 'Hail to thee,

Ra, who gladdens our hearts with the Boat of the Morning.'

Donata indeed felt her heart swell as she pronounced the second chorus: 'Beautiful art thou.'

'O Living Lord, rest thy rays upon the bodies of your servants!'

'Hail to thee, Ra, in thy rising.'

As the third and final chorus died away, the great gates of the temple swung open to reveal a magnificent replica of the barque in which the mighty sun god travelled across the sky by day and cruised the underworld at night. To frantic applause, the boat was wheeled into the open air by ten white-robed acolytes, five on either side, and Donata's heart skipped a beat as the light of early sunrise danced reflections off the silver and the gold, the lapis lazuli, the amethysts and the garnets. The Boat of Dawn! So lovely to behold, and soon – very soon – Donata would herself become a Bride of Ra.

'Let us give thanks,' intoned the priest, 'to the Great God, Lord of Heaven, the Giver of Life, without whom nothing can originate, that he has traversed the Realm of Night in safety and warded off the Serpent who waits in the dark lands beyond the West.'

'Thanks be to Ra.'

As the acolytes melted away, the priest moved forward to anoint the cedar wood with unguents while priestesses strewed rose petals into the boat and rattled the bells of their silver sistrums. The priest turned, reached into the soft moleskin sack which hung from his belt and threw a handful of what looked like soot into the burning brazier.

Whoosh! A soft explosion rang out, alarming the temple parakeets, and clouds of blue smoke filled the air, temporarily masking the entrance, so that for a count of, say, ten, attention was focussed on the hieroglyphs carved deep into the stone walls and on the alabaster sphinxes which stood guard. Then a handsome Negro began to beat on the shell of a giant bronze tortoise with a single fleece-covered drumstick, the resonant throb echoing round the packed enclosure.

Boommmm. Boommmm. Boommmmm . . .

The mist cleared, and to the tune of silver trumpets a procession of creatures half-human, half-beast glided out from the great temple of Ra. Led by Anubis, with his jackal head and wearing a golden cloak which swept the marble floor, the next in line was Osiris, a plumed crown upon his head, his blue-painted face covered to the mouth by a mask of pure gold whose cheekpads shone with the light of the sun god and whose almond-shaped eyes glittered bright with emeralds. Behind him followed other deities: Hathor, with her arching cow's horns; falcon-headed Horus; Bast the great cat goddess. With hands clenched into fists, Donata watched them form a V, with Anubis at the front, Osiris right behind him and the other gods fanning out on either side behind.

I am ready, Lord, I have prepared. Donata's heart fluttered. Could they hear her? she wondered. Did the gods recognise that she had followed her instructions to the letter? Her eyes alighted on Thoth, standing at the rear of the left-hand flank, his ibis beak pointed up towards the sky, his human hands holding out his sacred reeds and scrolls, and Donata knew instinctively that the holy scribe would know his servant had obeyed, for Thoth was God of Wisdom from whom no secrets could be hid.

Donata could hardly swallow. Suppose, she thought, suppose this time it fails.

The High Priest moved forward to Anubis and handed him a set of balances and an ostrich feather. Solemnly the jackal god accepted them and stepped to one side for the mighty Osiris to speak to his people.

'Know me,' he cried, holding high his sacred *ankh,* 'for I am the Lord of the Underworld and I am immortal.' A hush had settled over the congregation. 'Last night, the great Ra battled with the Serpent and passed safely through the twelve sacred gates to bring his light and warmth to my kingdom. At his hallowed touch –' the golden mask turned full force upon the sun, dazzling the spectators – 'the mummies of the dead shook off their bandages. Those who had been lame walked straight. Those who had suffered poverty in this life were given lands to own, and Ra breathed life into barren women that they might bring forth a child.'

An excited shuffle rippled round the crowd, and only Donata, it seemed, felt a weight descend upon her stomach. Don't let it fail, she pleaded. Don't let him die.

'Heed me, for I am Osiris, son of Ra. Follow me along the path to purity and blessedness, because only through me can you, when the time comes for hearts to be weighed against the Feather of Truth, advance to the Fields of the Blessed.' He paused and spread his hands in supplication to the sun. 'Father,' he said solemnly, 'Father, I am ready.'

Softly the drumbeat began again, this time with two fleece-tipped sticks. The High Priest lifted his eyes to an archer, stationed high on the wall and asked, 'And you, my child? Are you ready?'

The archer bowed, placed one hand upon his knee and said, 'With your blessing, master, I am.'

'Let it begin.'

At the High Priest's holy benison, the congregation fell to its knees. With his long shadow stretching out behind him, the archer straightened up and put an arrow to his bow. *Twang!* Straight to Osiris's heart! With a strangled cry, Osiris fell back, caught by falcon-headed Horus and by Thoth. Her hands to her feline face, Bast pushed past the others, who quickly gathered round the stricken body as the cat goddess cradled his head in her lap. Twice Osiris's legs thrashed, his arm twitched, then with an arch of his back, he slumped and lay still. Mumbling broke out among the deities as, wailing, they fell upon one another, hugging and weeping, the cobra with the crocodile, the vulture with the cow.

Down on her knees, Donata felt herself sway, oblivious to the moans and sobs which had broken out around her, and when Horus pulled a bloody arrow from the lifeless body of Osiris, Donata felt as though a knife had plunged into her own heart. What now? she thought, watching the plumed crown rock back and forth upon the ground. What happens to us now?

'Silence!' The High Priest tried to stem the mounting hysteria, as calls for the archer's own life grew stronger and more urgent. 'Our brother has suffered enough, let him be!' The devastated archer had broken his bow in two and cast his quiver to the ground. Now he beat his breast with a violence shocking to behold. 'Remember, it was the wish of Osiris himself that the archer should fire.'

Donata fought for breath. Shot through the heart with an arrow, surely Osiris could not return? But no, you must be strong, she commanded herself. Osiris has told us he is immortal and that, through him, the gift of immortality can be bestowed upon his people. Her eyes misted. Supposing, though, his heart was false? Supposing he had lied to her – to them all – and this was not possible . . . All her hopes and dreams would turn to dust, everything she believed in would tumble to the earth, crushed and broken.

The drumbeat changed again. Solitary strokes, loud and sombre. *Boom.* Anubis, with his jet-black jackal head, walked across to lay the Sacred Balance beside an alabaster sphinx upon a table of black granite. *Boom.* Black and white. Evil and good. *Boom.* On one side of the scales, Anubis laid a dripping lump of meat, and Donata's stomach turned when she realised this was Osiris's bloody heart. *Boom!* With the utmost care, Anubis placed the ostrich feather on the other plate and, with an audible hiss of relief as he stepped back, he watched them balance . . .

A cheer rose up, but Anubis cut it short. Osiris was dead and his heart weighed true, but could he be reborn? Yes, could he? wondered Donata. Purely through the way of righteousness, could Osiris be resurrected from the dead?

As cow-headed Hathor, her soft mouth offering up silent prayers, bent low over the corpse, Anubis replaced the heart into the bloody body and purified his hands in the bowl of holy water proffered by the shaven-headed priest. Donata held her breath as the jackal leaned over the corpse.

'Behold your son, O Lord of the West.' Even through the heavy mask, the voice of Anubis rang deep and melodious.

'Behold Orisis, whose heart has been found to be without evil, and whose virtue Thoth has recorded, Thoth from whom no secrets are hid.'

The ibis beak nodded solemnly and held up for all to see the Scroll of Truth where the judgement had been recorded.

'Once more,' cried Anubis, holding horizontal the sacred *ankh* and pointing it at the dead man's mouth, 'let the son of Ra walk among his people!'

With a collective gasp, the crowd goggled as the jackal lowered the holy *ankh.* It was true! Osiris *was* immortal! They could see for themselves the mouth below the golden mask opening at the same speed as Anubis moved the *ankh.* Donata felt tears roll down her cheek. Praise be to Ra, from whom all life is given.

Helped to his feet by Horus and Thoth, Osiris moved closer towards the congregation, that they might see the bloody robe for themselves. The arrow was then passed around, the head still wet and sticky.

'Know me,' he cried, 'for I am Osiris, Lord of the Underworld and I am immortal!'

Rapturous applause rang out, cheers and catcalls and whistles. Men and women wept openly, rejoicing in the resurrection of their lord, until the High Priest moved in to disperse the proceedings by pointing out that Osiris must rest after his ordeal in the Hall of the Dead. The remainder of his words were lost to Donata, because now was the time. This was her appointed hour. The moment she was to become a Bride of Ra!

Slipping away from the knots of joyous disciples, she edged round the wall of the House of Life in which the sacred scrolls were stored, past the holy pool and through a wicker gate in the temple compound wall. After the staggering events they had witnessed, no one else had yet left the temple grounds and quickly the high stonework muffled the babble of excited conversation until all Donata could hear was the song of birds celebrating the return of the Dawn Boat in their own mellifluous language.

The valley, in the early morning light, was never more beautiful, she thought. A perfect pear-shaped valley surrounded by lush wooded hills, protected by the Mount of Osiris at its north-west tip. The Cradle of Ra. The secret dwelling place of the Ten True Gods.

With no trouble whatsoever Donata located the ancient chestnut tree with its twisted, spiral trunk, for her directions had been clear and she had memorised them until she was word perfect. A gnarled old olive, twin hawthorns, an arbute still in full fruit, she clambered up the hillside past them all, hooking left, turning right, until she arrived, puffing and quite breathless, at the boulder shaped like a heart. For a moment, she considered sitting on the rock, quickly discounting the idea in case it held some holy significance. She had come too far to risk throwing it away!

Instead she plucked a twig of low-hanging poplar and fanned herself with the broad leaves. The last thing she wanted was to appear before her bridegroom out of breath and sweaty! She adjusted the lie of her shift over her bosom to better display her cleavage, and realised that the climb had twisted one of the straps which went over her shoulder. That's better!

Despite the solemnity of the occasion, Donata allowed herself a secret smile. Hardly the bridal attire her parents had imagined: a single piece of pleated cloth suspended by two thin cotton ribbons! No veiled headdress, no orange blossom, no carrying over the threshold. Or would she? Be carried over the threshold? For the first time, Donata realised she had absolutely no idea what this marriage involved.

True, she knew she would not be the only wife and that Ra came in many guises, both human and godlike – unfortunately, that was where her knowledge ended. Oh, well. She fanned a little harder. The uncertainly only added to the feeling of adventure, of a thrilling new beginning.

Peeping through the branches of a broom bush, from her lofty vantage point Donata looked down across the entire valley, over the high walls of the temple enclosure, over the shimmering rooftiles of the brewery, the bakery, the stables, and her pulse raced as her eyes scanned the royal palace of Mantu. Which of those rooms would be hers, she wondered? Glorious visions flashed through her mind. Of golden couches, lavish drapes. Food served on silver platters as harpists strummed in the corner.

A far cry from – where was it? oh, there – that puny arrowslit which represented her current bedroom window. Ha! Donata wouldn't miss that cramped crate of a room, devoid of furniture apart from a narrow bed, a chest and stool! Imagine her surprise when, two nights ago, she had returned from prayers to find a goblet waiting beside her pillow, full of wine. *Wine,* when only beer was served at mealtimes. Wine. The nectar of the Pharaoh.

Who left it there, or when, were mysteries, but Donata had drunk the wine and maybe she had drunk it too fast, because almost immediately her head had begun to swim, her limbs had felt weighted, paralysed. Figures had started to swirl before her in the mist. One minute Anubis, his black jackal head thrust close to hers, then the ferocious beak of Horus was peering at her, and then Thoth.

'Sister, you have been chosen,' Thoth announced, 'as the next Bride of Ra.'

With clouded vision and a drumming in her ears, Donata could not form a reply, but she recalled Thoth's ibis beak moving up and down as he informed her in a low undertone that the decision was, as always, secret and that if she told a living soul, just one, she would be discarded as unworthy for the god. Did Donata understand?

Donata understood. She had no intention of remaining among that lot of bitches any longer than she had to, and they'd find out soon enough that it was she, Donata, who had been the chosen one, and never mind their spiteful tongues about her squint. Ra saw beyond the physical and knew her spirit to be pure, and who would have the last laugh then, eh?

The following morning – yesterday – when she awoke, the goblet had gone and Donata feared it had been nothing but a dream. A raising of her hopes. A silly vision. But the directions had been so specific that, after the early hymn to Ra, she had slipped away and there, where Thoth had told her, she had found the twisted chestnut tree. And now, as she watched the hive of activity down in the valley below, the fetching in of vegetables from the fields, the harvesting of the beans and barley, she knew it had been no dream.

'You have told no one?'

Gasping with surprise, she turned, and saw that it was Horus who had descended silently from heaven to escort her to the bridal chamber. His falcon eyes glittered behind the mask, his long silver-threaded cloak splayed about him on the ground.

'Not a living soul, my Lord, and Thoth will bear witness, for he is the God of Wisdom from whom no secret can be hid.'

'Perfect.' The beak nodded solemnly. 'Perfect, my child. Now kneel you before this holy stone.'

Donata fell to her knees, grateful beyond words that she hadn't succumbed to the urge to sit on it!

'Close your eyes.'

Donata closed her eyes. She could hear a swish of clothing. Was it Ra? Osiris come to her? Or the blessed Pharaoh, Mantu? 'My lord, your servant waits,' she whispered. 'I am ready—'

The words ended in a gargle as something clamped round her throat and tightened.

'And so I am!' a harsh voice rasped. 'Oh, so am I, my beauty!'

Chapter Four

Claudia was taking breakfast in the shade of the peristyle when Julia came screaming in, clutching the message.

'Will you look at this!' she cried, waving aloft the scruffy piece of parchment. 'The monsters!'

Claudia speared a chunk of spicy sausage on her knife. Delicious. It had been smoked for months over pine ash until it turned red, and then grilled in the kitchen over charcoals.

'I should have thought, sister-in-law, you'd have affected at least a polite interest in the ransom note!' Lazy little baggage, breaking her fast at this ungodly hour, and her own stepdaughter's life hanging in the balance! Julia's eyes raked over the perfect complexion, the lustrous tresses, the immaculate gown and pictured Claudia rising late after a leisurely eight hours sleep, whereas she'd been tossing and turning all night with this bloody sticky heat, not to mention the worry, how typical that Claudia slept through it all! 'Aren't you even curious to read their demands?' The little cow didn't give a toss about Flavia.

Claudia popped a shrimp in her mouth. 'Not nearly as curious as I am about what the messenger who delivered it says. Ah, there you are, Junius. Did you catch him?'

There was no need for the head of her bodyguard to answer. Two burly henchmen appeared behind him in the doorway, dragging a ragamuffin urchin between them. Even secure in a double armlock, skinny legs thrashed out in raging kicks.

'Lemme go, you bastards!'

Julia swept over to the struggling youth. 'So you're the vermin responsible for kidnapping my niece!' A stinging slap landed on the boy's cheek, followed by a vicious back-hander. 'Where is she, you little shit? Where are you holding Flavia?'

'Gerroff me, you cow.' One foot caught Julia firmly on the shin and, as she doubled up in agony, the other kicked the soft part of her stomach.

'I'll see you skinned for that,' Julia hissed. 'Hot irons on your face, the bastinado on your feet!'

'Up yer arse, you ugly bitch!'

'Ladies, ladies.' With a flutter of her hands, Claudia indicated the henchmen pull back a pace or two and for Junius to escort Julia to a marble bench, whether she wished to sit down or not. 'This is no time for pleasantries. The Games of Apollo kick off tomorrow and the day after it's the Festival of the Serving Women. If little Flavia is to take the lead, we must have her catch up on rehearsals. Right then.' She bit into a peach, found it woody and tossed it into the laurels. 'From the beginning.' The raspberries were better, but the blue Damascan plums were juicier yet. 'Junius?'

The young, blue-eyed Gaul clicked his heels to attention. 'I stationed men around the house as you instructed, madam—'

'My house?' Julia was scandalised. 'How dare you take liberties!'

Claudia flicked her plumstone into the shrubbery. 'What measures did you take, Julia, to trace the kidnappers?'

'Me? Well, I – we . . . Good heavens, Marcellus and I never *imagined* . . . I mean, we were sick to our stomachs with worry—'

'Quite. Now, having established you did sod all, will you kindly let my bodyguard finish?'

'One hour after dawn,' Junius reported, 'this boy arrived with what I presumed to be a message from the kidnappers.'

'Liar!' The street Arab had by no means accepted his situation calmly, although the henchmen in whose arms he was trapped appeared not to stretch a single muscle between them in restraining him. 'This is a fit-up, lemme go!'

Junius didn't so much as glance at the wiry urchin. 'I

watched him deliver the note to the porter. The porter shouted to him to wait, but the boy was off faster than an elver.' The Gaul allowed himself a rare smile. 'Fortunately for us, we'd set an ambush and were able to follow the rat back to his den. *Un*fortunately, there was no sign of the gang.'

'One's a good start,' Claudia said.

Julia glowered at her sister-in-law. Smart as well as glamorous, she hoped that bloody wine the bitch was knocking back was poisoned. 'So you caught the messenger?' she sneered. 'That's no big deal. In fact,' her eyes narrowed, 'I wouldn't be surprised if your actions haven't signed Flavia's death warrant. Once the gang realise one of their number has been arrested, they'll probably cut their losses along with Flavia's throat!'

Claudia sliced a thick wedge off the green-striped melon on the table. 'What does the ransom note say, Julia?'

A sour taste filled the older woman's mouth. (Marcellus, how *could* you humiliate me like this, why couldn't *you* have seized the initiative? Why did it have to be this little trollop?) Julia flipped open the greasy scrap. '"Bring two thousand gold pieces, it must be gold, to the Camensis and leave them behind the right-hand statue at midday." Bastards!' She turned a venomous glare on the squirming youth. 'I wonder how haughty you'll look, my lad, facing down a charging rhino in the arena, you and your fellow scum!'

'Up yer arse!'

Claudia sliced off a triangle of pecorino cheese and thought, this is better than the Circus Maximus when it comes to entertainment!

'Just remember.' Julia picked up the hem of her gown and marched down the peristyle, wagging a long, bony finger at her sister-in-law. 'Flavia's life depends upon you.' And thus absolving herself of any further responsibility for her niece's welfare, she clicked her fingers for her slaves to follow and clippety-clopped out of the house, making sure to bang the door behind her.

'Midday, eh?' Claudia tucked her legs under her and perused the ransom note as she munched her way through a bowl of dark brown, sticky dates. The bastards make us wait all night, then force us to rush around like human whirlpools. Well, that still gives us three full hours. 'Junius, when I've sorted out the payment, I want you to take the chest and position it in the shrine, but be careful. They'll be on the lookout for suspicious behaviour, so no lurking behind trees, hoping you won't be noticed!'

The Camensis was a little wooded valley on the south side of the hill, consisting of a quiet shady grove, a spring and a shrine to the water nymphs who guarded it. But talk about a double-edged sword! Anyone hoping to stake out the area would be spotted instantly by the kidnappers, while the gang themselves would also stand out a mile!

Claudia drummed her fingers on the marble bench. 'This conundrum calls for subtlety and disguise,' she told Junius. The sudden appearance of a dozen heavies in a tiny woodland grove was hardly the answer! Three, maybe four men at the most to spring a trap. 'Hire a litter, wrap yourself inside a toga and—'

'Madam!' The young Gaul's eyes popped out of their sockets. 'I'm a slave! If I'm caught wearing the toga, I'll be—'

'Junius.' Patiently Claudia laid down the bowl of dates. 'Junius, try looking at this the other way round. Not what might happen to you if you're caught impersonating a Roman citizen. Rather what I'll do to you if you don't.'

She watched his Adam's apple gulp into obedience.

'Disguised as the spoiled son of a rich merchant,' her eyes defied him to so much as wince, 'you picnic beside the spring. You take a couple of girls, you sing, you play the lyre, you fool around a bit—'

'I can't do that.'

Why not? You're young. Twenty, twenty-one. But it was a funny thing about this Gaul. Claudia had never actually seen him look at a girl since she'd promoted him to head her escort. His eyes were always fixed firmly on his mistress, intense and rarely blinking. Which meant, she supposed, that he was either an extremely conscientious employee – or was otherwise inclined!

'Junius, if we're to get Flavia back alive, we have to make this look authentic. Since it's more than likely the gang are familiar with Marcellus and his family, friends, colleagues and acquaintances, you, as head of my bodyguard, will almost certainly be recognised.' Unless you go disguised as a rich man's brat with time on his hands, when your conduct would pass undisputed. 'Hire yourself a couple of whores – rent boys if you prefer – only for gods' sake, act the part. You're rich, you're idle, vulgar, brash. Draw attention to your profligacy, play on it. The more ostentatious your behaviour, the less anyone will suspect you're undercover.'

'Very good, madam.' His departing shuffle sounded sulky, but she knew he'd follow her instructions to the letter.

Claudia turned to the bruisers holding the ragamuffin prisoner. 'Am I imagining this,' she asked, 'or can I smell rose petals and lilies in my garden?'

The henchmen sniffed. 'I can't smell no flowers,' one said.

'Me neither,' replied the other.

'Then we are faced with the conclusion that something is masking the scent.' Claudia jerked her thumb towards the urchin. 'Take him to the bath room and don't spare the pumice stone!'

'Oi!' The voice was shrill in protest. 'You can't keep me here, I'm innocent!'

'Did I say you weren't?' She smiled. Deliver a message and then run off like quicksilver? You might not share a rat-hole with the gang, but you're in it up to your grubby neck, sunshine! Owing to the tight time-scale, interrogation would have to be postponed – but that was no reason to bring the smell of the sewers indoors! 'I am merely extending hospitality to a welcome guest,' she said silkily.

'Fuck you!'

'Oh, and be sure to wash his mouth out while you're at it,' she trilled over her shoulder. Sixteen years old and if this was his first introduction to a sponge, there'd be two days' hard scrubbing ahead!

'Hey!' Suddenly loud masculine voices filled the atrium. 'Hey, you! Come back here!'

From the corner of her eye, Claudia saw a flash of something brown and ragged hurtle past, saw him dive through the vestibule door. Dammit, I don't have time for this! She raced after the urchin, currently wrestling with the janitor. Behind, hobnailed boots echoed on the mosaic as they thundered to catch up. Claudia pitched in to help the troubled doorman. A hand lashed out like a cobra, and in the next instant both the oik and Claudia's bracelet were flying through the door.

Shit!

Bathed in summer sunshine, the streets were busier than ever. Boneworkers hawked counters, spindles and needles from trays round their necks, sackmakers praised their own seams and a water carrier sneakily filled his jugs from the sacred fountain on the corner while the warden turned his back. Claudia noted the progress of the tousled mop as it darted in and out of the shoppers. He was lithe, slim and supple, this youthful felon, but he had yet to understand that he was no match for a woman intent on retrieving a bangle set with pearls the size of ladybirds! Vaulting over a crate of clucking pullets and ducking beneath a bale of hemp, Claudia kept pace. Clouds of dust and feathers billowed in her wake, but she had no doubt she'd catch him – *and* her thick gold bangle!

Deftly he slipped down a sidestreet, and mentally Claudia punched the air. This was her cabbage patch this boy was on, and she knew every little sprout and floret! Swerving down the next alleyway, between the leatherworker's shop and the toy seller's, Claudia stuck out her foot.

'Oh, dear, you've tripped!'

Hobby horses, whipping tops, hoops and rattles went flying to all points of the compass as the urchin sprawled headlong over the counter, spewing out a tirade of filth matched only by that of the toy seller.

'I object to being robbed,' Claudia told the squirming youth as she hauled him off the counter by the scruff of his grimy tunic. 'I object to being lied to, and I object to foul language being used inside my house.' She jerked him round and slammed him hard against the wooden shutter of the shopfront, finding the crunch of his teeth under the impact eminently rewarding. 'But most of all, I object to the obstruction of justice when a young girl's life is in danger.'

'Please! Please, miss.' The street Arab's words rolled into a gabble. 'Here's your bracelet back, don't turn me in, only I need the money, miss, for me baby sister. She's very sick, I need to pay a doctor.'

'Nice try.' Claudia smiled approvingly at the trembling lower lip, the catch in the voice. 'Unfortunately, you need to practise those tears, and you somewhat overdid the wheedle.' She grabbed a handful of tunic from his chest and bunched it in her fist. 'Come along!'

'Never!' With a sudden twist, the boy squirted free, leaving Claudia clutching nothing more substantial than a lump of filthy wool. Bugger! Just when she'd got her breath back, too – and dammit he *still* had her bangle set with pearls!

Pie sellers and spice dealers goggled at the frantic chase, while those too slow to move out of the way found their toes crushed or else took to juggling their wares. The alleyways rang with shouts of encouragement, curses, howls of protests and cheers as the young woman whose long, dark tresses billowed out behind her snaked and slithered after a smelly, foul-mouthed youth.

What the hell have I got myself into this time? Claudia wheezed, charging through alternating smells of wood and molten copper, aniseed and paint. I'm so broke, I couldn't pay the ransom were my own life at stake, yet here I am, playing jackals and hounds through the mean backstreets of Rome to safeguard the life of a girl I don't even bloody like!

She hurdled over a box of squirming octopus and squid and ducked underneath a line of washing. Except, she thought, dancing out of the way of a small, black oinking piglet, personalities don't come into this. We're talking pond scum holding a fifteen-year-old to ransom, who foolishly imagine extortion is something they can get away with. They wish!

Dammit, this boy can run! There wasn't even time to pinch a date from the oasis Arab's stall. Up the hill they sped, along narrow twisty lanes, arching left, hooking right, and down the hill the other side, where paint peeled from the plaster on the tenements, windows were barred, and the stench from the runnels was vile. Twice Claudia slipped on cobbles greasy from rotting vegetation, blood, fishscales and discarded oil turned rancid in the heat, but still she pursued her quarry.

The boy was luring her deeper into the ghetto, but at least it wasn't a ghetto he was familiar with. This was the second time they'd passed that toothless drunk slumped in the doorway. Claudia's lungs were on fire. Her legs couldn't stand the pace much longer.

She thought of Flavia. This urchin was their only link with the kidnappers. Dammit, whose side were the bloody gods on?

Gasping, her lungs ragged, she lumbered behind him down another dark and sunless alleyway, no more than a double arm's span in width. What the –?

'Oh, Jupiter,' she puffed, and would have grinned had she had enough energy. 'I owe you one.'

The end of the lane was blocked by a twenty-foot wall.

The little fish was trapped!

Claudia slewed to a halt. At some stage, the owner of a town house on one street had wished to extend. Unable to go upwards, he'd bought a house in a parallel street and simply linked the two together, and to hell with the street in between.

Whoever he was, Claudia could have kissed him. Until she saw the knife in the boy's hand.

Chapter Five

It was a small knife. Obviously concealed deep within the urchin's tunic, probably in a specially sewn pouch. It was a last ditch-desperate knife, sharp and glittering, but it was held in a tight, professional grip.

'Back off, bitch!' The boy had turned feral, snarling and vicious in his fear and desperation. 'Don't think I won't use it.'

Frankly, the thought hadn't entered her head.

'I will. I'll bloody use it.'

Claudia's heart was pounding like a woodpecker on overtime. Her whole body shook. 'Go ahead.' To an outsider, her voice sounded calm. It was only inside her head that there was screaming.

'I mean it.' The boy's eyes bulged. Sweat cut runnels in the grime on his face.

Back off, a little voice cried. Leave it alone. You can't win them all, let it go. 'So do I,' she said, with commendable clarity.

Her mouth was dry. Her breathing had stopped. When fear meets an immovable force, there are only two possible outcomes. The boy had two choices: strike or lay down the weapon. Sweet Janus, there was no middle road.

The hand which clutched the blade trembled slightly. From anxiety or the strength of the grip? He had every right to be anxious. He'd backed himself into a corner, literally, and the error was of his own making. Pride, resentment, stupidity, weakness, the passions swirled around him like a whirlwind. Which path would he choose? The snarl meant nothing. Bravado. An authentic streak of viciousness. Only he could know.

Dammit, this could still go either way.

Crouched forward, the boy jabbed the air. To show he meant business? To stall for time?

Back off, Claudia. Now. While you can. Walk away. This simply isn't worth it. The voice nagged on in her head, but unfortunately Claudia Seferius had never been a good listener.

This was Life with a capital L. Precious. Precarious.

You had to taste terror to appreciate life, because without fear, there could be no highs to offset against it. You had to taste death to understand its opposite. *You had to gamble.* Claudia was a born gambler, and always the stake was the same. Adventure. The difference between tedium and the unknown; humdrum or the zest for living. And who in their right minds would settle for humdrum and tedious, when life turns on the spin of a coin?

The coin continued to spin.

Sweat stuck the cotton to her back, fear made the blood thunder past her temples. Time – precious time, maybe all the time she had left – became at once both meaningless and dear.

She thought of the coin. And wondered how long it would remain spinning in the air.

Time, already stretched to its limit, now became stuck fast at zero. In this dingy, narrow alley, street sounds from beyond were muted. Only Claudia's heart crashed like a boar in the undergrowth. Perspiration trickled down her forehead and dripped into her eye. She didn't blink. Couldn't –

Come on. Come on, come on, get it over with . . .

Suddenly – '*Bitch!*' With a wild lunge, the boy rushed towards her.

SHIT!

Frozen for so long, his mood shift caught Claudia off her guard. Almost. As he dived forward, she dropped to the ground. It was a move he hadn't expected. It knocked his knees from under him. Claudia latched on to his thin, bony ankle. He kicked free, but as he did so, they spun a full semi-circle together and simultaneously sprang to their feet.

The boy's furious expression told her all she needed to know about his feelings at being back at the point where he had started. Heart thumping, she followed his eyes. Frightened eyes. Angry eyes. Green as a feral cat's. Now the cat was cornered once again, and it did not know what to do.

With a high-pitched, ululating sound screaming from the back of his throat, he shot forwards, head down, and suddenly Claudia realised the coin of life had, after all, landed her way. The knife was held out to the side.

His body language told her his intention was to head-butt her in the stomach, not to kill. Just like the first time, she realised somewhat belatedly. Because by charging forward, as he had, he'd expected her to flatten herself against the house wall as he made good his escape. But still he ran towards her. With her breath suspended and his primitive cry ringing in her ears, she waited until the last possible second, made a feint to the left, skewed to the right. As she spun, she grabbed the boy's wrist and twisted as hard as she could.

'Aaargh!' With a sharp yelp of pain, the blade shot out of his grip and spun harmlessly back down the alley.

Jack-knifing him round, the momentum carried them both forward until they tumbled – praise be to Juno – on to a soft pile of fleeces, newly washed and ready for market. And this time, when she grabbed hold, Claudia made sure it was by the boy's hair and not by the tunic. White fleeces, brown fleeces, some with black spots lay strewn all over the cobbles.

There are times, she thought, blowing the hair out of her eyes, when life proves it can be worth living.

'This,' she wheezed, stuffing the scrap of tunic from their last encounter under his nose, 'is no fair exchange for my gold bracelet.'

The boy could barely see for tears of pain.

'Take a long, lingering look at the sun up there, because it'll be the last you see of it for some time.'

Claudia tipped his head up towards the sky, and her grip was as tight as a stonemason's vice.

'What do you reckon? Six years down the silver mines for conspiracy to kidnap? Add on theft and, oh dear, that's nine and whoops, I almost forgot the attempted murder charge, which I think you'll find neatly doubles your sentence.'

Claudia slid off the fleecy bank, jerking the thief to his feet.

'Still, dark as it is down the mines,' she said, and it was easy to be cheerful in victory, 'at least they provide their prisoners with decent clothing.'

Her eyes indicated the gaping hole in his tattered tunic and the urchin's grimy breast thrusting through the rip. A breast which also happened to be pert and round and full – with a rosy pink nipple peeking through!

'Janus!'

It was bad enough when Claudia had believed the guttersnipe was male. Now it transpired the hardcase was a girl!

Chapter Six

Due to increased congestion along the Appian Way, the horse carrying Marcus Cornelius Orbilio was forced to slow to a canter, and whereas a lesser horse would have registered its disapproval with several loud snorts and a repeated flick of its mane, this one kept its feelings to itself. The rider, however, being every bit as thoroughbred as the stallion, sensed the disappointment in the strong black shining flesh beneath his saddle. Comforting pats on its neck quickly mollified his mount and, with a twitched-ear acknowledgement, it continued at a happy trot, eyeing coldly, though, the plodding mules and oxen, the pedestrians and soldiers which had cut short its gallop on the open road. Look at them, the stallion snickered. Heat weary, trudging slower than a funeral. Poor breeding always tells!

Orbilio tossed a coin to a mother with a withered arm, whose toddler child was a mass of open sores.

'Bless you, sir,' she cried, 'oh, bless you,' and suddenly a crowd of beggars surged around him, attracted by the woman's vocal gratitude, only his thoughts had closed in to engulf him and Marcus rode on, as impervious to their pleas as he was to the beauty of the countryside, the dappled wooded hills, the shimmering heat haze, the waysides teeming with buttercups and campion, columbines and mallow. How could his boss do this to him? It's an administrative role, overseeing that the Roll of Honour was inscribed correctly on Mount Alban!

'Don't you think it's important, then?' sneered the fat toady who headed Rome's Security Police. 'Recording the participating luminaries in marble for posterity?'

'Of course I do, sir.' That aspect was not in dispute. Every year, both consuls plus all the other magistrates in Rome rode out to Mount Alban to make sacrifice to Jupiter at the long lines of semi-circular altars laid out in his honour. It was a solemn and religious ritual which culminated in the lighting of a giant beacon on the mountain, and naturally there had to be a record. It was his being assigned to the task that galled!

'Jupiter's balls, man, we're the Security Police!' his boss had bawled. 'We're not bound by bloody bureaucracy.' He snorted in derision. 'You don't expect spies and agents to be hampered by an army of clerks and scribes, now do you?'

'No, sir.' The sensitive nature of their work put them outside every government department, including the army. 'But—'

'The Mount Alban ceremony, Orbilio, involves every high-flier leaving the city at once. We have our bloody work cut out making sure that Rome remains secure on the one hand, while at the same time ensuring those illustrious dignitaries in the hills can sleep safe from the assassin's knife.'

'I realise that, sir.' If there was ever a better time to mount a coup, no one could think of one! 'It's just that—'

'Therefore, having achieved our objectives, I made a personal petition to the Senate to allow us to follow through this year and supervise the Roll of Honour.'

And in so doing, had tied Orbilio tighter than a hog for market! Stressing each official's individual significance in the government of the Empire, his oily little boss had added that he felt it only appropriate this should be reflected in the social standing of the officer appointed to oversee the Roll of Honour. It was his pleasure, he said, to assign the department's only patrician to said task, and naturally this was greeted with the predictable hum of approval. Bastard.

Reining in his horse at a water trough, Orbilio dismounted, patting the gleaming black flanks and inhaling the rich, leathery smell of the saddle. He knew damn well why his boss was doing this. To get him out the way. After all, you can't hurry a stonemason, not with that number of names to chip out!

Drawing a cup of water for himself, Orbilio sluiced it over

his face and allowed some to trickle down the inside of his neck. And with him duly sidelined, who would take the credit for averting that uprising in Gaul? None other than a short, fat, oily worm who would spread his pudgy hands and murmur, 'Oh, it was nothing,' and for him that's exactly what it was. *Nothing.* That slimy little bastard had sat back in his office, doing bugger all while Orbilio risked life and limb in Gaul.

Marcus replaced the cup beside the water trough and remounted. His boss, goddammit, had instigated no action, no policy, he'd not even sent him back-up. He'd just waited to see how events played themselves out. Then, once he realised Orbilio's hunch was on target, it was from his comfy office in Rome that he had distributed sheafs of propaganda and accepted the ensuing accolades. Indeed, by the time an exhausted Marcus Cornelius returned to the capital, having single-handedly settled the tribes and thwarted insurrection, it was to find his boss playing down the bloody incident and ordering him to supervise this sodding Roll of Honour.

As his horse's hooves resonated on the metalled road, the rich, sweet scent of honeysuckle, the low-pitched hoopoe's croon, the rasp of crickets in the long grass beside the road left no imprint on Marcus Cornelius. Somehow he had to find a way to dump this bloody quill-pushing job and knuckle down to some proper work. Rooting out forgers, frauds and killers.

But how? How? He wanted one day to take his own seat in the Senate, and he wanted it so badly sometimes it hurt. Apart from the obvious 'dereliction of duty' charge which would descend on him if he simply walked away from this wretched Roll of Honour, it would look as though he was sticking two fingers up at every senior government official as well as at the Senate itself. Damn. Damn, damn and damn his boss to hell.

You'd think he'd have given him at least *some* of the credit for taking on the Gaulish rebels single-handed. Oblivious to the chariots which rattled down the Appian Way or the melodious strains of a band of travelling musicians, Orbilio slowed his stallion to a walk. Well. Maybe not entirely single-handed. A smile played around his lips. He had had an accomplice.

Admittedly not a willing one, but nevertheless, without the help of a certain Claudia Seferius, the Gauls would still be at one another's throats.

True, *without* her involvement, it's doubtful they'd ever have considered a revolt, but that, Orbilio felt, was quite beside the point!

What mattered was that, together, he and Claudia had averted a national disaster, and what was his reward? A downgrading from what he did best, which was catching murderers and rooting out corruption in high places, capped, if you please, by rejection from the woman he . . . the woman he *what?*

Dammit, no, he wouldn't bloody say it!

An anvil slammed into his gut, as he pictured a girl with flashing eyes and flashing temperament, a girl who took life's corners on two wheels. Shared moments flickered in his memory: skirmish with head hunters; horrific wicker man sacrifices. The danger. The anxiety. Tense times when it might have gone either way. Through it all, though, whether crying tears of laughter or lying bloodied and bruised at death's door, there was not a single second when that wildcat hadn't been at the forefront of his thoughts. A lump formed in Orbilio's throat. How many times had he stopped himself from reaching out to touch skin softer than rose petals, from kissing the luscious dip inside her collarbone, from running his tongue inside her ear? He'd lost count of how often he'd imagined what it would be like to pull out the ivory pins holding up her hair, watch the heavy curls tumble down across the high swell of her breasts. Too many sultry nights had passed when he couldn't sleep for the desperate ache inside him; yearning to take her in his arms and make love to her, slowly and with care, the pleasure in the giving not the getting. Yet what had happened when he called at her house the other day?

'Do the letters FFO DOS mean anything to you, Orbilio?' she had asked.

'No-o . . .' Instantly, he was on his guard. 'Should they?'

'Try holding them up to the mirror,' she said, flouncing out of the room. 'See if they make sense then.'

Mother of Tarquin, did she think he had no feelings? 'Claudia!' He caught up with her in the peristyle. 'Claudia, you can't deny there's something between us, something strong and powerful and solid.'

She pulled up short, and turned her head away. 'No, Marcus, I can't deny that.' Her voice was soft. He'd had to strain to catch the words. 'Neither can I, in all honesty, deny that what's between us has a name.'

His breath had caught in his throat. Finally, goddammit, she was going to admit it! Admit to this surge of electricity which crackled in the air whenever the two of them were together!

'It's called,' she whispered, 'a marble sundial.'

Swallowing his grin, he'd tried another tack. He reminded her that wherever she went, trouble came up like a rash behind her. 'Someone,' he concluded cheerfully, 'has to bale you out of all your scrapes.'

'Marcus Cornelius, you are surely the most arrogant, the most opinionated, the most conceited man I have ever had the misfortune to meet!'

'You forgot to mention my devilish good looks.'

It was always like this. Bolts of white-hot lightning flashed between them, passion crackled in the air, yet whenever he tried to move in closer, to pursue the relationship, Claudia pushed him further and further away. Any further and he'd need to communicate by courier!

Why could she not acknowledge what existed: the passion and the sparks? Sure, she was scared of getting burned – she'd grown up tough, and that toughness had bred an uncompromising streak rarely found in women – but what did she have to lose by breaking the siege just for once? He'd never know, because that latest episode had ended in a quarrel, with her accusing him (him! a patrician, with lands and riches more than he could spend!) of being some seedy treasure hunter after her inheritance! Croesus! Orbilio had slammed his fist into the palm of his hand and reminded her that he was an investigator, not a bloody gigolo! He knew to the copper quadran how close she sailed to the financial wind and, unwisely perhaps in retrospect, he'd reminded her that she was, at that precise moment, stony broke.

It was an intimacy too far.

'How dare you!' she'd hissed. 'How dare you pry into my personal affairs, you grubby little ferret! I'll put up with many things, Orbilio, but I won't tolerate snooping, and if you ever so much as show your face around here again, I'll –'

He'd forgotten what exactly she'd threatened him with. A gelding knife, he believed, although that was immaterial. What he'd been trying to do, in his clumsy roundabout way, was to offer her his help, but would she listen? Would she hell! She'd drummed him out, with any headway he'd been making collapsing like so much rubble at his feet. If only he could find some way of making Claudia come to him for once, not the other way around.

The Appian Way became more congested the closer they drew to the city and he had trouble steering his horse through the crush. Peddlers up from Naples, fortune-tellers from Brindisi. Landowners departing the sticky city enclaves for fresher, cooler mountain air. Soldiers on patrol, making the roads safe for everybody, young and old alike. Along this stretch, tombs sprouted up to line the route, travertine or marble monuments to the lives of merchants, marshals and magistrates including, ahead there on the right, the circular turret of Gaius Seferius.

Orbilio reined in beside it, wiping his brow with the back of his hand. Remus, it was hot! Shading his eyes, he glanced up at the sun, directly overhead and casting virtually no shadow. Noon. No time to be out in this scorching, vile heat, yet he lingered beside the tomb, reading Gaius's life story in the frieze which ran around it. Like most others, it had been neatly edited, but there he was, the wine merchant, surrounded by his vines and scribes, and Orbilio placed his fist on his heart in salute. He had liked Gaius. Forthright, irascible, shrewd and funny . . . nevertheless he didn't mourn too deeply the big man's passing, for it left the field wide open for his widow!

The same widow who, at twenty-four, had inherited the whole shebang and found, almost immediately, that those men who had once been Gaius's friends were suddenly her enemies. Enemies who would not tolerate a woman merchant, who had first tried to buy her out and when that failed, set their course to freeze her out. Inasmuch as he had a vested interest in this human tornado, Orbilio knew she'd taken to passing on hefty bribes of late, as well as selling her wine at a loss to give people the impression the business was succeeding. Oh, Claudia. Why don't you ever let anyone help?

'Gee up!'

Marcus guided his horse through the army of herders steering pigs and sheep, goats and cattle into town. He picked his way past rickety wagons up from Campania, through squads of high-spirited schoolboys making the most of the holidays, through a veritable sea of servants, porters and slaves on errands, his horse snorting down its pedigree nose at this honking, braying, bleating throng.

Orbilio plodded on, up the Slope of Mars, past the temple of the god of war and along the covered portico, whose welcome shade invited many travellers to stop and snooze a while. What he needed, he reflected, was a meaty investigation to sink his teeth in, a case dramatic enough to justify delegating the Roll of Honour to a junior. Murder would be his first choice, although a juicy kidnap, a senator dabbling in a spot of forgery, a general up to his epaulettes in fraud, no, he wouldn't sneeze at those. Passing through the Capena Gate, he realised it would have to be a prestigious family involved, or he'd not be able to extricate himself from this administrative role, but where oh where was Orbilio going to find a family with such an obliging skeleton tucked up in its closet?

He sent a silent prayer to Jupiter, Bringer of Justice, to deliver him such a case and then, for the remainder of his ride, let his mind drift on a woman who not so much hit the ground running, as hit it like a spinning top. Why is it, he wondered, that whenever I'm with Claudia, I'm completely lost for words?

Outside his townhouse on the Esquiline Hill, Orbilio swung himself out of the saddle. Perhaps he ought to pay her a call? Pretend he was passing and—

'Master! Master Orbilio, come quickly!'

'Tingi?' In all the years this mournful Libyan had been his steward, Marcus had never seen him flustered. 'Whatever's the matter, man?'

'The new banqueting hall, sir. It's terrible! Really terrible.'

Mother of Tarquin, was that all? For a minute, Orbilio had thought it was something serious, not just a problem with the extension he was planning. Builders! Has one ever come and gone without leaving a bigger mess behind?

'Don't worry about it, Tingi.' He brushed the dust from his tunic with a ox-tail whisk and slapped his boots. 'The room will look fine when it's finished.'

Being a town house, expansion wasn't easy, but it had occurred to Orbilio that if he extended the room behind his office – that old storeroom no one ever bothered with – to run the whole length of the courtyard, then he could have a dining hall suited to entertaining on a grand scale and perfect for all weathers.

'No, no, sir. It's the wall.'

'Exactly, Tingi!' Marcus slapped his steward on the shoulder. 'I don't want a wall, that's the point.' He wanted sliding doors, which would open the length of the room to merge the dining hall with the garden. Perfect for summer banquets!

Inside the atrium, he paused to acclimatise to the dappled shade cast by a tall, honeycomb screen which brought a coolness to the room in stark contrast to the sweltering heat outdoors. Here, the air was fragrant with incense and myrrh, and with laurel which was sacred to Mars.

'I'll have a light lunch of cheese and fruit, then I'm off to the baths.' Followed (yes, he was sure now!) by a visit to Claudia Seferius.

'The wall, sir –' the Libyan paused, slowly shaking his head. 'There's no way I can describe it, you must see for yourself.'

Perhaps this torrid heat made him pine for his desert homelands? Orbilio decided to humour him, because Tingi wouldn't fuss over nothing. Woodworm? Dry rot? A prickle of unease ran down the young investigator's spine. There was a look on his steward's face . . . Commiseration? Sympathy? For what? Curious, Marcus followed him down the peristyle, past the kitchens, past his office to the little storeroom.

'Where the hell are the builders?' he roared. This dry weather won't hold for ever, I've got rafters, tiles, wooden panels piled up round my garden, where have the lazy sods sloped off to?

'I sent them away,' Tingi said, 'because, look!' He led the way over the rubble in the storeroom and pointed to the far wall.

That shouldn't still be standing, for a start! Orbilio fumed. What are the silly buggers playing at? Then he followed the ashen glance of his steward. '*Shit!*' He clambered over the rubble, skinning his knuckles and shins as he slipped on the stones. 'Holy bloody shit.' With his bare hands, he pulled at the plaster, enlarging the gap begun by the demolition men.

'As soon as I realised, I ordered work to stop,' Tingi was saying, but Marcus didn't hear. His head was spinning.

He had wanted a reason to abandon the Roll of Honour, hadn't he? Well, he'd certainly got one now! Wiping his mouth, he peered again into the cavity.

At the human skeleton walled up inside his plaster.

Chapter Seven

The old hag and her granddaughter pushed their way through the crowd. 'Alms,' the old woman croaked. 'Alms for a poor starving widow.'

'Sod off,' said the fishmonger.

'Get lost,' snapped the basket weaver.

'We don't want your sort round here,' growled the money-changers, goldsmiths and bards.

Bent-backed and with her moth-eaten shawl low over her face, the old crone shuffled on down the street, her stick clacking over the cobblestones. 'Alms,' she cried. 'Alms for a blind, starving widow.'

'Piss off,' the shopkeepers jeered.

And so the poor old dame was bulldozed further and further down the hill, every man, woman and child repelled as much by the sewn-down eye socket as the rags which hung limp on her body.

'Get out of here, you old hag!'

'You're putting my customers off, move along!'

Finally there was nowhere else to go. No one left to turn to. Exhausted by the heat and the jostling, the constant hammering of wheelwrights and the whirr of carpenters' drills, the sorry pair turned into the wooded grove protected by the sprites of the spring.

'I don't see why you had to lug me along!'

'Want doesn't come into it,' Claudia snapped. 'You owe me some answers, and you can start by giving your name.'

'They call me Flea.'

Don't ask, Claudia. Just don't ask.

'Dunno why you had to throw me in the bloody bath first, either.' Flea sniffed. 'Scrubbed up, I look like a bleeding girl.'

'I hate to be the one who breaks the bad news,' Claudia replied, 'but Flea, you *are* a girl.' Already, the shackles keeping them together were beginning to chafe. And that damned eye patch was itching like hell!

'Yeah, well I live on the streets, remember? As long as they believe I'm another bloke, I'm safe.'

'Really?' The old woman jerked her granddaughter against a sycamore trunk. 'Next time you're nabbed, you imagine it'll be another woman who accidentally exposes your breasts down some dark, lonely lane?'

'I can handle trouble.'

Claudia thought of the knife, and wondered whether Flea was deluding herself or whether this was merely bluster. 'All right. This man, whose purse-strings you've just cut. You think he'll let you go with a stern word of caution once your bountiful secrets are in the open? Grow up, Flea! We're talking rape!' A foul, degrading, painful violation, which will leave you scarred inside and out – trust me, girl, I *know*. 'Or do you imagine boys have bouncy bits on their chests, too?'

'I bandage 'em flat,' Flea retorted. 'I ain't bloody stupid.'

'Anyone who steals for a living is stupid – and spare me the hard-done-by expression, please. Mine wasn't the first bangle you purloined.'

'Ain't nothing wrong with thieving. I don't take from those what can't afford it, and it beats whoring any day.'

'There are alternative professions.'

'Not where I come from.' Flea sneered. 'You see 'em every day – pimps, ponces – prowling round the gutters in search of fresh brothelmeat to hawk. Well, you won't catch me selling me body to some greasy Sarmatian or letting some filthy pervert use me as his experiment!'

'And pretty boys are of no interest to these pimps?'

Flea's eyes narrowed suspiciously. 'You been there, have yer?' Her jaw dropped. The ghetto leave traces for those who know where to look. 'You have! You bloody have, an' all!'

'Me?' Claudia stuck out her tongue. 'My dear child, the imprint's still visible from the good old silver spoon.'

Flea's reply was nothing if not succinct.

The Camensis was quiet in the postprandial heat, only the odd sunbather, two slaves walking their masters' dogs, a blacksmith snatching a late lunch. Down by the spring, children watched by a laughing nursemaid squealed and splashed naked in the water margins, throwing bulrush javelins, while a middle-aged caulker, still in his pitch-covered apron, sobbed his heart out against the side wall of the shrine. A dearth, however, of young bucks cavorting with strumpets.

'You just leave me alone, will ya.' Flea wriggled and squirmed, but the manacles refused to slide past her wrist. 'Mind yer own bleeding business for a change.'

'Very well.' The old woman pointed a shaky stick to the shade of an oak. 'Let's sit there and talk about my business. One. You delivered the ransom note to Julia's house. Two—'

'I explained that, right? Some geezer slipped me twenty-five sesterces—'

'A chap you'd never seen before. Yes, you said. And when Junius ran you to ground, how strange you didn't have them on you, or stashed away in that rat-hole you call home.'

Flea side-stepped a pile of steaming horse manure. 'I told you that, as well. I'd spent 'em.'

'On what? Fancy clothes and fripperies? An alabaster lamp? A feather mattress?' The girl was lying through her pretty straight white teeth. 'Then, of course, you ran away.' Not just scampered down the street, either. This wretch flew off as though her heels were on fire!

'So? The bloke who paid me said, hand over that note and scarper. So I scarpered.'

'Olympic athletes rarely find that pace.'

'Hey,' Flea whined. 'I'd have told you if I knew the geezer – honest. Same as I don't know nothing about no kidnap, either.'

Ah, but you do, my parasitic friend. You know much more than you're letting on. What remains to be established, however, is just *how* much you're aware of, because it's possible someone is using you without you realising it. Unfortunately, the trouble with streetwise kids like Flea is that their trust can't be hurried. Like hunting tigers in the jungle, it requires patience, bait and cunning before you can to lure them into an admission. Interrogating Flea would not be simple. Or quick!

'Suppose the bloke what paid me comes to collect the ransom and sees me sitting here?' Flea tipped her head on one side. 'He'll think I'm a nark, my life won't be worth shit.'

Sorry, love. You haven't got the hang of manipulating people, have you? Keep trying, though. You're learning every day.

'Since you didn't recognise your own reflection after the bath,' Claudia said pointedly, 'it's doubtful your benefactor would.'

Amazing what a drop or two of water can achieve. Matted straw had been converted into burnished tawny tresses, ingrained grime had given way to clear, soft skin – although Flea's reaction had been blunt to say the least. She'd hurled a marble bust into the mirror!

Dammit, what was Junius playing at? Bent over her walking stick and dragging an unwilling Flea alongside, Claudia began to criss-cross the Camensis in a systematic sweep. That old man snoring open-mouthed under a poplar. Could that be one of the gang in disguise? A dribble of spittle oozing down his beard quickly ruled him out. What about those two scribes, comparing notes on the steps of the shrine?

'Alms,' she squawked, shuffling closer. 'Arms for a blind widder woman.'

'What? Oh. Here. Take this.' One of them tossed her a pie. 'Now should that be spelled with a ϕ or a ψ?'

'*Phi* or *psi*? Haven't a clue.' His companion frowned, and Claudia realised they were genuinely having trouble translating their Latin into Greek. The grief of the caulker could not possibly be an act, the man was distraught, and most of the other visitors to this quiet grove were drifting away as new ones arrived to take their place. But that's what it was, the Camensis. A crossroads, a place for passing through. Linger for a moment, take a minute to relax, then on with whatever business you were concerned with. Had Junius seen something? Someone he recognised?

'Shit!'

She'd never thought to check behind the statue! Suppose the ransom had been collected shortly after being placed in position? Junius might already be hot on their trail! Shambling sideways up the steps like a crab, the old woman's good eye scanned the park. No one seemed interested. No one was watching the beggars.

'You gonna eat this?' Flea waved the scribe's pie in front of Claudia's nose.

'No, but the sparrows – what on earth are you doing?' The girl was stuffing it inside her tunic!

'In my line, you never know where yer next meal's coming from,' Flea explained. 'It'll keep all right down here.'

Claudia thought of the mountain of food her steward reported the girl had packed away, eating like there was no tomorrow. How unfair that Flea remained as thin as a reed!

The shrine to the nymphs who presided over this gentle and inviting grove was circular and built of anio, a dull-brown building stone, which had the distinction of being durable and solid, but was ugly in the extreme. Clearly, though, the sprites had taken no offence. Perhaps they'd been mollified by the green marble flooring, the waist-high criss-cross fence which ran round the grove, or the fact that their likenesses had been captured in dazzling bronze. Or maybe they simply appreciated the fact that the shrine had been left open to the elements with no roof to cage them in and revelled in the freedom that it gave them. Whatever the reason, it worked. Finches twittered in the branches of the oaks, birches and almonds. Dog roses and yellow honeysuckle scrambled over trellises and pillars, much to the delight of droning bees. In winter, yellow aconites and hellebores flourished round the edges of the watercourse, but today, in high summer, dark purple helmets of monkshoods nodded alongside angelica, hedge hyssop and the great golden globes of the trollius.

Claudia glanced at the scribes, still unable to tell their *deltas* from their *kappas*, and thought at least we know where their *pi* has gone. Inside Flea's ragged frock! Finally, the two young men decided they couldn't give an *iota* for their *alphas* and, with a demonstrative snap of hinged notebooks, took themselves off to the baths. Even the caulker, his face blotchy, his eyes red and puffy, appeared to be over the worst and was now staggering off down the path – Claudia suspected to make a vigil over his dead child. Little else reduced a man to such despair.

She and Flea were alone in the shrine.

Slipping behind the right-hand statue, Claudia was surprised to see the chest still in place. Perhaps, though, they'd emptied the contents? A tiny key appeared from the depths of her rags and in seconds the padlock sprung open.

'Holy moly, look at that!' Flea's eyes jumped out of their sockets and bounced off the green-veined marble floor.

Golden coins winked in the sunlight like fish in the ocean. Quickly Claudia snapped the lid shut. Damn. She locked the chest. What the hell was Junius playing at? Why wasn't he here, watching the drop? She pulled off the eyepatch – a piece of pigskin marked with streaks of red dye to resemble stitches – and rubbed at her eyelid where the resin had held it in place. There was no reason, at least none she could think of, why her bodyguard weren't here, all four of them, watching and waiting and keeping close tabs. Junius knew where to come, for gods' sake. He'd put the wretched ransom chest in place! What had happened? What possible occurrence could have lured four big, strong lads away from their surveillance?

'How much is in there?' Flea's jaw was hitting her knees.

'Come along.' The old crone pulled her veil over her forehead and, patting the central nymph for good luck, limped off down the steps. They'd lingered long enough, she thought. Any longer will only draw attention, the gang might be watching covertly, who knows.

'It's gotta be a million.'

Leaning heavily on her granddaughter and scratching at her itchy woollen rags, the old woman shambled over to the spring. Bright Aegean blue to reflect the summer sky, bubbles coiled their way to the surface, making ripples like raindrops on a dewpond. She positioned herself on a log in the shade, resting on her stick, but only two young children approached the wretched shrine, and then only to poke fun at the statue with a patch over one eye.

'I've never seen so much flaming money,' Flea was saying. 'I can't hardly believe it. All that *gold*!'

Claudia continued to ignore her.

The afternoon wore on.

Come on, Junius. What's keeping you? I should have arrived earlier, she told herself. I shouldn't have placed the onus on him. Dammit, Flea, this is your fault! If you hadn't escaped and run me halfway round Rome, I wouldn't have been behind schedule in the first place. Claudia's thoughts turned to the ransom demand. Two thousand gold pieces indeed! Where the hell did the kidnappers imagine Julia and Marcellus were going to lay their hands on a sum like that at short notice? For that matter, how was she? It had taken some doing, filling that ransom chest!

Come on, come on, where the hell are you? Time flipped back a couple of hours to Junius, standing in her atrium resplendent in a toga, his fingers dripping rings and his hair oiled slick. The sight of him had made her feel as though the floor had been ripped from under her. Time had become suspended.

'Borrow my husband's stuff,' she had said. 'Help yourself, it's still in the cellar,' and he had.

So much so that, when she saw him, just for an instant, it could have been Gaius standing in the hallway . . . Something had pricked inside her, misting up her eyes. Overweight and overbearing, Gaius had taken Claudia as the ultimate status symbol, a trophy to be wheeled out at important functions, look-at-me-I'm-not-just-rich-I'm-lucky. She, in turn, had married him for money. They'd each struck a deal, no more than that, and throughout the four years of the marriage, both had stuck fast to their bargain. (All right, if you're going to be pernickety, maybe Claudia had stretched the rules from time to time, but who the hell counts gambling, adultery and debt?) The point was, it had worked. Then one day he was gone. Snap. As fast as that. Alive one minute, laid out upon his bier the next.

But Junius was no ageing lardball and the moment quickly passed. Time – and its urgency – slammed her back to the present and she'd dispatched him to the Camensis, after which she'd changed into these smelly rags and rubbed some resin on to the pigskin patch before positioning it over her eye. When yells from the bath room indicated the battle against grime had resulted in a home win, she'd grabbed the newly scrubbed parasite and made her way to the Camensis. Later than she would have wished, but with four big burly fellows keeping watch, that shouldn't have been a problem.

The smell of rodents began to tickle in her nostrils. Claudia had already suspected that Flea was a pawn in a very deadly game, and now it looked as though Junius had been lured away, as well. But the young Gaul was no fool. He'd be on his guard.

Dammit, the run-around is an integral part of every kidnapper's pattern, a reminder of just who's in charge here. More often than not, this was every bit as important as the money. *Was it more important?* Supposing they'd brought Flavia along to Camensis as bait? Would Junius have rushed over? Tried to free her? Claudia's imagination ran riot.

Two more hours passed as the old woman and her reluctant granddaughter moved round the park, making garlands here, snoozing there, gathering armfuls of fern for their bedding that night. Any fresh developments and someone would have fetched a message. Which they didn't. What the hell was going on?

'Oi! Clear off!'

'Yeah! Sling yer hooks, yer plague-ridden bags!'

Claudia's beggarwoman act had finally reached saturation point and, when the crowd began hurling rocks at her, she reasoned that this was indeed an appropriate time for hooks to be slung.

In fact, no one ever recalled seeing an old woman sprint so fast.

Chapter Eight

The Cradle of Ra rocked with the gentle rhythm of the breeze. Poplar trees shivered with pleasure as the hot, sticky wind played about their branches while the broader, flatter leaves of limes flapped like thin green hands, as though shooing the zephyr on its way across the valley. Far below the Mount of Osiris, goats clustered under the shade of a squat umbrella pine as workers in soft, wide-brimmed hats swished at the hay with long twin-handled scythes and piled it into mounds. Sleds fetched in carrots, peas and cabbages from outlying fields, also cherries, plums and pears. The sunlight caught a busy pitchfork here, a pruning knife there, the flash of an anklet or ring. Goosegrass was mercilessly winkled out with hoes, beehives inspected, an ox was being trained to the yoke.

Sitting on the heart-shaped rock high above the valley, the man, stark naked despite the searing sun, watched over it all. Distant bleats floated up from time to time, the occasional laugh, a honk of protest from the ox, a verse or two of communal singing from the men who swung the scythes. Bees droned around the thistles and the thyme, a lonely whitethroat trilled out its liquid melody and a flock of tiny iridescent purple butterflies explored the tops of oak and ash.

This, thought the man, is my territory and its beauty is everlasting.

He lay back upon the scorching rock, folding his hands underneath his head, and gritted his teeth against the burning on his skin. Endurance and the everlasting, the two went hand in hand. Without the former, the latter could not be attained and, if nothing else, the man was determined upon the course of everlasting life. He alone possessed the secret. He alone could win the battle against Death – against the serpent who lay in wait in the void which lies beyond the west – for he was the incarnation of the Dark Destroyer, Seth, and you dismiss the Dark One at your peril.

The Cradle of Ra! The very thought was laughable, the dwelling place of the Ten True Gods, my arse. The man sprang to his feet, fixing his gaze on the temple doors. They were closed now, as they closed every afternoon, once the morning ceremonies were concluded and those who wished to petition the sun god had finished their entreaties. Ten of them, indeed! The Dark One pictured them in their orderly little line, each cloaked to the ground in swirling black or silver, each masked by the deity they represented, and yet what were they? Nothing more than animals – the cow, the cat, the falcon, the crocodile, the jackal, the cobra, the vulture and the ibis plus those two human gods, Isis and Osiris. Ignorant and stupid, had they learned nothing? Could they not see what was in front of them?

'Oh, yes,' he whispered to the breeze. 'Ignore the Master of the Powers of Darkness at your peril.'

They had neglected him. In their arrogance, they had omitted Seth from their so-called Holy Council and yet had the temerity to call themselves the Ten True Gods. When there should be eleven at the table.

But in time there would be. Yes, indeed. Seth was working on it, and when the table was complete, he could once again reclaim his rightful place as king.

They would not – could not – dare to overlook him any longer. He was Master of the Darkness, the Sorcerer, the Measurer of Time. The powers of the night were his, he had magic in his hands.

He stared at his hands. Strong, tanned, you could almost see the magic rise up from them, like the heat which shimmered in the valley. Seth looked down through the treetops and recognised the woman Berenice, suckling her infant son. The child had grown fractious in the viscous heat, her breast was soothing to the boy. Seth closed his eyes and imagined himself in the infant's place, and the image sent a fire through his loins. He opened his eyes again. Berenice, her greedy son, all the flowers in this valley, one day (and soon) they would be gone. Dust, the lot of them. Beauty doomed by time.

Not Seth.

Oh, no, not Seth. Father of the jackal, uncle of the falcon, he had mastered the powers of darkness, and yet his fellow gods had spurned him. He, who had once ruled over Egypt with Osiris, had been cast out! Evicted! Allowed no place in society! Worse, he had been vilified because it was Seth who, at the Judgement of the Dead, had gobbled up the hearts of those who failed the Balance. But his fellow gods would soon regret their folly! The outcast would reap revenge in the only certain way.

He would transcend Time as he would transcend her sister, Death. As King of the Darkness, he would show those Ten True Fools *real* powers and then, for all eternity, they would bend their knee to him.

He watched Berenice move her son to her other breast, leaving both exposed to Seth's hidden stare from his eyrie on the hill. Such breasts. Such beautiful ripe, round breasts. He could almost see them thrusting themselves at the child, heavy with their milk, and he watched until his erection was complete. Turning, hard and primed, he stepped over the heart-shaped stone and pulled back the branches of a scrambling fig to reveal a cave gouged out of the pitted tufa rock.

'Mmmff!'

The girl tied to the high-backed chair squirmed and wriggled, and Seth stood in the cave mouth for several minutes watching the leather bonds bite deeper into the white and naked flesh as she struggled to break free from cords which never would release her. Seth was proud of his knots. They tightened with every twist she made.

'Mmmmf!' Wild eyes rolled above the gag across her mouth. '*Mmmfff!*'

'Endurance,' Seth whispered, running his hand down her cheek. Donata, wasn't she? Or was that the one sitting next to her? 'Endurance, my child. Through suffering comes everlasting life.'

His hands, his magic hands, moved down to mould her breasts, the blood from her wounds was sticky under his caress as he gazed with pride around his cave. Carved out of the soft rock for an unknown purpose by ancient Etruscans, who had left behind them only painted pictures on the walls, the cave had concealed its secret with trees and greenery through the ensuing centuries. But now, guided by his mystic powers, Seth had discovered it once more and here he had set up his table for the Ten True Fools, over which he would preside for all eternity, his own seat (throne!) at the head.

However, he could not proceed just yet. Not until *all* the gods had been assembled here.

As he took the hysterical Donata, Seth smiled. 'Hathor,' he crooned. 'Hathor of the Sky, now you are mine. Your womb retains the Sorcerer's holy seed, the seed that has transformed you from human to divine being. You belong to Seth, you have taken your place at his high table, you are Seth's for all eternity.'

Satisfied at last, he finally withdrew, washed himself from head to foot and anointed his body with the unguent of cloves and myrrh that everybody in the holy commune used.

'You see, Hathor? You have become divine, whereas I –' he laughed at the irony – 'I am about to become mortal again. The Dark One has the ability to move among the people without their knowledge or suspicion, and that is where his power lies.'

Donata was weeping openly by now, heedless of the vicious thongs which bound her to the chair, wishing she could turn back time to yesterday, even to this morning. This morning – when she thought the worst of it was being raped by Horus on the heart-shaped stone.

Seth had pulled on his clothes and was holding up a mask which had lain on the table in front of Donata, a mask identical in every respect to that worn by Hathor at the ceremony: the soft cow's mouth, the big, round ears below the arching horns. He stroked the long black lashes which surrounded the painted glass of the eye and tenderly planted a kiss on the broad snout between the gaping nostrils.

'Oh, Hathor, your time of destiny has come.'

He placed a thong around Donata's throat, similar to the one he'd used to subdue her earlier, and tied his special knot.

'Seth is not a beast, he does not kill,' he whispered. 'The choice of life or death is yours, sweet cow, mother of the falcon. Seth will return, to see which path Hathor has chosen.' He placed the heavy mask over Donata's head and watched her shoulders sag under the colossal weight. 'To continue with this life, knowing your heart will fail the Scales of Truth and sentence you to eternal desolation? Or to accept my gift of everlasting life by passing through the gate of death, like the others here?'

His hand swept around the table, to where the bodies of Thoth and Horus, Bast and Isis sat embalmed in eternal obedience to him. Which path would Hathor take? So far, none of his previous conquests had failed him, and four from ten leaves six. Hathor, should she choose to follow Seth, would bring the total up to five.

'Mmfffff. *Mmfff!*'

Carefully he fingered the unfilled replica masks, perfect to the feather, to the whisker, to the scale. Halfway. This was a confirmation of his power, of his domination over the other, lesser, gods. Soon his tableau would be complete and the Dark Destroyer could commence his eternal jurisdiction. But he must move fast. Despite the unguents and the heavy linen bandages, the four corpses seated round Seth's table were already demonstrating certain effects of this wearisome heat.

In the meantime, though, he must continue to move among the weaklings and the cowards of the commune, and this he could achieve, because, in their fools' eyes, they believed him to be one of them. They trusted him. Indeed, because of his position in the hierarchy, they actively sought out his advice and fulfilled his instructions to the letter.

Soon – oh, very soon – these idiots would see the Sorcerer for what he was. His power and his true identity would shine through. Their knees would knock. Voices would tremble at Seth's omnipotence. And they would see that Mentu was nothing more substantial than the King of Clowns, a Pharaoh ruling over fools.

True mastery and dominion belonged to Seth.

With conscientious thoroughness, he replaced the branches of the scrambling fig to conceal once more the mouth of his secret cavern.

Oblivious to Donata's strangled, helpless sobs.

Chapter Nine

There's something wrong here, Claudia thought, her long legs scissoring across the Forum. *Very* wrong! Four men don't just disappear into thin air. Junius would never bunk off without leaving word.

'Almond buns? Hot pastries, lady?'

Claudia's glare told the vendor what he could do with his delights, and the huckster melted back into the crowd.

Goddammit, there's a real smell of fish surrounding this affair, but I have an idea, a theory about this abduction, and I need to test it.

Claudia glanced at the angle of the sun, now over the Aventine and sliding fast. With her bodyguard missing and the threat as to what would befall Flavia, were the authorities to become involved, sour in her mouth, Claudia had had little choice other than to station untrained reinforcements in the form of slaves from her own household around the Camensis and to hell if they were spotted, she'd done her best, given the taxing circumstances. Verres the cook had taken two kitchen hands, ostensibly to collect herbs for the table. Leonides, her steward, had settled down beside the spring with a good book. Two beefy labourers chopped back shrubs and trusted to Jupiter that the kidnappers knew sod all about pruning techniques.

Barging through a group of acrobats, Claudia recalled something Julia had said when she'd delivered the first note from the kidnappers. One little clue, which Claudia should have picked up on earlier. Whose ramifications, if her suspicions were on target, would be momentous.

Behind her, the tumblers untangled themselves from the

pavement and called a warning to the tightrope walker up ahead. Too late. With a startled yell, he went pinging off his wire, straight into the bosom of a fat patrician wife.

But where did Junius fit in? she wondered, stepping over a small dog snoozing in the shade of an ivory carver's stall. Around her, hammers from a cobbler's last tap-tap-tapped its repetitious call. Bronze workers chipped out a hollow echo. And over the whole expanse of Rome, hot air from the marshes trapped everything from bread smells to fried fish, from the sulphur of the fuller's to the pungent stench of sweat. If Claudia's burgeoning hypothesis was correct, it would take one hell of a diversion to distract her bodyguard, who was by no means gullible nor stupid, from the task in hand—

'Out of my way, you!'

Claudia's hand flipped up the tray of oysters, raining crinkly grey shells on the travertine flags. She didn't wait to hear what the oyster-seller called her, ducking instead into the cramped premises of a basket weaver's. She tossed him a silver coin and put her finger to her lips as she ran up the wooden ladder to his attic. Here, the garret window gave a clear view across the Forum: the acrobats, the tightrope walker, the oyster man, on his hands and knees as he scrabbled to retrieve his lumpy cargo. Every colour of the rainbow swarmed beneath the basket weaver's window: scarlet shot with gold or silver thread in the rich robes of merchants; the white togas of patricians; the blue pantaloons the Persians wore; yellow shawls favoured by the Syrians; green turbans from the east. There were skins of every hue, mahogany and fair, ebony and olive; bald heads, veiled heads, goatee beards and sweatbands.

However, none of this swirling tide of humanity seemed lost. No one stood scratching his or her head in perplexity, looking this way and that, shielding their eyes or jumping over the heads of the crowd to see which way their quarry had gone. No one stood still. No one frowned.

One question answered, then. The dusty smell of willows prickled Claudia's nostrils. I'm not being followed. Dear me, a blind man couldn't miss that trail of destruction in the Forum. Her pulse raced that little bit harder. She was sure, now, she was on the right scent.

Outside the shop, she hailed a passing litter. The Field of Mars, she told the bearers, and could they run? Could they hell! Dispatch runners might learn a thing or two from these chaps as, panting heavily, they set her down outside the wooden amphitheatre. Around the makeshift seats, sawdust lay in heaps made soggy in the muggy heat. Bare-backed carpenters sawed and hammered, chipped and planed as the shadows lengthened. The killer breeze kept up its stealthy whisper. Wooden boards were hauled into place with the aid of ropes and ladders and suddenly the swirling waters of the River Tiber became hidden behind a painted backdrop of green rolling hills taken over by a hostile army encampment, while in the orchestra pit, a cacophony of drums and cymbals clashed, and horns blared out in uncoordinated practice.

Ordinarily, since it fell on the second day of Apollo's Games and was therefore eclipsed by the pageants and processions of the opening ceremonies, the Festival of the Serving Women was one on which every expense would be spared. Indeed, of the half-million sesterces which the Treasury poured into the Games as a whole, it was doubtful whether one hundredth made their way to this paltry, low-key celebration, such was the lure of the larger stage productions. Comedies by Terence, tragedies and epics – burglars were spoiled for choice, with every household in the city emptied for the shows.

This year, however, the Prefect organising the Games had a name to make. Young, thin and with a deathly pallor, he kept one eye on the scenery, an ear out for the orchestra, one hand sealed his correspondence with his ring while his brain kept track of the money he had sunk in sponsoring this venture. In fact, there wasn't one single component of his body which wasn't moving in some direction or another as he supervised the work.

'For gods' sake, find another tuba player!' His exasperated tones rang shrill. 'That idiot's tone deaf, and what cretin blocked the second exit with that statue? Get it out – no, I don't care where you put it, just move the bloody thing, and who the hell thinks that curtain is up straight? Croesus, you can see knees at that far end, now get it horizontal and make sure it sweeps right down to the stage.'

All the while, his hands made eloquent gestures to the carpenters and painters, the technicians and the dancers, in the way a man's hands would, of course, when he's ploughed a considerable amount of his own money into a dead donkey of a show.

'I need to talk to you,' Claudia said. 'It's urgent.'

'So's this,' the Prefect snapped. 'We're due our first dress rehearsal in the morning, and the bloody scenery's not up. Where the hell is my fig tree? *That?* Croesus, man, that's a crab apple! The serving women lit their signal from a fig tree in the camp. F-I-G tree, fig. Is this about my wife?'

For a second, Claudia didn't realise he was addressing her. 'Er, no. I wanted to ask you about—'

'Then it's not urgent. Come back at first light.'

Looking at him, growing paler with every inefficiency, Claudia wondered whether she was wasting her time here. His mind was clearly preoccupied with a whole series of disasters, not least his wife it seemed, but now a faint tinge of pink had appeared in the sky. Dammit, this could *not* wait till morning! Flavia had been kidnapped, it was imperative she tested her theory.

'Sorry,' she said firmly. 'But I need to talk to you about the girl who's playing the lead in Friday's re-enactment.'

'Get that herald out of here, he comes in *after* the – why do I waste my breath!' The young Prefect paused in his signalling and orders. 'Did you say the *girl* who spearheads the Serving Women's Assault?'

'Yes,' Claudia said wearily. 'Her name's Flavia.'

The Prefect pushed his fair hair out of his eyes and Claudia glimpsed, for an instant, the attractive young man he would have been, were he not bowed by the weight of ambition. 'You're in the wrong theatre, then.' He flashed her a short, harassed smile. 'Our actors are exclusively male. I say – are you all right?'

'What? Oh, yes. I'm fine.' Apart from that shaft of pain in the pit of my stomach.

It was just as Claudia had feared. There never was any kidnap. Flavia had set the whole thing up herself! And Flea was her accomplice.

Chapter Ten

Why use a tinderbox to start a fire, when Claudia's temper would do the trick? The little bitch, she stormed. The nasty, spiteful, unprincipled bitch! There had been no satisfaction in finding her conjecture proved correct, only anger, and Claudia was shaking with rage.

Flavia, the devious, self-serving little cow, had invented her role in the *Serving Women* drama as a smokescreen to fool her snobby foster parents. Deep breaths. Dee-eeep breaths. That's better. Keep calm, keep rational. Conserve your energies for roasting Flavia over a fire and to setting her screaming to music!

Screaming. Strange. Claudia could hear it clearly, as she approached her own front door. Screaming. Wailing. Screeching—

'What the blazes—?'

I've been gone less than two hours, suddenly all hell's broken loose! Moans and sobs seeped from every rafter of her household, wails came from the cellars, from the kitchens, from the gardens.

'It's Junius, madam.' It fell on her lanky Macedonian steward to explain. 'He's—'

Claudia's stomach flipped somersaults. 'He's what?' She wanted time to stop, go backwards, so she wouldn't hear the answer . . . her heart beat like a kettledrum.

'He's—' Leonides swallowed and could not meet his mistress's eye. 'He's in prison.'

'Jail?' Is *that* all? Mentally she pulled up her sleeves and prepared for battle. Arrest my bodyguard? I do not think so. 'On what charge?'

'Wearing the toga,' Leonides said. 'He was caught in the act . . .' The sentence trailed off into silence.

Claudia's blood froze in her veins. She became a living statue. 'When?' A frog croaked the question. The same frog which hopped up and down in her innards.

'Shortly after noon.' Leonides' own voice was a rasp. 'Someone apparently recognised him in the Camensis, dressed in a toga and surrounded by "his" slaves—'

'And felt obliged to report him to the authorities?' Around her, the atrium tumbled.

'Yes, madam.' His voice was barely a whisper as they both pictured the scene.

Soldiers clanking through the Camensis, their armour reflecting like gold in the sunshine. The detail would halt, surround the young buck and his happy band of picnickers. Junius would be hauled to his feet and clapped in irons. Shackled together in a neck brace, Junius, the hired whores and the other three members of Claudia's bodyguard would be marched off to the dungeons, pelted along the way with dung and rotten fruit.

Mighty Juno, tell me this isn't true. That this is Leonides' idea of a practical joke. That Junius will come bouncing out of the cellar any second. But Juno remained silent, and the cellar door remained shut.

And Claudia was forced to swallow the bitter pill of truth. That in her haste to save Flavia's life, she'd sent her own bodyguard to his doom.

The penalty for impersonating a Roman citizen is death.

In her mind, Claudia replayed their earlier conversation in this very hall. His protest. Her reply. 'Not what would happen if you're caught, rather what I'll do to you if you don't.'

'The whores were released after several hours' questioning,' Leonides explained. 'That's how the story got out, but the men remain under lock and key.'

He went there, he said. Straight away. But the Dungeon Master was refusing all access to prisoners, the cells were already too full, and all he could glean (and only then with the transfer of silver) was that the three henchmen would get off with a public flogging, whereas the Gaul – here Leonides drew a graphic finger silently across his throat.

On behalf of his mistress, the steward had proffered a substantial bribe and, when that failed, had lodged a protest. The stepdaughter of the Widow Seferius had been kidnapped, he explained. Junius was acting solely on instructions, they were setting a trap. But his pleas had bounced off the thick prison walls.

'Reasons don't matter, mate,' the Dungeon Master had sneered. 'A slave's a slave, as you well know, and the penalty for impersonating a citizen is death. Ain't no exceptions. Next case!'

Shit.

For several long minutes, Claudia stood alone in the gloaming, her mind whirling like a millrace. To stop by the dungeons would be a complete and utter waste of time. The death cells permitted no visitors . . . What should she do? What *could* she do? She had never felt so impotent in her life.

She paced, she wrung her hands, she sat, she paced some more. There must be something I can do. Frustration grew. Solidified into a heavy ball inside her stomach. A ball which answered to the name Defeat.

Wait, though, a little voice said. Aren't balls made to be kicked? Claudia obliged, and when the ball had disappeared into space, a small flame of hope kindled in its place. She might be powerless herself, but there *was* someone . . . Perhaps the only someone in the whole of Rome capable of pulling the right strings to get Junius off the hook. His name was Marcus Cornelius Orbilio. The question, though, wasn't could he, but would he?

The last time he'd called, she'd brandished a sharp little gelding knife, threatening to barbecue his bunions and make jam of his jawbone, saying that if he ever came near her again, she'd report him for harassing a poor grieving widow until finally it seemed Supersnoop had got the message: keep out and stay out, I do not want you in my life, not even on the periphery!

Because there was something about him which unsettled her. Not the hard muscles which strained against the linen of his tunic, or the way he turned unscheduled laughs into a cough. The emotion plumbed deeper, murkier waters. Waters where she had never swum before. Orbilio was the only person who made her feel . . . safe. That was the word. Marcus Cornelius made her feel safe and the feeling was strange to her. She distrusted it. For what it did to her insides, to her sleep, to her heartbeat. So she'd evicted the nuisance like an unwelcome lodger, and had discharged him from her life. There was no reason on Jupiter's earth why he should help her.

But for Junius' sake, she had to try.

'Fuss over nothing, in my opinion,' Flea scoffed, as Claudia clapped the manacles back on. 'Once you plead for Junius at his trial, the jurists will absolve him in a jiffy.'

'Jiffies are for free men,' Claudia snapped back, hauling the girl into the street. 'What you've conveniently forgotten is that because Junius is a slave, there will *be* no bloody trial.'

Don't think about it. Don't think of the innovative execution options facing that young bodyguard: crucifixion, trampling by elephants, being pitched against a bear in the arena, tied to a stake among a pack of starving hyenas . . .

'Well, it ain't my fault,' Flea whined, as Claudia hailed a passing charioteer to cadge a lift across town. 'You told him what to wear, not me.'

A millstone dropped in Claudia's stomach. 'Thank you, Flea, that point had not escaped me.' She looked deep and coldly into the girl's eyes. 'But remember it was Flavia, your accomplice, who shopped him! You two are in this together.'

Wait till I get my hands on that bitch.

The sky was dark, the air muggy when Claudia and Flea alighted from the chariot. Ordinarily the Argiletum was far enough away from the Tiber to be free of its pungency, but tonight the cloying heat intensified the stench of rotting fish, of bloated animals floating down the river, of its stinking yellow mud – and the viscous breeze was generous enough to ensure that everyone received their fair share of it, even the patricians who made the hill she was aiming for their home because the air there was reputed to be the purest in the whole of Rome.

'Thanks.' She proffered a coin at the scarred charioteer who'd so generously given her and her 'maidservant' a lift, but the old man waved it away.

'When you're accustomed to having ugly old warhorses on board, m'dear, two lovely ladies is a treat,' he said gallantly, before adding, 'Even if one of them does have a legionary's tongue on her!'

Flea stuck it out at his retreating back. 'Smarmy git.'

'Listen to me, you little wretch,' Claudia hissed. 'If you'd have been half as philanthropic with the truth as you are with your insults, Junius would not be facing death.'

'You can't pin that on me,' Flea protested sullenly. 'It weren't my fault.'

'Oh, wasn't it!' Claudia jerked on the shackles, making the girl wince at the red weal which formed as she was spun round to face her. 'Thanks to your stupid, selfish lies, a good and innocent man is being sent to the arena! Do you understand that, Flea? *Junius is going to die!*'

'I ain't no bleeding fortune-teller,' Flea began, 'how—'

But Claudia was sickened by the girl's irresponsibility, her refusal to shoulder any blame. 'You selfish little bitch,' she stormed. 'You think only of yourself, and then no further ahead than where your next meal's coming from.'

She drew them into a doorway to let a wagon past, then set a cracking pace up the Via Cavour, skirting wagonloads of sacks and crates and a cart of hide destined for the quayside. She spun right, down one of the narrow sidestreets, to avoid a brawl. Someone was ripping a shutter off the oculist's shopfront to act as a makeshift stretcher to carry home a battered, bleeding stevedore.

'Look, I'm sorry.' Flea jerked at the long frock which,

because she was accustomed to wearing short tunics which left her skinny legs bare, tangled round her ankles. 'I thought it was a laugh, a bit of a joke, all right? I never expected it to backfire.'

A joke? Helping Flavia stage her own abduction? Claudia could have kicked herself for not paying sufficient attention at the beginning. Goddammit, it was obvious, she should have seen through it straight away. Who knew the family well enough to know Marcellus and Julia would jump to ransom their niece? Flavia! Who'd think it funny to give her foster parents the run-around? Flavia. And who knew damned well they'd swallow that cock-and-bull story about her being invited to take part in the *Serving Women* drama without question? That was the bit Claudia should have picked up on. Janus, Croesus, no one in their right mind would ask Flavia to lead a *dog*, much less a civil performance before a crowd of hundreds!

'What did she promise you, eh? A share of the booty?'

Flea suddenly became preoccupied with picking her way through the debris scattered along the tangled network of slopes and alleyways, the broken toys, the running gutters, slops and meatbones and greasy cobblestones.

'Well, I hope the pair of you choke on the pebbles!'

'What d'you mean, pebbles?'

In the darkness, Claudia smiled. It had been a gamble, of course. A game of bluff and double-bluff, but with no way of raising two thousand gold pieces (and it had to be gold, the note insisted!), it was a simple question of expediency. Claudia had filled the ransom chest with rocks. A quick visit to the goldsmith ensured that only the thinnest smear of gilt covered the top layer of stones and hey presto, a box full of 'gold'.

'You rotten bitch,' Flea growled. 'What if Flavia really had been kidnapped?'

As I said. Bluff and double-bluff . . .

Torch-bearers appeared as though conjured up, lighting the way of those who could afford it, and laughter echoed out of a brightly lit tavern on the corner at the punchline of a joke, that hoary chestnut about the centurion and the barber's wife, hilarious no matter how often one had heard it. From the serried ranks of the balconies above came arguments and sneezes, meows and bedtime tears, the smell of frying mullet, onions and stale garlic. Slowly, though, the landscape changed. Cramped and overcrowded tenements gave way to spacious houses, whose inner secrets were muffled by high windowless walls, and the aromas were more of roasting boar and incense, fresh paint or the polish from the armoured vigilantes.

'I've never been up here before,' Flea marvelled. 'They,' she indicated the vigilantes, 'always ran me off.'

They would! Private security organised by those who inhabited these exquisite mansions ensured no crime took place in *this* district on the Esquiline. One glance at their mighty clubs, studded with nails, and you realised it wasn't called Nob Hill for nothing!

Outside the shops, the pavements still glistened where the shopfronts had been swabbed down at dusk and the gentle strains of a harpist drifted from one house, while doves crooned in their sleep from the courtyard of another.

'Some gaff, innit?'

Flea's eyes were the size of temple censers as Claudia stopped outside a white-fronted house of modest proportions, which screamed breeding and good taste. The door was highly polished, you could smell the beeswax even in this clammy heat, the bronze unicorn knocker gleamed in the light of the brands which burned either side the doorway in blacked-up iron brackets. 'Whose is it? Family or friend's?'

'Neither,' Claudia replied tartly.

Let people close and they hurt you.

Her hand hovered over the unicorn, then withdrew, uncomfortably aware of a churning in her stomach, the fluttering of a whole flock of starlings inside her ribcage. Anxiety – what else? Watched by half a dozen tough looking vigilantes, she lifted the knocker and pounded the unicorn with such force, it was a wonder Neptune himself didn't rise up out of the ocean to see what the fuss was about.

Suddenly, as the door swung silently open on its well-greased hinges, a fish hook tangled deep inside her and began to pull. Damn his eyes, why couldn't Orbilio be married, bald, fat or ugly, why did he have to have a twinkle in his eye? Bloody unfair that the Fates had bestowed on him an easy lope *and* that sceptical, lop-sided grin, because sometimes, when she couldn't sleep at night or when her mind drifted at the baths, Claudia would find herself musing on what it would be like, his lips on hers, his strong hands exploring nooks and crannies – although equally quickly she'd snap out of it. He was patrician, rich and clever, with integrity all but tattooed on his cheekbones. She came from an altogether different class and walked a tightrope between what was legal (very little) and what was not.

And as any rope walker will tell you, the last thing they need is some berk yanking on the balance pole, no matter how tall and wavy-haired and rugged!

Besides. Any lustful feelings were on her side only. He'd never even made a move, in all the months she'd known him, in all the adventures they had shared together.

His sights were on the Senate, not her bed!

In the shadows she noticed a small shape, dark and shifting. It slithered forward. Bending down, she scooped it up and thrust it in to Flea's disbelieving arms.

And as Claudia Seferius swept into Orbilio's lofty vestibule, she couldn't help wondering what propitiation the gods of this magnificent cedarwood threshold demanded.

She had a feeling it would be one colossal slice of humble pie!

Chapter Eleven

Marcus Cornelius Orbilio did not need the soldier stationed in his porch to tell him who had taken a fancy to wrenching his front-door knocker from its gleaming silver hinge. Only one woman in the whole of Rome possessed passion on that scale! Any other time and his heart would have lifted, but today, he realised, the gods had answered his prayers. *Every bloody one.*

He had prayed for a reason to be taken off the Roll of Honour.

He had prayed for a juicy murder case.

He had prayed for the ensuing scandal to be attached to a high-profile family.

He had prayed that one day Claudia Seferius would come to him and not the other way round . . .

Pinching the bridge of his nose, Orbilio recalled the old Corinthian proverb: Be careful what you wish for, it may yet come true. Remus, his head ached so abominably, otherwise he'd remember the name of the nymph who had, in return for a favour, asked the gods for immortality and, because she beseeched them so pityingly, had had her wish granted. Only later, of course, did she come to realise that what she should have sought was perpetual youth, because as the years passed she grew ever older, ever more shrivelled, her body bent and wasting away, but with no chance of her misery ending. Orbilio knew how she felt.

'Present for you!'

A black squirming object was suddenly stuffed in to his arms, although Claudia seemed to be experiencing a certain difficulty owing to the fact that there was a young woman manacled to one of her wrists. Orbilio felt the room – indeed his whole world – spin.

'His name is Doodlebug and he's a pedigree thingamijig, fully house-trained, of course. Now say thank you.'

'Er . . .'

'My pleasure, Marcus. What are friends for.'

'You . . . bought him? For me?' The day Claudia Seferius gave him presents was the day Hades put up a sign advertising day trips! Besides. There was something vaguely familiar about those big, amber eyes and the even bigger nose which pressed its icy wetness into the crook of his elbow then promptly fell asleep.

'A breeder on the Aventine,' she said breezily. 'Sound chap. Supplies guard dogs to the rich and famous. Now, while I'm here—'

Guard dogs! A shiver ran down his spine. No wonder the puppy looked familiar. That slavering monster three doors up had recently birthed a litter and as Orbilio tenderly stroked the solid rolls of fat, the bare pink podge of stomach, his ears remained pricked for the sound of Momma's claws skidding across the mosaic demanding her runaway babe's return. With his spare hand Orbilio protected his jugular vein.

'I need some advice,' Claudia was saying.

'You need a key.' He indicated the iron shackles linking the two women together.

'No, I don't. And for gods' sake, Orbilio, what's the matter with you? You keep twitching your neck. Do you have a sore throat?'

'Not yet.' For a small pup, Son of Disemboweller seemed extraordinarily heavy, but as Marcus lowered his arm, the look of censure from the two young women immobilised him faster than the Gorgon's glare. Marcus felt sure the gods were laughing.

'My problem,' Claudia began, 'is—'

'How long have you been into S and M?'

'Marcus Cornelius, will you please pay attention!'

'What does he mean, S and M?' It was the first time the chainlink had spoken. Until now, her eyes had been sweeping round Orbilio's atrium, and he had a feeling they had priced every item they landed on.

'Ignore him,' Claudia snapped. 'He's having a cheap dig at your cropped hair, the gangly gait and your obvious quarrel with that frock.'

'*What?*' Animal eyes burned into Marcus. 'Are you suggesting I'm some sort of pervert, mate?'

'Lesbians aren't perverts,' he corrected her, but the creature was taking no prisoners.

'Listen, I ain't here because I like it!' She jangled the chain at her wrist.

'I'm prepared to swap places,' Marcus offered generously, ignoring the twin fireballs which shot from Claudia's eyes.

'I'm here, coz she –' the girl's head jerked at Claudia – 'is trying to pin that sodding kidnap on yours truly and I ain't having it!'

'Kidnap?' Such were the shockwaves down Marcus's arm that the jerk woke the pup, who promptly relieved himself down his richly embroidered, lushly dyed, fine patrician tunic. 'And who might you be?' he asked, setting Doodlebug down and mopping his tunic.

'Flea, and I'm innocent, I tell ya. Get her to cut me loose.'

Huge amber eyes rolled up from the mosaic. Did she say, *fleas?* As a measure of his anxiety, the puppy deposited a more solid little mess and Orbilio wondered how much more Jupiter could pack into the space of one small day.

'Orbilio.' Claudia reached into her robe and drew out a key. In one fluid movement, the manacles were off her wrist and Flea found herself chained instead to the leg of a wrought-iron bench. Claudia's tone softened, became silky. 'Marcus.'

'What do you want?'

Claudia glided into the courtyard, where Flea's howls of protest couldn't carry. Here the sticky breeze was blocked out by high walls redolent with the smell of the climbing roses and sweet briar which scrambled over them and the blue glazed pots of heliotrope, night stocks, oregano and dill dotted beneath them.

'Tut, tut, you men, you're always in such a rush.' She positioned herself on a white marble bench beneath the statue of Venus and patted the empty space beside her. 'Why don't you pour us a nice glass of wine?

He closed his eyes, to try and shut out the curls piled high on top of her head (apart from three, which had tumbled loose over her left ear). He tried to ignore the gown which hugged the fullness of her breasts, showed the fierce points of her nipples and revealed hints of sun-bronzed cleavage in the breeze. He resisted the urge to inhale the spicy perfume which trailed around her, or hook those ringlets in his little finger and return them to their rightful mooring posts.

'Claudia, this is not a convenient time.' His eyes rested on the legionary standing in the shadows. 'What is it you want?'

Orbilio had not meant for the words to come out so sharply. He caught the brief flash of emotion in her eyes before the shutters hurtled down.

'I'm sorry,' he said. What on earth was he thinking of! 'It's just that—'

'How foolish of me to imagine I'd be welcome here.' Claudia's tone could have curled parchment. 'I'll make it brief.'

Shit. To buy time, he bent down to scratch the ears of the puppy who'd waddled out to find them, allowing Doodlebug to show his gratitude (and many other things besides) by flipping over on his back, squirming and whimpering with pleasure.

'It's a . . . work thing,' he explained, indicating the soldier standing at the far end of the peristyle, hopefully out of ear's reach. 'I'm under pressure—'

'Then I won't detain you.' Dammit, her face had set like a gemstone in a ring.

He jabbed his fingers through his hair and felt them tangle. Him and his big mouth! Between them, they were driving her away and without Claudia around to bring chaos to his life, he'd be consigned to nothing more than living death.

Existing in a vacuum: colourless, expressionless, without light or warmth or feature.

'Unfortunately, I need a favour and, regrettable as it is, you're the only one who can help.' She fixed a hard gaze upon his water clock, the one fashioned like a temple, and clamped her luscious lips. 'I shall pay you, of course.'

'*Claudia!*' A nail drove itself into his heart.

'The problem, you see, is Junius.'

Junius! The name cut through Orbilio like a Persian scimitar. Was this another Olympian joke at his expense? Mother of Tarquin, how many times had he lain awake at night, tormented by thoughts about the relationship between Junius and Claudia. Torrid images kept him from his sleep: the Gaul's corrugated musculature, his thick head of sandy-coloured hair, his strong, proud back – how familiar was Claudia with the body of her bodyguard? More than once Junius had been offered cash to buy his freedom, yet he'd never bothered and Marcus knew the reason. That fierce Gaulish scrutiny was directed on Claudia – and Claudia alone – indoors, and when outdoors his eyes would range in an ever-vigilant sweep to isolate potential threats of danger. That intensity burned deeper than any slavely duty, but the question was: was it reciprocated? Orbilio felt it a safe bet that the boy didn't always scowl and when his face was creased in smiles, it would become very, very handsome. A mongoose sank its fangs deep inside his gut and would not release its grip.

'Your . . . bodyguard?' Does he cup your face in his hands and cover it with kisses? Do you hunger for his touch, the way I yearn for yours? 'What about him?'

While bats squeaked as they foraged on the wing and moths fluttered round the torches in the garden, Claudia explained about the kidnap note, the later demand for ransom, how she'd set a trap to catch the messenger, Flea, who, it transpired, turned out to be Flavia's accomplice, and the reason Claudia was lugging her round like a monkey on a leash was that sooner or later that little bitch would tell her where Flavia was hiding and then she'd hang them both up by their earlobes and use them as a pair of dartboards. All this, her icy tones stressed, had not emerged till later. At noon, it had looked as though their only hope of getting Flavia back alive was to set a trap, with Junius in disguise.

And, granite-faced, Orbilio was forced to listen.

The mongoose sank its teeth in even deeper and began to shake its prey.

He pictured them, Claudia and the young Gaul, their faces so close together they could scent each other's breath, plotting, scheming, laughing softly. Were they sipping wine – eating sweetmeats – as they made their plans in secret? Were they touching? Mother of Tarquin, were they (here the mongoose tore out shreds) were they even clothed?

'As a result,' she finished coldly, 'Junius has been arrested and faces death without a trial.'

Good, he wanted to shout. There goes any further prospects of Claudia sharing secrets, wine and heaven knows what with that cocky little bastard! 'And you want me to bail him out?'

'Yes.' She spoke through clenched teeth and refused to look anywhere but up at his gutterspout. 'Will you do it?'

He listened to the chatter of the fountain, the clatter from the kitchens, the rumbles of the jars of wine and olive oil being rolled up from the cellars and the legionary's armour clinking when he shifted position. Nearby, in the public park, an owl hooted.

'Marcus. Please.' There was a catch in her voice. 'You can't let him die!'

'Can't I?' Involuntarily he let out a short laugh. At least he knew which way the wind blew with her and that bloody Gaul and the minute he could, Orbilio vowed to visit the Temple of Jupiter and throw stones at the King of Heaven's statue. 'Oh, can't I, really! Follow me.'

Like a concussion victim, he staggered down the path. Beyond the kitchens. Beyond his office. His hand, he noticed, was shaking as he plucked a torch from its bracket on the wall. All these months, he'd fantasised about Claudia sweeping in, begging him to extricate her from her latest escapade. In his imagination, he'd solved the problem swiftly and efficiently, winning her undying gratitude, so that next time they met, it would be with a pool of water at her feet where the ice had melted away. What happens, when she finally calls on him?

'Orbilio!' Her voice snapped him out of his reverie. 'Orbilio, have you been sniffing the hemp seeds again?'

No, he thought dryly. The only thing I've been smelling is my own goose cooking! He held the torch high above their heads to light the half-demolished wall.

'Janus!' Claudia leapt at its ugly revelations, but only to rip the torch out of his hand. 'That's one helluva hole in its skull,' she said, peering into the cavity, 'and – oh, yuk! A knife still stuck in the ribs.'

'I think we can safely rule out suicide.'

'Really?' she flashed back. 'And I thought you were a resourceful lot, your family. I'll bet, when they finish tearing this wall down, you'll find a pot of plaster inside and a trowel.' Her grin faded like the dog star at dawn. 'Look, I know this is murder, Marcus, and very serious, but I don't see how—'

'It affects your bodyguard?'

'Exactly. I mean, this is hardly last week's crime,' she said, running her finger over the skeleton's collarbone. 'Whereas Junius . . .'

She let her voice trail off, and Orbilio followed her thoughts. Tomorrow was Thursday, the start of the Games of Apollo. Traditionally the dungeons used the third day to dispose of their unwelcome guests in the arena.

Orbilio rubbed his weary cheeks. 'Suppose I told you I've been dismissed from the Security Police, my seals and passkeys confiscated?'

'That's preposterous!' Claudia spun round to face him. 'You didn't murder this chap!'

'No, I didn't. Neither did I wall him up inside my plaster. But while your confidence is appreciated,' more than words could ever express, 'it's unfortunate that my boss does not share your view.'

For so long it had rankled the Head of the Security Police

that Orbilio was a patrician while he himself came from an equestrian background. That Orbilio dined with magistrates and senators, never mind that these were his uncles and cousins and in-laws, all his boss saw was a jumped-up employee rubbing shoulders with men who in turn rubbed their own shoulder blades with the Emperor and who deliberately, or so he felt, excluded him from their 'club'.

His boss didn't give a toss about villains, corruption or insurrection. He had wormed his way up the greasy ladder of ambition, a rung here, a rung there, using bribery, flattery and blackmail as stepping stones until he'd reached the top. Where even here he believed himself snubbed.

What better chance to get his own back on 'Old Money'?

'You may have noticed my praetorian visitors,' Marcus said thickly. He paused and shot her a taut grin. 'Not an obvious choice of guests, but then the choice was not mine to make.'

His boss had wasted no time. Marcus Cornelius Orbilio was to remain under house arrest until this murder was solved.

Chapter Twelve

Down in the Cradle of Ra, the communal prayers for the god's safe transport through the Realm of Darkness were long over. Dinner had been cleared away hours ago, a simple repast of bacon, onions and lentils washed down with barley beer, and soft snores emanated from the dormitory blocks. Berenice was not close to sleep.

She felt old.

Older than her two and twenty summers, older than the hills which surrounded this lush valley, older than the Mount of Osiris which watched over them. Tears welled in her eyes. She had missed both prayers and dinner, the first because she'd been banned from attending while her baby continued to cry (some bitch called it grizzling), and the latter because she had no appetite and was truly sick of bacon. Why couldn't they have fish for a change?

'We are self-contained,' the High Priest had replied, when she took him to task over the matter. 'Our valley sustains us with wheat and fruit and vegetables, we have a garden for our herbs, pastures for our cattle, sheep and pigs. Ducks and geese and chickens give us eggs, and Ra himself has favoured us with a spring of sweet water from which issues forth a stream to wash our linens and flush out our latrines and bath house, but there is no trout stream running through our valley. We have no salmon spawning. Are we therefore not prepared to live without fish, Berenice?'

She had felt her cheeks burn with shame, yet he pressed relentlessly on.

'Do you, Berenice, deny that this is Paradise and that we

are the Children of the Blessed?'

'Blessed are we, thanks be to Ra.' The automatic chorus could hardly skip past her tongue, she felt selfish, mean and ungrateful. She had spoken to the High Priest as though this was some holiday retreat and, quite rightly, he had put her firmly in her place. This was her home. Did she not like it? The question was risible! It simply took some adjusting, that's all, and perhaps it was this contrast which spurred people – Romans, no less – to tear down what the Pharaoh Mentu had built. No matter how hard she tried, Berenice could not begin to guess at their motives. Jealousy? Spite? Revenge on those who'd turned their back on the Roman way of life?

'Beware the enemies of Ra!' Mentu, dressed as Osiris with his blue painted face and gold mask, repeated his warning every night as the Boat of a Million Years returned to the temple to make its voyage through the underworld. 'For they seek to destroy us!'

To destroy this idyll? Berenice would die – no, she would *kill* – to preserve what the Ten True Gods had founded in this valley. The High Priest, with his shining shaven head and low brow ridge, was right. This *was* Paradise. Ra had given her hope and love and self-respect, and if this meant spending her days pollinating fig trees, clipping fleeces or following the harvesters to glean the ears of barley left behind, so be it.

But for two days now her son had been fretting, his face was flushed and, as of this afternoon, a light purple rash had spread down his back. Berenice ran the back of her little finger across his burning forehead. He was only five months old and there had been moments, especially today, when she regretted leaving behind the squad of nurses and nannies she would have had fussing around him at home.

'Ssssh. Ssh, little one, you'll be all right in the morning.'

Berenice looked up at the silent, thickly wooded hills. She was tired, she thought. Overwrought and over-reacting. The very notion of leaving here, of returning to her former, pampered life, was disloyal both to Mentu and to Ra, and her cheeks flushed with contrition. Yet, as she rocked her infant son, the thought still niggled that a commune without slavery, with everybody equal, was all very well, but when one is used to having servants do this, servants do that, the days can be pretty exhausting.

Stop this, Berenice! Stop it at once. You're tired, worried and exhausted by the heat. Once the baby recovers, you'll be fine.

The pungent smell of chives and basil wafted from the herb garden. Suppose, though, her son had fallen ill, because its mother was unhappy? That had to be a possibility.

How she wished she had someone to talk to! Family, friends, someone to confide in, help her get a perspective. Dear me, they were friendly enough, the folk here, but they weren't the type one could indulge in with weighty, in-depth discussions, or have a laugh or a gossip. They were serious, pious and dedicated and, unlike Berenice, not stifled by the constant repetition. The endless succession of prayers, the repetitive rituals, the fact that one never thought for oneself, was even allotted the clothes on one's back – one set for work, the other for rest, and each set identical to his neighbour's, right down to the conformist jewellery and unguents. Weeks ago, Berenice had stopped using that sickly concoction of myrrh and cloves, it had started to make her feel queasy. What was wrong with using lemon balm on her skin? Or having fish for a change for her dinner!

'Sssh, darling, ssh. I'll make you better, Mummy promise.'

As the long night wore on, she tried to recall what might be happening back home, but because she'd abandoned the Roman calendar willingly in favour of the Pharaoh's ten-day weeks, his ten-month years, Berenice had lost track of 'proper' time. According to the High Priest, this was the Month of the Crocodile. Did that mean it was July already? Berenice could not remember, everything was the same every single day.

Why should this concept grate? she wondered. Why on her and her alone? The others were happy enough, why wasn't she? Tears welled in her eyes. Crumbs, this was what she'd wanted, wasn't it? Longed for? Her whole life orchestrated for her, removing the responsibility of thinking for herself? It had been worth every silver denarius she'd donated for a routine which had been soft and soothing on her mind, but today – why did she long for home all of a sudden?

'Come on, darling, take a drink.'

But the child refused her breast. It must be the baby. She sighed. This is so beautiful, this valley, so calm and peaceful. When he's better, I'll be better. She kissed his downy head. Or *was* he sick because of her? Picking up on her anxiety?

Spinning thoughts jumbled her mind as Berenice closed the door on her darkened bedroom. She laid the snuffling infant in his cradle, undid the straps of her gown and let it fall to the floor. Heavens, had she ever known such heat! She moved to the basin on the table to rinse her face and body, when she pulled up short. A goblet had appeared! Berenice sniffed. Wine!

'Will you look at that!' she whispered softly to the baby. She hadn't tasted wine since she had arrived here last autumn, pregnant with the child who was not her husband's. 'A gift from the gods!'

Only the Ten True Gods were allowed wine to drink, the faithful were given beer. Berenice gulped it down, savouring the richness as it trickled down her throat. Strange, not drinking it for so long, she'd forgotten what it tasted like. Far sweeter than she remembered.

'Oh!' The room began to spin. 'Silly Mummy.' She giggled. 'Drank too fast and feels all woozy.'

She slumped down on the bed, black waves sweeping over her. When she tried to move, she couldn't. The door to her bedroom opened, and misty eyes saw Hathor in the doorway, her coppery cloak sweeping the floor, the soft cow eyes turned on Berenice. She ought to be afraid, she thought, seeing visions in the early hours, but she wasn't. Hathor had come to help. Hathor had given her the wine.

'Hathor looks after mothers with their calves,' the vision said, and Berenice thought it odd, such a deep voice for a goddess. 'Hathor has seven of her own.'

I know, Berenice wanted to say. The Calves of Hathor weave the web of life. But her throat was paralysed, and she could say nothing as the goddess began to stroke her heavy, naked breasts.

'As I thought, Berenice, the problem is your milk.' With each caress, the cow's breathing became heavier, turning into fast, rasping snorts. 'Give this,' Hathor said eventually, 'to your baby.' A small phial appeared from the folds of the loose metallic gown and was placed softly on the table. 'When he falls asleep, take him to the gates of the temple and leave him in his cradle.'

Berenice wanted to cry in gratitude, but no tears, no words would come.

'Providing you do as I say, Berenice, your son shall live.'

The girl closed her eyes as the healing hands of Hathor squeezed the poison from her breasts.

'When Ra brings the Kiss of Dawn to the valley, so shall he breathe the Kiss of Recovery on your son, but only – *only* Berenice! – if you lay this sacred amulet on the heart-shaped stone at the precise moment he turns his light upon your child. Will you do this, Berenice?'

I will, she said inside her head, gazing with adoration at the pebble which, when one came to look carefully, looked just like any other little pebble. Who would imagine it held such strong healing powers? Silently, she repeated the directions. Twisted chestnut, blah-blah-blah, heart-shaped stone. I've got it. The directions are etched in my brain. Hathor swirled away into the night and Berenice, naked and cleansed, sighed contentedly. Oh, praise be to Ra! Surely I shall worship him all the days of my life!

Chapter Thirteen

Claudia sat on the pile of rubble in Orbilio's half-demolished storeroom and rubbed at the pain which throbbed in her temples. Like an invisible demon, the breeze from the marshes picked up splutters of sulphur from the torch, added to them the dry dust of cement and stirred the whole lot around to make a sticky, foul, unbreathable porridge called air.

Face facts, Claudia. You're staring defeat in the whites of its eyes.

In a few, very short hours, eight days of Games to honour Apollo will kick off with a procession from the Capitol, with people lining the streets, dancing, singing, everyone wearing floral garlands. The parade will then end at the Circus Maximus under the Palatine and, to a hymn accompanied by sacred flutes, an ox, a cow and two white goats will lay down their lives to Apollo, their horns gilded and beribboned, while banners hang from every balcony and roof. Claudia had organised kingfisher blue for hers, hundreds of them, streaming from the window sills and gutterspouts, draped around the thresholds front and back, and Junius, goddammit, would not live to see one of them!

'I don't understand,' she said, as the pain in her forehead intensified. 'How can Flavia be innocent in law, when there's no question that she set up this abduction?'

Orbilio perched on the pile of bricks beside her. 'People can't kidnap themselves,' he said wryly. 'The most she could face is conspiracy to defraud, but you said yourself, there were only rocks in the box and, before you say anything you might regret, Mistress Seferius, don't forget the goldsmith's a witness. No modifications to your testimony acceptable!' He shifted uncomfortably on the rubble. 'Therefore, since no monies have passed hands, no crime has been committed.'

Bitch! Claudia chewed her lower lip. Of course, if Flavia hadn't actually collected the ransom, there was still time for a switch . . . oh, don't be stupid! The chances of Flavia leaving two thousand gold pieces lying untouched in the Camensis was about as likely as this skeleton dancing off into the dawn!

'It's bloody unfair!' she said, spiking her hair. She knew that, at that moment, she would not have trusted herself with Flavia, fifteen years old or not. 'She walks away scot-free, while Junius gets to face a starving leopard.'

And the only man who is in a position to flex both family and official muscles to secure the young Gaul's release is under house arrest for a crime he didn't commit!

Despair shuffled that bit closer. She could smell its foetid breath.

Orbilio rubbed his jaw and began to pace the room. 'There might be a way round this,' he said slowly. 'Were Flavia, for instance, to swear to the Dungeon Master – on Jupiter's oath, naturally – that Junius was no slave but her ex-lover, the son of a Parisian horse breeder, say, who'd jilted her and that she'd sought revenge, and providing I sent a letter backing this up, it won't matter whether the Dungeon Master believes it or not. An oath is an oath, he'll be forced to act on it.'

Claudia felt the room spin. No food and no sleep on top of this cloying heat, what else could it be? Surely not a reaction, because he – Mister Honest and Upright himself – was prepared to compromise his position by lying?

'When I get my hands on that girl,' she said, 'I'm going to skin her alive and make books of her hide, then I'm going boil her flesh in vinegar and pickle her miserable bones in brine.' Claudia bounced up off the demolition heap and kicked the plaster wall. '*After* she's sworn her oath, though, so Junius can help with the pickling.' By the gaping cavity, she paused. 'There is a stumbling block to your master plan.'

Life is never a straight road, is it? More crazy paving, and worse, you have to lay it yourself!

'We have no idea where the scheming bitch is holing up.' By all that is holy, Flavia, you will pay for this.

'I presume you've questioned the parasite?'

'Flea?' Claudia snorted derisorily. 'That girl is tighter than a clam!'

'Then,' he grinned, 'perhaps you need a bigger hammer to crack that tough nut's shell. Walk this way, madam, if you please.'

In the atrium, Flea lay fast asleep on the floor, her manacled hand hanging limp from the wrought-iron bench leg, her face looking cherubic and heart-wrenchingly young. Across her lap, Doodlebug lay sprawled, his four paws facing different directions with Flea's free hand supporting his head. Something constricted in Claudia's stomach as she watched their ribcages rise and fall in unison.

'Leave this to me,' Orbilio whispered. 'I'll join you in the garden in fifteen minutes.'

Fifteen minutes? Fifteen years and you still won't reach the truth, she thought, but the garden was peaceful and the honeysuckle was sweet . . . and the legionary almost invisible.

The quarter hour had not passed before Orbilio came bouncing out to join her. 'Faced with being put to the torture by men who have never clapped eyes on a virgin not previously made of marble, Flea has miraculously turned into a linnet,' he said. 'Why don't you go and hear the birdie sing?'

Claudia looked up at the night sky, to where stars were hidden by a blanket of fug, and wondered how the Security Police would ever hope to manage without him.

Indoors, a very different scene greeted her eyes. Doodlebug had woken up, full of beans and in the sure knowledge that he was everyone's friend and that they wanted to play with him. Flea still looked hauntingly young, but hers was no longer the peaceful, pretty face of a few minutes before. Oh, sweet Janus, what's in your past? What horrors have you lived through?

'All right, this is the truth, I swear it!' and if Flea, that moment, had claimed she was the mother of Helen of Troy, Claudia would have believed her. This girl's emotions were pared to the bone. 'I met her a week ago, right? Flavia was sitting on the steps of the Temple of Luna and sobbing her little heart out and, I dunno why, but I just felt sorry for the poor cow.'

I can tell you why. You're nowhere near as tough as you like to make out, my girl!

'Flavia, see, was going on about how unhappy she was, how she'd seen a chance to break free from her horrible family –' Flea flicked an apologetic glance at Claudia, then grinned to see that no offence was taken. 'Anyway, the gist of it was, she couldn't leave. Not without money, any road.' Absently, she tickled Doodlebug's floppy, daft ears. 'Gold was the actual word,' Flea said. 'She needed gold, she said, for the brothers of whores.'

'For what? Flea, if you're winding me up—'

'I ain't, honest I ain't. The brothers of whores,' she insisted, and her luminous green eyes shone with the truth. 'I swear I dunno what she meant by that, it weren't my business to ask and I didn't much care, but I told her, I'll give you a plan to raise the money you need and then, if it works, you give me ten of them gold pieces and she said, it's a deal.'

'So the plan – this kidnap – that was your idea?'

'Reckon it was,' Flea admitted in a tiny voice. 'Will I . . . will I still be put to the torture?'

Doodlebug began to tug at her skirt, growling and skidding on the polished mosaic.

'Flea.' Claudia felt rotten pressing on. 'A man's life is at stake, I need to find Flavia and I can't believe you don't know where to find her.'

'Well, I don't.' Tough and streetwise, Flea hated the tears which began to fill up her eyes. 'Flavia said she'd come to me, so I told her where I lived, and . . . well, she'd visit, I suppose you'd call it. See, we got on, Flavia and me.' Her long lashes turned downwards. 'Can't understand that, can yer? Us being friends.'

Oh, but I can. Two lonely misfits and, for one, a burgeoning sexual awakening. 'Did she know you were a girl?' Finding no satisfaction with a lump of old cloth, the puppy turned his attentions to Claudia's sandal.

'Course not!' Flea was horrified. 'But that didn't have nothing to do with it. We just clicked as pals, that's all.'

Maybe to you, but I'll bet my bottom denarius Flavia fancied you something rotten. 'This talk about the brothers of whores—'

'Uh-uh. She didn't talk about them at all. Clammed up tight, she did – mind, once she mentioned something about Westerners. I remember that. Westerners.'

'You mean, people living on the west of the city? The Palatine Hill?'

'I dunno.'

'Did she mean over the river? Come on, Flea, think! Did she talk about Ostia?' That's west of Rome. 'Try to think, please. This is very important.'

'I know it is,' Flea said weakly, 'but she said it was her secret, and I didn't push. Look,' she shifted to stare Claudia squarely in the eye, 'I'm sorry about Junius, I mean that. And I'm sorry I gave Flavia the plan and I'm sorry I delivered the notes and I'm sorry I didn't press her about where she was staying while all this was going on. But you ain't seriously gonna put me to the torture, are you?'

'Actually,' Claudia said, disentangling sharp puppy teeth from her shoe, 'we never were. That was simply a ruse to make you confess!'

And with that she made a fast, strategic exit, leaving the soldier in the vestibule to take the brunt of Flea's foul-mouthed curses.

'So?' Orbilio asked, and she could smell his sandalwood. 'Do you have Flavia's address? I've written the letter to the Dungeon Master, all she has to do is swear an oath and – oh. Your expression tells me Flea doesn't know Flavia's whereabouts.'

'This might seem difficult to believe, Marcus Cornelius,

but for all her streetwise ways, that girl has been kippered as efficiently as we were.'

Call us a horrible family would you, Flavia, my sweet? Well, brace yourself, kiddo, *you ain't seen nothing yet.*

To the east, the first faint tinge of pink began to glow in the sky. Hollow-eyed, Orbilio stared up as though mesmerised. 'The army is coming this morning,' he said, and his voice was little more than a rasp. 'Trench-digger types accustomed to siege engines and catapults rather than the delicate task of removing skeletons. They'll destroy any evidence.'

As well as all trace of his innocence.

A blackbird began to let loose its warbling trill, and almost immediately a dozen other birds weighed in with tunes of their own.

Claudia plucked a sprig of lavender and held it up to her nose. 'Then perhaps,' she said, with a sly smile, 'we had better put into practice that old hunting technique of felling two deer with a single spear.'

A quizzical eyebrow rose lazily upwards. 'And how, pray, do you propose to do that?'

'Praying doesn't come into it.' She laughed. 'You can't effect Junius's release, because you're under suspicion of murder, and you will stay under suspicion for as long as the murder remains unsolved. The only solution is to solve the murder ourselves.'

'In three days?'

'Why not?' she asked, kilting up her skirt and marching down the peristyle. 'If we don't want the Catapult Kids trampling the evidence, the only way to preserve it is by tackling the job ourselves. Here!' She tossed him a chisel. 'We've only a few hours to get this wall down.'

'You,' he grinned, chipping away at the cavity, 'are wasted in the wine trade! You're a builder through and through, I've never seen anyone so instantly at home with a hammer.'

'Then you'd better not cross me.' She grinned back. Plaster dust was flying everywhere, and she thought, so this is what he'll look like when he's grey.

'But what about Flavia?' He coughed. 'Shouldn't you at least try to trace her?'

'Later.' Claudia stepped back as the claw on her hammer pulled a large section of wall tumbling into the storeroom. 'After all,' she added cheerfully, 'it's not as though she's in any danger, now is it?'

Chapter Fourteen

Once the High Priest had held up a golden facsimile of the Sacred Feather of Truth and blessed the Boat of the Morning, the worshippers drifted back to their quarters. There they would change into their working clothes, in preparation for the day ahead: some would filter off into the fields, to harvest the beans and the barley. Others would make their way to the threshing floor, the bakery, the brewery, the kitchens. Goats and cows had to be milked, cheese turned, geese fed with grain.

For the man who called himself Seth, it was a simple enough matter to slip away. To climb to his secret cavern in the hill.

Beside the heart-shaped stone, he divested himself of his Egyptian clothing and allowed Ra to rest his warming rays upon his nakedness. Dawn had been sweet this morning, he reflected. Very, very sweet.

He pushed aside the scrambling fig, to where Berenice writhed and thrashed in her high-backed rush seat, straining against knots which tightened with every squirm and wriggle. He had made a good choice in Berenice. Plump and rewarding, oh yes. A good choice. That's why he'd come back a second time this morning. Berenice was the best so far.

Donata (he believed that was the last one's name, he couldn't quite remember), but Donata had been, frankly, disappointing in comparison. She had been a virgin and as such hadn't quite known what to expect from a man. Berenice had. She certainly had, and Seth liked that.

'Oh, Hathor. How well you have served your master.'

He picked up the replica mask from the table at which

his servants sat and replaced the cow's head over Donata's bulging, bloodshot eyes rolled up in death. I have chosen well, he thought, because all five of my disciples have chosen what was right. They have walked the True Path of their own accord, and their hearts and mine will weigh light in the Balance.

'I shall stand before Ra with no killing on my hands, no death on my conscience,' he told Berenice. 'The choice is theirs, as it will be yours, my child, now you have my holy seed implanted in your womb. Do you wish to live and face eternal desolation? Or be reborn, a servant of the Dark Destroyer?'

'Mmm, mmmm, mm-mmm!'

Berenice was trying to communicate through her gag. He wondered what she wanted to say. He ran his hands, his magic hands, over her heavy, milk-laden breasts and realised that Berenice was special.

'You have killed your child to serve the Sorcerer,' he whispered, letting his hands work their holy magic on her body. 'Such sacrifice will not be forgotten in the afterlife. You shall be Seth's favourite for all eternity.'

He took her again, harder than before, and as he washed himself afterwards, he counted the places at the Table of the Ten True Gods. The ibis and the falcon, the cat and the cow now waited patiently for eternal resurrection, as well as Isis, who had been the first to take her seat. Which mask should he place on Berenice while she deliberated on her future?

Seth walked along the table, ruffling the feathers of the vulture, drumming on the solid scales of the crocodile. Because Berenice was special, he could not sit the jackal's head on her, the jackal was a scavenger. Perhaps the striking cobra? He looked at his chosen one, his favourite, the blood seeping from where her leather bonds dug in. This was proving a difficult decision, and Seth would have liked more time to make his final choice.

'Mmmmm!'

Of course! Berenice was right, he didn't need to decide now! He could think on the matter and when he came back after nightfall to embalm Donata, he'd be able to take Berenice again. That would be nice. And then he could tie his special knot and leave her to contemplate her future overnight. Perfect!

He anointed his holy body with the commune unguent which rendered the Master of Darkness invisible among his people and pulled on his neatly folded clothing. Tonight he would have something special to look forward to, but meanwhile, there was work to be done. Seth, in mortal guise, had a position to uphold. He must not neglect his duties, lest someone began to suspect.

Also, he remembered, there was a new arrival to greet this morning. A fifteen-year-old girl, contributing two thousand gold pieces to the Solar Fund.

Seth liked them young.

Chapter Fifteen

Installing an indoors bath room, complete with piped water and underfloor heating, had depleted Claudia's inheritance considerably but never once had she regretted it. At times like this (and lord knows, times like this came thick and fast of late!), a long, hot soak in lemon-scented waters, listening to the strumming of a harpist followed by a hired masseuse trouncing the last few knots of stress was all it needed to restore equilibrium. Except today! Claudia waved the musician away, her throat too constricted for words to squeeze past.

Today, time was running out for Junius, the slave boy.

Cypassis, her broad feet encased in wooden sandals to prevent them burning on the hot mosaic, clopped around with towels, strigils, scented oils and tweezers, picking up discarded laundry, sweeping up curls which had been snipped by the hairdresser and left where they had fallen, her face puffed and blotchy from crying.

'They'll split us up, madam, I—'

'Cypassis, no one is going to split my household.' Over my dead body! 'How many times do I have to tell you, there's no question of the army carting you away to test your loyalty to the Emperor with hot irons!'

Like dye in water, the idea that they'd be viewed as accomplices to Junius passing himself off as a Roman had spread around the staff, until suddenly the entire contingent expected be dragged off to the arena on Saturday! Even level-headed individuals, such as this big-boned Thessallian maid, had worked themselves up to such a frenzy that the very *least* they expected was a flogging at the post before being despatched to some new and cruel owner in the darkest corner of the Empire!

'This is the work of the gods,' Cypassis muttered. 'We mortals are being punished—'

'Spare me the superstitious claptrap and fetch my tortoise-shell comb!'

Cypassis made the sign to avert the evil eye before scuttling away, noisily blowing her nose. Divine retribution, indeed! Claudia squeezed her eyes shut and sank below the water line. All because the kitchen hands and gardeners who'd stood watch in the Camensis swore on the lives of their mothers that the ransom chest had been spirited away! Claudia blew bubbles under the water. Did these men not have one brain cell between them? Up she came, spluttering. Even Leonides, her lanky steward, could find no explanation for its disappearance.

'The shrine in the Camensis is circular,' she'd reminded him sharply.

Returning home from the Esquiline, white with Orbilio's plaster dust and covered with nicks from flying chippings, what Claudia had needed most was sleep not a discourse on divine intervention! Her head ached, her eyes pricked, someone had filleted every bone from her body.

'The shrine is open to the elements, apart from a waist-high criss-cross fence, and is approached by six stone steps, which means the far side, where it drops away, stands so high.' She'd indicated her own neck. 'Of the three statues on the podium, we were instructed to leave the chest behind the right-hand figure, and I suppose it did not occur to you to check the far side of the podium?'

'Madam?'

'I'll wager there's a deep impression in the grass where a heavy chest has landed.'

It was a human being, real live flesh and bones, who had visited the wood nymphs' shrine yesterday, not some invisible deity, and who, concealed by the bronze statuary, had hoisted the box over the side. They would have returned under cover of darkness to collect it by sneaking up from the back.

'You were in the Camensis, Leonides. Tell me what you saw.'

'That's the whole point, madam. I saw nothing! No one went near the shrine, only an Egyptian noblewoman and I can personally vouch that hers was a sightseeing trip— Oh. Oh. Oh, I see. That was Flavia, wasn't it?' His face turned ashen and waxy as he saw the auction block beckon and, sensible chap that he was, scurried off to see to madam's bath!

But the soak hadn't helped. Claudia was dizzy now from exhaustion, weak from lack of sleep, but she must press on. Time was trickling away. Too precious to waste. Must keep going.

Cypassis returned with the comb, knocking over a small phial of oil, which shattered on the tessellated floor to release a concoction of seaweedy smells into the steamy atmosphere. Claudia didn't notice. Her mind was reliving the ransom drop in the Camensis. The *bitch!* The scheming, cold-blooded, cold-hearted little bitch. Claudia saw it clearly, as though she'd been there herself: Flavia, disguised as an Egyptian noblewoman; recognising Junius, of course, at once; so greedy to get her claws on two thousand gold pieces, she throws him to the wolves. Time passes. The commotion dies down. Secure in her disguise, Flavia saunters through the Camensis. Up the steps. One-two-three heave. Over the side and thud.

Fancy yourself as an Egyptian, do you? Claudia would be the first to pickle her in natron and inter her mummified remains in a sarcophagus!

She climbed out of the sunken tiled bath. The voluminous linen towel was soft and fragrant, smelling of clove pinks and lavender, but the scent caught in her throat. Already, it was approaching noon. The Games of Apollo were well into their stride and with the morning parade faded to memory, the sacrifice to Apollo would be in full swing. Soon, hundreds of post-processional parties would spring up, discussing how encouraging the auspices had been, how succulent the sacrificial roast and, oh my, did you see that black eye on the senator's wife? Don't tell me she got that shiner tripping over!

The gossip would range from I hear peach blight's pushed up the prices to did you know you can reach Cadiz in under a week these days? Any other time and Claudia would be taking her place at the feasts. With her eagle-eyed bodyguard stationed behind her.

Two days. Two days were all she had left.

Must press on. Can't stop . . .

'Are you ready for your massage?' Claudia's favourite beautician, a fresh-faced young Syrian, had been promised the earth by Cypassis to shut her shop for the day and attend to her mistress at home. 'I brought along a special moisturising balm which contains honey, almond milk and the sap of aloes, much favoured by Queen Cleopatra. You'll find this soothing.'

For all Claudia cared, the girl could rub nettles into her skin. *I'm sorry, Junius. I am so very sorry.*

She squeezed away the tears which welled up and pricked. This is not the time for self-pity. You've dug out the skeleton, rescued the evidence, save your self-loathing for Saturday. Claudia rolled over on to her stomach, folding her hands under her chin. You still have two days left, stop bitching and put them to good use! Her father's motto echoed in the vaults of her memory: never go to war angry, that merely strengthens the opposition.

The philosophy wasn't his, of course, it was a standard army axiom, dragged out whenever a barbarian war band swooped down to slaughter soldiers or civilians in a merciless guerrilla attack, their aim being to goad Rome into quick retaliation and lure them into ambushes and the enemy's strategy. Wait! the generals would urge. The time to remember this outrage, to avenge your friends and colleagues, is the moment right before we strike. Because *when* we strike, *where* we strike, *who, how* and *what* we strike must be Rome's decision, not theirs.

The generals were right. Claudia followed plumes of steam coiling upwards to the ceiling. Her father was right, but then, wasn't he always? Mental lips kissed his whiskery cheek as he marched off to war, waving and grinning to his ten-year-old daughter. Not to march back ever again.

What would he have thought of her now, she wondered, begrudging the time spent catching up on sleep or relaxing in a bath? Those are necessities, girl, not time wasted, he'd have said. Look upon them as an opportunity to give your brain a workout while your body rests.

Claudia's head throbbed behind her eye sockets as it invariably did, when she thought about her father. Why *hadn't* he come home? The army had had no answers for her mother. There was no record of him being killed, they said, but then again, fighting had been fierce. Bloody and brutal, they added. Especially hard on the camp followers over the ridge. What they failed to say, however, was who, in the midst of so much hand-to-hand fighting when the battle might go either way, who gave a damn about one individual? So what if an orderly ran off in the melee?

Claudia flipped over on to her back, tilting her head so the Syrian girl could reach under her chin, and frog-marched her mind back to the business in hand. Namely saving Junius from ending up as the main course for a hungry lion!

But before she could proceed, Doodlebug had taken it upon himself to investigate the pleasures of the bath and was waddling round the rim trying to lap the water, urging the level to rise closer to his tongue.

'Out you go. Shoo, shoo!' Cypassis might as well have asked the sticky breeze to stop blowing. 'He'll fall in,' she warned.

'Then he'll add another string to his bow of accomplishments. Swimming.' Claudia was smiling in spite of herself.

To his delight, Doodlebug discovered a playmate in the water. Another small, black, podgy creature with amber eyes and floppy ears who ran when he ran, stopped when he stopped, leaned forward when he leaned forward too.

'I don't know what Drusilla will say when she finds out you've brought a dog in.' Cypassis sighed.

So far it had taken scheming on an Olympian scale to keep the two apart, but on one point everyone was agreed: disaster loomed ahead! But what was Claudia supposed to do? Leave Doodlebug at risk of being trampled under careless hob-nailed boots? Crushed under rubble? With Supersnoop's front door open as the army tramped back and forth, anything could happen in the street. Now Flavia, she would have happily seen run over by a chariot or kicked by a horse. Not an eight-week-old puppy!

Tipping forward at a precarious angle, Doodlebug dredged up what he thought (bless him) was a bark. Strange, the other fellow didn't respond! He let loose a second yelp-cum-cough and still nothing came back. Not even a whimper. He was teetering perilously close to himself, when Cypassis swooped to his rescue.

'Come on, you!' She tucked him up under her arm and marched him away, telling him that they'd have to call him Narcissus, if he kept up that relationship with his reflection and what would he like for his tea? A piece of stewed rabbit?

The beautician chuckled as she massaged an unguent of sweet-smelling calendula into Claudia's fingers, and suddenly the world was back in kilter and Claudia knew what she must do next. She must sleep. Deep, healing sleep, after which her judgement would no longer be clouded by emotion or hysteria or this overpowering sense of defeat. Like any good general, she could then line up her clues like troops and view the evidence objectively.

She slept.

And later, in her office, in a flowing linen robe scented with thyme and her hair hanging loose around her shoulders, a very different Claudia set out parchment, quill and ink. Her efficient rustle alerted the blue-eyed, cross-eyed cat stretched lengthways on the maple chest.

'Now then.' She unrolled a crisp sheet of parchment and anchored its corners with ivory figurines representing the seasons. 'With no idea of Flavia's whereabouts, we have to get Hotlips off this hook of house arrest. Why? In order for him to use his official clout to set young Junius free, of course, and we can only do that by solving the riddle of the body in the wall. Now, what clues do we have, Drusilla?'

'Prr.'

'I agree. Precious few.' Claudia leaned across to tickle the cat's pricked ears. 'But let's set them down on paper, anyway.'

'One.' She dipped her pin in the inkwell. 'Skeleton stripped of tell-tale clothes and jewellery.' The cat jumped up on the desk and knocked Autumn flying. 'Two. Skull has all its own teeth, bones show few signs of damage.' Which leaves us with a young person and no indication of their status! 'Three. Killer too squeamish to pull out knife, yet composed enough to pull rings off finger!'

'Prrrrr.' The cat rolled on to her back so Claudia's fingernails could work their magic on her tummy.

'Good thinking, poppet! Four. Is body a slave, a skivvy? Who wouldn't own rings in the first place?'

Better-placed slaves, such as Verres, Leonides (Junius, of course!), earned healthy bonuses and could often be seen at the races, bow-backed with the weight of their jewellery. You see, that was the irony. No one minded slaves getting rich. Indeed, many owned shops, businesses – taverns were a popular choice – they even owned slaves of their own. It was impersonating a citizen which carried the ultimate forfeit. To wear the toga, meant death.

Claudia rolled the figure of Autumn around in her fingers, absently feeling the bunches of ivory grapes, the carved basket of olives. 'Five,' she wrote, uncurling the corner and anchoring it back with the figure. 'No hasty cover-up. No hasty crime?'

The body had been stood against the original storeroom wall and pinned there with leather straps nailed into the brickwork. One, which had come away when the first hammer went into the wall yesterday, ran round the forehead, to stop the head sagging forward, and a second went under the armpits to support the weight of the corpse. The killer knew what he was about.

According to Orbilio, the force of the blow to the head would have killed her. He certainly hoped so, he added. Rather than the knife first driven into her ribs and then being coshed to prevent her from screaming.

'Mrrrp?'

'How do we know the corpse was a girl?'

Claudia's stomach flipped somersaults as she recalled that gut-wrenching moment, shortly after dawn, when they realised that it was not one body they were staring at, but two. Inside the pelvic bones, lay the remains of a second, minuscule skeleton.

She leaned back in her chair and saw past the floral painted wall, the leaping antelopes, the flying cranes and leopards. Was the victim's pregnancy the motive for her murder? It had happened before, the mistress threatening to tell the wife, cause a scene, demand he divorce his wife and set up home with her and the baby. Sometimes it's blackmail, sometimes the product of rape, but whatever the reason, the end was as brutal as it was tragic. The mother murdered, the baby dying – later – inside her.

'Unable to identify the victim, we'll have to work back from the killer.'

'Frrr.' Drusilla squirmed with pleasure, her eyes closing to slits.

'And the one thing that anyone who knows him can tell you, Marcus Cornelius Orbilio would not kill a woman, and never like that!'

Anyone, that is, except his boss! Unlikely, the trumped-up little jackass had grudgingly conceded, when he had finally bothered to call round late this morning. Though in his view that did not let Orbilio off the hook, and if he was covering up for someone, he said, may Jupiter help them both, because he bloody wouldn't, and get that bitch out of here, he knew about the Widow Seferius and her activities were not always legal! So much as another toenail across this fancy carved threshold and never mind house arrest, he'd lock her up for conspiracy.

The cat poured herself over Claudia's shoulder, purring into her ear.

'That man, Drusilla, is an imbecile.'

Unfortunately, though, his logic was a hill fortress which could not be stormed. Fact, he said. The house had been in

Orbilio's family for three generations. That rather cut the possibilities. Fact. It was impossible to date the remains, sufficient to say they weren't recent, but then Orbilio had lived there for eight years, was it? Oh, nine . . . he'd forgotten how young aristocrats are when they marry! Fact. There were no records of work to the storeroom, but then a murderer would hardly keep any, and none of the current household had been there for more than three years. The previous incumbents sold lock, stock and barrel one sunny morning down by the Tiber by Orbilio's wife, he believed, who had then absconded with the money she'd raised and, dear me, yes, the contents of Orbilio's money box, as well. Fact. Divorce followed soon after, did it not? Oh, and by the way. Where was his ex-wife these days?

Claudia had been ushered out of the door at that point, with Doodlebug squirming under her arm and Flea manacled once more to her wrist, and the last thing she'd heard was Orbilio calmly reminding his boss that his wife had eloped with a Lusitanian sea captain and was currently living the life of a lotus eater and also, as a point of order, she hadn't taken one damned coin from his money box. She'd sold the slaves instead.

Drusilla's purring stopped abruptly, giving way to a low growl. Hackles began to rise. Out in the courtyard, with the sun opaque and watery as it began to sink below the heavy, honeyed clouds, Doodlebug spotted the demon and proved again that he was perhaps not as fully house-trained as Claudia had led Marcus to believe.

Animal expletives filled the air. Quite an unusual sight, she thought, a cat treeing a dog. But no sooner had Doodlebug recovered from the biggest leap of his eight short weeks, he was off again, having learned that demons are also capable of reaching the flat surfaces of sundials. Round and round the monster chased him – through the roses, past the purslane, tearing up the chives and oregano, until . . . *splash!* Doodlebug found the one place where he was safe. Slap, bang in the middle of the goldfish pond.

'There you go, tiger.' Claudia waded in to rescue the

soggy bundle and thought, I'll wring Flavia's neck the way I'm wringing out this poor puppy. I'll wring it so she turns midnight blue and squeaks! 'And as for you, you should be ashamed of yourself, you contemptible Egyptian feline—'

Egypt! Claudia dumped Doodlebug into the arms of a passing gardener. Egypt. Why, for instance, would Flavia choose the dress of an Egyptian? Her hem making tiny puddles on her office floor, Claudia spread out a second sheet of parchment.

On the left, she wrote 'Why Egyptian?' and on the right, wrote 'Dreadlocks.' A plaited wig would disguise Flavia's hair as kohl would alter the shape of her eyes, and the dynamic costume would draw eyes away from the face. No greater significance than that. Pity.

She shook the spare ink off her nib. 'Why the need for money?' Was Flavia planning a trip? Say, to Egypt? For gods' sake, forget Egypt. It was only a bloody disguise.

The quill hovered above the inkwell like a hawk poised to strike. 'Westerners.'

Was Flavia planning to move west? To Ostia? To Sardinia? (Heaven forbid, to Iberia!) What scrambled logic went on inside that seething teenage brain? And who the hell, she scratched on the parchment, were these wretched 'Brothers of whores'? A giant blob of ink deposited itself on the parchment and slowly spread itself outwards.

Claudia allowed her mind to radiate outwards with it. Something Julia had said, right at the beginning. Her fingers drummed the desk. Not the *Serving Women* re-enactment, something else. Connected with music . . . Apollo. That was it. Flavia's preoccupation with Apollo. Typical teenage crush, of course, this yearning for the long-haired son of Jupiter, who plays a mean tune on the lyre. Show me a girl who hasn't fallen for a balladeer at some stage in her life and I'll show you a heart made of granite! But Apollo. God of music, poetry and healing. Apollo. Who drives his fiery chariot across the sky. Apollo, the sun god, worshipped by the Egyptians as Ra—

Egyptians! In a swirl of pale-blue linen, Claudia raced across the peacock mosaic to the atrium, to the great Nile fresco which covered the wall. Egyptians! To whom the land where the sun sets, the land to the west, represents the dark realm of death. The underworld. Goddammit, the *land of the Westerners.*

Her eyes scanned upwards. Beyond the yawning hippos and the thrashing crocodiles. Beyond elegant papyrus plants, date palms and soaring pyramids. Higher, even, than the disc which represented Ra himself. Because there, in the top right-hand corner, was what she was looking for. Stylised symbols of birds, of human body parts, of animals proliferated in meaningless, vertical blocks, but there, nestling between the owl and the foot, was the hieroglyph Claudia had sought. The eye. The painted eye of the falcon god, Horus, the sacred emblem of the Pharaoh.

Not brothers of whores, you clot. No wonder it made no bloody sense – Flea had misheard.

Flavia had talked about that self-styled mystical cult who called themselves 'The Brothers of Horus'.

There was an Egyptian connection, after all.

Chapter Sixteen

The cult's headquarters comprised two rooms on the top floor of an apartment block in the artisan quarter of the Viminal, right on the corner where Pear Street meets the herbalist's. To advertise its presence, a stylised kohl-rimmed eye – the Eye of Horus – complete with trademark 'teardrop' was painted on the outside a full cubit high. Claudia paused in the alleyway where, thanks to towering six-storey buildings, the sun never penetrated and cricked her neck upwards. The lines were strong, the colours fresh on the giant almond eye which stared out across the city with such haughty indifference and, as she pressed her way up the stairs through the breakfast bustle, Claudia dredged up what few snippets she'd gleaned about this mystical religious body.

An Egyptian called Mentu, in an imagined belief that his claim to the royal throne had been usurped, had set up his own court sixty or so miles north-west of Rome. Here, styling himself Pharaoh Mentu I, he rigidly practised all things Egyptian, from civil law to agriculture, religion to apparel and Rome – ever tolerant of free speech and foreign religions – laughed its pixie boots off.

'Silly bugger,' they hooted. 'Hasn't he heard Egypt joined the Empire? The province has been ours these eighteen years!'

And far from putting a stop to Mentu's practices, Rome set him up as a laughing stock, the butt of a million jokes in which he was derided as a harmless, gormless fool. And that was pretty well the limit of Claudia's knowledge. From time to time, she'd seen his followers shaking sistrums and spreading what they called 'The Word of Ra' and had dismissed them as mindless automatons. They might style themselves the Brothers of Horus; Claudia preferred the term Pyramidiots!

This being the school holidays, the stairs of the apartment block rang with the clump of eager little feet, with bouncing balls and rolling hoops, a dropped marble here, a toy soldier there, women bustling home with loaves hot from the baker's, jugs of wine from the taverns. Men in stained work tunics blew hurried kisses to their wives and ruffled the heads of their children as they skidded down the corridor, their satchels slung over their shoulders, scurrying off to work. On the top floor, Claudia leaned against the rail to get her breath back. It was quieter up here, the only traffic being a rheumy-eyed crone in black widow's weeds setting off with her market basket in the crook of her elbow, and an old greying mongrel nibbling at his flea bites. Advancing towards the Brothers' door, the appetising aromas of fried sausages and fresh bread which had accompanied her up the stairwell were beaten back by the smoke of incense resin.

'Sister!' A moon-faced youth whose eyes were rimmed with green malachite bade her welcome. 'Join us, we beseech you, for the end of prayers.'

Typical fanatic. Entrenched in his own beliefs, not interested in anyone else. Didn't occur to him that she might want, say, the door of the goldbeater's assistant, or had he seen her missing tabby cat?

'Come.' In his pleated white kilt, held in place by a broad knotted sash, the boy beckoned for Claudia to follow. 'We make our devotions back here.'

Her eyes took in the sparse furnishings, the unpainted white plaster, the simple rush stools. Flavia had opted for *this?* Two tables and three plain wooden chests lined one wall, with a rough stove in the corner over which a variety of meat hooks and ladles hung higgledy-piggledy above cauldrons and skillets. Jars and pots stood askew on a shelf, their dribbled contents left to harden and stick in thick runnels, much to the delight of the flies. Her eyes swivelled to the five mattresses which lined the right-hand wall, two not slept in, and a washbasin full of water you could not see your reflection in, which stood guard at the end.

'Hail to thee, Ra, in thy rising,' intoned a voice from the room which had so far been obscured by choking incense smoke.

'Mine eyes adore thee,' answered the moon-faced youth, placing the palms of his hands together in reverence. A second acolyte, a girl, adopted an identical position, her eyes closed tight in piety, while the third member of the trio – the speaker – appeared to be sprinkling water on something with his fingertips. All Claudia could see clearly through the gloom was that his head, eyebrows and chest were shaven.

'Gladden,' said the priest, 'our hearts with the Vessel of Dreams, the Barque of One Million Years. Blessed be the Boat of the Morning.'

Boat? Halfway up the Viminal Hill, this man's talking boats? But incredibly, as her eyes adjusted to the darkened room and swirling smoke, Claudia realised that – yes, on the top floor of this six-storey apartment block and some half a mile from the river, there was indeed a boat filling up the whole of the back room!

And not just any old boat!

She coughed, perhaps from the fumes, perhaps from the vision which crystallised before her. Its high prow covered in gold and its ribs inset with amethysts and pearls and lapis lazuli, the vessel glowed luminescent in the darkened back room, and the curls of smoke from braziers which dotted the floor were like eddies of water, blue and swirling, carrying the boat on their tide.

'O Living Lord, rest thy rays upon thy servants.'

If Midas himself had owned a yacht, it wouldn't have been half as spectacular as this, and now she understood what had attracted Flavia. And it was not a life of rustic simplicity! Overhead, the star-spangled ceiling glittered with silver and gold, and the blue of the walls was so dark as to be almost black, highlighting reliefs of gilt and copper and bronze.

'The events depicted on these walls,' the bald priest explained, 'show Ra's journey through the dark Realm of the Night. Over here –' a manicured hand swept to the left – 'his battle with the Great Serpent who waits nightly to devour him, and over here –' the hand swept to the right – 'his journey through the Twelve Great Gates of the Underworld. I am Zer. Will you break fast with us?'

Claudia recalled the dirty jugs and bowl of filthy water. 'Love to.'

The female acolyte tossed handfuls of rose petals into the barque's prow, extinguished one by one the bowls of smoke and, reversing reverentially, closed the door of the back room behind her.

Zer pulled up a rush stool and indicated for her to be seated. 'You wish to join the Brothers of Horus, that you may enter the Fields of the Blessed through the path of resurrection?'

Whoever called life a learning curve was right. Claudia had just forgotten how steep it was in places. 'I do indeed.'

'You swear to abide by the laws and the customs of Egypt?'

'Yes.'

'To worship Ra, through his son on earth, Osiris, our own Pharaoh, Mentu?'

Talk about a man with a split personality! 'Naturally.'

'And you are prepared to renounce your life, your family, your friends, the Roman pantheon?'

'I am.'

Humility, she'd decided, was the key. Awed as she had been by the riches hidden away in the back room, she'd quickly noticed that the two acolytes, glowing with righteousness as they were, said nothing. The pair were content to watch the priest, mirror his actions and gaze adoringly at him, reminding her of dogs trained to perform tricks. Except there was a sinister feel to their adulation. That they would be prepared to go to any lengths to protect their lord. *Any lengths at all.*

At the priest's nod, the boy passed her a beaker of black, foaming beer and the girl handed round platters of flat bread and cheese. Despite his name and exotic taste in barbering,

Claudia suspected that Zer was not actually of Egyptian extraction. She glanced again at the soft, well-manicured hands, so much at odds with their simplistic surroundings. Zer was patently not averse to a bit of pampering from time to time! So then. Not Egyptian, not an ascetic and not a fanatic like these other two. Claudia sensed a sharpness about this shaven-headed priest. A probing quality. Assuming this building was the funnel for sending new recruits off to the commune, then Zer was the man doing the pouring.

'We are proud of the society we have built,' he said, tearing off a chunk of the bread, 'and the barque which honours Ra.'

Barque? I'll say you're barking!

'It is never too late to purge the heart of its sins, to fill it with goodness and truth.' He gulped at his beer, wiping the froth away with the back of his hand. 'I assure you, you will not regret joining.'

Damn right. The sooner I clap hands on Flavia and bring her home, the quicker Junius will be free of his death sentence. Already this was Friday. Executions were scheduled for tomorrow afternoon. Time was fast running out.

While Zer explained about the council of the Ten True Gods, their role in the Judgement of both the Living and the Dead and how, through them, the heart would find purity to weigh light at the Balance, Claudia studied the transfixed acolytes from the corner of her eye. The boy's Caesar haircut marked him out as the scion of a well-to-do family, as did the girl's cosseted complexion and, as though a beacon had been lit, Claudia saw Zer's reason for targeting that particular corner of the Forum to sing Ra's praises. Coincidence? That this spot just happens to be where the young blooms of patrician families hung out to exchange news and gossip over an open-air goblet of wine? I don't think so!

'How quickly might I be able to join you?' she whispered.

'Sister.' Zer took both her hands in his and gazed deep into her eyes. 'It is obvious you have problems.' His voice was low and mesmeric. 'But once you devote yourself to Ra, these problems will be as dust upon the wind.'

'It's my stepfather. Since my divorce –' she kept her lashes well lowered – 'he's been pressuring me to sign a contract to marry his own son, that he might get his hands on my inheritance.'

'Ah.' Something flashed in the priest's eyes, and he began to take a closer interest in the quality of her gown, the rings which decorated her fingers, the emeralds which hung from her pendant. 'I see.' He smiled, and she thought, I'll bet you do!

He shuffled his stool closer and topped up her beer.

'Under Egyptian law,' he smiled oilily, 'men and women share equal rights and since we have abolished slavery in our commune, there are no constraints on who one might marry, a craftsman, a dentist, a poet, if that's who takes your fancy. Alternatively, should you wish, my child, there's no pressure to re-marry at all. Indeed, most of the ladies who join us do not take a husband, while others –' he paused, assessing again the jewels and the gemstones. 'Others might be chosen by Mentu to become his wife.'

'He has more than one?'

'The Pharaoh can take a hundred wives, if he so desires. It is the supreme honour, my dear, afforded to very few, to become a true bride of Ra.'

Claudia's heart began to pound. Assuming her suppositions were on target, any minute now and he'd broach the subject of money.

'There is, of course, the little matter of the Solar Fund.'

Good boy! 'The Solar Fund?' she asked guilelessly.

'The community is self-contained,' Zer explained. 'It is the temple which requires upkeep and naturally the greater one's contribution, the more favourably Ra smiles upon his servant.'

Naturally, indeed!

'This is entirely a voluntary contribution, you understand.' The smile became more unctuous still. 'New members are under no obligation to make a donation, although if they do, it is wise to remember that the sacred metal of Ra is gold.'

Another brick fell into place: the reason why the ransom had to be paid in gold.

'Oh, dear.' Claudia placed her hands together, the way the acolytes had done earlier. 'I have precious little by way of liquid assets – my stepfather, you know . . . Spent it all.' Careful, now. Don't overdo it. 'On the other hand, I have an olive grove in Campania and vineyards which stretch across three hills in Frascati. Would they be acceptable, do you think?'

The priest all but licked his lips. 'More than,' he said, adding with a reassuring pat on her hand, 'Ra's gratitude will be warmly rewarding, I assure you.'

Believe me, Zer, I am assured! Men and women might have equal rights in the land of Mentu and the commune might be self-sufficient, but a girl doesn't need to be a Socrates to work out that those who contributed handsomely to the Solar Fund were not the ones who worked the fields and toiled all night kneading dough in the bake house!

Claudia's thoughts flickered towards her wilful stepdaughter. Without her precious gold pieces, Flavia's contribution was the jewellery she had been wearing. Quite a haul under ordinary circumstances, a street thief's for example, but you had to remember Mentu was not about spiritual comfort. There were no slaves in his commune, because no slave could enter without the consent of their master – and, dear me, the Brothers of Horus were not targeting the poor! Mentu was on a simple get-rich-quick scam and with her paltry contribution, Flavia would be way down the line when it came to dishing out Ra's sunny favours.

Hey ho, Claudia thought happily. A few days scrubbing floors and mopping out latrines will make her view her ideals rather differently. In fact, had Junius not been facing the fangs of a ravenous tiger, she'd have left Flavia to rot for a month!

'This.' She stood up and hugged the priest. 'Is the happiest day of my life. You don't know how much this means to me, being free of my tyrannical stepfather.'

'It means a lot to us, too.' Zer beamed back, and she knew he was already calculating the value of her mythical olive groves and Frascati vines.

'I shall have the contracts drawn up immediately,' she said breathlessly, 'they'll be with you tomorrow, Sunday at the latest.'

She moved across to the window. In the street below, six hired henchmen filled up shopfronts and doorways and tossed dice on the pavement, one always keeping a tight grip on an gamine creature with green eyes whose puppy happily chewed the end of its leash.

'How soon can we leave?' Claudia asked, with a commendable catch in her voice. 'I'm desperate to get away, to begin a new life, and I don't want my stepfather to find me.'

'Can you be ready to travel within the hour?' the priest suggested, because he didn't want the stepfather finding her, either!

When the latest recruit's handkerchief fluttered out of the window to be carried away on the malarial breeze, the priest was not aware of any redistribution of pedestrian activity below. He simply sketched a blessing in the air and assured her – in his gravest manner – that her lost kerchief was an augur. A symbol that her old life was discarded. On and on, his solemn tones droned in an effort to convince her that the Pharaoh Mentu was the only true bridge between heaven and earth and that now their sister had chosen the path of peace and harmony, immortality in the Fields of the Blessed was assured.

Silly sod.

Chapter Seventeen

For the second day running, the sticky breeze throbbed and pulsed like some invisible vampire, sucking energy from whoever it touched, and the breeze was unforgiving. It made sweat run in torrents down the necks of the fully armoured legionaries guarding Marcus. It trickled down their legs, their arms, their foreheads, their bronze plating, causing it to boil beneath their vests and sizzle against their cheekpieces and greaves. The scarves around their throats to prevent the armour chafing were dark with perspiration, their skins darker still from the heroic effort of standing guard in this crushing killer heat. The triumphal breeze blew gently in their faces, breathing lethargy, marsh sickness and mocking human fallibility.

Despite the eight unhappy men stationed round his house and the platoon of slaves cleaning up the house, Marcus was alone. Isolated in an emotional, rather than a physical sense.

There was no Claudia breaking her nails as she pulled at the plaster to remove the bones of the murder victim, whose ribs, even when they'd pulled the body out, still bore the instrument of the crime. No Claudia, weeping silently at the tiny skeleton lodged within the larger frame. No Claudia, white with cement dust and wearing a tiara of brick chippings in her hair.

No Claudia, being bodily evicted from his house, yet still managing to re-shackle Flea, down a libation for the family gods, curse Orbilio's boss to Hades and scoop up a squirming Doodlebug all at once!

Orbilio looked out upon the building site that was his garden and missed them all.

He missed Doodlebug, gnawing on the chair legs, ploughing up the dust and – may the gods forgive the little sod! – running off with the skeleton's kneecap. He even missed that outrageous street thief, Flea, with her wide green eyes and tawny hair and language which would make any self-respecting sailor blush. And he missed Claudia.

Especially Claudia. Propounding theories as she spat out chunks of plaster. Sprawling backwards over the rubble when her claw hammer jammed. Accusing him of showing off because he'd ripped away more of the wall than she had. It was, he thought, as the morning sun beat mercilessly upon his back, the closest thing he'd had to a family. The warmth, the banter, the pulling together, like oarsmen on a trireme. It had felt right, somehow. Natural.

So different from his own family, who were cold and clever and distantly proficient in everything they put their mind to. Laughter did not figure in an Orbilio family childhood. Just the brisk snap of efficiency, extending even to play, which took the form of music, poetry and painting. He'd never known a father who wrestled with him on the atrium floor, played a game of hide-and-seek, or the family banding together to play 'sardines'.

And yet, he reflected wryly, one member of that callous crew had sufficient passion to drive a knife deep into another's ribcage.

The heat was unbearable and, with no desire to retire to the office adjacent to the cause of his grief, Marcus crossed the courtyard to the atrium, whose honeycomb screen neutralised the sun's scorching rays. One day. Twenty-four hours since he'd first been confined to house arrest and already he was bridling like an incarcerated felon. The baths were out of bounds, and that was a bugger, too, particularly in this stinking heat, because it wasn't the same, splashing around in a tub. He needed a good soak, a massage in the steam room, a deep-cleansing scrape with the strigil. Dammit, he'd get spots on his back at this rate!

Up and down he paced, scratching at the stubble on his jaw,

the tangles in his hair. Who? he thought. Whose was the body bricked in the wall? *Who put her there?*

His steward, Tingi, was doing his best to track down the slaves Orbilio's wife had sold the day she ran away, in the hope that they might shed light on who had been living here when the . . . let's call it, building work was carried out. Marcus slammed his fist into the palm of his hand. The bitch! He didn't mind her leaving him – good riddance. It was tearing apart the lives of forty-seven slaves which was so bloody unforgivable! How *could* she? Croesus, she'd known where his money boxes were kept, she could have taken any amount she pleased. Instead, the cruel bitch had waited until he was halfway to Macedonia on campaign before she set about splitting up families and friends with not a thought for their feelings. Just in order to feign some kind of independence and claim it was 'her' money she was leaving with!

Now, as then, Orbilio felt nothing but sympathy for the Lusitanian sea captain with whom she had eloped.

'Ah, Tingi! Any luck?'

The mournful Libyan, arriving home, spread his hands. 'No more than I had yesterday, sir.'

Finding where his slaves had been taken after the auction had been a doddle – records were kept of all transactions – but even in this, his bitch of an ex-wife had been cunning. Aware of the bitter feud between Orbilio's father and one Lucius Afer, she'd contacted Afer prior to the auction, and he had promptly snaffled the slaves up then gloatingly refused point-blank to sell them back to Orbilio. Shortly afterwards, the bastard distributed the slaves around his vast and scattered estates, thereby transferring the feud to the next generation.

Tingi mopped the sweat from his forehead. 'I'll try again later,' he said, 'but it would help if we knew just how long the body's been there.'

'Don't I know it!' Orbilio retorted.

Fifty years in the wall and the crime would never be solved. Contagion would cloud his family name for eternity.

Five or six years bricked up in the plaster and Orbilio's

chances of reinstatement to the Security Police, already perilously slim, would vanish into thin air, along with any prospect of the Senate. But, no! The crime could not be that recent, the body *had* to have been here before he inherited the house. He was sure he'd have noticed a wall creeping forward!

Then again. Marcus tasted acid in the back of his throat and, flipping back a mental calendar by a full nine years, saw a callow youth of seventeen exchanging marriage rings with his fifteen-year-old bride in what was not a love match, rather the political merging of two powerful clans. The mists swirled in his memory to reveal that same young man lifting weights and working out in the gymnasium to build up his muscles, and different swirls revealed different facets of the young Marcus Cornelius. The serious frown, as he pored over maps and considered his forthcoming stint in the army. The laughing youth, out on the town with his riotous friends. The experimental lures of his marital bed.

What the mists of time did not reveal, of course, was a boy interested in the walls of old storerooms!

The calendar flipped rapidly forward and, standing in the cool of his atrium, with his loyal steward at his side, Orbilio knew in his heart that if, say, an uncle had bricked up a wall six, five, even four years ago, he would not have known. Much less cared.

But the boy had matured into the man and the man experienced a tidal wave of guilt. Suppose he had unwittingly concealed a murder?

'Is everything all right, sir?'

Suddenly, Marcus knew he could not rest until he knew the truth. However bitter that might be.

'What? Oh, yes, Tingi. Everything's fine, thank you. I need a shave, that's all,' he told his concerned steward. 'Can you see to it? And, er –' he lowered his voice – 'any joy with that other matter?'

The Libyan glanced round, checking the legionaries' positions at their post. 'The favours you called in, you mean? No, sir. I spoke with the Clerk of the Dungeons, he said there's nothing he can do, the Gaul's committed a capital offence, the papers have already been signed.'

'What about the Dungeon Master? He owes me big time.'

'So he said, sir, but the problem is, he can't just tear up the execution order, twenty-two other names are on the same sheet and duplicates have already been filed in the Record Office.'

Marcus felt a stab of pain behind his eyes. 'Tingi, you go back. You tell him that Orbilio doesn't give a toss about his bloody administrative procedures. You remind him that Orbilio saved his son's arse, and you point out exactly *where* Orbilio caught the little bastard and what he was doing at the time. I'm sure,' he added, 'that after a moment's gentle reflection, the Dungeon Master will see a way to excusing Junius the Gaul from Saturday's outing in the arena.'

In truth, he felt less than confident. One lesson Marcus had learnt during his appointment with the Security Police was that loyalty was an elastic commodity. People were effusively grateful on the occasion that their skins were saved, less so over the passage of time, and that they rarely repaid the favour without some kind of prompting. The Dungeon Master was very much the type who separated the past from the present as though they were the yolk and white of an egg, and to lean effectively on people like him required a physical presence. Not some diluted, second-hand message!

As in so many areas of Orbilio's young life, waiting was always the hard part.

The herald was calling the first hour before noon and the barber was stropping his knife on a sturdy Spanish whetstone when the letter arrived. Orbilio, buried beneath a mound of hot towels, suggested his secretary read it aloud.

'My dear Antonia –' The secretary, a plump individual with wide set eyes which bestowed on him a false sense of innocence, cleared his throat. 'Oh, dear. There uh – appears to have been an error in the address.'

Orbilio grinned. 'I doubt that,' he said. This could only be one woman's doing. 'Carry on.' *Now* what was that scheming witch up to?

The barber stripped away the hot towels and pulled taught Orbilio's cheek as the secretary read on.

> This is goodbye, but please don't be sad for me. I am starting life anew, in a place where my stepfather can't get his hands on my olive groves or the vines in Frascati, and since I have no need for these estates any more, I am dedicating them to Ra. Yes, Ra, Antonia! Isn't it wonderful? I am joining the Brothers of Horus, to walk – if my heart should prove worthy – the path to the Fields of the Blessed. I shall think of you always, dear friend, and pray that, one day, that brute Marcus will stop beating you senseless.
>
> Your sister in harmony,
>
> Claudia (soon to be known as Anuket)

The barber was quick to apologise as he mopped the bleeding cut, but Orbilio waved short his protest. 'It's not your fault,' he said, and it wasn't. '. . . that brute Marcus . . .' He'd been laughing so hard, the barber couldn't follow the contours, 'beating you senseless' indeed!

Clever letter, though. Obviously written in the presence of the – shall we say – membership committee, the message seemed on the surface nothing more than a fond farewell to a girlfriend. Underneath, however, its code revealed that Claudia had discovered Flavia's whereabouts. That in order to bring her back to save Junius, Claudia was pretending to join these mystical Brothers. That in order to enlist, one had to, sinisterly, change one's identity and finally – that to join involved the transference of large sums of money!

Orbilio's humour faded. He for one had never believed Mentu harmless, even though the enterprise had been the subject of official investigation. In the end, the Treasury line was that as long as Mentu paid his taxes and endowed a college or two, what was the problem? Mentu, whether he liked to call himself Pharaoh, Osiris, Ra or Slinky Sue was not committing any crime. No fraud, no forgery, no theft, no plots against the State. Oh, sure, one or two families complained about their (mostly) daughters running away, that they were allowed no physical contact and that the few short notes received didn't come across like the children they'd raised, but so what? These 'runaways' were, in legal terms, adult, and while theoretically their absconding might be against the law, inasmuch as children remain the property of their fathers until marriage (and, for women, their husbands thereafter), everyone felt that those who chose commune life were either unstable, unloved, unwanted, immature or simply inadequate.

Or, to put it another way, no one really wanted these people back.

And to some extent, Marcus sympathised with that view. If human beings are stupid enough to give up everything to follow some quasi-religious nut, then that's their choice. What worried him was that, of all the people who'd joined, none – not a single one – had ever returned! Twice he'd pressed for a closer investigation into the activities of the cult – indeed he'd even volunteered to go undercover himself – but the official line held firm. *Don't rock the boat.* Which had culminated in yet another clash with his superior.

'Even if Mentu is operating a swindle,' his boss had said, 'this is not a job for the Security Police, whose role, as you obviously need reminding, is to oversee the security of Rome by rooting out forgers, conspirators and the like. So get your arse out of my office and start bloody rooting!'

When the barber moved to rinse Orbillio's face with clean water, he pushed him away. Everything in Claudia's letter underlined his suspicions about the self-styled Pharaoh Mentu. Members had been targeted with cold-blooded precision, picked because no one would press too hard for their return while at the same time ensuring that not so much money changed hands that it warranted making a fuss. Sisters/brothers/friends might show concern, but what the hell? They have no clout in law.

The Brothers of Horus, as Claudia's letter told him only

too clearly, were in the business of mind control. They brainwashed the 'faithful' with new names and new rituals as a means of keeping them focussed on Ra and off their money, although until now the cult had been nothing more than a vague and nagging worry niggling away at the back of Orbilio's mind and, like the buzz of a wasp trapped in a room, annoying, though hardly a major cause for concern.

Until now.

The words echoed round his empty bed chamber.

Until now.

Never had Marcus felt more paralysed than by this damned house arrest. Soldiers at every entrance. Vigilantes posted outside.

Until now. Until Claudia joined up with the cult . . .

Marcus dabbed at the nicks on his chin with a spider's web soaked in vinegar. He didn't imagine for one second that the headstrong widow would be swayed by the Brothers' mind games (in fact, he almost pitied them), but surely over the past year or two, *one* of the faithful would have wanted to leave?

Immediately, the wasp became a whole swarm.

Exactly what did happen when you tried to leave the cult? Why had no one ever come home? Suddenly, looking into the mirror, Marcus realised it was not Claudia's sanity he feared for.

Marcus feared for her life.

Chapter Eighteen

Several things happened that Friday afternoon.

First, the clouds descended lower and lower, trapping the heat, funnelling the breeze and making the rancid air fouler yet.
The weather was showing signs of breaking at last.

In a wooden amphitheatre on the Field of Mars, the pallid Prefect failed to notice the perspiration which slowly weighted his elegant tunic. Transfixed, he watched his troupe of male actors rehearse a centuries-old drama and, to his utter astonishment, such was their professionalism that none of the audience noticed the wonky scenery and dodgy props, or even that the Serving Women lit their signal to the Romans from a crab apple tree not a fig.
Indeed, computing on a wax tablet during the intermission the cost of his production, the Prefect found the enterprise pleasantly profitable on all counts.

The same could not be said of the girl who had misled her foster parents into believing she was taking a starring role in the show. As rumbles of thunder rolled in the distance, Flavia leaned over the stoneblock latrine and was comprehensively sick. Why? she wailed. Why did they make her do that? Help out in the kitchens, they said, and she thought maybe peeling root vegetables, shucking peas, it sounded romantic, and besides, she rather liked the look of the boy who fetched hot loaves from the bakery.
Instead, they made her . . .

At the memory of the stinking, steaming, purple viscera spilling over the yard, Flavia vomited again, and wanted to die. It wouldn't be like this, she sobbed, if I'd had those two thousand gold pieces. Two thousand gold pieces buys you cushy jobs like potting honey, mixing perfumes, making sweet music on the strings of a lyre. Not gutting a . . .

At the very thought of the mess on the cobbles, she retched a third time, then a fourth, more noisily still. She hated it here. She wanted to go home. Nothing was at all like Zer had promised.

Zer had promised a new life, a world filled with happiness, where brother loves brother and the Pharaoh is father to all. He had said nothing about disembowelling a *pig*! Come to that, she thought gasping for air, he'd said nothing about everyone wearing identical workclothes, or attending prayers twice a day, or communal eating, or wearing these itchy reed sandals. He hadn't said she couldn't choose her new Egyptian name, either. She'd earmarked Nefertiti (for preference), Cleopatra as second choice – instead they addressed her as Magas. Ugh. She shuddered at the ugliness of the name. And why did women have to wear these horrid shift dresses, which only flattered the thin?

'Magas!' The voice was harsh and insistent. 'Magas, stop babying around. It's a pig! We need to eat, and you must pull your weight in the commune. Remember, child, we are all sisters of Ra.'

Flavia-Magas wiped her mouth with a sponge. 'I can't,' she wailed. 'I can't face that disgusting stench, I can't!'

'There's no such word,' snapped the voice. 'Now clean yourself up, flush out the latrines, and hurry back to your work. This is not the weather for guts to be lying out in the yard!'

'This ain't no weather to be outdoors in.'

The party was making excellent progress in the four-horse trap, the roads being quiet, the hills relatively gentle, when Flea blurted out her sulky protest. Claudia flashed a radiant smile at

Zer, which also encompassed his two mooning acolytes, and hissed under her breath to the thief, 'One more squeak and you'll be picking teeth from your tonsils.' Aloud, she said, 'Sweet child. So concerned for our health and well being.' She shrugged helplessly at the priest, whose shaven head ran with beads of perspiration. 'Wouldn't leave me, you know. I did try . . .'

Zer smiled his oily smile at the girl with the puppy sprawled across her skinny legs. 'We have no servants where we are going, but love and loyalty transcend all emotion. Ra will richly reward you.'

Translated, of course, as meaning Ra will richly reward olive groves in Campania and vines stretching across three hills of Frascati, and should the new recruit wish to bring her maid and a fat, un-house-trained puppy along, Zer would most certainly raise no objection, she could bring a troupe of dwarves and dancing elephants for all he cared. Zer's job was to ensure financial transitions flowed smoothly.

'Why don't you close your eyes, dear?' Claudia was anxiety personified. 'Rest a while?'

The question may have sounded solicitous to priestly ears, but the thief wasn't fooled. Substitute mouth for eyes, was the message. Bitch, she mouthed back, when Zer's head was turned, but Flea wasn't really sorry she was on this trip. It was kinda fun, tagging along with Claudia. She saw things she'd not normally get to see, people she'd never normally meet – well, not unless you could call cutting their purses a meeting! And it bloody hurt, binding up yer tits, it was nice to wear a proper breastband for a change, something which supported 'em, made them comfy, and besides, casing this place sounded cool!

She leaned her spine against the woodwork and considered the heavy, grey clouds overhead. There was this bloke, a master thief, who she could approach when she got back to Rome. He was that bloody smart, this bloke, he'd be able to fence the Emperor's personal seal!

The trap joggled along, its cargo of humans and bits and

pieces for the commune bumping in time with the wheels. Cauldrons, griddles, in fact lots of iron stuff, she noticed. Three rolls of linen. A sack of hemp, a barrel of pitch, a block of salt – stuff they weren't able to produce on site. Can't imagine what Flavia would want with them. If it were Flea, she'd stick with Claudia, you'd get a ride and half with her, but there was no accounting for tastes, and – funnily enough – she was looking forward to seeing Flavia again. Talk about opposites attracting! But they'd got on well, Flavia and her. An instant rapport, although what Claudia would say when she copped hold of her, Flea didn't like to think, and Flavia deserved it, too. Narking should be punished. She should not have shopped Junius to the rozzers, that was out of order, that. Especially when she, a rich man's brat, would know it entailed certain death.

Idly, Flea fondled Doodlebug's floppy ears and wondered what it would take for Claudia to let her have him for keeps.

She shifted the dead weight of the sleeping pup and glanced at the creepy priest and his pair of followers. Barmy, them two. Pity they weren't wearing jewellery, she'd have whipped it off them in no time, gormless twonks wouldn't even notice! But there'd be stuff at this commune to nick and sell on, she'd stake her life on it. Flea's thoughts settled on the thief master in Rome. Play your dice right, girl, and you could make serious dosh out of this.

As it happened, they were trading in a very different currency in Rome.

Deep inside the dungeons – converted stone quarries which ran underneath Silversmith's Rise – the heat was fiercesome, the stench appalling and the Dungeon Master held half a peach under his nose as Orbilio's steward rattled off a list of his son's misdemeanours. The Dungeon Master listened attentively, amazed by both the range of his son's proclivities and the fact that Marcus Cornelius knew so much about them.

'All he is asking,' the steward concluded, 'is that you let

the Gaul go in return for your son's transgressions being, shall we say – overlooked.'

The Dungeon Master considered the steward. A Libyan. A foreigner. A wog. And held the peach that bit closer to his florid nostrils. It was true, then, the rumour that Orbilio was under house arrest, else he'd have come down here personally. Orbilio wasn't the type to be put off by a bit of a stink! Carefully, the Dungeon Master made some holding remark while his mind worked gymnastics, then said (with a firm handshake), 'Tell Orbilio I'll do my best for the Gaul.'

He waited until the Libyan had left before strolling down the rank, stinking corridors to where shackled prisoners languished, raged, pleaded or sobbed against the implacable stone quarry walls. Strangely, Junius the Gaul had done none of these things. No protest, no struggle. In fact, the Dungeon Master believed he had not spoken one word since his arrest. In the spluttering light of a reed brand, the jailer studied the impassive face of the slave who'd been caught red-handed wearing the toga and noted that in spite of the filthy conditions, the intolerable air, the heat, the oppression, the beatings, hard blue eyes stared levelly back. The Dungeon Master tossed a ring of keys from hand to hand. Not a bloody flicker.

'Cocky bastard, ain't yer?' The type who gives the crowd good value for money when it comes to public execution.

Taking a good, long look at the Gaul made the warden's decision easier.

He sighed and wondered how it was that his son, his own flesh and blood, had become such a thoroughly bad lot. Where had they gone wrong, him and the boy's mother? More importantly, perhaps, where would it end? At this rate, someone would die, or at the least end up seriously injured. The warder wiped a hand over his face. What kept the scandal hushed up was an agent of the Security Police who wished to trade the life of a cocky young Gaul. No contest, was it? A half-smile lifted the Dungeon Master's top lip. Gaul . . . He sniffed the ripe peach. Yes, indeed. Now, were his son to leave, say, tomorrow for Gaul, or Iberia, anywhere distant, there would be no case to answer here, would there? His own position as Dungeon Master would not be compromised and whichever way the wind might then blow for Orbilio, the investigator's wings would be clipped.

The Dungeon Master looked at the scroll listing tomorrow's executions.

And patted it.

Who was he to deny the crowd a worthy competitor?

The Clerk of the Dungeons, delivering yet another batch of paperwork to the Dungeon Master, studied the execution roster, which seemed to be growing longer by the minute. Must be the heat, he reasoned. Tempers fray, feuds boil over, and it can only get worse, now the cloud cover's low. And wasn't that thunder he'd heard in the distance?

The Clerk toyed, just for a fraction of a second, with confiding in the Dungeon Master, man to man, as it were, that he owed Orbilio a favour for the time when he . . . ahem. Well, he would not mention the actual nature of the debt – not to this burly, tough ox – but the point was, he could perhaps let drop that he owed someone a favour, and that if the Dungeon Master could perhaps see his way clear to excusing a certain young Gaul . . .

Uh-uh. The fat bastard was more likely to throw him to the tigers as well, for trying to bribe an officer of the Empire!

Nevertheless, as he deposited the product of what some called bureaucracy, others a meticulous attention to detail, on the warder's cluttered desk, the Clerk genuinely regretted that he had not been able to repay the favour that he owed.

In his hidden cave high above the valley, Seth washed himself thoroughly and regarded Berenice. He was wondering now whether he had been right to make her his favourite. Look at her, the bitch. Slumped. Not so much as a shudder of protest when he ran his hands over her, not a ripple of revulsion in the engagingly innovative way he took her.

'God knows, I've tried, Berenice,' he said wearily.

A few tricks that he knew, plus a few more he'd invented, but pain no longer made any impact.

'You can't blame me, if I find myself a new favourite.'

One thing, though, it wouldn't be Flavia. Seth had watched the new arrival carefully, quickly marking her as a firm candidate for his dinner table. She was not the type to make friends easily and that was good, because once they bonded, these girls, there was no chance of picking off one of a crowd. He took loners. Misfits among the misfits. Girls whose abrupt departure no one noticed, much less grieved over, and this Flavia was a perfect candidate – indeed, Seth had already allocated a mask. The vulture. Appropriately ungainly, appropriately ugly, but then her face wasn't important. Only her expressions mattered to him, her reaction to his deviant attentions.

All the same, the Dark One wouldn't choose a lump like that for his consort in the afterlife! He really wished Berenice had tried harder today. Outside, thunder roared like the Minotaur.

'It's your own fault,' he said, 'that you're displaced.'

Berenice did not respond. She sat, staring numbly, mutely, as though looking beyond the Master of Darkness, the Sorcerer, the Measurer of Time. With the full force of his weight behind his hand, Seth sent her neck jolting sideways with a crack, but those dumb, numb eyes didn't register. As though Berenice was half-dead already, having given up the struggle for life.

Suddenly joy surged within him, and his loins stirred once more.

'Of course!'

Of course, Berenice would not fail him! Berenice *wanted* to be his favourite, his consort, it was her only way of telling him that she wanted – yes, *wanted* to die. To walk the chosen path with Seth. The others – he cast his glance round the table, at Thoth and at Horus, Bast, Isis, Hathor – the others he had left alone while they made their decision whether to live on and be damned to eternal desolation, or to struggle against his special knot which tightened with every effort and, in death, achieve blessedness.

His loins were positively jolting again.

Berenice was the only one who had actively *shown* him which path she wanted to take! Seth was a fool for not understanding before. Hadn't Berenice fed her own son a poisoned draught to be with him? Only through death could she find resurrection alongside her lord. Only through death could she find her true place for eternity.

Fire shot through his veins. Alone among the figures seated round his table, Berenice understood that the past stands for nothing, it's the future that's significant, and the future lay in Seth's magic hands. He knew now which god Berenice should become. Tenderly, he picked up the mask of the striking cobra, Wazt, the royal serpent who protected the Pharaoh by spitting her poison in attack, and he gently stroked the sacred scales.

'You want to die, don't you?' Seth ripped away Berenice's gag. 'Tell me, my child, how impatient you are to be with me!'

A flicker showed in the dullness of her eyes. 'Kill me,' she whispered. 'Please kill me.'

Seth made her beg while he raped her again.

The count was now up to six.

The sky had turned to an ominous purple as the group of travellers dismounted. Rain was surely only minutes away, it was dark as night in the hills, and all hands pitched in to secure the canvas awning over the trap. Nearly there, Zer said. Another couple of hours if it rains, less if the weather holds off.

All the same, they were glad to be stretching their muscles, Doodlebug in particular. He tried cocking his leg against one of the wheels and failed with spectacular success, and the look of pride and affection on Flea's face did not escape Claudia as nimble fingers threaded ropes round hooks, through eyes, pulling, knotting, testing the rainproof protection.

Satisfied with their efforts, the group clambered back on board, and Claudia thought, time is undoubtedly tight – just forty-eight hours before Junius is due to face death – but the commune is closer to Rome than I'd even dared hope. A band of hired henchmen (cynics might call them thugs) were following at a discreet distance, all she had to do was grab Flavia and ride off with the girl.

She glanced around the wooded, rolling hills, whose tops were smothered in granite grey cloud, and asked herself, what could go wrong?

Dash in. Dash out. Swear an oath.

Nothing on earth could be simpler.

The first of the raindrops fell as Marcus Cornelius assimilated his steward's report. The raindrops were the size of dinner platters, and sounded like someone was breaking eggs on the path. He listened wearily, and made the man repeat his account, and the rain came faster and faster, spattering the tiles and bricks and timbers which lay in wait for builders to transform them into his dream of a grand banqueting hall.

Whatever the Dungeon Master's handshake had been supposed to convey, Orbilio knew damn well the bastard would weasel out of his debt. There would be apologies, conciliations, excuses, mitigations, but that fat son of a bitch intended Junius to die, and since a man without honour is no man at all, Orbilio would deal with him later. It meant, of course, that the Dungeon Master had devised a way of saving his son's skin – presumably by sneaking the scumbag out of Rome – but Orbilio could deal with that later, as well. Well, no. He might as well see to it while he considered his next move.

He called for his secretary and dictated at speed, as the rain drummed on the roof.

In no time at all, his messenger's heels splashed through the streets to deliver an oilskin package which would ensure the immediate arrest of the Dungeon Master's son together with an investigation into the Dungeon Master's own financial affairs (with the specific objective of determining how so modest a wage could run a large country villa), and as the courier dodged the drips from the gutterspouts and vaulted the puddles, Orbilio considered the time scale ahead.

Twenty-four hours and the arena would be empty. Only the cleaners would remain, raking up sand sticky with the blood of the dead and hooking up the corpses to load them on to carts for the furnace. Tigers, lions, leopards would be skinned first, the stench would be vile, flies would swarm thicker than dust storms.

He could be wrong, of course, about Mentu's followers being forbidden to leave. Perhaps, now they were back in Rome, they were too ashamed to talk about their foolhardiness and mingled with contrition and anonymity in the backwater of family life? Balls. Nobody left because nobody *could,* and that would apply equally to Claudia Seferius. Marcus felt his mouth go dry. Her tongue might scare the spots off a cheetah and her glare strip the bark off an elm, but Orbilio was willing to bet that Mentu had armed guards stationed round the place, as well as drugs to keep recalcitrant members in line. He did not envisage for one second that she'd be home in time to save the Gaul.

He rubbed his knuckles into the hollows of his eyes. If he could solve the murder, that would free up his movements, but so far, his efforts had proved fruitless. A veritable army of scribes and secretaries, even his accountant, had been despatched to track down the slaves who'd previously lived in this house but although they'd located a handful, no one recalled any building work to that bloody storeroom. Bugger. Orbilio's main hope now lay in tracing a groom who'd bought his freedom about six months before the great auction and had set himself up as a mule doctor. He might recall something. The question was, where were the groom's stables located?

The hunt went on . . .

Lamps were lit round the atrium. Out in the courtyard, the legionaries at the back gate stamped their feet to shake off the trickles of water which ran down their legs, a dog's howl cut through the hammering of the rain and the thunder. The mother of the puppy, Orbilio imagined, conducting a head count and finding one mouth short at the teat!

Marcus watched the slanting torrent, the lightning whose

brilliant flashes were blurred by the clouds. Jupiter, it was hot! Rose petals lay stripped and battered on the path, most of the herbs and flowers had been flattened by the rain, their heads bobbing in puddles slow to drain, and the clove-like spice of basil filled the air, along with the intoxicating scent of earth.

What would he be doing, were he not under house arrest, that was the question?

The body in the plaster would be high priority, but hardly topping his list. A visit to the jail would be pointless. No matter how hard he leaned on the Dungeon Master, the rotten bastard would still protect his son, covering if not condoning what the boy had done (and would, of course, continue to do, be it in Rome, Sardinia or Gaul). It was too late at this stage for bribes and escape from the dungeons was, by design, quite impossible. Shackles. Locked doors. Iron grilles. Armed guards. *Quite* impossible!

No. Were he able to walk free from his house, Orbilio would ride straight to the court of Mentu. He could not be certain that Claudia's life was at risk from the Brothers of Horus, but by the gods, he could not be sure it was not!

Very quickly she would be exposed as an impostor and whilst they would not dare imprison her, he did not doubt that at some stage – and soon – a tragic accident would befall her, her food poisoned, perhaps, or a snake might find its way in to her bed.

As the storm thrashed and writhed overhead, Orbilio thought of Junius. His vehement defence, his passionate protection, contrasting so starkly with the cool stare, the solid, unwavering stance. He pictured the hard blue eyes, the sandy hair, the solid musculature. It would be the cocky bugger's arrogance, rather than his dignity, which carried him through his ordeal in the dungeons and on Saturday, goddammit, the Gaul would walk with back straight and eyes uplifted into the baying crowd and, even as the jaws of death clamped over him, he would not blame his mistress for what befell him.

Marcus rubbed at his temples and acknowledged the pain in his chest for what it was. Jealousy. The thought of the boy pressing his lips, his hands, his body to Claudia's skin pierced him like a dagger through the heart. And maybe it was because he didn't want the Gaul to end up a martyr that Orbilio's eyes misted up, but whatever it was, Mother of Tarquin, he didn't want the boy dead. Not like that. Yet there was sod all he could do. Eight legionaries guarded his doors, vigilantes patrolled in the streets.

Junius was destined to die.

Claudia's life was in danger.

And Marcus Cornelius was powerless to act.

In desperation, he reached for the wine jug.

'Tingi!' He called louder, and only partly to be heard above the pounding of the rain. 'TINGI!'

'What?' The steward came running. 'What is it you want, sir?' His eyes took in the pitcher of wine which had been full just a half hour previously, and the lopsided, foolish grin plastered on his master's slack face.

'Why, Tingi, old friend, I want what everyone else ish getting, this shecond night of the Games.'

The steward took a step back from the blast of the wine fumes.

'I want entertainment,' Marcus said, punching a limp fist into the palm of his hand, 'and if I'm not allowed out to enjoy it, by the godsh, I'll bloody well have it brought here.'

From the vestibule and from the courtyard came the sound of sniggering.

'By entertainment,' the Libyan frowned, silencing the guards with a glower, 'you mean . . . ?'

'Women, Tingi.' Marcus reeled forward and clapped him on the shoulder. 'By entertainment, I mean *women.* Big, tall, lusty, busty girls. I want them to be able to sing, to dance, to tell dirty jokes, I want girls who can drink me under the table and then bonk me to oblivion, two at a time.'

'Two at a time?'

'Whatsha matter? Have I developed a stutter?'

He appeared to have developed a weave, though, and groped for a pillar which would support his drunken weight.

'There's only one course of action under circumstances like these. Throw a party.'

'Sir!' But the steward's protests were waved away.

'Hey . . .' Marcus slid gracefully down the pillar. 'Thish is my party, all right? I want my boss to know what a bloody good time I'm having under house arresh and that I don't give a tosh. So you jush make sure there's plenty of wine, Tingi, my old son, and even more plenty of women.'

The last words the smirking legionaries caught before he passed out were, '*Big* women!'

Chapter Nineteen

Claudia had misjudged Mentu. He was not like the man in that Macedonian legend who came to clear rats from a village and ended up piping the children away. There was a whole cross-section of ages and skills and abilities milling around inside the Pharaoh's commune.

The storm had, miraculously, held off for the journey, although it seemed to be following them northwards at a steady pace and, being a valley, once it arrived, would set in for hours, swirling round and round as it gathered in strength, faded, then gathered in strength once again. Meanwhile, the heat throbbed like a Nubian drum, and the viscous breeze sucked out your vitality and carried it away over the hills. Stiff-limbed, she clambered down from the trap. Long-horned cattle huddled in groups to protect themselves from the flies. Wilting fieldhands trudged home with the last wheelbarrow-loads of the day, but it was the scale – the sheer organisation – which took Claudia's breath away.

So many people! Somehow she'd imagined fifty or so gullible souls lured from the bright city lights, universally young and stupid, whereas there were ten times that number here! Claudia's opinion, she appreciated with the benefit of hindsight, had been influenced solely by the gospel spreaders of the Forum, cranks and fanatics like the two who'd accompanied her today, and by the fact that her fifteen-year-old stepdaughter had joined up with the Brothers.

Mentu's vision was never so narrow!

Every age was represented, including toddlers who had doubtless been born here, yet most astonishing was that

Mentu's specious ramblings had actually attracted craftsmen: weavers, carpenters, wheelwrights. Claudia had passed a potter's kiln, a brewery and, adjacent to the bakery, a flour mill, whose quern was turned by a sad-looking mule in a collar. On the drive in, she'd caught the distinct tang of a charcoal kiln in the woods as well as the less pleasant smell of the fuller's yard. She'd heard the thud of an axe, watched huntsmen return home with nets full of pigeons and a deer slung between two shouldered poles.

Her gaze roamed round this idyllic pear-shaped valley nestled in the soft, Etruscan hills. Fields stretched its length and breadth, there were orchards, pastures, beehives, olives, cattle, sheep and goats. You couldn't pick a city matron, plonk her in the country and then expect her to know how to clip and shear and geld, oh dear me, no. Animal husbandry required specialist skills, as did farm work, building maintenance and hunting.

Wily old Mentu had left nothing to chance.

He did not see this commune as a flash in the pan.

Yet, sinisterly, the commune was devoid of human discourse. Small children should be piggy-backing, hopscotching, skipping with ropes or rolling hoops, squealing as they punched each other's lights out in the dust. Instead, they sat in obedient silence, huddled over their counting frames, skeining wool or shucking peas and beans. Mentu would doubtless call it duty. Anyone else would suspect that subservience was being drummed into them from the earliest stage and that the adults fared no better. Sure, there were plenty of discussions about which-size-nail, how-many-onions, who-borrowed-my-awl, and can-someone-help-me-find-my-thimble floating about, but how odd that no one was debating politics, slandering their neighbours, climbing on their pet high horse or passing on unsound rumours as folk are prone to do in village groups! No faces here were red from exasperation, creased up in laughter, or rejuvenated by the latest gossip. By and large, members walked silently, heads bent and quiescent.

'To be sure, we're not all from Rome here, y'know!' The ripe brogue of Brindisi rose above muted accents ranging from Naples, Ancona, Cremona. 'Come. I'll help you wash and change, and then I'll show you the ropes.'

The brogue belonged to a stout, middle-aged woman whose greying hair was never going to be contained by something so insubstantial as a bun. Wisps stuck out in all directions, like a hedgehog who'd found himself caught between pestle and mortar or struck by a particularly spiteful bolt of lightning.

'That's the Pharaoh's quarters over there, me lovely.'

Setting a predictably gentle pace across from the stables, the woman indicated the far wing of a well-appointed set of buildings. Once, this had been a traditional villa set in the heart of its rural estate. However, instead of four blocks built round a rectangular courtyard, one wing had been demolished completely, the two long ones extended and a jumble of wooden buildings clustered between. Even so, Claudia reckoned accommodation would be pretty cramped!

'That far wing's off limits to anyone who isn't either a Pharaoh, a Pharaoh's wife or the Holy Council. Not forgetting Min, of course. He lives there, too.'

'Is Min the commune cat?'

'Cat?' Mercy roared with laughter, and several more grey hairs jack-knifed loose. 'Lordy, child, Min's the Grand Vizier!' She wiped away the tears. 'And before you ask, yes, it's his real name. They're brothers, Mentu and Min, but you'll get used to these Egyptian monikers after a while. Would you believe the name I was given when I joined was Mersyankh? Mersyankh! I could hardly pronounce it, let alone spell it.' She drew Claudia close. 'I told them, I'd settle for Mercy.'

Claudia laughed with her as they walked up the steps to the ladies' bath house. Mercy was by no means simple-minded and it was difficult to see this robust, happy, well-adjusted woman kowtowing to commune rules, but then escape routes come in many guises.

As though reading her mind, Mercy said, 'Ach, to be sure, I've never looked back! I dedicated the best part of forty years to me family, doing what's right for them, what's best for them, until it's time, I thought, I did something for meself before it's too damned late.' She relieved Claudia of her discarded gown and held it up admiringly, before folding it away in a chest. 'So I up and left the lot of 'em.' Claudia's rings, armbands and pendant she placed in a dish shaped like a water lily, and Claudia knew that would be the last she'd see of her lovely jewels!

There was something in Mercy's manner which prompted her to ask, 'Left, as in "without a word" you mean?'

'Best way, me lovely,' Mercy said, helping her into a pleated shift dress, white and patterned with diamonds of green, blue and turquoise, identical in every respect to her own. Identical, in fact, to everyone else's.

'Me husband was a bastard,' she added matter-of-factly. 'Beat me when he drank and beat me when he was sober, a proper brute, and I don't care what anybody says, I recognise his type in Geb, and so I do! Geb's Keeper of the Central Store – he oversees the domestic side, the cooking, laundry, that kind of thing – you'll know who I mean when you see him. A Barbary ape on two legs. Are your shoulder straps too tight? Anyway, you'll have no trouble with Geb. He hates women – men like that do – he avoids them when he can, which is, of course,' she laughed, 'most of the time.'

Her hand dithered over two small wide-rimmed, flat-bottomed pots, finally reaching for the one in the form of a duck.

'Black,' she pronounced, and Claudia realised they were eye paints she'd been choosing. 'Later,' she said, 'I'll show you to the rabbit hutch which passes for your bedroom, but first it's prayers. My, my, you look a picture!'

She steered her charge towards a tall mirror of polished bronze, and what shone back was not Claudia, but a replica of the three hundred other women in the commune. Hair had been twisted into a simple bun at the nape, eyes rimmed with kohl, a shift and sandals identical to everyone else's. Incredible. In the space of ten minutes, Mercy had bestowed upon Claudia a veneer of invisibility . . .

'Tomorrow,' she said, replacing the disc-shaped lid on the kohl, 'I'll henna your palms, your fingernails and the soles of your feet, ooh, it's a heavenly sensation. Tomorrow's a public holiday, and tonight we celebrate the passing of the crocodile—'

Whoa! 'We're mourning the death of a future piece of luggage?'

'Tch! Hasn't that lazy sod, Zer, told you anything about your new way of life here?' Outside, thunder rolled and rumbled, lightning streaked the sky. Glancing up, Mercy prayed aloud that the rain would hold off until after the ceremony had finished. 'We operate a ten-day week, a ten-month year in the commune, and the months are named after the festivals. Hathor's marriage to Horus, for instance, is one, which we abbreviate to 'the cow'. Gets too complex otherwise.'

Otherwise? Claudia was already confused! But then that's what this whole place was about. Disorientation. New clothes, new regime, new identity. No personal possessions. No contact with home or even with the outside world – come on, that double set of gates wasn't to impress local wildlife! Memories would be eradicated by ritual, by work, by devotion to Ra through homage to his Ten True Gods working on earth and this, of course, suited cult members as well as cult leaders. It would be wise for Claudia to remember that. People were here, because they chose to be here. Because they had a need for dependency, for numbing, for sublimation of self. They did not want the responsibility of thinking for themselves, they were content with being set repetitive, mindless tasks which relieved them of personal accountability, even on the most menial level.

Brainwashing, she belatedly realised, works both ways . . .

Large raindrops began to fall, loud and hot. Grabbing Claudia's arm, Mercy ducked her head and dashed towards a high wall, whose enclosure was covered by a huge blue canvas awning worked by a contraption of wooden laths, poles and ropes. Quite a crowd was already assembled, which didn't stop Mercy from pushing her way to the front for a good and clear view, and what a view! If Claudia had thought the boat on the upstairs floor of the apartment block was a knockout, here was surely its mother.

No replica, this! The barque was full-scale, a vessel fit for a king – for a god – its high prow and stern glowing with gold. Due to the heavy, dark sky, lanterns and torches had been lit around the temple front, making the jewels and gems shimmer and turning the rubies to living red eyes. Zigzag fangs of lightning turned the overlaid silver to incandescent flashing waterfalls. Behind the boat, stone hieroglyphs covered the white temple wall – Claudia recognised the Eye of Horus (why this preoccupation with body parts?) – and alabaster sphinxes lounged haughtily either side of the great, gaping doors.

'How many wives has Mentu got?' Two? Three?

'Twenty,' Mercy said, without blinking an eyelash. 'Why?' she chuckled. 'D'you fancy your chances?'

As more and more people huddled under the awning, Claudia was blown back by this overpowering odour of cloves and myrrh. The unguent, she realised, was yet another erosion of personality and decision-making, and in small quantities – well, you couldn't say it was pleasant, far too pungent for that, but nevertheless the fragrance was tolerable. En masse, though, and exacerbated by the heat, the smell was truly awesome! By now, the rain was drumming heavily on the canvas carapace, splattering over the side in thick torrents, and for a few moments, Claudia noticed no change in the background noise. Then she became aware that a different kind of drumming had started.

Booom, boo-boo-booom, boo-boo-booom, boo-boo-boom.

A broad-shouldered Negro beat a giant bronze tortoise with a fleece-covered drumstick, and the slow pulsing rhythm made the hair prick on Claudia's neck.

Booom, boo-boo-booom, boo-boo-booom, boo-boo-boom.

A man moved into the spotlights cast by the high, mounted torches, and at first, she thought it was Zer. It was not. Zer had already left on his return trip to Rome. But this man was also clad in priestly garb, and the strong, broad ridge of his skull showed a man of courage, strength and character, a man for whom wool would not easily be pulled over shaven eyebrows.

Booom, boo-boo-booom, boo-boo-booom, boo-boo-boom.

'He's permitted only goosemeat and beef for his protein intake,' Mercy whispered. 'Not allowed to touch fish, the poor darling, and as for beans. Tch. Can't so much as *look* at the divils!'

Small fry, Claudia thought, to being forced to bath in cold water twice daily. Fine in this weather, but winter?

Behind the High Priest, ten white-robed priestesses swayed and rattled their sistrums, the tune from their silvery bells almost inaudible against the rumbles of thunder. *Booom, boo-boo-booom, boo-boo-booom, boo-boo-boom.*

Then the eerie drumming stopped. An air of expectancy sizzled round the crowd. The High Priest reached into a moleskin bag at his waist and threw what looked like grit on to the brazier. *Whooosh!* Clouds of smoke billowed up, and when they cleared, Claudia gasped. Emerging as though airborne from the building came the most extraordinary procession she had ever seen!

Led by a man with his face painted blue and covered to the mouth with a dazzling gold mask, other figures filed out of the temple. Each wore a long, floating cloak of either gold, silver, copper or black which scraped the marble floor and, all except one other, bore the mask of an animal. Claudia recognised Horus, the falcon god, Bast the cat (oh, Drusilla; she's the spitting image of you!), a cow, a cobra, a vulture – ten in all. But then, as Mercy said, everything here came in tens.

Claudia used the opportunity to glance over her shoulder, and nobody noticed her backwards inspection, because five, maybe six hundred pairs of eyes were entranced by the theatricals (sorry, religious observances). Goddammit, which one was Flavia among this herd? Her eyes swivelled round. The girl was shorter than Claudia, but then so, it appeared, were three-quarters of the women gathered here. She was fatter than Claudia, but then so, it appeared, were three-quarters of the women here . . . Claudia let out an impatient sigh. With their regulation frocks and regulation eyes, it would be easier to tell sheep apart! Somewhere, she imagined, Flea would be snaking her way through the crowd, pocketing fistfuls of blue scarab amulets, although quite how a dungbeetle was supposed to protect a person from harm, Claudia had no idea.

'Hear me, for I am Osiris!' The rich tones of Mentu carried over the lashing rain. 'Tonight my holy father, Ra, departs to do battle with the Serpent and traverse the Realm of the Dead.'

The High Priest stepped forward. 'Hail to thee, Ra, in thy departing.'

Around Claudia, hands clamped together and a reverential chorus rang out. 'Mine eyes adore thee.'

'May thou cross in peace the Underworld in thy glorious Boat of the Evening.'

'Beautiful art thou.'

'And may thou rise in the horizon of heaven to give life to all that thou hast made, those who worship when they behold thee and sleep when thou dost depart.'

'For the joy thou bringest, O Lord, we adore thee.'

Two drumsticks now feathered the shell of the tortoise, faster but softer, and as the priestesses rattled their silver bells and showered the barque with rose petals, ten white-robed acolytes, five on either side of the boat, hauled the vessel back inside the temple buildings, the silver, lapis, amethysts and emeralds flickering wildly in the torchlight. The door closed behind them, but before the crowd could disperse, Osiris held up his hand.

'Brethren,' he said, and all eyes were upon him. 'You all know me, for I am Mentu, father to the fatherless, husband to the widow, protector of the poor. Through me, and my holy father, Ra, we bring you goodness, peace and harmony, that when the Day of Judgement comes, your hearts may weigh true at the Balance. And yet.' He paused for a count of three. 'There are those among us who do not believe.' This time the pause was longer, to take account of the astonished gasps, the shuffles. 'There are those among us who wish to destroy what we have created!'

Expressions of disbelief rippled round the horrified crowd, and Claudia thought, so this is Mentu, the man who controls this herd of mindless peabrains. She squinted across the dancing lamplight to get a better view of the Egyptian who sold himself as a Pharaoh, as Osiris incarnate, son of Ra – and no doubt many other things besides! Min and Mentu, the Brothers of Horus? More like two barrow boys from Memphis with an eye to the main chance – an eye that most certainly did not belong to Horus!

Impossible to see much under the blue paint, the mask and the voluminous floor-sweeping cloak, except that, unless Mentu had exceptionally long legs or disproportionately short arms, the people's beloved Pharaoh wore built-up heels to compensate for a distinct lack of height.

Bored with the liturgy, Claudia had daydreamed her way through much of his monologue, but her attention was drawn back by a young man being escorted up the temple steps to stand before Mentu on the platform. He was a handsome enough lad, eighteen and muscular in his linen loin cloth, but what made her sit up sharp was that, flanking him, stood two guards armed with scimitars.

The storm's vicious scything of the sky mirrored the contours of their weapons. Claudia's blood ran chill. Armed guards. Tall double gates. Fences. Claudia swallowed. She was glad, now, she'd hired those henchmen. The first sign of trouble, and they'd swoop down like a shot at her signal.

'How will we know it?' one of them had asked.

Inspired by the *Serving Women* re-enactment, Claudia had said simply, 'I'll light a fire, of course.' (Although, unlike the pallid Prefect, she would not pedantically insist on a fig tree!) Absently, she wondered how she'd manage to kindle one in such a tempest, and reassured herself that any storm would have burned itself out by then. Not, she added hastily, that she imagined there would *be* a problem.

A second youth had jumped on to the stage (Claudia! it's a religious platform, behave yourself!). An unprepossessing creature, being podgy and sallow and prone to spots, but dazzled by piety, this second youth had sunk to his knees, sobbing, saying that he, too, once believed he would be better off back in the old world. He, too, had wanted to leave. Mentu floated over to him and placed his hand upon the fat boy's head. The boy was blubbering in earnest, telling everyone he'd been a fool, a narrow-minded fool, because *this* is his family, *these* are his friends, *these* are the people who love him.

The crowd, gripped by the boy's penitence, were surging forward, urging him on with avowals of love, and a flock of bats fluttered beneath Claudia's ribcage. Like the first youth, hauled up half-naked before them by the guards, she was less than convinced.

She had not realised how deep the indoctrination was planted.

Oh, shit. It was something she hadn't considered – the fact that leaving might not be an option. This boy had obviously tried and had been carted back under armed guard to be put on show for everyone to gawp at.

Something happened.

For a moment, Claudia did not understand its significance, this subtle movement of the animal gods. One moment they were standing in a V formation behind Osiris, now they had surrounded the youth who'd tried to escape. Their voices were soothing, almost cooing, but when the V fanned out again, the boy – and the armed guards – had disappeared.

Every hair on Claudia's body stood on end.

'It saddens me,' Mentu said, 'whenever a brother or a sister leaves us. What saddens me more, however,' and he brushed at his face, as though wiping away a tear, 'is that our brother Sorrel here sought to sneak away like a common burglar. He is free to depart, you all are – no!' He held up his hand. 'Anyone who wishes to leave is free to do so with the blessing of Ra, only come to me, first, I beseech you.

Seek the wisdom of Ra, through his son, Osiris, for outside this valley our enemies surround us. It is not purely the soul which imperils itself beyond these hills.' He voice rose a pitch. 'Rome seeks to destroy us, brothers.' The volume rose, too. 'To cast down Ra and the Ten True Gods, to smash what we have built.'

The baying of the crowd made Claudia's flesh crimple.

'But we shall resist! We shall fight to the very last breath for the right to resurrection, to eternal blessedness, *they shall not deny us!*'

The howling grew louder.

'I say, our enemies must perish!' Mentu was bellowing to make himself heard. 'They have no hope of salvation. If they attack us, we –' he made stabbing signs in the air – 'must – fight – back.'

'Fight!'

'Kill!'

'Die for the cause!'

'Brothers!' With a cutting gesture, Mentu held up both arms and silence descended at once.

Claudia, terrified, had never experienced anything like it. Her breathing had stopped. Her heart was hammering. She had never been more alone in a crowd.

'Sisters.' His voice was mellow once more, almost coaxing. 'If Rome breaches our defences, we will meet the enemy head on and gladly. That's why we have men in the hills, to protect us, to give us advance warning of hostile attacks.' The gold mask shook sadly. 'If you want to leave, brothers, I beg you to leave openly through the gates. These men are mercenaries. Trained fighters. They cannot see in the dark and we do not want to suffer,' there was a catch in his voice, 'any more grievous accidents.'

The silence which followed was almost as frightening as the animal sounds the herd had made before, when it had risen to the mood of its leader.

'Accidents?' Claudia turned to Mercy, who was gazing enraptured at the speaker on the platform.

'Tch. Terrible, it was. Terrible.' Her eyes focussed again. 'One, gored right through by a rutting boar, poor soul. Another tripped and fell and impaled himself on the very stakes designed to keep the enemy out, while the third lad our noble watchmen mistook for an assassin, poor lamb was cut to pieces. Terrible. Such a waste of young lives.'

'But people do leave, right?' Claudia was not sure her voice was as obedient as she had hoped.

'There's been a spate of silly geese,' Mercy admitted, 'who've taken to stealing away in the night as though it's fashionable or something, although for the life of me I cannot see why. This is paradise on earth, is it not? Mind, they were young, the girls, and who knows what goes through empty heads at that age? Not that I'm suggesting they were touched like Berenice, you understand! To be sure, I'm not.'

On the platform, as though nothing unusual had occurred (perhaps it hadn't), the High Priest began to intone his thanks to Ra for the prosperous past month, the bounteous harvest, the plump cattle and ripening fruits. The figure wearing the crocodile mask stepped forward, to be garlanded with flowers by the ten white-robed priestesses and sprinkled with incense by the High Priest.

'Berenice?' Claudia prompted. Her voice was a rasp.

'Let's be charitable and say the heat got to her and she couldn't cope,' Mercy said, lowering her voice. 'He'd been running a temperature and grizzling, poor wee mite, so to shut him up, Berenice poisoned her baby. Aye. Fed him hemlock and left his wee body on the temple steps to stiffen, then –' she snapped her fingers – 'off she swanned. Not a word, the irresponsible besom. You're beginning to get the drift of this, aren't you?'

For a wild moment, Claudia wondered what the hell she meant, then she realised Mercy was talking, incredibly, about the ceremony taking place under the lights. The tragedy – the breathtaking horror – of Berenice, her poisoned baby, the fate of the boy, Sorrel (Sorrel? who dished out these weird names?), who'd tried to walk out, none of these things had actually touched Mersyankh. This worldly, stoic creature had merely been saddened by what had happened.

'That's the end of the crocodile,' said the woman whose husband used to beat her. 'Tomorrow we greet the new month of Ibis.'

Oh, Mercy! Won't you ever learn? First your husband, now Mentu, they've taken out your spirit and you've just rolled over and allowed them to do it. Like a rag mopping up a spill, they've sucked up all your spunk – and along with it, your ability to question!

'Not difficult once you get the hang,' Mercy continued cheerfully. 'And because it's a special occasion, tonight we get palm wine with our supper.'

Claudia reeled. She pictured the guards. Noble watchmen, my armpits! Those were mercenaries, trained killers, Mentu openly admitted it. She thought of the scimitars. The double perimeter fence. Stakes to repel the enemy. High gates. And she thought, if three well-built young men can't escape this ring of steel, what chance has a girl?

Stranger still, what chance have several girls?

And at night?

Moreover, why would a young mother, even under pressure, kill her own baby? Why wouldn't she simply abandon him? He'd be in good hands, for heaven's sake!

A hymn had broken out, with clapping and much waving of arms, and despite the throbbing heat and torrential warm rain, gooseflesh rose on Claudia's arms.

The sooner she got Flavia out of here the better, but the sky was black as night and only the temple platform was lit. Under this awning, she couldn't see diddly, let alone Flavia. She'd have to wait until supper.

But time was fast running out.

This is Friday night. Junius will die tomorrow afternoon.

And suddenly Claudia knew she'd need something stronger than palm wine to sustain her through the next few hours. She'd need courage, she'd need strength, she'd need all her wits about her, because this wasn't going to be as straightforward as she'd hoped. But more than that, Claudia felt that what she really needed was a scimitar like the guards carried.

Because right now six henchmen stationed on the far side of the hills didn't seem like any protection at all.

Chapter Twenty

An eagle owl, swooping over the seven hills of Rome, had a clear view of the wreckage left behind by the midsummer storm. Flash floods. Clogged and overflowing drains. A tenement struck by lightning, palls of smoke and flames ripping through the night along with the sickly stench of burning flesh from those trapped inside.

The owl did not wish to singe its feathers. It moved on.

Soaring above streets whose stinking, rotting refuse had been flushed downhill by the torrential rains, piling the debris against buildings and in the doorways of those not privileged enough to live higher up on the bluffs, the owl's penetrating amber scrutiny picked out some interesting enough titbits in the wreckage – a drowned kitten, several live rats – but the bird was a creature of the open woods and forests and in any case of a size more attracted to fawns and wolf cubs. It was simply passing through.

Northwards it swept, on silent, eerie wings, over the shrine tended by the Vestal Virgins, above the coins twinkling at the bottom of Juturna's healing pool, above dungeons awash under two finger widths of filthy water. The owl could not see, even if it wanted to, the small phalanx of soldiers splashing their blood-stained prisoner through the foetid underground chambers of this former stone quarry. The prisoner was a slave, an Armenian, who'd stabbed his master twenty-seven times in the chest and neck and stomach. His only regret was being captured before he'd been able to stab him another twenty-seven.

'Name?' the Clerk asked wearily.

The prisoner sympathised. It was late. It was hot. Outrageously hot, the storm hadn't cleared the stickiness, if anything it had added to it. The Clerk would be tired, because weather such as this forces a man to breaking point and as long as the jails continued to fill (which they would, while this heatwave continued), the shift would get no reprieve. Standing ankle deep in sludge, the Armenian wondered whether the Clerk might be sickening for marsh fever. He looked ghastly. Haggard. Lined. As though he carried some terrible burden. The prisoner regretted his lack of consideration, not killing the vicious bastard at a more convenient hour so men like the Clerk could go home to their wives and their families.

He did not wish to cause any trouble.

He gave his name.

'It's a sad day,' said the Clerk of the Dungeons, staring past the shackles and the soldiers, 'when decency is repaid with inhumanity.'

The prisoner, smelling his master's blood on his hands and tunic, saw no point in trying to explain to this hollow-eyed Roman the true definition of savagery.

'Yes, sir,' he said meekly, his heels sinking deeper into the sludge.

What use was there in telling them he was glad the cruel bastard was dead and that in killing him, he'd spared others the same ordeal? He really did *not* wish to be any trouble. Saturday was not far away. He watched the gaunt Clerk lay down his nib. No point in trawling for remorse where it didn't exist, even though a grovelling apology always went down well with the crowds. The Armenian was under no illusions as the guards led him away.

Nevertheless, he felt for the Clerk, wearily rubbing his temples and feeling the strain of this terrible heatwave.

Poor overworked sod hadn't even written down the prisoner's name.

To the north and west, rain continued to lash at the Cradle of Ra, flattening the remaining unharvested barley and swelling the apples and the berries and the pears. Seth, dry inside his cave, had almost finished bandaging Donata's corpse, only the neck and head remained. Ideally, he would have had the bodies professionally embalmed, but the logistics of arranging that were far too complex. For a start, he'd have had to travel to Egypt and that was out of the question, and in any case, even if, by some remarkable coincidence, he had found an embalmer locally, he'd have had to keep the man prisoner in this cave while the repellent business was being conducted.

Impossible. Not only would the fellow be permanently trying to attract attention, he'd have the use of a very sharp knife!

And besides, Seth leaned back to admire his handiwork, he was not sure he'd want to know about brains hooked out through the nose, organs removed through the flank. Messy. Unnecessary. The job for a butcher, and for heaven's sake, this cave was no slaughterhouse! His disciples took their own lives, quietly and willingly, the decision entirely theirs. Because not everyone, he acknowledged impartially, would want to be deified, to sit at Seth's Holy Table for eternity. He wouldn't force them, no, no, no, but my word, he had chosen wisely. All six had favoured the path to blessedness, and Seth promised each and every one that they would not regret their decision in the afterlife.

Nevertheless, the smell in the cave was fast becoming intolerable.

He secured the last of Donata's bandages and replaced the heavy cow mask. There were, he knew, other ways of preserving the body, which did not require professional help. One could, for instance, inject the corpse with oil of cedar through the anus and insert a bung. So powerful is the action of the oil, that it liquefies the soft internal organs, but while Seth did not believe himself squeamish, there was no way he could bring himself to remove that loathsome plug and then dispose of the contents.

Alternatively, he could do what the poor settle for in Egypt, simply pickle intact bodies in a bath of natron. Only how would he get his hands on the substance? So much salt would attract attention.

His only solution was to move fast.

The rain hammered down, channelling itself into waterfalls on the rocks, as Seth stood naked in the doorway of his cave. The same cave which had kept the ancient Etruscans dry all those centuries ago and whose paintings still survived in brilliant colour on the walls. Leopards. Lions. Dancers. As grand an entrance to the underworld as Seth could wish for.

He stood there, watching the night. The realm of darkness over which he was Lord and Master. Seth, the Sorcerer, the Measurer of Time. To be fair, he had no real complaints at the speed at which his project was forging ahead. Six down. One earmarked. No problem. Three more was all he required, maybe two, because one of the girls in the laundry was starting to look as though she could be talked into something. Also, he had studied carefully the new arrivals Zer fetched in today. Three of those four recruits had been female – and one of those, Seth reflected happily, was just up his street.

In the meantime, though, he must return to the commune. He'd be missed if he didn't leave now.

But the next time he visited his cave, he resolved to bring herbs to hang here – basil, balm, oregano – to mask the stench, while he bandaged Berenice.

The first real flutterings of panic began to beat inside Claudia's breast. Supper, including the palm wine, had come and gone, and still she had not caught a glimpse of Flavia. Or Flea, for that matter. In fact, Flea, in particular, because the thief would know how to move around unseen and two pairs of eyes are always better than one. The reward for helping would be that Flea could keep Doodlebug, but even the puppy was nowhere to be seen.

The commune was carried along on its own sinister current.

Claudia was being swept along with it.

Resistance was useless. She had tried a direct assault, the

I'm-trying-to-find-my-friend-Flavia routine, only to have it quickly pointed out that no one used their old Roman names here and they were very sorry, unless she could tell them her friend's Egyptian name . . . and of course she could not. The fact that Flavia was a recent arrival counted for bugger all, as well. Immediately a newcomer arrived at the commune, she was Egyptianised in dress and hair and face paint. Claudia wasn't too sure that Egyptian women wore their hair in buns, but then again, there wasn't much about this place which was genuinely Egyptian when you boiled it down! This was Roman life pasted over with a veneer of the exotic. Nothing threatening, nothing too alien, just Egypt sanitised and repackaged and sold back to them as sun worship. This commune was nothing but a token gesture.

Nevertheless, the machine was brutally efficient. New members arrived and were assimilated instantly.

For her part, Claudia had been adopted by Mercy's 'cell', an ominous title for an innocuous group comprising women aged between sixteen to sixty in age, and in mentality between nought and nil. Sitting with them over supper, she realised their brains were nothing more than sponges which had soaked up Mentu's teachings and Mentu's rites and rituals, with the result that what seeped out was simply a re-hash of Mentu's mindless drivel.

Indoctrination, brainwashing, call it what you like (Mentu, incidentally, called it 'instruction'), had purged them of whatever demons they'd carried on their backs before they came, so that now they were so clean of their old life that they almost squeaked, and with all this holiness and blessedness and paths to righteousness dripping off their tongues, Claudia feared she might be physically sick.

The cells were (predictably) ten apiece, Claudia filled Berenice's place, and that made a good starting point. She might be able to track Flavia that way, because she was also recently arrived and was bound to have filled a vacancy. Were Claudia to establish who had disappeared before Berenice, she might hit home.

'Oh, that was Donata,' Mercy said, topping up the palm wine. 'Odd creature, thought herself a cut above the rest of us and very conscious of her squint.'

A ripple of muted giggles rang round the cell, suggesting that Donata had had good reason to be sensitive. But when Claudia tracked down Donata's cell, she found that her place had been taken by Zer's acolyte from Rome who had arrived with her today, and that was depressing, because she was beginning to run out of leads.

Leads!

Knocking back a shot of palm wine, she set off for the kitchens. Where else would a young puppy aim for?

'Sister.' The greeting was gravelly and low, and not quite as touchy-feely-friendly as the voices in the refectory. Anywhere else, and you might think it was a warning.

Claudia turned a beaming smile upon the voice. Geb, who else, she thought, remembering Mercy's description: a *Barbary ape on two legs.* The description was apt, too. He had it on his chest, and he had it on his back, and he had it in great tufts underneath his arms. Even the hair on his head, damp and plastered down, was straggly, having grown beyond its natural length. Claudia suppressed the shudder which threatened to engulf her. Civilised men razored off their body hair, kept their skin supple and oiled. But the fact that Geb was hairy (how could one man grow so much fur, did he feed it?) didn't necessarily mark him down as a wife-beater. Mercy would be prejudiced. And the reason Claudia could see so much of his body was that at the moment he was stripped to the waist while a second man with blue-black, slicked-down hair wrapped a bandage round his torso with practised fingers.

'Oh, dear.' She frowned. 'That looks nasty.' Actually, she couldn't see the wound through the thick wodge of linen.

Geb. Keeper of the Central Store, in charge of the smooth domestic running of the commune. Geb. A kind of godfather figure. The hairy godfather, who might well have allocated chores to Flavia.

'Less serious than it looks,' said the second man. His skin

was dark, verging on swarthy and there was a blue stubble line round his jaw. 'Light scalding, no more.'

'Light?' growled Geb. 'That lousy bitch tipped half a ruddy pan of sauce over me.'

'An accident, I'm sure,' and now the second man held a warning in his voice, except this time the warning was for Geb. He glanced up at Claudia and she noticed his clothes were damp at the back from the rain. 'You're new here, aren't you?'

She wondered how he could tell. 'Yes,' she gushed. 'Praise be to Ra.'

'Praise be to Ra,' they both echoed back, but the enthusiasm was dim.

'Put your finger there,' the bandager instructed his patient.

'I can't reach.' Geb winced as he twisted, and Claudia stepped in to fill the breach.

'Allow me,' she said cheerfully, holding the linen while the knot was tied off. Neither man smelled of anything except the regulation commune unguent – cloves and myrrh.

Neither man offered his thanks, either! The first concentrated on checking his new fabric skin, the second on rolling up the remaining bandage and stuffing it, plus a pot of creamy yellow unguent, back inside his satchel. 'I'm Shabak,' he grunted. 'Doctor, dentist, apothecary. Any problems, see me.' And with that he was off, striding down the corridor, his blue jaw shiny in the lamplight.

'Want something, do you?' Geb refused her offer to help him back in to his shirt.

'My puppy,' she said. The search for Doodlebug would take her to places where Flavia might be skivvying. 'I expect he's in the—'

'No brother is permitted personal possessions.'

'I know that and you know that,' Claudia trilled, 'but unfortunately Doodlebug is too young to read the rule book. He'll be pining for me.'

'I dare say,' Geb said dryly. 'But he won't be doing it in my jurisdiction. Only animals allowed inside my kitchens are dead ones.'

And just in case she didn't get the message, Geb, the hairy godfather, the Keeper of the Central Store, stood with his broad hands on his hips, blocking her way.

On the other side of the wall, a fifteen-year-old girl who hated the name she'd been allocated, sobbed into her greasy, splattered tunic. It was an accident, surely Master Geb could see that? She'd turned round, struggling with the heavy pan and with the burning heat which was coming through to her fingers, despite the cloth around them, and she'd cannoned into him.

It was an accident.

Around her, pans and skillets clattered and scraped, iron upon iron, bronze upon bronze. Steam and smoke bubbled up from the ovens and cauldrons and washbowls, obscuring the overhead hanging bunches of herbs, the smell of frying fish and baked bread, roast goat and garlic vying for attention. Now that the main hall had been fed, it was time to serve the Pharaoh and his Holy Council, and *they* didn't settle for poxy beans and onions and a chunk of braised pork!

The reminder of the cooked pig made her snivel louder. So much for equality. Flavia sniffed. Tasks are allocated according to contribution, and hers had been a few trinkets. Bastard! Not for the first time, she cursed her foster father for diddling her out of the ransom. Stingy, rotten, skinflint bastard. Thanks to him, she was scrubbing dishes and . . . and tipping anchovy sauce over the Keeper of the Store!

With a wail, she ran out of the kitchens, tears of self-pity streaming down her cheeks as she hunkered behind the charcoal shed.

'I didn't mean it! I didn't mean to scald him!'

She gulped back the sobs. They said he had a fearful temper, Master Geb. Not the type who beats you then forgets it. Geb liked to simmer for a while and then devise the punishment.

She blew her nose hard.

She wished she'd never come here.

She wished she'd never *heard* of the Brothers of Horus.

She wished someone would come to rescue her.

She wished she could get out. Go back home.

But in her heart, she knew that she couldn't. That, somehow – she couldn't say why – but somehow Flavia knew she was destined to stay in this valley for ever.

Claudia had tried sailing with the current. It had not found her Flavia and goddammit, the sand in Junius' hourglass was running perilously low. She looked at Geb, standing four-square in front of the doorway to the kitchens, his damp hair sticking to his forehead and decided to sail upstream.

'My puppy is only eight weeks old.' Oops. Her elbow accidentally nudged Geb's bandaged body as she swept past. 'I'll check the kitchens anyway!'

Perhaps flinching slowed him down. Perhaps Geb was the type to note a grudge and retaliate later. Perhaps he truly didn't care. Either way, Claudia swept unchallenged into the hustle and the bustle, the clouds and the condensation and, using her search for Doodlebug as cover, checked out the kitchen staff. Patently unused to charcoal ovens and iron griddles, to spits and spatulas and strainers, nevertheless they were having a whale of a time. Gales of laughter mingled with chopping, pounding, pouring, whisking, while controversy over which way up the gridiron went combined with tastings and testings and estimates on quantity.

'Where's that clumsy bitch sloped off to?'

Geb had either forgotten Claudia, or his priorities lay elsewhere. He was intent on finding the girl who'd mistaken him for a herring and dressed him with anchovy sauce.

'When I get my hands on her, I'll stripe her hide, she'll think she's a bloody zebra for a week! Have you finished yet?' He turned his bellowing on Claudia. 'I told you, before, you won't find a live animal inside my kitchens.' He swiped his damp fringe out of his eyes. 'Now you're in the way and I've a fucking schedule to adhere to.'

No Doodlebug. No Flavia!

Since kohl around the eyes wouldn't last a minute in this vaporous atmosphere, faces were scrubbed and clean and clothes were comfy tunics. Claudia would have picked Flavia out at once.

If she'd been here.

Big cats keep quiet at night. The night is for listening. For waiting, for sleeping, for hiding. The night is for keeping your own counsel and your own silence. The night means not giving yourself away.

Different codes applied to those caged up inside the dark caverns under the arena. They had not been fed for a week and they were mad with starvation, with anger, with fear and with loathing. They did not know when they would eat, indeed, if they would eat. They roared their resentment at the whole human race, and few in Rome failed to hear it.

For those humans chained in underground chambers nearby, the echoing rage was especially bloodcurdling.

In his shackles, the Armenian who'd been brought in earlier sat in a pool of filthy sludge which showed no signs of draining away and listened to the angry beasts roaring their hatred into the hot summer night. He had no fear of death, not after the cruelty his master had put him through these past seven years, and was merely glad that, in killing him, he had spared others a similar ordeal.

Aye, he thought, flexing his stiffening muscles. It's a strange thing, life. Never how you plan it. Subservient by nature, the Armenian had only ever wanted to serve others. Finally, in his last act on earth, it looked as though he had. But in a manner more intricate than he could have imagined.

He was not afraid of death, or what lay beyond it. Once Saturday was over, the real adventure would begin.

So while the prisoners around him cursed and prayed and sobbed and raged, the Armenian closed his ears to the big cats' savage growls and plaintive roars which echoed into these subterranean chambers and set his mind to wondering what crime the prisoner who'd occupied these chains before him had committed.

And what sort of adventure he was having now.

Chapter Twenty-one

Did you know, ears never stop growing? Everything else – lungs, bones, lips, veins – reaches a certain stage and then cuts out. Ears, it seems, were never given guidelines. Or maybe they're programmed to quit at the age of 125, only no one lived long enough to find out.

Quite what the individual facing Claudia would look like when he clocked up his century, she couldn't imagine, but elephants sprang to mind. As did rabbits, and not necessarily because bunnies have big ears. His whole face was rabbity. That sort of softened wedge shape which, while attractive in small children, becomes off-putting in an adult.

'. . . feeling unwell, I can take you to Shabak.'

'What?' Mesmerised by the length and breadth of the ear flaps, and intent on rattling the gates to the temple compound, Claudia had paid scant attention to his wittering. He seemed to be concerned for her health. 'No, I'm fine, I'm looking for my puppy.'

'He won't be in there.' Long, twig-like fingers pulled her away. 'I'm Penno, the Temple Warden and Chief Petitioner, Servant of the High Priest, and unless they're for sacrificial purposes, beasts are forbidden to set foot on sacred territory.'

You aren't.

Maybe it was the ceremony earlier, with those realistic animal masks flickering in the torchlight, but all the men Claudia had encountered tonight conjured up images of beasts. For if Geb was the Barbary ape on two legs, then surely Shabak, with his narrow waist, narrow hips and (alas) narrow shoulders was the monkey – and now she had Penno's coneylike features to contend with!

It's this place, she thought. It's overloading my imagination, I'll be hallucinating next.

The rain had eased off temporarily, but the storm still cloaked the hills, sending out brilliant splashes of white and ominous rumbles of thunder. And the heat throbbed like a kettledrum, and the cicadas rasped in the waterlogged grass, and dolphins leaped through hoops in Claudia's stomach.

She shook herself free of Penno's grip and hoped it was the lightning which twisted his face into a sinister leer. 'The storm will frighten him,' she said, 'I need to check for myself.'

Dammit, I'm down to a few hours.

'Sister.' There was an edge to the temple warden's voice. 'Only initiates are allowed inside these walls outside of the times of prayer and petition, that's why the gates remain locked. Your dog's not in there, believe me, and even if he was, *you* wouldn't be.' The tone softened, became almost wheedling. 'It's late, my child. You'll be tired. I'm sure he'll come home in the morning.'

It *was* late. Without a herald to call out the hour or stars to check the time by, Claudia could not be certain, but she imagined it was more than two hours past midnight. Only one window in Mentu's wing showed a light, otherwise the whole commune slept, and the temple warden had every right to be suspicious of a member wandering around at this time of night. The question is, what was he doing prowling about on his own?

A celestial rumble broke overhead, signalling the storm's intention to return. Back in Rome, there'd be brawls and barter, the lowing of oxen pulling the delivery drays, wheels clattering, crates banging, shouts, ribald laughter, singing from the taverns, creaks from overburdened axles. Thunder would not get a look in!

'Ordinarily,' Penno said, 'I'd be a gentleman and escort you back to your quarters. Unfortunately –' he jangled a set of keys,

– 'Ra will return to us in less than three hours and there is much work to be done. Excuse me.'

With a curt nod he disappeared behind the wicker gate, and at least that answered her question. Tomorrow (today!) was the start of the month of Ibis. There'd be another festival to prepare for. A public holiday to organise. More prayers. More ritual. More opportunity to befuddle brains and step up the mental treadmill so that people became too scared to come off.

Mentu's scam might be earning him a packet, but the number of people he was damaging was growing by the day. Zer canvassed Rome, but there would be other Zers dotted around, bringing in members from Naples, Ancona and, like Mercy, from Brindisi. Damaged individuals, who Mentu and his money-grubbing cronies sought to damage further.

Damage . . . and possibly worse.

Six girls, Mercy reckoned. Six girls aged between fifteen (Donata) and twenty-two (Berenice) had skipped this valley without trace and, if gossip was to be believed, Berenice had deliberately poisoned her five-month-old son before leaving.

Leaning her back against the high temple compound wall, Claudia felt something lumpy dig into her flesh. What the . . . ? It was an ear. Glory be, it was a pottery ear stuck on the wall. How very odd. Her hand followed the contour of the wall at the same level, until she'd counted ten cemented at regular intervals on to the stonework. Ears? At first, she couldn't believe it, but yes. Human ears made of terracotta . . . and as she walked the perimeter, she cast her mind back to dinner. To something Mercy had said about the wall needing to be high to keep evil and impurity from Ra's holy place of worship. And since mortals were only allowed to worship Ra through an intermediary god, there was the facility for them to come at any time when access to the temple was barred to whisper their hopes and prayers (and indeed worries, should they have them!) to any one of the Ten True Gods who would always be on hand to listen to their pleas and pass the message on to Ra, through his holy son, Osiris.

Meaning, Claudia assumed, this was some form of spying!

She wriggled her finger deep into an earhole and was not surprised to find it wasn't stopped by masonry, only by the fact that her finger wouldn't reach that far. She plucked a scabious, growing underneath the wall. Well, well, well. Wouldn't you know, that stem just kept on going! He was a wily old bugger, Mentu. What odds that behind each ear would be one of his cronies, writing down everything the petitioner said? Reporting back.

Claudia's thoughts returned to the six missing girls as she stared up at the sky. Heavy clouds, black as Hades, hung over the valley, muting the zigzag flashes. Mercy's explanation didn't make sense. Tonight's charade showed that young men in their muscular prime don't make it through the double barriers. What chance had pampered young women? And the Berenice business bothered her. 'Touched' had been Mercy's description, but to feed hemlock to your baby and simply walk off was way, way beyond 'touched'.

The rain began to fall again. Chip. Chip. Chip-chip-chip. What was Claudia to make of the so-called tragic accident, in which a boy who'd tried to escape had been cut to pieces by Mentu's thugs? Was it truly an accident? Or an convenient way to dispose of a problem?

As the hot raindrops hammered down, Claudia began to have a very bad feeling about Mentu's paradise valley.

And it didn't help that she could not locate Flavia.

Chapter Twenty-two

Morning.

Prayers were over. Petitions were over. Ra had been duly venerated, despite today's Boat of the Morning docking more like a humble fishing vessel than blasting in, a trireme in full sail, all trumpets blazing. But at least the storm had abated, the rain temporarily holding off, and who really cared whether dawn burst in on a rip tide or simply sidled into its berth and dropped anchor? The Great God had returned, he had battled the serpent of the night and traversed the twelve realms of the underworld, let us be thankful. Praise be to Ra.

Claudia pressed her hands over her eyes and tried to control the churning within. Executions commenced in nine hours' time. She could not let Junius die.

Her skin was clammy, her mouth dry, her stomach sick with anxiety. This was her fault. She should never have made him don that toga in the first place, she should have foreseen the problems.

The knot inside tightened. She could not even pin this one on Flavia! True, the wretched girl had set the train in motion with her phoney kidnap and her demands, but it was Claudia who had given her bodyguard his orders. It was she who shouldered the blame. He was a slave, a Gaul, a foreigner, with no option but to do as he was commanded by his mistress. Claudia's eyes misted. She'd lost count of the times Junius's pained look of protest had returned to haunt her.

'Madam! I'm a slave! If I'm caught wearing the toga . . .'

She remembered laying down that bowl of dates, fresh

and sticky from their oasis homeland, and suggesting Junius consider the matter from a counter position.

'Not what might happen if you're caught. What I'll do to you if you don't.'

The threat had been issued light-heartedly and Junius, used to her ways, would have taken it as such.

Junius.

She would never nibble another date again! The very thought made her stomach heave.

How old was he? Twenty? Twenty-one? He'd hardly lived! He should be looking towards raising a family, to rafting his way through the white waters of life. He did not deserve to die because he'd been found draped in a piece of white wool. He did not deserve to die simply because some silly bitch told him to wear it.

Intense blue eyes swam before her, the sandy coloured hair, strong hands which hovered like hawks over his dagger. Oh, shit . . .

He's not going to die, stop thinking like that. You can save him. Find Flavia, get that oath sworn.

You can.

You can save him. There's still time . . . *just.*

Around her, the commune laughed and babbled and acted as though this was another normal day. Better than a normal day, in fact, because this was the first day of Ibis, a day for rejoicing. A holiday. Sacrifices, hymns, dancing and music, wrestling, feasting and fun. Bitterness rose in Claudia's throat. These people, jigging around in their festive wigs and blue scarab amulets, were not touched by tragedy, impending or otherwise. Misfortune was a thing of the past, because in this valley life was fresh and new and you didn't have to watch ageing parents die a painful, lingering death or worry about unfaithful spouses, wayward kids, politics, jobs, the threat of war. Moneylenders, debt collectors, robbers, muggers might as well belong to another world, strange and mythical creatures with horns, wings and claws – for Mentu's cult members had left their financial burdens behind at the gate.

Someone else had taken over their problems. Someone else was in control of their lives. Here existed only a simple pecking order, safe boundaries behind which they could hide. These people – these happy, clapping, dancing people – had relinquished reality along with their responsibilities. Nothing could shock them. Nothing could touch on a nerve. They had abdicated. Real life no longer happened.

But you can't leave behind your own shortcomings.

Look at them! Dressed up in their best bib and tucker, in thick plaited wigs which had been handed out for the occasion, every one identical, irrespective of the wearer's sex. Women gyrated, in sharply pleated shifts with straps which passed over their shoulders, garlands round their necks and kohl around their eyes, with men who wore white ankle-length kilts fastened with a broad sash round the waist. They couldn't give a toss whether their brothers or sisters were sick or miserable, how their pet rabbit was faring, whether Cousin Lucia had bowed to pressure from her family to marry that gap-toothed old widower, or found happiness with the man she loved.

And suddenly Claudia realised they were not harmless, gormless Pyramidiots buffered by the rigid conformity of commune life. These were hard, self-centred, selfish scum who'd absconded with the family silver and – like Flavia – had thought only of themselves, and to buggery with everyone else. They could not be touched, because they were incapable of making deep emotional attachments for the simple reason that they did not have the equipment in the first place. These miserable sons of bitches damned well deserved each other and Mentu – may the gods smile on him – was welcome to feast off their selfish inadequacies.

She hauled off the heavy, black wig, running the myriad plaits between her fingers. Reality would catch up with them soon enough, of course. They'd become ill. Some would die. They would tire of the brewing, the baking, the slogging in the fields, simply because they hailed from soft, middle-class families with soft, middle-class values. But in the meantime, this was the day of the Ibis and the day was all that they lived for! For them, there was no yesterday, not even any tomorrow. They certainly wouldn't lose sleep about nebulous concerns, such as the welfare of a few retainers: whether they were well, being schooled, actually receiving the bonuses they'd been promised. That was not their affair any more. Physical and moral welfare was someone else's responsibility, they'd left all that behind, and who cares whether one more poor sod ends being torn apart by a pack of ravenous dogs?

I care. Oh, Junius, I care . . .

Eight hours and counting.

Fat tears trickled in black, kohly streaks down her cheeks. I shouldn't have made him wear Gaius's toga. I should not have left him alone in the Camensis. I certainly should not have come on this wild goose chase! All I've done is waste valuable time.

A vice clamped round Claudia's throat. Play fast and loose with your own life, if you must – but don't balls up anyone else's! Tears of self-pity pricked in her eyes. Conceited bitch. Miss Know-it-all! You think you can handle this stuff on your own, when the stark reality is you're nothing but a rank amateur and a bloody poor one at that. You bungle the kidnap, you get a loyal bodyguard thrown in the dungeons, and you can't even find a fifteen-year-old girl in an enclosed valley.

What shall I do? Someone help me. Someone tell me what I should do.

But as usual, Claudia Seferius was on her own.

The valley began to swim around her as she twisted the plaits of her wig into knots. Should she cut her losses and go back to Rome? If there had been anything Claudia could have done to bail out her bodyguard, she would have taken that action in the first place and not come swanning out here!

Yet it had seemed so right at the time. Grab Flavia, and carry the troublesome bitch back to Rome where the oath had already been drafted.

Seven hours and counting.

As the vice tightened round her windpipe and an eagle clawed at her heart, she pictured the dungeons. Dank, dark, smelly at the finest of times, the heat and the deluge would have made them unbearable. The wardens were brutes – they had to be. She pictured the Gaul, one side of his face battered, swollen and raw. So vivid was the image, that she could see clearly the contusions and cuts, matted hair, one eye almost closed, his face filthy.

No. Not filthy, the dark colour was from bruising. His skin was actually quite clean . . .

Claudia blinked. She'd eaten little last night and nothing this morning, dehydration and heat had finally got to her. She began to laugh. The picture was so bloody realistic! The laughter became manic and high.

'Ouch!' The slap to her face stung like hell.

'I'm sorry, but you were getting hysterical.'

Hysterical? Me? When my delusions slap me and then apologise? Claudia reeled. So this is what it's like. *Cracking up.* Losing your mind . . .

'Did I hurt you?' The phantasm was shaking her now! 'Madam, are you all right?'

'All right?' What sort of insanity is it, that lures people into conversations with apparitions? 'When I'm talking to someone who's locked up seventy miles south in jail. Of course I'm all bloody right.'

'Actually, it's sixty-four miles and I'm not in jail,' Junius grinned. 'Didn't you know, you can't chain a Gaul for long.' He shrugged his broad shoulders. 'It's our nature,' he said, 'we get restless.'

Chapter Twenty-three

There were many things Claudia did not understand. She did not understand how he'd escaped the inescapable. She did not understand how he'd discovered this beautiful valley of Ra. She did not understand how he'd been able to distinguish his mistress among the mass of identikit kits.

Most of all, though, she did not understand why Junius had never troubled to buy himself his freedom! Heaven knows, it was not from lack of funds or opportunity and while some foreigners might envisage Roman slaves as downtrodden drudges, reliant on meagre kitchen scraps and a blanket to wrap themselves in at night, the myth could not be further from reality. Many slaves were downright rich. Saving their salaries, they bought businesses such as hairdressers, wigmakers, tailoring, which they ran out of hours, while others, for instance, hired out their talents as artists, musicians, wrestlers. Indeed, more than one barbarian had learned his lesson the hard way, when he came face to face with the Emperor's administration and discovered a vast army of slaves beavering away inside the Imperial Palace, issuing mandates and supervising appointments, enforcing laws and implementing Senate initiatives on Augustus's behalf on everything from the judiciary to public roads to tax. Few governors and magistrates, provincial prefects and aediles dared look down their noses at the Emperor's vassal bureaucrats! However, Junius was no imperial civil servant in a cushy sinecure, he ran no business out of hours, which meant his wealth was simply clocking up. Why would he not wish to buy his independence?

'I'm sorry, Junius.' Claudia's mind had been wandering, as

minds tend to do with relief. 'What did you say?' Her knees were knocking like castanets. She could not believe it. He was alive! Junius was alive! Reprieved and well and in no danger of being fed to the bears!

'I was merely thanking you for bribing the jailers.'

Me? 'Oh, Junius!' She patted his arm reassuringly. 'Good heavens, it was the least I could do!'

'When I returned home, Leonides brought me up to date with events,' the young Gaul said. 'How Flavia staged her own kidnap to join the Brothers of Horus and that, with us lot languishing in the cells, you'd hired yourself another bodyguard, but he was worried, he said, because he had no idea where you were.'

That's because I didn't know myself the location of Mentu's funny farm.

'Security.' She winked, tapping the side of her nose.

Strange. He'd made no mention of Flavia shopping him, suggesting that either Leonides had drawn a veil over the issue or . . . or Junius was here on a mission of personal revenge! Indeed, what else would lure him so far from Rome, where no one would blame him for staying home and nursing his rather nasty-looking wounds? His mistress was perfectly safe. He'd said himself, he knew about the hired henchmen, so what plan, she wondered, fermented inside that bruised and swollen head? What form would his retaliation take?

And how the hell had he walked free from Death Row?

'How the hell did you find me?' she asked.

'Leonides told me you'd gone to see the patrician.' Around them, the dancing continued to a haunting mix of sistrum and drum, harp and pipes which carried on the breeze down the valley. 'I paid a visit to his house.'

'Orbilio told you I was here?'

'Him!' Junius executed a uniquely Gallic gesture then unceremoniously spat on the damp earth. 'He was in no position to speak, that one, much less give directions!'

'You do know he's under house arrest?'

'He was under a pile of half-naked, slobbering Amazons!'

Junius somehow managed to convey that Junoesque wasn't the word to describe these slappers, while also leaving Claudia in no doubt as to his feelings on finding the one person she had looked to for assistance helplessly drunk. 'The guards said he'd been partying since—'

'So how *did* you find me?' Claudia had no desire to hear about Orbilio's indulgences. He was single, free, could do what he liked. And the pain round her heart was indigestion, because she'd eaten no breakfast this morning and very little dinner last night.

'His steward put me on to the Brothers of Horus, where some bald bloke in a squalid apartment told me where I could join. I spun him some yarn about being the son of a Gaulish horse trader who'd been to university in Alexandria and had "found" Ra while I was there, and since the patrician's steward lent me this expensive tunic, a jewelled dagger and a few of the patrician's baubles, the priest accepted my story.'

'He'll accept any story,' Claudia replied tartly, 'so long as you have a suitable donation.' A jewelled dagger wouldn't buy him beyond a job in the fields, although he might be promoted to the back-breaking threshing floor, depending on the quality of Orbilio's 'baubles'.

'I'm down to help out in the brewery,' Junius said, with a suspiciously innocent air, and Claudia grinned.

Junius had availed himself of a few extras while Tingi's back happened to be turned . . . 'Your education with me isn't entirely wasted, then!' Hadn't she always said the boy had shown promise?

'These people.' He frowned. 'They're not what I envisaged.'

Me neither. Claudia followed his eyes to a couple in their sixties who had apparently lived such dull and blameless lives that they felt more than eligible for resurrection in the Afterlife, especially since, for one or the other of them, that gentle tap on the shoulder might not be far away.

'Only the young ones make the headlines,' she explained.

In her few short hours here, Claudia had assimilated pretty much all there was to know about the Pyramidiot way of life.

'And because there's no direct contact with the outside world –' scribes pen any letters to families on Central Store papyrus and arrange their despatch – 'no one hears about couples who simply calf off from society, or the likes of middle-aged women' (e.g. Mercy) 'who walk out on violent husbands. What's particularly worrying, though, is that seemingly rational adults' (e.g. Mercy) 'swallow so many dubious tales.'

'Such as?' Junius prompted.

'How about not one, but *three* men coming a cropper when they try to leave? One gored by a rutting boar, another mistaken by the guards for an assassin creeping in, and an unlucky third tripped backwards and impaled himself on the protective stakes.'

'Wouldn't the assassin have been creeping the wrong way?'

'And how can one impale oneself on an outward, downward facing spike? But that's not the half of it,' she said, licking her finger and wiping away the thick runnels of kohl from her cheek. 'Where three burly fellows failed, no less than six of the weaker sex have succeeded in sneaking through unseen *and* unchallenged, yet nobody questions the official explanation. I find that extremely odd.'

What tactic do you employ, Mentu? How do you control their very reasoning?

'That bald priest in Rome,' Junius said, 'fed me some crap about Rome wanting to wipe out the Brothers of Horus, but that was tosh, surely. I mean, who'd buy that rubbish?'

'Look around,' Claudia said dryly.

Apart from those involved in running the scam, the only two members who weren't taken in were Claudia and the Gaul! Yet surely, at some stage, others must have smelled fish in the air. *What became of them?* And what had happened to the young man who'd found himself surrounded by the animal deities on the platform last night, and had then been spirited away? The only place they could have taken him was into the body of the temple.

'Luck of the gods, boy!' A coarse grey bun thrust itself

between Claudia and her bodyguard, its own wig stuffed into an accommodating dress strap so that Mercy appeared as though some black, hairy succubus was hitching a lift on her shoulder. 'What in blazes happened to you?'

Claudia performed the introductions, adding that it was a long story, but it seemed the new recruit's family were none too enamoured with him joining the Brothers and had sent four of his cousins to dissuade him.

'Ach, men! Won't use Latin when they can use fists.' She turned to Claudia, her eyes narrowing. 'You two know each other, then?'

'Not at all,' Junius said quickly. 'As you can see from my clothes, I've only just arrived and the good sister here befriended me.'

Mercy's face relaxed. 'We'll get you cleaned up and into some proper clothes later, but the sacrifice is about to begin, you won't want to miss that.' To Claudia she lowered her voice. 'You've scored there, me lovely! That boy fancies you rotten.'

Claudia couldn't help smiling back. Junius? Attracted to a woman four or five years older than himself? Poor old Mersyankh! No judge of character.

'You really think so?' she simpered.

'I know so!' A stout elbow nudged her in the ribs, accompanied by a coarse chuckle. 'And they might be the size of rabbit hutches, our rooms, but that don't stop the rabbits from breeding! Wigs on, then.' Wrestling the succubus, Mercy steered the two young 'lovers' towards the front, butting them up against each other with a wink, and Claudia raised no objection to the matchmaking. This way she and Junius could confer without arousing suspicion.

After just two ceremonies, Claudia was already familiar with the routine. The sinister brow ridge of the High Priest no longer made her shudder. The explosion, the smoke, the eerie drumbeat on the giant bronze tortoise, the silver bells of the sistrum no longer made her scalp tingle.

'Different animals are sacrificed for different occasions,'

Mercy explained, pulling Claudia's dreadlocks into line. 'A hog for the Feast of Osiris, a heifer for Isis, Anubis the jackal gets geese and for the crocodile, a black ram.'

Thoth, it seemed, in order to reflect his status as the God of Wisdom from whom no secret may be hid, warranted a bull so utterly enormous, the poor beast had to be brought to the sacrificial knife on wheels, and whilst this suggested force feeding on a scale that verged on cruelty, Claudia had to admit the flesh was absolutely delicious. Only she and Junius, though, seemed to find the ceremony unduly protracted.

First Penno, old Rabbitface himself, came up to inspect the bull from nose to tail. Apparently the presence of just one single black hair on an otherwise pure white hide would deem the beast impure. But no, after much zealous searching, the fat bull passed the test, its eyes no doubt still watering from where Penno's studious tweezers had plucked out any offending black hairs earlier. No matter. The fact that six hundred gullible souls were happy with his pronouncement was sufficient, and Penno's twig-like fingers twisted a band of papyrus round the animal's horns to show that it was ready.

The High Priest moved in next, taking great pains to light the sacrificial fire himself and pour libations of wine to both Ra and to Thoth, the ibis god to whom this month was sacred.

Unfortunately, unlike Rome where sacrifice was both gentle and reverential, there was nothing subtle about the decapitation of a bull or the flaying of its carcass. And who the hell wanted to watch the creature being disembowelled and the cavity stuffed with honey, raisins, figs and myrrh? Thank god, the middle section was cast upon the flames to be consumed by sacrificial fire, but the leg and shoulder meat which was passed round was juicy, rich and tasty.

Somehow, Penno and his shaven-headed master managed to spin this out for an incredible two hours, during which time only Claudia's feet shuffled in impatience. But those boys weren't finished yet!

'The first day of the month is for purification,' Mercy explained, reminding Claudia of what Penno told her last night: that the temple was the house of Ra, not accessible to common oiks and that communication with the sun god could only be through his servants, in other words, through any one of the Ten True Gods (hence the terracotta ears) or, when the temple compound was open to the public, through the High Priest or his long-eared Chief Petitioner.

As though a flood gate had been opened, people surged forward to Penno and the High Priest, kneeling so that the waters of purification could be poured over their heads to wash their sins away.

'Come, brothers. Step forward, sisters of Ra.' The High Priest's voice rang out across the courtyard and Penno's twiggy fingers beckoned more forward. 'Come up and seek forgiveness from Ra.'

He added something about how each of us should strive to become a better person, blah-blah-blah, and Claudia wondered if there was a bowl to be sick in. Even Mercy went forward, to join Penno's queue.

And above them, on the temple platform, Mentu with his blue face, gold mask and rich Osiris garb watched with singular impassivity over the proceedings, flanked by his inanimate animal gods. Were they in on it, the cat, the jackal, the cobra, standing stationary as statues? Or had he suckered them, too, this Egyptian strutting in his built-up shoes? According to Mercy, Mentu overruled even his brother, Min, the Grand Vizier (are these people for real?), if the occasion so demanded, and he initiated all matters of policy. Therefore, Claudia reasoned, Mentu must manipulate the priestly functions.

Now, she couldn't be certain, not being an expert, but this didn't seem to bear much resemblance to the Egypt over which Julius Caesar and Mark Anthony had fought each other to the death. Too few gods, a suspect calendar, a suspiciously Roman-looking temple upon which a few hieroglyphs had been hacked out and dodgy religious observances which bore little affinity to that exotic culture reliant on the inundations of the River Nile.

No, no, no. This was theme-park Egypt, a human zoo, sold

to credulous Romans on the premise of what they imagined Egypt to be like, with just sufficient difference about the place for them to feel they'd set foot on foreign soil without feeling in any way alien.

Which made Mentu crafty, as well as clever.

He'd sold them Ra, he'd sold them resurrection, he'd sold them Roman ways repackaged as Egyptian, and he'd also sold them this business of doing everything in tens, including changing the names of the days of the week and the months of the year to disorientate them, the months being named after the gods, weekdays being named after plants. In addition, Mentu had sold them Thoth, from whom no secret can be hid, and you can bet your bottom denarius that any secrets whispered into the terracotta ears were repeated back to the whisperer as proof of Thoth's omnipotence!

What devious machine did Mentu employ to keep these sheep believing? Somehow he contrived to hold their absolute trust – how else could they swallow that guff about the enemy massing outside? By default, therefore, Mentu must also be behind the strength of the security. Did he order the deaths of the three men caught escaping?

Did he know about the six missing girls? Did he, sweet Janus, arrange it?

Anything seemed possible in this hidden valley of Ra. Anything at all.

'You'll need a hyssop poultice on those bruises.' The accent was neither female nor from Brindisi. 'Plus an opobalsam salve on that eye.' A professional thumb lifted Junius's battered eyelid, indifferent to the wincing it induced.

'Shabak.' Claudia nodded. 'He's our doctor, dentist – and what's the other thing?'

'Apothecary,' Shabak said, without turning a hair of his slicked-down blue-black head. 'And should that gash to your knee prove as stubborn as I suspect, you might consider a light treatment of herb paris.'

Claudia fluttered her eyelashes. 'Oh, but surely that's poisonous?'

The shiny blue jaw swung round, the cruel eyes piercing. 'Not with the correct dosage, sister.'

'Is that what happened to Berenice, you do think?' In for a quadran, in for one of the Emperor's shiny gold pieces. 'That she intended to slip her baby a mild dose to calm him down and soothe his pain, and miscalculated?'

It was equally possible, of course, that the poor misguided woman mistook hemlock leaves for parsley in the dark. Or the roots for a parsnip? Or believed the seeds were aniseed? No mother, surely, would deliberately poison her baby, especially since there was no suggestion Berenice was anything other than a careful and attentive parent. There had to be some other explanation.

'Berenice fed her son enough hemlock to fell a horse,' Shabak said bluntly, and there was no mistaking the hostility in his voice.

Damn.

He'd recognised Claudia from last night, when he'd been bandaging Geb's burn near the kitchens. Now here she was, poking around again, muddying waters which ought by rights to be left placid, asking questions where none should be asked.

Claudia flashed Junius a quick catch-up-with-you-later look. Her priority now was to rootle out Flavia, Flea and the puppy, then get the hell out of here.

This whole place gave her the creeps.

No one missed her, because this was a public holiday, the first day of Ibis, and everyone was entitled to join the festivities, however lowly one's role.

A cold collation had been laid out in the dining hall the previous night, and the kitchens were eerily still. No steam, no clattering pans, no spillages, no fingers nicked from sharp knives.

No bodies getting in each other's way.

No one to notice that several bunches of herbs hanging from the ceiling had gone missing.

Tomorrow, when normal service would resume, Mentu's great agricultural machine would crank back into action, along with the kitchens, the scribes, the brewhouse, the charcoal burners in the woods, the small squad of healers who mixed potions for Shabak. No one worked in the laundry today. The large, flat scrubbing stones lay piled in neat heaps, airing lines hung limp and bare after last night's deluge.

It would be tomorrow before anyone noted the absence of a moody girl who had never mixed with the crowd.

It would be much later before anyone cared.

Chapter Twenty-four

Whether you liked to call this public holiday by its Mentu-name of Lotus or simply preferred the idea of it being a good, old-fashioned Saturday, there was no disputing the jollity of the occasion. After the sacrifice and the ensuing penances, the band struck up again and off the cult members twirled, in their wigs and kilts and diamond-patterned shifts, dancing and clapping and singing at the tops of their voices like . . . well, like proper Pyramidiots!

But they were happy. For all his faults, Mentu made these people happy, by giving them, Claudia supposed, exactly what they wanted. A refuge from real life, with prayers and work to control and discipline their minds, interspersed with festivals like today when they could let off steam. Supply and demand, it kept the world turning; Claudia had no real objection to that.

'I simply don't wish to be part of it!' she told a small toddler, picking her up and swirling her round so her legs fanned high in the air.

The toddler chortled and gargled and made giggly noises and Claudia's arms were aching badly by the time she set the girl down, but as she turned away, tears of disappointment welled up in the huge, doe-like eyes, forcing her to pull off the tot's nose at least seventeen times before hunger pangs took over from fun and little fat legs waddled off to scavenge the last of the bull meat from the sacrificial platters. Watching her, Claudia felt a pang for this beautiful, happy creature for whom outsiders would always be enemies, who would never experience the cut and thrust of bartering in a street market redolent with spices and liniments and vellum, never even see cloth bales fluttering in every colour of the rainbow, much less encase herself in floaty tunics or diaphanous, feminine wraps. Sweet Juno, those little fat feet would never learn to walk in soft, tooled-leather slippers, no perfumer would mix a personal scent for the grown woman to wear. She would not smell the sea, not even a river, or gasp at the wonder of a flotilla under full sail, canvas bellied out in the wind. She would never see olive groves tumbling over the hillsides, or the breathtaking spectacle of an army marching off to war. For that little girl, the excitement of two Titan gladiators battling it out in the arena would remain a mystery, as would the thrill of a chariot race. In their place, she was doomed to a life of servitude, in a valley from which there could be no escape.

Claudia watched the grease dribble down the child's chubby little chin, and felt a tear trickle down her own cheek.

With a sideways peep she noticed Shabak leading Junius towards his hut for treatment and knew enough about her bodyguard to know he'd raise the subject of Berenice, the baby and the hemlock, man to man, as it were, over the dressings. She doubted he'd get far with his interrogation. Shabak was not the rugged boys-together type!

Over on the temple platform, Mentu and his nine cohorts clapped and swayed, the crocodile dancing hand in hand with the vulture and the cat, the ibis garlanded with flowers to mark his special day. She looked at them. Glanced at the Pharaoh's domestic wing. Glanced back.

And felt a spark of mischief kindle in her breast.

The wing was deserted as Claudia slipped through the door and, in the silence, heard herself gasp. Good grief! Dazzling mosaics spread themselves across the floor and stretched away to infinity. Lurid paintings covered the walls, hunting scenes, battles, gods versus giants, all the way up to the gilt, stucco ceiling. The first room she entered was Mentu's, and it was clear the simple life was not for him. A bed of pure bronze lay smothered under piles of swansdown cushions and sheets of iridescent damask. In the centre of the mound, sprawled flat on its side, a jet-black tomcat encased in rolls of fat lifted half an eyelid.

'Sssh!' Claudia placed her fingers to her lips.

The eyelid closed. Not even a stiff white whisker twitched as the intruder poked around inside chests of maple wood inlaid with mother-of-pearl and inspected gold statuettes, ivories, hinged jewellery boxes filled with rings and amulets and cloak pins. If he wore one pin for every tunic with a different amulet and, say, three different rings each day, Claudia calculated that it would take several months to wade through this lot.

The cat was snoring as she slipped into the adjacent room. In here, a sunken bath was surrounded by white marble statues whose lifeless toes pirouetted on glazed floor tiles lit by a score of alabaster lamps. The finest linen towels stood stacked against a chest containing oils and unguents, strigils, scissors, clippers. Water lilies floated in the water, which was warm.

She moved on to what had served the previous owner as a lofty, vaulted atrium and where, in pride of place, a throne of pure gold in the shape of a couchant lion stood beneath a tasselled awning which had been suspended to fan the Pharaoh as he rested. Fragrant resins pumped out their expensive aromas from braziers mounted high on the walls, and ribbons, ivies and garlands of bright scented flowers wound their way round pillars of the finest Parian marble to the red-painted capitals.

So many colours, so many scents, each and every one vying for attention. The golden stucco ceiling was adorned with flying beasts. A drunken Bacchus was surrounded by leering satyrs, all pawing the same weary nymph. Leopards were disembowelling a stag. So much colour, so much heat, so much movement. So much coming at you at once and none of it pleasant. Claudia's instinct was to step back. To retreat. To escape.

Then she remembered the delighted squeals of a little girl spinning through the air, and instead of turning round, her long legs marched her purposefully forward down the wing. Quite what sabotage Claudia planned to carry out, she wasn't sure, only that Mentu must be stopped. It was sickening enough what he was turning decent people into, and irrelevant that his victims queued up willingly in droves.

Mentu had no right to deny that child her proper destiny.

Other rooms led off from the central corridor, equally opulent, equally lavish in their decoration. In a line, five scented chambers each comprising four beds divided by shimmering drapes and compensating with onyx, tortoiseshell and silver what they lacked in privacy. These, then, were the chambers where Mentu's twenty wives slept and, across the hall, their recreation room. More pillows. More diaphanous drapes. A lyre propped against a chair leg. A tapestry loom. Goblets of gold, salvers of bronze piled with apricots, peaches and plums. Claudia ran her finger over the polished maple-wood couches upholstered in scarlet and green before closing the door on this room where intimate, cloying secrets swapped in hushed whispers still drifted in the sultry air.

An office. Full of scrolls and counters, money boxes, chests and desks, the smell of ink and parchment stamping their own scent above the aromatic resins and wild-flower garlands. Hmm. Nothing here to vandalise; trashing records wouldn't mean a thing. The damage had to be something personal which would strike deep into Mentu's heart, as well as spike his guns.

She moved on. Smaller chambers, elegant and expensive. A woman's room, decorated with cat paintings, cat statuettes, even (yuk!) a cat mummy. Bast's room, obviously, and Thoth's was next door – a stuffed ibis in the corner proved it. Watery scenes around the walls of the room opposite betrayed the bearer of the crocodile mask and – Ah. This is interesting.

Claudia listened. Only a lazy bee, buzzing round the garlands, disturbed the hush. She slipped into the room. Talk about repression! Whoever slept here was so withdrawn, you could mistake him for a tortoise. She lifted the lid of the clothes chest. As expected, creases you could cut yourself on, sandals scrubbed so clean they might be new. Nothing out of place. A tidy mind to reflect an ordered personality? Or the room of a martinet who never let himself go? The name, Neco, inscribed on the cover of a wax tablet told her nothing, except this was the room of the commune's Chief Scribe, responsible for overseeing the members' correspondence and—

'Uh. Uh. Uh-uh-uh.'

Amid the graveyard silence, the grunting put Claudia on instant alert. She froze, straining in the stillness of the hall.

'Uh-uh. Uh-uh. Uh-uh.'

Sweet Janus! Someone's in trouble! Her thoughts flew to the boy, Sorrel, who'd been caught by the guards last night trying to escape. They were keeping him here, then, a prisoner. She tiptoed down the corridor, careful lest the boy was guarded. She was no match for a scimitar . . . Four doors down she stopped. The grunts came from here.

'Uh. Uh. Uh.'

Now she listened carefully, there seemed to be a second sound. A mewing . . .

Quietly, Claudia eased open the door.

Whoops!

Not the boy from last night. Not a guard. Not, in fact, anyone in trouble at all. And the naked man pumping away at the girl who knelt face down on his crumpled couch with her skirt up around her waist probably wouldn't thank Claudia for rescuing him, either.

Beating a silent retreat, she identified the man as Min. Apart from the distinctive curly-toed sandals, his room was larger, more spacious, the décor more elaborate than the others she'd seen, except one. Mentu's. Whose couch was buried under a mountain of iridescent pillows, and where the gold was only marginally more dazzling.

Min and Mentu, the Egyptian siblings behind this elaborate scam.

Min and Mentu, lovers of fine arts.

Strange how their footwear was really all she knew about the brothers: one wore built-up shoes to disguise his lack of height; the other was in such a hurry to consummate his lust that he hadn't bothered to untie the sandal straps which were wound halfway up his calves.

The majestically titled Grand Vizier, Second-in-Command, Min would be responsible for overseeing the commune's finances, for booking in the contributions to the Solar Fund and salting them away. How did he feel, taking orders from his brother – occasionally, as Mercy pointed, being overruled? Min's unprepossessing back view had given her few clues about his personality, only his appearance. He was older than she'd imagined – early sixties – with what was left of his hair wiry and grey. Min, like his brother, though, was short and he was also stocky with it, plus—

A scraping sound from his room sent her ducking behind a gilded statue. For six or seven heartbeats nothing happened. Then the door opened and the girl came scurrying out, tears streaking her cheeks, her face crumpled in anguish.

A battering ram hammered into Claudia's heart.

Rape.

'I could have stopped it,' she whispered. 'Dear sweet Jupiter, I could have helped that poor girl.'

She replayed the scene, and saw it from its genuine angle. Min: his sandals still tied. The girl: skirt round her waist. No foreplay, no lust, no mutual passion.

What Min wanted, Min took.

Claudia's weight could not support her, she slid to the floor, her heart crashing wildly in her chest.

I could have prevented that attack.

Could you? a little voice asked. The violation was already under way, the bastard had nearly finished. All you'd have done was shout and scream and raise the roof, and who the hell would take your word over his?

Huddled in the corner, Claudia's teeth began to chatter. Who indeed? Two silly girls would have been hauled up before the Holy Council. Raped by Mentu's Grand Vizier? Slander! Defamation! Spiteful, vicious smears! One branded jealous because she hadn't been the chosen lover, the other branded bitter because she'd been cast over. No one would listen. No one would believe.

Croesus! Was that what had happened to the six missing girls? Claudia buried her head in her hands. Had Min raped them as well, forcing them, in anguish and despair, to kill themselves? It would explain Berenice's strange behaviour, certainly, because her baby had died a truly horrible death. Hemlock would have paralysed his lungs, his limbs, every tiny muscle in his tiny body, and no mother whose mind was running lucidly would choose to kill her child in such a manner when she could have smothered him painlessly in his sleep. But poison him she had. To spare him the indignity and shame of growing up to believe his mother had spread malicious allegations?

Assuming, though, the six girls had committed suicide, why had no one found their bodies? Surely one of them would have wanted to make a statement with her death, perhaps drowning herself in the ceremonial pool or hanging herself from the gateway? Or was this yet another angle to Min and Mentu's cover up?

'What are you doing here?' The voice was openly antagonistic and carried a slight whistle. 'This wing's out of bounds.'

The curly-toed open sandals were familiar. But not the skinny legs which they encased.

Claudia said nothing. Still shaking from shock, she simply couldn't. Dammit, she hadn't heard him sneak up! Frantically, she reassembled her composure as a bony hand gripped her arm and hauled her to her feet. The light which flickered in his eyes told her that he enjoyed feeling her wince.

'What's going on, Neco?'

Min, spruce in white clinging shirt and pleated kilt, came striding out of his bedroom. His whole mien was military, his voice clipped, and Min, she realised at once, was accustomed to giving orders and having them obeyed without question.

'I found this bitch snooping around.' Neco's whistle was the result of two front teeth which stuck out and crossed.

Claudia blasted him with a glare that could have uncurled

his sandalled toes. 'I'll have you know, you imbecile, that I contributed an olive grove in Campania and vineyards which stretch across three hills of Frascati to this organisation. I've come to see exactly where my money's going!'

There was something reptilian, repellent, about the Chief Scribe, even more than his nauseating master. Repressed, undoubtedly. A martinet, no question. But with Min, one suspected the battle lines would be drawn up from the beginning. With Neco, you would never see the blow which felled you.

'How dare you—' he began, but a podgy hand forestalled him.

'Why don't you rejoin the festivities, Neco?' There was steel in the faded blue eyes of the Grand Vizier. 'I'll deal with this.'

Cold glances flickered between Vizier and Scribe. No love lost here, then. Eventually Neco's thin lips curled in acquiescence. 'Sir.'

Claudia followed his retreating back. Hair tortured to within an inch of its life by hot curling rods. A slight stoop from years bent over a desk. Stomach muscles flabby from too much time in a chair. Everyone here looks inwards, she thought, to their own needs. Proof that self-absorption can lead to obsession.

'Never mind Neco,' harrumphed the Grand Vizier. 'Holds a senior post, y'know. Don't tolerate familiarity.'

It wasn't clear whether Min meant Neco or himself.

'Vineyards, eh?'

'In Frascati.' Claudia smiled, and wondered whether it reached as far as her eyes.

'White stuff, presumably.' His full mouth formed a ghastly, kissy pout. 'Too dry for my taste. Prefer the sweet stuff, don't yer know.' And still there was no softening in the steel. 'New girl, are you? Don't believe I've had the pleasure.'

Damn right!

'Heard about you, though.' They were still standing in the middle of the corridor, outside his own bedroom door. 'Caused a bit of stir, what?'

If he grabbed her now, say by the hair, he could drag her

inside his room and no one would ever know. Those hands – those big, strong, army hands – could clamp around her throat and within a count of thirty she'd be dead.

'My puppy's missing,' she said with commendable mildness.

'So he said.'

Who? Geb? Penno? Shabak? It wasn't lost on her that someone had reported back, but then Min hadn't intended that it should be! Heatwave or not, suddenly it seemed icily cool.

Claudia swallowed.

In the eighteen hours since her arrival, she'd been unable to find Flavia anywhere, and, by heaven, how she'd searched. Another of Min's conquests? A picture swam before her. Of a chubby fifteen-year-old, sobbing into the sheets as she struggled helplessly beneath the Grand Vizier.

Sweet Janus.

Suppose the total was now *seven* missing girls?

Chapter Twenty-five

For what seemed like eternity, Min's faded blue eyes stared at Claudia from beneath his wiry, grey brows. She stared back. He couldn't hear (how could he?) the thrashing of her heart. Only Claudia could feel the dampness of her palms.

'Little black fellow, is he?'

Huh? Then she remembered Doodlebug.

'You'll find him in the stables.' The Grand Vizier made a noise in the back of his throat. 'Other dogs, y'know. Companionship.'

Claudia turned to leave. Any excuse. The urge to sabotage Mentu's operation had dulled. She just wanted to *go*. Get out of here. Before she was sucked in any deeper.

'Bit of a problem, though,' he harrumphed.

Visions of Doodlebug kicked to death by a mule flashed through her mind. Attacked by the other dogs. Torn apart, bleeding and helpless.

'That girl you brought along—'

'Flea?' The hysterical images were replaced by much more realistic pictures of Doodlebug snuggling into his new make-shift family, gallumphing along behind the pack, tumbling, tangling up his stubby legs and rolling in the cowpats.

'Is that what she calls herself?' Min's kissy pout was back. 'Not surprised, frankly. Filthy mouth. Anyway. Been caught stealing. Serious offence. Trial tomorrow.'

Oh, Flea, you silly bitch. Thieving's bad enough, but *getting caught?* 'The girl's a street thief, Min, stealing's what she does best.'

'Force of habit, you mean?'

'Exactly.' Claudia loaded honey into her voice. 'There's no need for any trial. Confiscate the booty and tell her not to do it again, she'll understand.'

The Grand Vizier snorted.

Shit. 'I had hoped' (another spoonful of honey) 'that by bringing her here, she'd find Ra—'

'She found him all right,' Min retorted. 'Helped herself to half of his bloody offerings! Not allowed, y'know – commoners inside the temple. Restricted area, accessible only to the Pharaoh and his Holy Council. To trespass inside the holy of holies is serious. To steal from it – gad, that's treason.'

Flea, you stupid child, why couldn't keep your sticky hands to yourself for just ten minutes? Surely that wasn't too much to ask?

'I'll have a quiet word with her lawyer,' Claudia said. The silence of the corridor was beginning to grate. Strange, how the eyes of every statue seemed to bore right through you. 'See if we can't thrash this thing out.'

'Don't have lawyers.' Min patted the solid paunch under which his white kilt swung to his calves. 'Defendants plead their own case before the Pharaoh or the Grand Vizier. Witnesses called, judgement pronounced.'

Claudia saw a chink in Flea's plight. 'And who will be presiding over Flea's trial?' Please say it's you. However much I despise you, I'm sure there's a mutual currency to deal in.

'For offences against Ra, the Pharaoh always sits in judgement.' Min produced that throaty noise again. 'But remember, we're all equal in the eyes of Ra. Men and women. No distinction here. Each of us is expected to acquit ourselves well, that's our god-given duty and we shall not falter. Hear what I'm saying, do you?'

'I think I may have missed the point.'

He leaned close, and she could smell parsley on his breath. 'The point,' he said acidly, 'is that equality tolerates no prima donnas.'

Ouch.

'And no histrionics, either,' he snarled, his blue eyes blazing hatred. 'Provoke any further disruption and I'll personally see that you regret it.'

So he'd known all along that she'd seen his tearful victim flee his room.

'On the other hand,' he added, with a lightning switch of personality which sent his eyes raking over the curve of her breasts, 'stay on the right side of me, little lady, and you'll be surprised what I can do for you.'

'This little lady is prepared to live without surprises.'

'Your prerogative.' A strange smile twisted half his face. 'Just bear in mind, Flea's won't be the first death sentence we've pronounced.'

An icy blast blew straight in from the Arctic. It sucked her breath away. 'You—' Claudia cleared her throat and tried again. 'You don't execute someone for stealing a few trinkets off a boat,' she said, and her voice carried only the faintest hint of a quiver.

'We do here,' Min replied cheerfully. 'Unless, of course, I put in a word for her tomorrow.'

'And what would it take for you to plead her cause, I wonder.'

'Oh, I think you know the answer.' His faded eyes cast the merest flash towards his bedroom door before they stripped the linen from her body. 'Woman of the world like you.'

'Go to hell.'

'Highly unlikely,' sneered the Grand Vizier. 'I don't force any woman into anything she doesn't want to do.'

'Find yourself a dictionary and look up "tyranny" then.'

The insult rolled off him like raindrops off an oily rag. 'Just ask yourself, m'dear, how much is that scrawny kid's life worth to you? Bugger all to me, I'll tell you that!'

Min's mocking laughter echoed in the empty corridor long after he'd closed his bedroom door.

In the arena in Rome, the executions were well under way. Fourteen hardened murderers and rapists had cried and begged and pleaded for the mercy of the people, only to have their mangled corpses hooked away, fresh sand thrown over their coagulated blood.

The Armenian waited with a patience he had grown used to over the past seven years. Whatever beast the executioners had lined up for him could not be half as bad as the horrors inflicted by his master – the abuse, the beatings, the rapes, the humiliation. He was glad the bastard was dead, unable to inflict any further torture. Whatever he faced now, would be swift.

His turn came. The charge was read out.

'. . . slave charged with wearing the toga in public . . .'

What? For a moment the Armenian could not believe his own ears. I killed my master, he wanted to shout. I stabbed him. A cruel and terrible man, he deserved it, I'm glad, I would cheerfully do it again.

Then his endless patience kicked in, and he accepted that the nature of his crime didn't really matter. The Armenian had known, the instant he'd been shackled in that empty slot, that the previous occupant had only recently departed. With prisoners pouring in at such a rate, a gap doesn't hang about for long!

He recalled the strange, faraway look in the Clerk's eyes. His words. 'It's a sad day,' he had said, 'when decency is repaid with inhumanity.'

At the time, the Armenian thought he was addressing him. Later, though, he had not been so sure and now, with the stench of blood gagging at the back of his throat, he understood the Clerk of the Dungeons had been talking to himself.

So then. The Clerk had released the slave who had been caught in the act of wearing the toga and had set the Armenian in his place. Not an oversight, then, the Clerk not writing down his name.

Idly, as a wolf mad with fury was prodded with red-hot irons in its cage, he wondered what name he was scheduled to die under. And whether it mattered much that in the Afterlife he would arrive with a set of false papers.

Fire was brandished at the wolf to enrage and terrify it further. The Armenian could see the poor beast had been starved. Its ribs showed through its dull and unkempt pelt, and there were scars on its back from ancient battle wounds. Naked, the Armenian made no attempt at modesty by turning his back on the crowd. The scars on his own back were not for public consumption.

Finally – mercifully – the wolf was released from its cage. Maddened by the smoke, disorientated by the baying mob, it ran around in uncoordinated circles, until amber eyes flashed fire at the only living soul within its reach. It stopped and snarled out its hatred of mankind.

The Armenian threw down the bar he'd been given for defence, and heard the crowd boo. They wanted a fight. They didn't want to see a man's throat ripped out cleanly. The stamp-stamp-stamp of feet began to reverberate around the pit.

Stuff them, he thought. This is my day. I have earned the right to do what I want.

The wolf began to bound across the sand, picking up speed. He could smell its rancid breath. Felt flecks of its saliva hot on his face. It sprang. He could see its fangs, long and yellow. In its amber eyes shone death.

One. Two. *Now!* The Armenian slashed his arms against the beast's flying forelimbs. Snap. The wolf's eyes bulged. A racking sound came from the back of its maw. It jerked. Then fell on top of him. Stone dead.

Mesmerised, the crowd roared and this time the stamping was ecstatic. To wild whistles, the umpire – dressed, as always, as Mercury, messenger of the gods – stepped into the arena. He prodded the wolf's nose with a hot iron and when the beast didn't move, pronounced life officially extinct. He turned to the audience and asked, should the victor live? Or shall he face a second encounter with the beasts?

The spectators screamed so loud the Armenian couldn't hear. Didn't try. But this strange pounding in his heart was a sensation for which he would die happy.

Eventually he identified it as pride.

Through misty eyes, he gazed into the crowd. To a universal raising of the thumbs.

'Junius, the Gaul,' the umpire intoned sombrely. 'You are free to return home, on the strict understanding that you never again impersonate a Roman citizen. Do you agree?'

'I do.'

'Can you confirm your mistress resides at the following address?'

With tears drizzling down his cheeks and splashing in the sand, the Armenian was forced to admit that he didn't have a clue.

They sent him to Claudia's anyway.

For the young girl who'd been working in the laundry, the prospect of a wolf cleanly ripping out her throat was heaven.

She would give anything for that.

To be spared what Berenice had suffered. What she, herself, would have to endure.

Straight away she'd recognised Berenice under the striking cobra's mask, even though the corpse was naked. There was no telling what had killed her. Not the bonds, they'd only ripped open the flesh as they dug in. Perhaps he'd slit her throat? Quick and clean. That way, she wouldn't see it coming.

The girl's heart sank. Berenice's wounds had not been cleaned. Surely the blood from a cut throat would not have been mopped up and the others left to dry? There were no tell-tale arcs of red across the painted walls or on the bandaged remains of the others seated round the table. The laundress shuddered under her gag.

Three chairs remained empty.

Four masks lay on the table.

One for her.

Beyond tears, beyond pain, beyond hope, the girl wondered what terrible sins she had committed to warrant so barbarous a death.

Outside the cave, footsteps crunched up the path. So far, she had not even seen the face of the man behind this sickening tableau – he'd worn the mask of the falcon, which he'd obviously taken from the corpse sitting opposite. She knew that, if she saw his face, she would recognise her killer. She wondered how much trust she'd placed in him in the past.

The footsteps stopped. A strong hand pulled back the scrambling fig. Light flooded in. Her heart was pounding, she felt sick. Sweet Ra, she didn't want to die.

At that point, the processes of decay began to take their inexorable toll on Berenice. And when the cobra mask lolled forward of its own accord, the girl from the laundry fainted dead away.

Chapter Twenty-six

Orbilio's head weighed a ton. While he was napping, someone had taken out his brain and replaced it with a lump of granite. His eyeballs were on fire, his mouth had been filled with sand, there was a white-hot burning in the region round his liver. When a whiff of stale wine tickled his nostrils, he willed the nausea to pass. He did not want to think about what he had done. His memory gave him little choice. He leaned forward and was sick.

Demons began beating the granite block with cymbals.

He wanted to groan, but his tongue had trebled in size and in the process had cemented itself to the roof of his mouth.

Green spots danced before his open eyes. Red ones when he closed them.

Resting his groggy frame against the wall, he reached inside his tunic and extracted the crumpled letter, waiting patiently until the handwriting settled into focus.

> Dear Sir,
>
> Further to your recent request, please be advised that we are right out of Gaulish hunting dogs at the present time. However, Armenian hounds are every bit as reliable and, in view of the urgency of your requirement, we shall ensure our best champion attends the forthcoming hunt.
>
> Your obedient servant, etc., etc., etc.

Against his better judgement, Marcus smiled. No question this letter, which had been delivered late last night, came from quill of the Clerk of the Dungeons who had somehow swapped the prisoners around, putting an Armenian criminal in Junius' place and setting the Gaul free. Orbilio was relieved. Not only because Claudia's bodyguard was out of danger, but because he'd always believed the Clerk to be an honourable fellow. Unlike that rat of a Dungeon Master, whose son – ho, ho, ho – would already be mourning his misfortune in a cell. The difference in his case, is that at least he'd get a trial.

So then. Orbilio dragged his hands down over his face. Junius was off the hook, that was one problem solved, though two still remained:

One. Whose was the body in the plaster?

Two. How to get Claudia free of Mentu's steadfast grip?

Claudia. His pulse quickened as he pictured those high, fine, chiselled features. Her long, curvaceous legs, her luscious breasts. Mother of Tarquin, how he yearned to nibble his way down that swan neck of hers, feel her tense with pleasure as he slipped the soft cotton from her shoulders, hear the gentle swish as it landed at her feet. At the thought of her naked, silky skin his loins began to stir and, in spite of the demons clashing cymbals in his head and the burning pain behind his bloodshot eyeballs, Orbilio began to laugh.

Oh, yes. She'd really fancy you right now. Face white and waxy. Stubble on your jaw and breath little better than a drainage ditch in summer. What a catch!

He thought about the whores he'd hired last night, seven in the end, who had met the stringent requirements he'd demanded.

And hoped to Remus that Claudia never got wind of his involvement with those lusty, busty Amazons.

He'd never live it down.

At that moment, the object of Orbilio's introspections sat slumped against the storehouse wall, her head buried in her hands. Some distance away, like so many seething maggots, the black dreadlocks of her wig soaked up a puddle of last night's rainwater where she'd hurled it.

Now what!

The gods of Olympus must be laughing their socks and slippers off. 'Better than turning nymphs into trees and mortals into stags, don't you think, watching the antics of that Claudia Seferius down there?'

How right they are! To save Junius from certain execution, Claudia follows Flavia to this quasi-Egyptian commune, and what a waste of bloody time that turned out to be! An administrative cock-up (what other explanation?) frees the Gaul without her wretched meddling, so all Claudia has to do now is find the silly bitch and leave. Only there's a problem. That grasping little street thief gets herself locked up in the temple jail, and the circle joins itself, except that this time it's Flea's life Claudia has to save, and the only way is by sleeping with Min!

Claudia threw a stone at the plaited wig, and missed.

Well, sod Olympus.

A bombardment of stones rained over at the wig.

And missed.

Claudia could almost hear Juno purring up there on her celestial throne. 'Mahvellous entertainment, dahlings. Do come and watch.'

One treat they'd miss, though, the gods gawping down from Mount Olympus. Venus and Eros could wreak what mischief they wanted, but there's no way Claudia would be lifting her skirts for that randy Vizier! The thought of his solid paunch pressing against her naked flesh brought goose-pimples to the surface. Never mind divine intervention, I'll turn myself into a tree – an animal – a goddamned constellation – before he gets his pudgy paws on me! Just let him try.

Flea's trial was not until tomorrow, though. Ample time to work on a plan of escape and typical of Min, dishing out his ultimatum and leaving Claudia to sweat on it. He'd want her to squirm. To reflect long and hard on the deal she would be making.

Bastard!

This time the rock hit the dreadlocks square on, and three more landed on their target before another thought occurred to her. The five men charged with the daily running of this commune – the superintendents, so to speak – were not weak, compliant or submissive chaps, content to take life's easy road. On the contrary, they were forceful characters in positions of authority, accustomed to dishing out orders as much as to obeying them, and who revelled in the fact that they had minions of their own dancing attendance.

Min, the Grand Vizier, who uses emotional extortion to get what he wants.

Neco, the martinet, with a preference for physical rather than emotional torment.

Shabak, the blue-jawed physician, so lacking in compassion.

Penno, thin, suspicious, relishing his religious rites and rituals.

Geb, the Barbary ape on two legs, the Keeper of the Central Store, with the fearsome combination of vile temper and slow-burning grudge. The hairy godfather, who beat his wife.

Five bullies, with two traits in common:

– they each have a need to control.

– they share a universal hatred of womankind.

Five men, moreover, who are able to move freely round the commune and talk to people – girls – without drawing notice to themselves. Five men, all of whom are trusted by every member present, each in a position to cover his tracks, should his aversion to women become a deadly obsession.

Claudia stood up, brushed her skirts and looked around. Six girls had gone missing. Loners who had not been missed in either sense of the word. Six girls . . . yes, six (sweet Janus, please don't let it be seven!) Not Flavia! I know she fits the profile, but please, please don't let him get her.

Find Flavia. Grab Flea. Get out.

Find Flavia. Grab Flea. Get out. She repeated it like a mantra in her head. Find-Flavia-grab-Flea-get-out. But this was not going to be easy. Far from it. Everyone in the commune is allocated a task, and depending on how generous one's contribution, the softer the number. Claudia had not yet been allocated her own role, but anyone handing over olive groves and vineyards across three hills of Frascati would get a cushy one. Mercy, on the other hand, had fled Brindisi clutching next to nothing. Why wasn't she scrubbing floors or kneading dough, grinding corn or weeding lines of vegetables with a hoe?

And of the ten women in Mercy's cell, which one had a personality? True, her views were loyalist, her devotion unequivocal, but in Mercy there was a distinct lack of sameness. Who had latched on to Claudia from the start, offering to show her the ropes? Mercy would call it befriending. Claudia called it keeping tabs.

Remember Mercy's concern that Junius and Claudia might know one another, her relief at finding they did not?

Unless Claudia very much missed her guess, Mercy's job here was as minder. *Mercy was a spy.* Sooner or later, too, she'd catch up again with Claudia and, like the very best of barnacles, would cling firm next time. Claudia vowed to be vigilant.

Across the courtyard, three figures shambled into view. Anubis, in his jackal-headed mask. Bast, the cat goddess. And between them, his arms firmly linked in theirs, trailed a third and the third man wore no mask. Claudia's breath came out as a whistle. She waved. The trio speeded up.

'Hello, there. Sorrel, isn't it?'

You don't forget a name like that.

'Didn't I see you last night?' she yelled after them. 'On the temple platform?' Hauled up wearing nothing but your loin cloth by guards wielding scimitars after you'd been caught trying to escape? The boy's vacant expression didn't change. His legs were dragging.

'Mistaken identity,' Bast hissed. 'This boy's simply fainted in the heat.'

'We're taking him to Shabak,' Anubis puffed. The strain of dragging a muscular youth at the double was beginning to tell. 'For a potion.'

Claudia's own knees wobbled.

I'll bet you are, you bastards.

Hugging her arms to her body, she now saw the full extent of Min's threats and how trouble-makers were dealt with in the commune. For who could mistake the purpose of those bright poppy heads waving in the breeze at the back of the orchard?

At first the dose would not be voluntary. Like the boy, Sorrel, it would involve some form of temporary incarceration. But quickly the addiction would kick in of its own accord, eliminating any need for detention. Within a week, Sorrel would be pleading not to leave this beautiful valley.

And – unless she trod carefully – so would Claudia Seferius.

Was that what had happened to Flavia? Had she protested at being put to work in the fields, the kitchens or the brewery? 'Another trouble-maker, Shabak, for you to deal with!'

The insidious evil of the valley began to clamp round her, crushing, squeezing, forcing the breath from her lungs.

I must get out.

Claudia could not explain the feeling. But hanging over her was the spectre that soon – very soon – something terrible would happen.

Wait a tick! If Flavia was being held prisoner until she became addicted and pliable, then it stood to reason she and Sorrel would be held in the same place. Right. Follow Bast and Anubis, see where they take him, and find out whether Flavia's there too.

Min's threat echoed in her brain. 'Provoke any further disruption and I'll personally see you regret it.' Did this constitute provocation? Claudia had a feeling Min would construe it that way.

With wings on her ankles, Claudia flew across the open courtyard. She looked left, right, peered ahead. Shit. She had dithered too long. There was no sign of any animal gods. No sign of any drugged prisoners. Damn, damn, damn. Where are you, Sorrel? Where have they taken you?

From the corner of her eye, she caught a shadow. Just a hint, before it ducked backwards to mould itself into the shade of the storehouse wall. She scurried after it.

Nothing.

Then – yes, there it was again. Darting to the left.

As before, the merest hint.

She sped past the windowless store. Hooked to the left. Caught up slightly. Enough to see that the shadow was a man's. Alone. Should she follow him? What about the trio? There he goes. Her sandals skidded on the stone. He's trying to double back. Cut down here.

Racing after him, still undecided, Claudia turned the corner. And cannoned into him.

Too late she saw the sharp swing of the scimitar.

Chapter Twenty-seven

'Will you unhand me?' wheezed the shadow, flat upon its back. 'Or do I have to cry rape?'

Claudia blinked. It can't be! 'Orbilio?'

'I used to be, before your kneecap changed all that.'

'What? Oh.' She removed the offending joint and his skin ceased to be grey. 'Marcus Cornelius, what the hell are you doing up here? Last I heard, you were being eaten alive by seven slobbering Amazons.'

'Me? I'm strictly a one-woman man,' he said, but all the same she rather thought he winced.

'You look terrible,' she said, peering closer.

'Thanks.'

'Whey-faced. You need a shave. And your eyes are a particularly unattractive shade of bloodshot.'

'You know how to cheer a man up, don't you? Well, if it's any consolation, my head hurts, too.'

'Classic case of Amazon overdose.'

'I needed them,' he said miserably.

'Only seven? You must be getting old.'

'No, no. I needed them to help me sneak away from the house.'

Claudia felt a bubble burst. Relief? From what? She didn't care how many women he slept with, that pain inside was where she'd jarred herself in falling. Then – slowly – laughter began to rise in her diaphragm. 'You *didn't?*' No wonder he'd asked for big women!

A similar vibration came from his. 'I bloody did.' He grinned, propping himself up on both elbows. 'What's more,

I was that convincing, dressed in drag, that three erstwhile respectable businessmen propositioned me as I crossed the Forum!'

'Well, I hope you didn't sell yourself too cheap.'

'The whiskers put them off, otherwise I'd have made a mint. In fact, when this thing's over, I'm seriously thinking of changing my career.' He flopped back on to the cobbles and sighed contentedly. 'Alternatively,' he said blissfully, 'I could become a gigolo.'

'You'd starve.'

'Nonsense. I'm already experiencing the effects of women giving me the old once-over.'

'Have you been sniffing those hemp seeds again?'

'One look, and *you* were all over me, for a start!' He closed his eyes. 'Still are, in fact.'

Ah . . . As she scrambled off his prostrate form, she thought she heard him mumble 'pity' but she wasn't sure. There was something curious going on inside her body. Heartbeat playing up, funny breathing. Her cheeks must have caught the sun, they were burning, even in the shade of the storehouse wall. Clearly, she thought, I'm out of shape. What else could cause this disruption to her system? She vowed to visit the gymnasium, the minute she returned to Rome.

'I'll do a deal,' Marcus said, brushing down his tunic. 'You don't tell anyone I wear women's clothes at night and I won't tell about how you chased me through the streets and pinned me flat against my pommel.'

'Oh, that's a pommel?'

'Behave yourself.' He grinned again, adjusting the hang of his scimitar and pulling straight his belt. 'Respectable Egyptian maidens don't make advances to the guards. You'll have to restrain yourself until we're both back home in Rome.'

'Who says I intend to leave?' Strange. He was standing three feet away, yet she could still smell his sandalwood unguent as strongly as if he was just three inches from her, and that faint hint of mint upon his breath. Also, the hardness of his muscled torso, the warmth of his flesh felt as though they still pressed against her skin.

'I do,' he said, leaning closer, and suddenly his eyes were smoky dark. 'I know you, Claudia. I know you inside out, and I know that even in the unlikely event that *you* might be tempted to swap a life of idle luxury for toiling in the fields, your bodyguard will be keen to get away.'

He was aware that Junius was here? Of course! His steward would have put him in the picture. 'You know about the cock-up at the jails, then?' she asked, but since he looked puzzled, Claudia realised he didn't have the full picture after all and explained about the administrative error in the dungeons.

'Admini –? Error –? Oh. Yes. Right.' His face lost some of its bounce and, crestfallen, he stuffed a crumpled piece of parchment back inside his tunic.

'Junius won't be unduly keen to get away,' she added. 'He's wangled himself a cushy number here.'

'Only because while my steward lent him some appropriate gear, he appropriated some extra for himself.' Marcus scratched at the stubble on his chin. 'All the same, he *will* be hot to leg it once he knows the rules.'

'Rules?'

There was a wicked glint in his eye. 'Hadn't you heard?' he said innocently. 'Good Egyptians that they are, the Brothers here practise circumcision.'

'Then it's high time they stopped practising and damn well did it properly.'

Goddammit, he had no right to smell this good. Look at him. Haggard and unshaven, he's deliberately using his masculinity to try and win me over. Tough luck, sunshine! For all your silver tongue and witty speech, don't think I don't know why you're here. You can't fool Claudia Seferius. You want that seat in the Senate House, and see me as a means to win it.

Oh, I sympathise; don't think I don't. You're under house arrest, it's unfair and unjust, and your boss has you by the balls. How best to wriggle off the hook? By wrapping up a tasty little con trick, which you can hand to your boss in return for him dropping those ridiculous trumped-up charges. You're back on track, no harm done – hell, you might even earn yourself some laurels. Fine. Good luck to you. Just find someone else to use as stepping stones.

'I don't air my soiled linens in the street.'

'Excuse me?'

'I said, there's no way I will be a witness at their trial.'

'Have I blacked out or something?' he asked, cocking his head to one side. 'One minute we're laughing and joking, the next you're thrashing like a mustang on a rope and I don't know what the hell you're on about. Whose trial?'

'Min and Mentu's. And I won't be party to it.'

'Claudia, I'm not here to—'

'I'll swear an oath that I encouraged Flavia to join and was so taken with the commune that I decided to bring Junius and Flea along with me for a break.'

'Flea!' He threw up his hands in exasperation. 'Claudia, why in the name of Mars did you cart that wild child out here?'

'Good grief, man, isn't it obvious? To knock her's and Flavia's heads together.'

'Right.' His tone said that Orbilio didn't believe it for a second.

Too bad.

Long before Claudia had become aware that Flavia was the instigating force behind the kidnap – in fact, the instant she discovered the boy messenger was actually a girl – she knew there was no way she would allow Flea to return to living off the streets. The danger was too great, and Claudia knew – by heaven, she did – because she'd recognised in Flea a mirror image of herself ten years back down the line. Therefore if, by some crazy chance, it was true that the Unlovable One had actually found a friend in the Untameable One and (more crazy still) those feelings of friendship were reciprocated, then there was no reason Flea could not find a niche in Flavia's household, and consequently in Flavia's life.

Apart, the girls were less than adorable. Together?

'Together, who knows . . .'

Marcus repeated her last sentence aloud.

'Orbilio, what are you drivelling on about now?'

He buffed a fingernail with unnecessary care. 'I rather think I was asking you to marry me.'

Her heart stopped beating. Limbs turned to wood. The world had stopped revolving. Then – 'Do I look the type who marries men who hoard bodies in their plasterwork?'

'Well, actually you do.'

With a crash, her heart muscle cranked back into action. Silly bitch. What made you imagine for one second he was serious? Look at the brightness of his eyes, the high spots of colour in an otherwise chalky face. It was a joke, Claudia. Supersnoop was cracking a joke. Making light of things. Good grief, you didn't seriously think he'd—

'Talking of bodies,' she said. Anything to change the subject. 'There's something weird going on in this hippie-happy valley.'

'Weird, *apart* from grown men and women handing over all their worldly goods so they can dress up as Egyptians, work the land and worship that yellow thing up in the sky?'

'That's not weird, that's cranky.'

'And on which subject – yours truly ducked, because he didn't know who was after him – but that doesn't explain milady's behaviour, chasing armed guards round the outhouses.'

'What breathtaking arrogance you have, Marcus Cornelius, to imagine I was chasing you.' The party in the compound was still in full swing, you could hear the drums and trumpets, even from this secluded spot. 'I was merely following the jackal and the cat, because they were dragging a limp Sorrel between them.'

'I take it back,' Marcus said. 'That's not cranky behaviour. That's *weird!*'

Men. Never listen to a word you say. Patiently, she explained about Bast, Anubis and the boy called Sorrel, who'd been drugged because he'd had the temerity to try and leave. Then she told him about the three so-called accidents – the goring, the mistaken assassin and so on – and finished up with the rumours about the missing girls, including Berenice, who had killed her baby boy with hemlock.

'Claudia, you have to leave this place,' he rasped, and there was no trace of amusement in his eyes. 'Right this second. It's too bloody dangerous to hang about.'

'I will,' she promised. 'I'll leave just as soon as I find Flavia and rescue Flea.'

Orbilio rolled his eyes to heaven. 'For gods' sake, woman, just this once will you please, please, please do as you are told and leave it to the boys to sort things out? Between us, Junius and I are perfectly capable of finding Flavia and – what do you mean, *rescue* Flea?'

'All right, so I forgot to mention she's under lock and key for stealing. It's no big deal. I'll get her out, and then we'll leave. Oh, Doodlebug is doing fine, by the way. He's in the stables.'

'Doodle—' Despondency cut short his words. 'Claudia Seferius,' he said wearily, 'you must surely be the only person in the whole damned universe who would think to bring her entire household to this valley.'

Claudia debated whether to tell him about the six men stationed in the hills, and decided ignorance would be better for his health.

'I realise you slipped past the legionaries disguised as a rather large courtesan, but how did you manage to inveigle your way into becoming a member of staff?'

'Long story,' he said, and his face changed colour. Must be the light, but she could have sworn it took on a greenish tinge. As though he was about to be sick. 'I uh – I'll tell you all about it, sometime.'

It didn't work, his trying to make a joke of whatever turned his stomach. 'Does it include the reason you were hiding?'

'What? Oh. No. It's just that the guards aren't allowed past the second perimeter fence unless there's a damn good reason, and once they're inside the commune, they're under strict instructions to report immediately to Geb.'

'Geb?'

'He's responsible for the security arrangements.' Orbilio's knuckles knocked against the storeroom wall. 'It's the logical step, since all the building keys are in his care – outhouses, storehouses, sheds – everything, in fact, except those within the temple compound.'

The facilities had to be locked, because equality ruled this society. No favouritism, no extras, everyone had the same as everybody else.

Unless, of course, one lived in Mentu's wing.

Idly, she wondered where Geb and Penno and the other supervisors slept. She had a suspicion it was not in the dormitory blocks, and wished she'd been able to complete her inspection of the off-limits wing.

'Leave finding the girls to the professionals,' Marcus said firmly. 'I know it sounds a lot to ask, but keep your head down just this once. Please! With the festival going on, you won't be missed and I'll be back here in no time. So then.' He briskly rubbed his hands. 'Is it a deal? You'll stay put till I return?'

For all his calm efficiency, there was a hint of pleading in his voice which tugged at something in her stomach.

'Vestal Virgin's honour,' Claudia assured him. 'I won't budge, I promise.'

Except it didn't really count, because she had her fingers crossed.

Chapter Twenty-eight

Few cult members were affected by the sweltering heat of the afternoon. Today was the first day of Ibis, a holiday, a day of celebration. Singing, dancing, poetry and games occupied their thoughts today, and when their bodies needed sustenance, there were limitless supplies of palm wine and fig cakes, honey bread and beer. The best beer, too. Black beer. Thick and potent, it went straight to their heads and made them happy. The musicians played on.

Amongst the frenzied jubilations, it was easy for the man who believed himself to be the incarnation of the Dark Destroyer to slip away unseen. This time of year, high summer, the grass was lush, the vegetation thick. From his eerie on the hill Seth could see and not be seen. As he would for all eternity, once he had worked his special magic.

'Tonight,' he reminded the girl from the laundry, 'we celebrate the Festival of Lamps.'

Would it be too risky to make his move during the actual ceremony? The danger stirred his loins, but he, being Seth, Controller of Man's Destiny, must repress his own desires. He must take no chances. Seven now, and only three to go. Too close, now, to his goal to gamble. He was the Measurer of Time, he must gauge his programme with care.

Studiously, he bandaged his favoured consort, Berenice, wrapping every finger individually, making sure the linen strips were taut and overlapped. The little laundress made no sound.

'It's not going to be easy,' he said, heaving Berenice on

to the table, 'luring away that delightful creature who arrived with Zer from Rome.'

He paused for breath. He'd forgotten how plump his consort was. He wiped his brow, then proceeded to bandage up her thigh.

'That girl is smarter than the others, but she's worth persevering with.'

Seth liked a bit of spunk.

'All the same, the strategy requires careful planning, and it doesn't help that that Flavia-Magas bitch has gone to ground.'

One fucking burn – an accident, at that – and she's scuttled into hiding like a rabbit.

'I'll find her, of course.'

Seth can go anywhere he pleases.

'Oh, I'll find the timid cow.' No one can escape the Dark One when he is in pursuit. 'My magic, little laundry girl, is written in the heavens and the writing is the stars.'

He planted a parting peck on Berenice's cheek before applying the final bandage and then, with sturdy ropes, tied the mummy upright to its seat of woven rushes. By the time he'd finished, Seth was lathered like a racehorse.

With both hands flat on the table top, he waited for the wheezing to subside and as he did so, a daring plan occurred to him. What if he moved now? This afternoon, while the revels were in progress? Not such a gamble, really. Most of the common rabble were half-cut down there, it was only the other supervisors that need concern him – and that was where he could use his position to advantage.

'Why not!'

That's what he'd do. He needed to act fast, the stench was overwhelming and the herbs he'd hung had made precious little difference. There was, as his mother used to say, no time like the present.

She was wrong, of course.

The present is meaningless, it is the future which counts, and the future was in Seth's power and the future belonged to him. Why not bring the future forward? Advance the holy schedule?

He moved to the mouth of the cave, gazing down upon the bewigged heads of the drunken, swaying proselytes. They did not know the Dark One moved among them, seeking vengeance, wreaking his destruction. Therefore, in his mortal guise, he should easily be able to winkle out the little rabbit from her hole or, failing that, there was no reason why he couldn't reverse the order and get that spunky bitch from Rome up here instead. The quickness of the hand deceives the eye, and – oh, sweet Ra! – suppose he got the two at once! Flavia and whatshername. His loins jumped into action. *The two together.*

His breathing was harsh and ragged. After that, I only need one other.

And by then it wouldn't matter who he'd seized, or how, because by the time the hue and cry was raised, Seth would have worked his spells and turned these women into gods, *real* gods, not fakes like those who assembled in the temple and conned the people out of money.

'I,' he said, positioning the striking cobra mask on Berenice, 'am The Master of Darkness, the Sorcerer, the Measurer of Time. Only I have the power to transform my disciples into divinities and rule over you for all eternity.'

It occurred to him that the girl from the laundry was keeping very quiet while all this was going on. He hoped she wasn't jealous.

Shit! The bitch had gone and died on him! He kicked her hard on the shins, and slapped her face.

'Bitch!' He kicked her in the stomach. 'I haven't finished with you, yet.'

Laying into her with fists did not dampen his arousal, and he looked sadly at his magnificent erection. For a moment he considered taking the bitch anyway, but Seth was no barbarian.

He was the Commander of the Dark, Controller of Man's Destiny, Master of Restraint.

He did not shag dead whores for his satisfaction. Even when they cheated him.

He'd make her pay, that one. In the Afterlife, he'd bloody make her pay, you wait. Meanwhile, four masks remained unclaimed upon the table. He ran loving hands over them all. The vulture he'd allocated to that ugly duckling, Flavia and the gold mask of Osiris he would save till last. Oh, but how Osiris would be last! He thought of Mentu, with his wives and gold and cushions, and felt a prick of happiness at how the bastard would react when he finally realised that Seth the Dark One had prevailed.

Seth, who he had ignored and who had taken the ultimate revenge!

In resurrection he would rule the gods for all eternity. And when he died, that bastard Mentu would know who he would face the day his heart was weighed. Seth! To whom he for ever must bend the knee.

But he was doing something, what was it? Oh, yes, the masks. He had two choices, didn't he? The black jackal or the crocodile.

'There you go.' The man who had convinced himself that he was Seth set the heavy mask upon the shoulders of the little laundress. 'You worked with water, you treacherous bitch, you might as well spend eternity in it.'

The crocodile grinned inanely back.

Chapter Twenty-nine

The stables smelled of horse dung, donkey fur, fresh-mown hay and leather. Claudia, the city girl, pinched her nose and thought, this is a funny place to find a dog, among the mokes and mules. Stranger still the dogs weren't running free. Why kennel them? As she leaned over the rail, a variety of canine greetings issued forth, from low-pitched growls to yelps to barks and a score of hounds reared up, backed off, hunkered low or bared their teeth. And from this seething forest of paws squeezed a round, black roly-poly pudding.

'Hello, champ!'

Such was the little fellow's hurry that his jellified legs were going every which way except the right direction, then whoosh! all four were in the air at once as he tried to reach her, whimpering, squealing and (oh dear) wetting his little self in the happy process.

'Doodle-noodle.' Claudia lifted him out of the pen, ruffled his hard, black head and scrunched around his floppy ears. 'Much more of your exuberance, and I'll leave you behind!'

Doodlebug didn't fall for that one. His fat pink tongue continued swishing round her face and neck, his button eyes brighter than a dozen beeswax candles. Dogs, he licked, might be my species, but I'm much more at home with you and Flea. Can we go now? He rolled over, while he asked the question.

A shadow fell across his bald, pink tummy. 'Thought I'd find you here.'

Two curly slippered toes appeared beside the squirming pup. Dammit, with all that barking going on, she hadn't heard the Grand Vizier approach.

'Thought over my proposal, have you?'

Claudia felt a chill run down her spine. She stood up and looked him in the eye before she answered. 'You mean, your proposition?

Min smiled. 'I mean trade, m'dear. Man in my position carries influence. Be nice to me –' two hot hands closed over Claudia's breasts – 'and I can save that girl the ordeal of a public trial and, hrrumph, inevitable execution.'

Claudia willed her own hands not to swat his away. Flea's life hung in the balance, she daren't risk Min's wrath. His vengeance. Spurn him now, and he'd kill Flea out of spite.

'So I'm supposed to go to your bedroom and—'

'Bedroom?' Pudgy hands moved in loathsome circles. 'Consider my getting your friend off the hook deserves something rather more adventurous than a quickie, don't you, m'dear?' Min tweaked her nipples before releasing them. 'You have imagination. Use it.'

'I'm using it right now,' she said. Bastard. 'I'm imagining you're bluffing. I'm imagining that, when Mentu sits in judgement, the Grand Vizier has no influence whatsoever on the outcome of Flea's – ouch!'

The stinging slap had sent her sprawling backwards on the hay. The dogs, on the far side of the barrier, went wild.

'Never misjudge the influence I carry,' Min hissed, breathing over her. 'Never underestimate my power, you don't know the half of it!' Then he straightened up and, just like earlier in the corridor outside his room, there followed a lightning switch of personality. 'Tonight we celebrate the Festival of Lamps,' he said pleasantly. 'I'll be outside the House of Life at midnight. Don't,' he snarled, 'keep me waiting.'

As quietly as he arrived, the stocky Grand Vizier departed, leaving no trace other than a throbbing, swollen cheek and a foul and sullied memory.

Claudia brushed her gown, as though she could brush away the reminder of his touch. Min wasn't bluffing about this kangaroo court and Flea's summary execution, it was another way of weeding out the trouble-makers, with no stain on anybody's conscience! She rubbed the linen where his hands had touched her breasts. Damn that fat toad to hell! Oh, Flea, you stupid, stupid bitch. What possessed you to go stealing from the Barque of Ra, for heaven's sake? Claudia recalled the girl who Min had raped, and knew he hadn't taken her so much for sexual pleasure as control.

Claudia had a feeling that gratification came in many twisted forms round here.

'I'll be back,' she promised Doodlebug, kissing him on his cold, wet snout before returning him to his excitable companions. 'Only there's something I have to do that's rather urgent.'

The task entailed a return to Mentu's wing, and when Claudia smiled, it was like a lynx playing with a lizard.

Afternoon prayers were under way, a change in schedule to take account of some extra ceremony which had to be squeezed in before the Festival of Lamps began. Good. Under cover of these observances, Claudia could move freely when and where she chose. She cocked an ear, and caught a couple of 'Beautiful art thou's already being trotted out, followed by a few 'Mine eyes adore thee's. Brilliant.

'What in hell's all this commotion?'

Startled, Claudia spun round, stubbing her toe on the wooden board of the doggy pen. Standing right behind her, his face dark with an emotion she couldn't read, was Geb. The hairy godfather, whose fists were at this moment clenched into hams. Claudia pictured them laying about his battered wife.

'The noise,' he growled. 'What set the dogs off? You?'

She looked at him. Dark eyes, darker in the shadows of the stables. He advanced towards her, breathing heavily. He's enjoying this, she thought. The Keeper of the Store likes to watch his victims squirm. Waiting, while they cower into meek obedience.

Dream on . . .

'No,' she said, and watched her denial throw him off his balance. 'I saw someone moving around and came to investigate. The dogs were already barking.'

'Liar.' His face twisted in a sneer. 'You came for that damned puppy-dog down there.' Geb's wits were sharper than she thought, it had taken him merely seconds to recover. 'I told you yesterday, no personal possessions in the commune, and— What happened to your face?'

'Heatstroke.'

His lip curled. 'Yeah.' A man who beats his wife would recognise the symptoms on another!

She glanced at his big, broad, hairy knuckles and observed a bruise on his right hand, which she did not recall seeing last night. With a sharp bark of command, Geb quietened the dogs and cast his glance round the stables.

'Who was it you saw snooping about?'

She wondered whether he meant Min, and shrugged. Let him make of that what he wanted!

Too late she realised that what Geb wanted to make was an enemy, and her insolence was all the excuse he needed. 'Spies,' he said, baring his teeth, 'die by Ordeal of the Lakes.'

A bolt of ice shot through her. 'D-drowning?'

'Oh, no, no, no, no.' It was the first time she'd heard him laugh, and hopefully the last. 'First, we burn our spies in the Lake of Fire, then we throw them in the Boiling Lake.'

'*Set alight then boiled alive?*' Claudia felt the icy terror grip her throat. He was on to her. Geb was on to her! She pictured the torture which lay ahead. The fire which would sizzle up her flesh, the boiling cauldron which would cook it on the bone.

Nausea washed over her. Would Orbilio rescue her in time? Would fire bring her henchmen running? And what of those who came here with her? Would Flea be doomed to the same fate? And suppose Mercy voiced her suspicions about Junius? Sweet Jupiter, he'd have been better off taking his chances in the arena.

'Enemies of Ra must face hell on earth before their Day of Judgement. Fire and oil purifies their soul, and then –' unbelievably, he tickled her under the chin – 'yes, only then will their hearts weigh light at the balance. Come with me.'

'I—' she couldn't speak, her teeth were chattering. 'Look, I—'

To her astonishment, Geb threw back his head and rocked with laughter. She noticed that several of his back teeth were missing, the rest were brown or yellow.

'Scared you shitless, didn't I? Ho, you should have seen your face, when you thought I was accusing you.' The roaring subsided, and she'd guessed right. By one means or another, The Keeper of the Central Store terrified his victims into submission. 'So now whenever I ask a question, little missy,' he snarled, 'you bloody answer me. Who – did – you – see – here?'

'The light's too dim to tell.'

Thick fingers closed around her earlobe and pinched hard. 'Really?'

'All right, all right. I do know who it was.'

'Who?' Grinning, he let go.

'Min. The Grand Vizier was here, we . . . spoke for a few minutes.'

'Min?' The news seemed to unsettle him and several seconds ticked past before he said warily, 'No guard? Or someone dressed up like a guard?'

'No!' It came out as a shriek. Jupiter! It's not me Geb's suspicious of, he's on to *Marcus*. 'No.' She cleared her throat and forced her voice to be level. 'Just me and Min.'

'Very bloody cosy,' he growled, then glanced across the stables to the entrance. 'Well, if you see anyone else snooping around, you come straight to me, you hear? Not Min. To *me.*' He leaned forward, and his eyes bored into hers. 'Got that?'

She nodded. A meek sister, cowered by the master.

Geb grunted his approval, or at least she presumed it was approval, then said, 'It's time for the test, we'd better hurry.'

Test? 'I – um.' Think, girl, think. 'I need the latrines,' she said urgently. Dammit, she had to get away from him.

'No time,' he said savagely. 'You'll have to cross your legs, and by the looks of you –' his eyes raked over the curve of her breasts, then followed the contours of her belly,

– 'you're the stuck-up sort of cow who keeps her knees together quite a lot.'

'For you, I'm prepared to use glue.'

Something growled deep in his throat, but whatever rejoinder he'd planned to make was cut short by the braying of silver trumpets from the temple. He grabbed her by the elbow and propelled her into the yard.

'You and I, missy, have unfinished business, but this is not the time.' He pressed his face close to hers, the commune unguent sticky in her throat. 'Later,' he rasped. 'Later, you'll account to Geb, you mark my words.'

With that, he strode off away and out of nowhere Mercy was at her side. 'Luck of the gods, girl, what did you do to get on the wrong side of him?'

'Oh. Is he cross?'

'Are you serious!' Grey hairs stuck out like a porcupine from Mercy's bun. 'His expression is like thunder, he's in a right old mood!' She linked her arm through Claudia's, and Claudia prayed it was a kindly gesture and not one of imprisonment. 'Steer clear of him, child, he's a bad one, trust me.'

Trust you, Mersyankh? I don't think so.

On the temple platform, the Holy Council was already assembled. Horus, with his falcon head. Hathor, the cow. Bast. Anubis. Thoth, the ibis, from whom no secret may be hid. White-robed priestesses rattled silver sistrums, the negro beat the great bronze tortoiseshell, and the High Priest with his shaven head gleaming with the heat sprinkled sacred water all around. Coils of choking incense rose from braziers set around the Boat of Ra, ablaze with its inset jewels and gold, its oars lifted high into the air as though shipped in some celestial harbour. To a low hum from the assembly on the platform, a set of balances was laid with reverence upon a black table set in front an alabaster sphinx.

Hang on. Claudia ticked off the deities. One of them was missing. The leader himself was absent. A figure rippled up alongside her shoulder and Claudia felt her heart thump with relief. She did not need to turn her head to know that Junius had found her.

'Any luck?' she whispered from the corner of her mouth.

'Flavia's here all right.' He shuffled forward, so no one else could hear. 'Last night, she accidentally caught Geb with a hot pan and scalded him.'

Claudia heard her own sharp intake of breath and passed it off to a curious Mercy as the closeness of being near her beau. Mercy, glancing at the handsome lad beside her, produced another of her famous coarse winks. Dammit, so close to Flavia and I didn't bloody know!

'Unfortunately,' Junius continued under his breath, 'she was that scared of repercussions, she's gone into hiding, and that's not all. One of the laundry girls hasn't been seen, either. It's not that unusual, she's a bit of a loner by all accounts, but in view of what you told me, about six missing girls, I thought it might be relevant.'

This boy gets better and better! She was about to give him further instructions, when Mercy gave her a cautionary dig in the ribs, and suddenly Claudia was aware of how the mood had changed around her. Tension rippled round the silent crowd. As one, the commune held its breath . . .

Booo-ooom.

The single drumbeat made her jump and sent a ghostly echo round the valley.

'Behold your son, O Lord of the West.' The resonant voice of the High Priest carried far across the temple forecourt. 'Behold the Pharaoh, Mentu, father of the fatherless, husband of the widow, protector of the weak.'

Reaching into the moleskin sack which hung around his waist, the priest tossed a handful of what looked like black ash upon the fire and whoosh! smoke exploded into the air, beclouding everything.

Booo-ooom. Booo-ooom. Ba-boom.

To the new drumbeat, the smoke subsided, and as it did so, a throne rose upwards from the middle of the boat. Seated upon it, in full pharaonic regalia, was Mentu and for the first time

Claudia was able to see the man beneath the golden mask. For this new ritual – this test, whatever it might be – his face was no longer painted blue and the only embellishment to his natural features was a false chin beard of plaited hair held on with straps. Claudia leaned forward for a closer view.

Min was not, as she expected, the younger brother. Mentu was at least ten years his junior.

Around his broad and stocky shoulders hung a cloak of vulture feathers. A cobra of pure gold entwined itself around his forehead. The twin protectresses, she thought. The vulture, gentle and sheltering, whose broad wingspan gives asylum to the Pharaoh and his people, and the royal serpent, its hood raised, spitting venom. In his left hand Mentu held something which looked like a tiny shepherd's crook, and in the other what looked like a fly whisk. Claudia had a suspicion they were neither!

'Tonight,' he said, and every eye was on him, 'tonight we set a vigil for Ra, as he wrestles with the serpent in the void, to give our thanks for the joy which he has brought us in the past and which he will again bestow upon his children in the future.'

'For the gladness that thou bringest, we adore thee.'

The Pharaoh, high upon his throne, let his gaze wander over his enraptured audience. The tension in the group tightened like a spring.

'What's happening?' whispered Junius, but Claudia had no answer. Only an uneasy feeling that she was about to witness the mechanism that bound six hundred people to one man.

The silence stretched on. A buzzard, mewing in the hills, was answered by its mate. A horse whinnied in the stables. Cattle lowed.

'When I tell you,' Mentu said at last, 'that there are enemies of Ra who seek to destroy what we have built, do you believe me?'

'We believe you,' rose the chorus. 'We place our trust in thee, O lord Osiris.'

'Suppose, though, I were to tell you that, even now, there are those who seek to destroy us from within?'

The collective gasp which rose up from the crowd told Claudia that there was no set rejoinder, that Mentu had sprung a surprise on them. Was it coincidence, that Mercy's hand had now linked up with hers? She thought of Geb, suspicious of a man dressed as a guard. The minute this ceremony was over, the hairy godfather would follow up the scent. A shiver rippled over Claudia, as she wondered why the presence of one guard should so unsettle him.

'I hope,' Claudia told Mercy, disengaging her fingers, 'Mentu's not referring to that nice young couple who came with me from Rome.'

Mercy said nothing, and slipped instead a protective arm around her shoulders. Oh, you're good, Mersyankh. You're *very* good.

Mentu waited for his flock's discomfiture to settle. 'Seth, the Dark Destroyer, the Devourer of Souls, moves among us daily,' he said solemnly, 'tempting us to join him in his anarchy and chaos, to undermine what we have built.'

'Seth, the Dark Destroyer cannot touch us, we are pure.'

Aha, the sermon was back on track. From the way the chorus tripped neatly off their tongues, the members were used to responding to references to this Seth character who, it would appear, represented disorder and annihilation, the antithesis of what the commune stood for. Vaguely, Claudia remembered snippets of the myth. Seth was the evil god, whose lust for power eventually got him ostracised and thrown into the desert, and whose rage whips up dust and sand storms.

'Unless our hearts are pure,' Mentu said, 'unless we can assure the Judges of the Dead that we have committed none of the Forty-two Deadly Sins that deny us access to the Underworld, Seth will gobble up our souls and condemn us to eternal desolation.'

'O Lord Osiris, let our hearts weigh light against the Feather of Truth.'

'I cannot expect you to accept my word on trust,' said the Pharaoh. 'I must earn the right to your respect – oh yes!' He held up his hand to quell the protests. 'Only by seeing for yourselves can you truly follow me along the Path of Righteousness to walk the Fields of the Blessed for eternity.'

All around her, the chorus rang out *'Praise be to Ra!'* and Claudia knew she was about to be shown Mentu's secret weapon at long last.

'Through my father, Ra, I can bestow upon you my own immortality . . .'

So that was it! The key to Mentu's power! A giggle simmered deep inside her breast. Roll up, roll up, come and join the circus! She looked at the Pharaoh, sitting on his royal throne and scratching at his royal birthmark. You cunning son of a bitch. Eternal life in return for a few offerings of gold and silver, jewels and gemstones . . . Ha! You're nothing but a common charlatan, and any minute now you'll start a game of 'Find the Lady', fooling everyone with your tricks and sleight of hand!

Well, it wasn't necessarily these people's fault. Pyramidiots they might be, but many a fool has been parted from his money for less! Let's see, how *do* you prove yourself immortal, Mentu? A padded vest, in which a bag of blood has been concealed, so that when you're stabbed through with a sword, you're seen to bleed – to die – and then, hey presto! A few words of mumbo-jumbo, a few rites and rituals, and yippee, it's a miracle. The Pharaoh lives!

Penno, the temple warden with the big ears, was leading forward a small black goat by its gilded horns to where the High Priest held a goblet high above his gleaming pate. Claudia nodded. The potion would be fed to that poor goat, who'd die of whatever deadly concoction Shabak had knocked up, and then the great man himself would step up to 'drink' the poisoned brew.

Fine. If these peabrains were so stupid as to imagine Mentu could die and be reborn in twenty minutes, then Claudia was not complaining. As far as she was concerned, this drippy bunch could stick their invidious fawnings where Ra's rays didn't shine.

Meanwhile, she had work to do!

Chapter Thirty

For Orbilio to imply that he was on the staff had been a slight embellishment on the actuality. In fact, it had been a downright bloody lie.

He pushed aside the heavy door which opened in to the bakery. Outside, the quern was still, the horse collar dangling forlornly from the pole which traversed the rotary grinding cone and Marcus rejoiced for the absent donkey, who must get pretty dizzy going round and round, even in short shifts. Indoors, the dry air tickled at his nose and made him sneeze. Baskets of grain lined up for milling queued patiently against the back wall. Sacks of flour hunkered beneath scrubbed trestle tables, over which tomorrow scores of bare-backed workers would sweat buckets kneading dough. Orbilio placed his hand flat against the chimney wall, not surprised that the great oven in the wall had been kept going. Fires like that took too much time to build up once they'd died, it was best to keep them ticking over. There was still plenty of charcoal in the leather bucket.

He fondled the wooden handle of the mighty iron paddle on which the loaves were pushed into the oven, and thought it wasn't all a lie. That bit about reporting to Geb, for instance – that was true. One of the security guards had told him. He'd also told him that sentries weren't allowed down here, not unless they'd captured someone, otherwise they were not permitted past the inner fence, which, like the outer barrier, ringed the far side of the hills. No, the guard had admitted, neither he nor his fellow mercenaries knew much about what went on here, it meant certain death to even gossip or conjecture, and since they were paid such bloody good wages, he for one wasn't prepared to piss into his own honey pot. Their job, he added firmly, was to patrol the perimeters – to keep outsiders out and to keep insiders in and yes, that included women, although to his certain knowledge no girl had escaped, much less half a dozen.

Nevertheless, under pressure, he did admit that, despite the restrictions placed upon his movements and his lips, he'd picked up enough about this mongrel organisation to know that the Brothers were packaging Egypt more as untutored Romans imagined it, than a true reflection of real life in the province. Orbilio tended to agree. From regular dinner parties with a man who had served under the Governor of Egypt he'd learned that the genuine culture, with its religious beliefs and laws, daily practices, had little in common with this bastardised society. This valley here was way off key. A distinct duff note in the music of the Nile.

Checking that the coast was clear, he closed the bakery door quietly behind him and, keeping to the shadows, crossed over to the brew house. Hm. The door was locked. He rattled the handle twice, put his shoulder to the woodwork and, when it wouldn't budge, moved on, the sour smell of barley beer clinging like a leech.

It had bothered him, at first, that people were prepared to follow Mentu blindly like they did. Then he realised that the trick was to make them believe something which, on the surface, was so utterly unbelievable that then they'd swallow anything, no matter how incredible it seemed. Two years experience in the Security Police suggested that Mentu would need to pull a pretty fancy stunt to have them swallow the bullshit that he fed them, and the guard had pretty much confirmed this. Something to do with a padded vest, an archer and a pig's heart, he had said.

Next on the right stood the granary. In the doorway, Marcus paused. Not a whisper. He slipped inside. The threshing floor had been swept so thoroughly there was not a single ear of wheat or barley to be seen, not even wedged down in the gaps between the paving slabs. Winnowing fans hung from hooks and an upper gallery ran along one wall overhead. He sniffed and recognised the aromatic scent of tansy. Useful herb, he thought. Its jagged leaves add a bit of pep to stews and sausages, its yellow button flowerheads brighten wreaths and garlands, and – according to the mystics – tansy wine can make a man immortal. (Or so Jupiter told Ganymede, and look what happened there!) Tansy, however, is also effective at keeping mice at bay and that's why he smelled it here, inside the threshing house.

Soft of tread, he climbed the wooden steps. A field mouse, had it not been deterred by the liberal sprinkling of herbs, could not have moved more quietly. A pulley mechanism operated up here, cranking up baskets of wheat and barley fresh from the threshing floor which were then swung through this hatch here (he squeezed his own body through the narrow doorway) and emptied into the corn bins for storing until the following harvest. Gazing down on to the soft golden hills below, Orbilio felt the chill contrast between the gentle art of reaping grain and his own chosen occupation.

Sometimes, he thought, his hand automatically closing round the scimitar which hung around his waist, sometimes his work was bloody hard.

Take that guard, for instance. The one who'd told him so much about the commune and its security arrangements. The bastard had actually *boasted* about how he'd impaled 'some stupid little jerk' to make his death appear accidental, even to stuffing a gag in his mouth, and laughed when he said it took the kid fourteen hours to die. Marcus pinched the bridge of his nose to quell the nausea. No matter how many times he re-lived that episode where the mercenary bragged about his killing skills, the edge was never blunted. Each time it made his skin go clammy, hurt his head and made his stomach churn.

Almost as much as it had when he brought the rock down hard upon the braggart's head.

Orbilio shuddered. He was not sorry the man was dead, the bastard had been a sadist and a thug who had enjoyed killing for its own sake, but he himself felt only sadness and revulsion when he was forced to take a life – and make no mistake, he'd had no option with the guard. To leave the man unconscious was too risky. Apart from his own life, there was Claudia's to consider, also Flea's and Flavia's, plus – although he had to admit he didn't give a toss here either way – Junius as well. Therefore, it was with a clear conscience, if not exactly a light one, that Orbilio had slipped into the dead man's clothes, buckled on his weapons and concealed his body in the undergrowth.

And it was precisely because the taking of a human life, however necessary, did not lie easy with him, that Orbilio did not hear at first the footsteps on the gallery outside. He turned. Saw a lump of wood swinging violently towards him.

Smelled something which was neither corn nor tansy.

Then his world turned black.

Claudia found it easier than she'd envisaged to give her female minder the slip.

She waited until after Mentu 'swallowed' the deadly poison but, while biding her time, found nothing but admiration for the theatrical skills of the Holy Council. The way Isis gasped and Thoth dropped his scrolls of wisdom, you'd think the High Priest had slipped up and given Mentu the stuff he'd fed the goat! That was the clever bit, she decided. The High Priest, with his bare arms and shaven chest, could not possibly conceal a second potion on his person, therefore the crowd would readily accept that Mentu drank the same draught as the goat. They would not suspect that, concealed inside the goblet, might be a tiny phial of foxglove, henbane, celandine or belladonna, which would have been rammed down the poor animal's gullet.

However, if the Holy Council were born thespians, Mentu took the laurel crown. Claudia almost applauded as the fat Pharaoh's twitches mirrored that of the dying goat. The cramps, the rigidity, the ghastly noises in the back of the throat. Well done, Shabak! Her eyes had flickered across to old Bluejaw over there, a walking testimony of apothecary skills! He daren't dose the goat with cowbane, spurge or fool's parsley which induced a messy death by vomiting (and worse!). He'd picked a 'clean' quick poison which attacked the heart.

Ah, yes, the heart! That same dripping lump which the black jackal, Anubis, placed upon the Sacred Scales of Truth and which – surprise, surprise – balanced perfectly with the ostrich feather on the other side. What is it, Mentu? A block of gold, fashioned as a feather? Or won't you waste your precious metal, are we looking at a lump of painted lead?

Reverently, the cow and the falcon bent over the corpse, their floating robes conveniently blocking the view as Anubis replaced the heart into the Pharaoh's bloody, lifeless body. Not too fast, now. Don't let the punters think it's easy. A few more rites and rituals, let's string it out a bit – that's the stuff! A spot of handwashing, some mumbled prayers, a splash or two of holy water on the 'corpse'. Well done. Keep the audience on tenterhooks! Taking advantage of Mercy's absorption with the resurrection drama, Claudia slipped away.

'Behold your son, O Lord of the West.' The voice of Anubis rang out smooth and harmonious, as the voice of every conman should. 'Behold Osiris, whose heart has been found to be without evil, and whose virtue Thoth has recorded, Thoth from whom no secret can be hid.'

When the ibis's beak wagged up and down as his human hands held aloft the Sacred Scroll of Truth to show the people where judgement had been recorded, Claudia all but laughed. To think they'd paid good money to be part of this, as well! She could just imagine the sales pitch in the Forum.

'Roll up, roll up. Bring us your gold and silver, and in return we'll dress you in itchy, shapeless clothes, feed you meagre meals and work you harder than a mule.'

It's a wonder the barkers weren't crushed in the rush!

She was still grinning when she slipped through the temple forecourt gates. Oh, little terracotta ears cemented to the wall. What secrets have you heard?

'You've heard, then?'

Claudia sucked in her breath. Who—? What—? Then she realised that Penno, old Rabbitface himself, was striding towards her, his thin face pinched and drawn, and that he could not *possibly* have read her thoughts. The tips of his gravity-defying ears were pink.

Heard what, she wondered? 'Yes, of course I have.'

'Don't know how she did it,' he muttered, twisting his twig-like fingers in his hands. 'Locked her in myself, can't imagine how the thieving bitch escaped.'

'*Flea escaped?*'

Penno didn't seem to notice the obvious contradiction – that Claudia had patently *not* heard the news.

She smiled. Being so scrawny, it would have been relatively easy, she realised, for Flea to squeeze through the bars. Thieves sneak through small gaps all the time. Their size and flexibility is their stock-in-trade.

'I think I know where she might be,' Claudia told the temple warden, who stopped shaking his rabbit head and muttering about poor security to twist his face into an unclassifiable expression.

'Really?'

'I'll go and check, if you like.'

Penno's eyes narrowed. 'You will?' Thin, suspicious, he didn't trust her.

'Well, there are two places Flea could be hiding.' She chose two in opposite directions. 'So you take the bakehouse, and I'll check out the ladies bath house.'

He had no choice. But casting a glance over her shoulder, Claudia felt a prickle of unease when she realised was Penno following her with his eyes.

His face was ugly. His ears were a curiosity.

But his eyes were just plain creepy.

'Hey!' The voice startled her. 'What the hell do you think you're doing?'

Damn. Outside the doctor-dentist-apothecary hut, Claudia turned a radiant smile upon her blue-jawed accuser. 'Where

I come from,' she said sweetly, 'it's customary to venerate the gods with flowers. I plan to do the same for Thoth, by weaving him a garland.'

'There are plenty of wild plants,' Shabak growled, 'without you buggering up my medicine garden.' His attention focussed on the bouquet in her hand. 'Why those two in particular?'

Ah. 'Because . . . where I come from, purple means honour and, er, yellow symbolises devotion.'

'Just where *do* you come from?'

Glad you asked me that. Claudia took a leap into the dark. 'Originally,' she breezed, 'Iberia, but of course I've lived in Rome since I was a child.'

'Iberia?'

Juno, sweet Queen of Heaven, if you're listening to this, I beg you not to give him Spanish ancestry. Claudia had attributed his swarthy skin and blue-black hair as hailing from the East, possibly as far afield as the Indus Valley . . .

'Baetica, to be precise,' she said. 'It's in the south.'

'Arid country, then?'

'I'm afraid I remember very little – apart,' she added with a girlish smile, 'from the customs which my family preserved.'

Shabak grunted and that, dammit, meant nothing. 'Those flowers,' he began.

'Pretty, aren't they?'

A frown knitted his dark brows. 'You do know what they're used for?'

'Me?' Time for a light, silvery laugh. 'Good heavens, botany's a black art to me, I barely know their names. This is a buttercup, I know that much, while the other one – don't tell me, it's ajuga, right?'

'Globe flower,' he said dryly, 'and purple columbine.'

He chewed his lower lip for several seconds, and again Claudia was struck by the thinness of his wiry frame. She recalled seeing him with Geb, and the contrast between the two men. One large and forbidding, the other small and unsmiling. If one was the Barbary ape on two legs, she remembered thinking, then Shabak was the agile monkey.

'This garden is reserved for me and my trained assistants only,' he said at length, although his mind seemed to be preoccupied with something else, she wondered what. Why wasn't he at the temple service? 'I must ask you to respect our Hippocratic laws.'

You did say hypocritic?

With a few tinkling apologies along the lines of being new here, she had no idea, so sorry and all that, Claudia left the doctor standing in the middle of his path, stroking his long blue shiny jaw in thought. There was something on that man's mind, and no mistake. She prayed it wasn't her! And that it had no connection with the flowers in her hand, because Shabak would know damned well what effect these two would have. Nothing serious, of course, and the symptoms would be temporary. But by the time Claudia had finished, Min the Grand Vizier would be in real discomfort! Cramps. Cold sweats. Nausea. He'd have difficulty breathing (that'll worry him!) and, best of all, the problems he'd encounter passing water would make the strongest bull's eyes water!

Surprisingly, Shabak's gaze was still riveted upon her, so she pretended to have trouble with her shoe while she collected up a few more wild flowers and stuck them in the bunch. Her plan was coming along nicely. The juice of this little wayside blossom rubbed into his pillows, sheets and mattress and Min can look forward to a few lovely raised blisters here, a delicious skin rash there.

Claudia made a mental note to focus on his loin cloths. Shabak finally lost interest, by which time it was quite some bouquet she had accumulated. Ah, well. No reason not to spread her generosity to others.

The black tomcat in Mentu's chamber hadn't moved, and even when Claudia had finished doctoring the leader's wine and clothes and bedlinens, the lazy creature only yawned and tucked its paw in. Cats, thankfully, were immune to the effects of her pot-pourri, although in this one's case, she acknowledged that it probably would not have noticed.

She breezed around the deserted wing. A little bit for Bast, a little bit for Horus, a nice big squeeze of juices in the bath. (That'll heat the water up!) She treated their towels, paid particular attention to the feathers in their bolsters. Things were going well. The theatricals outside the temple would continue for a while longer – Mentu would milk his happy resurrection for all it was worth – Claudia had time to poke around here at her leisure.

Because it seemed to her, that under cover of Mentu's carefully constructed con, a sick killer could mingle freely in the crowd.

He would be cold, compassionless, selfish to a T – and would be at pains to put on a front to disguise his brutish ways. The mantle of a caring physician, for instance. Or might he prefer to dramatise his role, such as the thug-like Keeper of the Central Store? Then again, clipped speech disguises many moods—

Stop this, it's nonsense! The cloying atmosphere is getting to you, don't fall into its trap! If six girls (seven if you count the little laundress) have gone missing from this commune, the most likely explanation is that they've been sold on as slaves, probably to brothels in the Orient. The trade was not unknown. Claudia felt her spirits lift. In which case, my girl, there'll be documented evidence here somewhere.

Her search began with Min, taking care, of course, to doctor every surface thoroughly along the way. Shabak *might* put two and two together and mix up a fast antidote, but with luck (and whatever had occupied his thoughts back there) the meeting in the medicine patch would have slipped the physician's mind. Nimble fingers riffled in Min's trunks and chests.

Everyone has secrets. Most people write them down. Not necessarily directly, although some do like to keep a diary, but they retain mementoes which, in isolation, mean precious little, but which – when put together – carry a great deal of significance. Like Min's collection of pornographic sketches, for instance, in which women were uniformly humiliated and abused. She skimmed through the illustrations and concluded that, in Min's eyes, women were born for man's use and his pleasure. No doubt he also kicked his brother's tomcat, should it ever venture into this room!

The only other papers hidden in his strongbox were accounts and, judging from his ticks and comments in the margins, Min worshipped money even over Ra. Women might not be respected. Gold was. He was salting stashes of it away in secret – and, according to these records, in places Mentu didn't know about. Oh dear, oh dear. You naughty boy. You're out to double-cross your younger brother.

Well, that was their affair, perhaps they'd come to blows when it came to light and kill each other in the process. But certainly any receipt for the sale of young girls to brothels would be lodged among these papers. And, dammit, there were none—

She backtracked to the office, where the papers were in neat order, and could tell from the registry that Neco was obviously right at home overseeing a large number of clerks and scribes, secretaries and accountants. As she had suspected, records were kept of every confessional heard at the terracotta ears – time, date, confidante's name, all listed alongside – but there was nothing suggestive of sales to Oriental brothels.

Penno's room was decorated with hieroglyphics depicting the Day of Judgement – Anubis, weighing out some poor sod's heart, with Osiris set to lead him to the Underworld should the feather in the jackal's hand balance on the scales. Below the scales, there squatted a hideously misshapen monster licking its chops. Seth, of course. The Devourer of Souls. She peered closer at the long, curved snout and stiffly tufted tail. No wonder the dead man was looking worried!

Laid out on Penno's long low table was a hand-sized replica of Ra's famous barque, a bowl of holy water, a set of ten carved priestesses, two ivory musicians and two carved horn dancers. Puzzled, Claudia considered the arrangement as she dripped the irritant juices on his bed and rubbed petals, leaves and sap into the temple warden's mattress. Then she saw! Old Loppylugs here conducted his own religious ceremonies in the privacy of his room, inevitably acting out the role of High

Priest himself, and no doubt Penno made several changes – improvements! – in his little dramas. What other fantasies did he harbour? Men who are addicted to rites and rituals make ruthless killers. Like Min, they have a need to control.

Each of the superintendents here thrives on control – terrorising, intimidating, bullying, even prescribing drugs to keep the commune pliable. That's their job. It's why they were given these commands.

Claudia gazed round the bedroom of the Keeper of the Store. Give him one thing, she thought. He's a stickler for his own rules, the room was barren. No paintings on the walls. No tasselled drapes. A couple of spare tunics, nothing fancy. No jewels. Not even a razor for Geb! It therefore did not take her long to find his secret cache of letters, and there were only two.

> You bastard. You killed her, and you didn't even bother coming to her funeral. You are no father of mine.

The second one was clearly a response to Geb's reply.

> You are more evil than I thought. You killed my mother and now you lay the blame on her, you say she drove you to it. I hope you rot in hell, you vicious bastard.

The raw emotion was too much for Claudia. She felt the child's pain (instinctively she knew it was a son's), sensed the anguish in his heart. Mercy's feminine intuition had not been wrong. Geb *was* the type to beat his wife and he'd beaten her once too often, so it seemed. No, wait! Claudia was jumping to conclusions here. She only had Mercy's gut feeling that Geb had used his fists. There are many other ways to die . . .

But the son's suffering embedded itself like a fish hook as Claudia continued to doctor the clothes and bedlinens of the remaining members of the Holy Council and she could not dislodge the barb. Was it possible, she wondered, that Geb had joined the Brothers of Horus to clear his conscience through their rigid, self-imposed regime of abstinence and penance? It might explain his violent temper and the punishment he inflicted cold. Through suffering, was he saying, you too can achieve blessedness? The notion did not sit well with his loutish behaviour.

Blast! Zigzagging back and forth, she realised she'd missed a room. Neco's! Bugger, she'd used up all her irritants, as well! She imagined the Chief Scribe's superior air when it became obvious he'd escaped the mass contagion. By heaven, he was a smug bastard now, he'd be bloody unbearable then! Stupid cow, how could you have overlooked him? Neco, of all people, would keep his documentation neat and tidy. Any sales slips would not be hard to find – Claudia's hand was on the door when she realised someone was already in the room. She put her ear to the woodwork and heard a thwack, followed by a whistle, followed by a groan. Thwack, whistle, groan. Thwack, whistle, groan.

Her immediate thoughts were of Min, and the girl whose rape she had not prevented. She'd not fail another girl, whatever the consequences. Without hesitating, Claudia burst in.

She had indeed interrupted something nasty. The whistle was caused by the breath being expelled through the scribe's crossed teeth. The groan was pain. But the cause of the groan was a three-tailed knotted rawhide lash with which a kneeling, naked Neco thrashed himself.

Chapter Thirty-one

No light, no sound, no scent ever penetrated the charcoal shed, except when the hatch was opened either to fling in new supplies or shovel out existing stocks. Flavia, curled foetus-like in the corner, wanted to die.

She was hungry, weary, dirty, hot and thirsty – yes, above all, she was thirsty. Merciful Minerva, help me, she pleaded in her dark and silent tomb. I didn't mean any of this to happen.

She was beyond tears now.

Curled up in a ball, staring into blackness, she had no concept of time. It seemed like days had passed, and her throat was dry and dusty from the coals, the thirst was killing her. What's happening to me? she cried. Why hasn't anyone come to open up the hatch? They need coals for cooking, for the bakehouse, for hot water for the Pharaoh's bath house. Why has no one come to take the charcoal? How much longer must I wait?

Her nails were split and broken from picking at the wood, her knuckles and her shoulders were raw, but the bolt on the outside of the hatch stayed fast. She had cursed it, pleaded with it, prayed to every god and nymph, but nothing changed. What had started out as Flavia's refuge had become her prison.

She daren't think about what would happen to her, once they found her. Geb would ridicule her in public, black and drenched with her own sweat, her hair plastered to her body. Then he'd beat her. He had promised her a hiding for that scald, even though it had been an accident. After this, he'd thrash her for everything from insolence and disobedience to throwing his horrid schedule out of kilter. She began to tremble. She'd seen the lash he used. Three strips of rawhide knotted at the tips.

Someone said that he once used so much force that the knots became embedded in the victim's flesh and that he'd had to hook them out with his little finger. She shuddered in the dark. Please spare me that.

Memories of Marcellus flooded in. Julia. Suddenly Flavia didn't hate them any more. She wanted them to take her home.

None of this would have happened, she sniffed, if only they'd sent those two thousand gold pieces like I asked. With collateral behind me, I wouldn't be in this mess, cowering like a common criminal, a cornered rat. I wouldn't have to gut pigs and slave in the hot kitchens. Oh, no – a thought occurred to her – after this, Geb would not allow her back inside the kitchens! Sweet Janus, he'll send me to the fields. I want to go home. Please. She clamped her hands together and squeezed up her eyes. Please let me go home . . . I'll be good, I promise. I'll marry whoever you want me to, I won't run away again, I swear upon my father's grave.

Her father! Oh dear Jupiter, if I die in here, she thought, I'll have to face my dad across the River Styx. He'll be furious that I've let the family down, brought the name of Seferius into disrepute – and Flavia daren't imagine what he'd say about her friendship with that smelly street urchin called Flea.

Tears began to roll again. They were hot and salty and tasted of the bitter charcoal. She wanted to be sick. She wanted to be home. Home and warm and safe, looked after by her slaves and wrapped in cool, fresh linen towels. She wanted—

What was that?

In the blackness, Flavia tensed. Someone was twitching at the lock.

'Help!'

She scrabbled over the slippery coals.

'Help me, let me out!'

Clunk! The bolt flew back. The hatch opened slowly, and she recoiled at the brilliance of the light which flooded in.

'So then.'

Flavia shielded her eyes. The voice was one she recognised, but she could not make out the face. That voice, though . . .

'That's where you've been bloody skulking!'

Flavia must surely be mistaken. Why would this person be the one to rescue her? It made no sense.

'Come on.' A firm hand closed around her wrist and jerked. 'Out you get!'

Junius winced when the crowd surged forward because someone caught him on the hip where that vicious Dungeon Master had landed several kicks. White fire thrashed behind his eyes, muzzing up his vision, but he hadn't told the doctor, let alone his mistress.

His throat constricted. When he arrived here, in the commune, he'd been worried that he might not find her among the herd, but – inwardly he smiled – it wasn't very difficult in the end. Who else marched around as though she owned the place, nose in the air and chin held high?

He was now convinced something bad was going on. Six girls had vanished to date, and he felt sure another girl, the little laundress, was a casualty.

Junius was worried for his mistress.

'Stay here,' she'd said. 'Watch for my signal. This way, we can all get out together.'

So here he had remained. Alongside the woman from Brindisi, whose grey hair would not obey the rules and coil up in a bun, and resisting her every effort to go and change his merchant clothing for Egyptian costume. But it wasn't his out of place clothes making Junius jittery.

It wasn't right, the bodyguard doing nothing while the mistress laid her life out on the line.

It should be him, who took the arrow for her. Him, who stopped the slingshot meant for her.

Around him, the crowd were cramming forward to give their praise to Ra, to strew petals on the temple steps and swear allegiance to Osiris, through his son on earth, Mentu.

Since leaving Gaul, Junius had seen some bizarre spectacles, but this was way beyond him, this business about worshipping a boat . . .

Where the hell was she?

His eyes roved round the commune, alighting that fraction longer on the supervising staff who had been coming and going with such regularity throughout the so-called resurrection. He distrusted them all – the hairy one, the shiny one, the fat one, the bony one. He paused. Hang on a minute. The weirdo, the one with the wonky teeth and the lip. He was missing.

And so was his mistress.

He chewed his thumbnail and shifted his weight from foot to foot. His mind heard again the command to stay put, the way it brooked no contradiction, and Junius rubbed his good eye. Which would be worse? he wondered. To stay while her life might be in danger, or disobey the order and try to seek her out in the crush?

'It's a miracle, isn't it?'

Beside him, Mercy's eyes glowed with fanaticism.

'Mentu dies and is reborn before our very eyes, he will lead us to eternal resurrection, and soon, when darkness falls, we'll celebrate his rebirth with the Festival of Lamps.'

She wrapped her solid arms around him and hugged him tight.

'Isn't this the happiest moment of your life?' she asked.

Junius said nothing.

Marcus lay on his back in the granary, unaware of the setting sun, the lamps which flickered round the temple compound, the heavy summer heat which throbbed, the sticky breeze which brought sickness to the city. Sprawled on the grain and wearing a dead man's clothes, he was unaware even of the bloodied bruise just above his ear from the blow which had laid him out, unaware of ribs which had cracked when he had pitched forward on a heap which was by no means as soft as it appeared – or as he would have wished.

In his unconscious state, he did not dream.

He did not know that, back in Rome, his faithful steward, Tingi, had tracked down the groom who had left his household six months before his wife sold off the slaves and was about to divulge some interesting revelations. Revelations that would lead, although Marcus did not know it, to the identity of the murder victim – a distant cousin of his uncle's who had come to stay before Orbilio had taken over the house. The groom, having fathered eight children of his own, had recognised the signs of the girl's – shall we say – condition straight way, and his wife mentioned rumours about the cousin's affair with the master of the house. How the cousin and the wife had had a blazing row one night, resulting in the cousin leaving shortly afterwards.

Neither could Marcus, in his cocoon of oblivion, know that his boss was sitting, at this very moment, in the theatre, unable to concentrate on the comedy by Terence, because it niggled him that any scandal attached to Marcus might blow back in his own face. Suppose Orbilio *had* killed his wife and bricked up her body in the plaster? How would that reflect on the Head of the Security Police, who had checked his references and found them impeccable? While the audience clutched their sides and howled, his boss was wondering whether he'd acted too hastily in drawing attention to the body in Orbilio's storeroom. Mopping at his brow, he glanced across to the box where Augustus sat with his wife and daughter and a few close friends. Suppose word got back to him? Presumption of guilt went very much against the Imperial grain and the Head of the Security Police must – like the late and Divine Julius's wife – be above suspicion. He shuffled miserably on his cushion. He had never found Terence funny, anyway.

Night fell and Marcus, lying on his back, snored softly in his coma and did not see the human shadow which fell over him.

Luckily for him, he hadn't heard about the fate of spies. That they were condemned to die by the Ordeal of the Lakes, first by being roasted in a fire. Then by being boiled alive.

Marcus did not see the figure which leaned over him.

He slumbered on . . .

* * *

All across the valley, the exhilaration and excitement generated by a whole day packed with festivals and games and culminating in their Pharaoh's proof of immortality slowly gave way to a different kind of optimism. Soon, the vigil would begin. Ten thousand tiny lights would flicker through the night, guiding Ra's boat through its perilous journey in the Realm of Dark. The flames would scare away the Serpent of the Void and navigate a safe route through the Twelve Gates of the Underworld.

Ablaze with these mortal illuminations, mummies would awaken from the dead and cast off their bandages. The lame shall walk, the blind shall see, the barren shall bring forth a child. *Praise be to Ra, O lord of lords and king of kings, whose limbs are gold and emeralds are his eyes. Grant us peace in heaven, health on earth and acquittal on the final Day of Judgement.*

The High Priest, with his ten priestesses, laid out flat dishes filled with oil and salt and his ten white-robed acolytes lit the floating wicks around the Barque of Ra. In the darkness, the gold prow glinted brighter than midsummer sunshine and as the hundreds upon hundreds of twinkling lights were lit, the Boat of a Million Years drifted on the waters of their hope.

Up in his secret cave, Seth felt his whole body glow with happiness. His skin tingled, his pulse skipped, he could not believe his luck. *Another one!* He danced around his table, unable to keep still. Tonight, while those fools down there celebrate the Festival of Lamps, The Master of Men's Destinies can begin the slow process of putting his own magic into practice. Dark, powerful magic which will make divinities of mere disciples.

He clasped his hands together and gave thanks to Ra. Ra, who had shown him the secret path to immortality. Ra, whose goodness shone on Seth by day and whose power guarded him by night.

Power! The knowledge of his own potency stirred his

manhood into action and he took the new arrival roughly and without care. In his heightened state of emotion, Seth could not recall her name, or the mask he'd allocated her – in fact, he could not recall any of their real names now. Thoth and Bast, Horus and Hathor, that's who they were. They had become the Ten True Fools, seated round his table for eternity, with Osiris coming last to bend the knee, as it must be. As it was ordained to be.

Seth climaxed.

The girl whimpered.

'Shut up!' He silenced her with his fist. 'Shut up, you bitch, I need to think!'

Think. Think . . .

But he couldn't think. He was too light-headed at the moment. He laughed. By heaven, it had taken him by surprise, back there on the stage, when Mentu actually mentioned Seth by name. For a minute, he'd wondered if the bastard was on to him – about to denounce him on the spot – and he didn't mind admitting, his heart had nearly stopped! But now, in retrospect, he was glad the subject of the Dark Destroyer was back out in the open. For some reason, Mentu hadn't mentioned him for a week or two, and Seth badly wanted the people to know about his power. To understand who they were dealing with.

He loped over to the back of his cave, to the set of scrolls hidden in the corner. He had set it all down in these books – everything, except the secret of his magic, naturally! That secret was his and his alone, it had been passed to him by Ra and would travel with him in the underworld. But when the time was right – and that time was fast approaching – he'd deposit his Book of Knowledge in the House of Life, along with the Forty-two Sacred Books of Wisdom, so that everyone might know who they'd be dealing with.

That Seth was no mere Dark Destroyer, Devourer of Souls.

That he was also Master of Eternity, controller of men's destiny, the Sorcerer, the Measurer of Time.

That he, with his ten disciples, could change the future of mankind.

He replaced the scrolls and looked around. His majestic seed had transformed mortal women into gods who now sat around his table and awaited the stupendous moment when Seth and Seth alone could breath life – eternal life – into them.

He counted. Eight. And only two to go!

Seth really could not believe his luck.

Chapter Thirty-two

Like other rites and rituals practised by the Brothers of Horus, the Festival of Lamps was another mishmash of Egyptian heritage blended and jumbled so effectively that they emerged at the other end as a single hybrid. A chimera. Like the sphinx, the ceremony was part this, part that, part something else, until eventually it took on its own identity.

Claudia was in danger of losing hers.

Marcus was not where he was supposed to be. Junius was not where *he* was supposed to be. Flea – am I repeating myself? – was not where *she* was supposed to be (because Claudia would have staked her life Flea would have headed straight for Doodlebug), and Flavia, bless her little cotton socks, was nowhere to be found.

So much for organisation!

Under the oppressive clouds, no moon shone down. The wooded hills stood black against the sky. Implacable. Remote. In the lampglow, the ceremonial pool shone like molten copper and around it women clutching burning brands huddled close, their bodies stiff with prayer, as the High Priest stood, hands outstretched and raised, entreating that this holy water receive the blessing of the sun god, from whom all life is made.

Resurrection. Regeneration. Fertility and potency. Powerful stuff, Claudia thought, powerful stuff the brothers were brewing.

And these Pyramidiots guzzled every last drop, their tongues even hanging out for more. How weird can you get, believing the sun's propelled by a bloody boat? For gods' sake, the sun's the sun! Apollo might look after it, but he doesn't *drive* the damn thing.

More and more lamps were lit, until thousands of tiny flames flickered in the blackness, many stationery but others moving, tiny torches carried in the hands of individuals. A honey glow surrounded white-robed acolytes as they swung flaming censers outside the temple doors, others rolled a blazing hoop between the alabaster sphinxes, and still more carried shallow dishes of flames which dangled on triple-chained stems. You'd think that so many lights would make it bright, but in this twinkling maze Claudia couldn't see a sausage, much less recognise anybody, and frustration frayed her temper. Around now, Min would be keeping his appointment for their amorous liaison behind the House of Life. She smiled a wicked smile, and wondered how erotic itchy loin cloths were to him.

'Nasty place to have a rash, old chap. Why don't you take a dip in the heated indoor pool, followed by a long lie down?'

This was midnight, where the hell *was* everyone? Claudia had checked out the yard behind the storehouse. No Marcus. She'd hung around the stables. No Flea. She'd waited for Junius in the temple compound, and been handed a small lighted stick by a sanctimonious priestess. The torch was handy, because it was easy to become disorientated in this labyrinth of lamps, but surely five sensible adults could contrive to meet up at an appointed place?

Five. The number made her flesh crawl. Five men, one a certain killer, while who knows what hideous deeds the others might have perpetrated. They all had the capability. She shivered as she recalled Neco's fury when she'd burst in on his bout of self-flagellation. With his front-toothed whistle, he had reminded her of a striking cobra as he had reared up on his knees and hissed for her to get the fuck out of his room.

His venom clung. Long after she'd left the wing, long after the sun had set, oh how Neco's venomous whistle had stayed with her.

Despite the throbbing heat, the rasp of the cicadas, the flicker

of the flames, Claudia felt a chill run through to her bones.
And felt the breath of evil on the breeze.

Four men responsible for the daily running of the commune listened to the High Priest's chants and did not hear the words. Each man's thoughts were turned inwards, and their thoughts were turned on hell.

One saw it as a vision – literally the hell on earth spies and traitors must endure before they walk the Path of Righteous to the Fields of the Blessed in the Afterworld. *The Ordeal of the Lakes.* In his mind, he heard again and again the terrible screams of a youth, trussed like some sacrificial beast, roasted slowly over an open fire. That, the overseer thought, was bad, but the animal screeches when the poor kid was thrown into the boiling cauldron had haunted his dreams ever since. They made him fractious. Jumpy. Each day thereafter, he had relived the boy's execution, knowing in his heart of hearts that it had been wrong. Wicked, even, but although he held a powerful office in the commune, no one could overturn Mentu's decision once it was decreed. Therefore, each day had become a living hell, as he feared for fate of the next unfortunate . . .

For the second overseer, hell was something far more personal. He had fled his previous life because of the scandal which had been about to erupt, expecting to put it all behind him in the peaceful running of this commune. Hoping that, by immersing himself in daily commerce here, he might forget: pretend that he was normal; convince himself that he was just like any other man. Oh, how quickly he'd found out! How soon he'd realised he could not leave this dreadful thing behind! Each day he was tormented, each waking hour – yes, each and every minute plagued him. Forced him to resist his natural urge. From the corner of his eye, he watched a young man's muscles ripple in the lamplight. And by all that was holy, lusted after him. The overseer's fists clenched with his pain. To his eternal mortification, he knew he had not left his hell behind. It sat with him, on his back. Always. And cursed him . . .

The third overseer's hell was equally carnal. It involved

him and an older woman, making love. Perverted love, at that. That's why he'd left her and come here. To get away from her, from the things she'd made him do. He didn't mind so much that she liked him to tie her up and whip her, but other times she made him do things . . . things he couldn't talk about, couldn't bear to even think about. Degrading things. And the tragedy of it all was that the woman was his mother . . .

Hell for the fourth overseer was no less agonising, but it was at least wide-ranging. Lately he had come to believe what he had suspected for some time. Not so much that the reincarnation was a sham – Mentu had told him from the start that his health would not stand proving his immortality with such regularity, that on some occasions he'd have to pull a stunt and he'd need help. That was not the problem; the fourth overseer could live with that. But recently it had come to his knowledge that the contributions to the Solar Fund were not going to the upkeep of Ra's holy barque and temple. In fact, he was not convinced there even *was* a Ra. Lately he had come to believe this whole commune was a con. A means of making money from a lot of trusting innocents and, if this was true, what on earth was he do to? There was no one to confide in. It was hell.

The fifth overseer's thoughts were as far from the abyss as human thoughts might be. The night was hot, his blood was up.

He was having fun . . .

Chapter Thirty-three

The heat and the dark and the mass of twinkling lamps was as disorientating as anything Mentu could have organised for his band of Pyramidiots. Cicadas buzzed like blunted woodsaws in the grass. The low, oppressive clouds hung like heavy, winter cloaks over the hills which enclosed this fertile, pear-shaped valley. In the distance, thunder rumbled and the summer storm, never far away, pawed the ground like an angry bull preparing to charge.

The analogy was apt, thought Claudia. This whole place reminded her of the lair of the Minotaur, and not just on account of the thunder. So many tiny lamps – thousands upon thousands dotted round – coupled with the moving torches and the swirling wheels and censers turned the commune into an unfamiliar maze and, just like the Minotaur's labyrinth on Crete, she was going round in circles. But somewhere in this flickering web was an aristocrat dressed like a guard and a bodyguard dressed like an aristocrat, surely one of the two would stand out, even in the dark?

The bull roared louder, and the earth trembled with his bellow.

Dammit, for the third time, possibly the fourth, Claudia found herself back at the ceremonial pool, where the High Priest blessed the holy water and the women, including Mercy, chanted out their prayers as they sat in vigil through the night. One of the temple parakeets screeched inside its cage and shook its feathers, then the aviary fell still. Only the cicadas and the chanting competed with the thunder.

Claudia fumbled her way out through the wicker gate which

enclosed the temple forecourt and wedged her torch into a terracotta ear. Damned thing was neither use nor ornament, she couldn't see with it and she couldn't see without it, so she might as well have both hands free in case— She pulled up short. In case of what, Claudia? She shivered, because she didn't know and that was the horror of it.

The not knowing . . .

The nameless dread she felt inside but couldn't – wouldn't – allow her mind to dwell on for too long.

What's that? She squinted into the gloom. That figure, in the silver cloak which billowed out behind, was one she didn't recognise. Not a member of the Holy Council – she was familiar with the cow, the jackal, the ugly crocodile, and Mentu's mask was gold. This figure wore a mask of silver and a shimmering silver-plated wig, whose dreadlocks tinkled like a thousand sistrum bells. Curious, Claudia followed the figure with her eyes, surprised that it did not turn into the temple forecourt but swept on past, unaware of her presence in the shadows. This figure was not disoriented by the labyrinthine lamps. It marched with purpose across the grass towards the bushes.

Claudia felt a beat of unease pound inside her heart. Unless she missed her guess, that figure also clutched a bundle of white rags in his left hand. They looked like bandages.

The beat grew stronger. And as she watched the figure disappear into the bushes, she felt compelled to follow. He (Claudia presumed it was a he) was not difficult to spot – the silver glittered like a full moon in the dark, but that alone would not have been sufficient. The figure carried with it a tiny lighted brand to guide his path. Claudia followed the glow-worm up the hillside, along what seemed to be a beaten track. An assignation?

(Which reminds me, Min, how *are* the blisters coming on?)

Oh, damn, I've lost him! Up here, it was so dark she could not see her hand in front of her face, and there was no longer any glow to follow.

Hot and weary from the climb, Claudia leaned her weight against a tree and listened. For a minute, all she could hear was the blood pumping through her ears, then – was that a voice? It was. A man's. Talking deep and low, but strangely. There was no answering female. (Or male, come to that!) As she acclimatised to the terrain, Claudia realised the path looped round.

'Ouch!'

She rubbed the toe she'd stubbed against a heart-shaped stone and thought she saw a luminescence in the bushes. Correction, through the bushes! There was a horrible smell coming from somewhere, too, but it didn't put the man off singing.

Lost! Lost! Lost! My love is lost to me.
She passes by my house and does not turn to see.

Nice voice, but what's it doing behind a bloody bush?

Sweet! Sweet! Sweet! Her lips upon my mouth.
But now my heart is scorched, as the desert to the south.

Acoustics such as these are usually achieved by an echo like . . . well, like in a cave! Claudia shrugged. But then, why shouldn't there be a cave up here? The ancient Etruscans who had once worked these lands, pockmarked hills left, right and centre. In fact, in the vineyard adjacent to Claudia's own estate, they'd gouged out so many holes that the vintner used the whole damned hill for storage. Why shouldn't Mister Silver use one for his assignation?

Ra! Ra! Ra! O Father, great of might!
My sacrifice and prayers, do not they you delight?

Claudia listened to the haunting refrain of a young man

thrown over by his lover and whose heart aches because she will not take him back, despite his fervent prayers. Perhaps, though, the mysterious silver figure was not bent on an amorous liaison. Why the need for so much pomp if he was just after a fumble in the dark? Perhaps, like the ancient Etruscans, this cave was used for the Brothers' ceremonies – an extension to the Festival of Lamps? After all, if the Etruscans turned caverns into temples, why not the Pyramidiots? Claudia had only *assumed* this figure was up to something secretive and furtive.

Come! Come! Come! Death come to me, today.
For only in my tomb can I find the peace I pray.

That was the other thing, of course. The Etruscans also used their caves for burials, and Claudia could well believe it of this one. She did not recall ever smelling such a putrid stink!

Above her head, the man repeated the tune and Claudia had the strangest feeling that he was whistling while he worked. Worked at what? There was only one way to find out. Go and take a peep!

But before she had taken one step across the heart-shaped stone, the puff of light was extinguished. There was a rustle of greenery, then the silver figure emerged into view. Quickly, Claudia crouched behind a bush. The figure passed so close, the hem of his billowing cloak brushed her cheek, and it smelled only of myrrh and cloves, the commune unguent. Claudia waited until he was out of sight, then, humming, 'Lost! Lost! Lost! My love is lost to me', softly under her breath, climbed higher up the path.

'Janus!' Overcome by the hideous stench, she pinched her nostrils between her thumb and forefinger. What the hell's this bugger up to?

The cave was behind what looked like a wild fig, but as Claudia tried to scramble through the branches, the whole bush sprang away, to reveal the entrance. The stench was loathsome. The ancients used to paint their cavern walls with scenes of riotous celebrations, but that smell isn't paint . . . more like rotting meat!

Squinting eyes made out the table. Sweet Janus, what evil practice are they up to? The Holy Council wearing tight, white costumes were seated round it, wearing their masks and . . . and what? Making some kind of magic, obviously, and using god-knows-what filthy brew. Claudia was now gagging on the smell, but strange. Her retching did not alert the seated group. Slowly Claudia realised the figures were not moving. Stuffed dolls? Or . . . or . . .

She could not help the strangled scream which escaped her.

Trembling violently, Claudia counted the figures round the table. Eight. Holy Jupiter, until now, they had believed only seven girls were missing.

She buried her hands in her face. Tell me it's not true. Sweet Janus, tell me this is some sort of doll council. That some madman hasn't abducted eight young girls and killed them. 'What else do you think would cause this vile stench?' a little voice sneered. 'You said yourself, it smelled like rotten meat.' Claudia refused to hear the truth and stuffed her fingers in her ears. No, she screamed silently back, these are stuffed replicas. These are not mummified remains! 'Really?' the voice inside her asked. 'Then why was he bringing bandages up here?'

Claudia's teeth were chattering. Eight girls, not seven. Who – she closed her eyes – who was number eight?

She reeled away, flattening herself against the hard rock face, because already she knew the answer to her question. Oh, Flavia! All the things she'd planned to say to her – about the worry she'd heaped upon her anxious step-parents, how selfish she'd been to betray Junius just for a few gold coins to throw in Mentu's money box and what did she think she was playing at, the selfish cow? I'm so sorry, Flavia, I didn't mean them. I didn't really mean them.

Tears rolled in rivers down her cheeks.

Fifteen years old and she'd ended up the eighth victim of the most perverted killer ever to have walked this earth. Poor

Flavia, she hadn't lived! Never sailed the oceans, never felt the soft touch of a man. *Or had she?* And Claudia knew the answer to that question, too.

Scrubbing her tears away with the back of her hand, Claudia forced herself to look at the table once again. There's something wrong with the tableau. Eight white bodies, but . . . but one of them wasn't white from bandages. One of them was white from naked flesh, glistening in the dark.

Racing across the stone floor, her heart hammering, it occurred to her that it was possible, just possible, that Flavia wasn't dead yet. Using both hands, she hauled off the jackal mask.

And screamed.

The face did not, after all, belong to little Flavia. The face was thin, the complexion flawless, the cropped hair tawny brown.

His eighth victim was Flca.

Pain speared through her. White hot, searing, it ripped and clawed and savaged at her breast.

Oh, Flea, Flea. What have I done?

Claudia cupped her hands around the urchin's cheeks. They were warm, but they were not warm with life. Those luminous green eyes bulged forward, her tongue protruded from her lips. And the ligature around her neck told its own horrific story.

She felt her head spin. Flea, Flea, what terrible price did I make you pay? What was I thinking of, bringing you here? Orbilio's description echoed inside her head: 'Wild child.' Skinny – scrawny – foul-mouthed – funny. She thought of the feral beast, wielding a knife down the cul-de-sac because she'd been trapped. Trapped. Flea was born to be free. To be wild . . .

Suddenly, in the midst of her horror and her grief, Claudia caught a whiff. Scent. Myrrh and cloves.

She made to turn, but something flashed before her eyes and closed around her neck.

'Wha—'

The word was cut off sharp. The ligature tightened. She tore at the cord. Heard heavy breathing. She heard a wailing in her ears, and a drumming.

Someone said, 'I have you now, my pretty one. You belong to Seth.' But Claudia was not listening.

Her legs thrashed out. She at clawed the air, there was a monumental roaring in her ears. With a twist, she arched herself backwards, kicking, writhing. The noose continued to tighten. She heard a rasping sound. A rattle. And knew it came from her own throat. A fire burst behind her eyes.

Then everything turned black.

Chapter Thirty-four

Marcus found it hurt when he tried to sit up. It hurt his ribs, it hurt his head, it hurt his numbed arm from where he'd been lying on it. But most of all, it hurt that he had failed Claudia.

And now it was dark. He must have been unconscious for hours. He rubbed tenderly at his poor cracked ribs, and as he did so, became aware of movement on the grain. A shadow, darker than the rest, fell over him. He reached for his weapon, but the scimitar had gone.

'I took it,' the voice said. 'In case anyone came in.'

Orbilio blinked. '*Flavia?*'

'You came to rescue me, didn't you?' Her eyes were bright from emotion. 'I recognised you immediately, even though you were in disguise. I *knew* you'd come to save me.'

The emotion, he realised, was neither relief nor satisfaction and he remembered that, although he'd only figured once in Flavia's short life, she'd had something of a crush on him. Obviously, the passage of several months had made little difference to her feelings! He groaned, and this time it was not from pain.

'I would have brought you water,' she said, crouching down beside him and wiping a damp curl from his forehead, 'only I didn't want to leave you. Spies, you see, have to face death by Ordeal of the Lakes. That means they first roast you on a spit over the Lake of Hellfire, then they boil you alive.'

Orbilio felt he ought to be grateful. Instead he snatched the scimitar from her hands. 'Give me that,' he said brusquely. Dammit, the girl wasn't even holding it properly.

'Here, let me.' Eagerly, Flavia helped him to his feet. He towered over her.

'Are you responsible for this?' he asked, rubbing the goose egg which had risen up behind his ear.

'Me?' The idea horrified her. 'Flea did that.'

She would, he thought. Act first, think later, that was that little street thief's motto! 'I suppose she saw me in uniform, and thought I was part of the act.'

'Did you know she was a girl?' Flavia looked puzzled. 'I had no idea, until she pulled me out of the coal hole.'

Even though it hurt his ribs, Orbilio grinned. What a pair, those two! And what a difference ten years makes. Suddenly he felt old enough to be their father. Weary enough, too . . .

'The pair of you deserve a damned good spanking,' he said, although he had a feeling his voice lacked the authority he meant it to carry. 'You for running off, her for knocking me out cold.'

'I told her, you'd come to rescue me,' Flavia gushed, trying unsuccessfully to link her arm in his. 'She said afterwards that she was sorry.'

Like hell, he thought, putting his foot on the rope ladder. Flea would be glad to get her own back. Dammit, he liked Flea. He imagined that was what Claudia had been like at that age, too. Feisty, spunky, sharp and streetwise. But with more intelligence!

'Where's Claudia?'

'Is she here, too?' Flavia spiralled into a sulk.

'So's Junius,' Marcus added happily.

'Is he mad at me?'

Orbilio heaved himself on to the gallery which ran around the grain store. 'What do you think?' he asked mildly. 'You left the poor sap to die.'

'But –' Flavia's face was deep red, and he hoped it was not purely from the exertion of climbing the ladder. 'But he was only wearing a toga,' she said.

'For a slave, that incurs the death penalty,' Orbilio said, 'so you'd best be nice to him from now on. Now keep close and follow me. Uh, you don't need to keep that close.' He disengaged her arms from round his waist, and thought it doesn't take long, crush transference. One day she's in love with Ra, now it's me again. Now if it was the other Seferius woman snuggling up against me in the dark.

'What's so damned funny?' Junius, stepping from the shadows, did not let his harsh eyes so much as drop to Flavia.

'Where's Claudia?' Marcus fired back.

'She's not with you?'

Another time, Orbilio would have enjoyed watching his opponent squirm. But tonight the stakes were not coins, they were not even human emotions. The stake was flesh and blood and had long tumbling curls.

Quickly he explained to Junius how Flea had mistaken him for part of the commune security force, how she'd discovered Flavia's hiding place and, finally, how Flavia had sat with him until he came to consciousness. 'Why weren't you bloody guarding her?'

'She told me to stay put,' the Gaul growled back, and Marcus knew this was not the time to fight.

'That woman,' he said, spiking his fingers through his curls, 'is a law unto herself. Let's find her and move out.'

'She'll be with Flea,' Flavia suggested. 'And Flea won't leave without some puppy she's got herself attached to. Let's try the stables.'

Doodlebug went wild, but there was no trace of two spirited young women.

'Here.' Orbilio slipped a leash around its neck and handed the puppy over to Flavia. 'You stay here with him.' To Junius he said, 'We'll organise a search. You take from here northwards, I'll take the southern half. Meet you in an hour.'

The young Gaul also felt the stakes were too high to fight over. 'No point,' he said. 'I've covered every goddamned inch, they're not here,' he added solemnly, 'and I'm worried. Gut-wrenching worried, if the truth were told.'

Whey-faced, he outlined Claudia's theories about the missing girls and her suspicions about the overseers. He did not say that he feared his mistress and the street thief had also been abducted, but Marcus read it in his face and in his voice. Flavia had begun to weep, noisily and clumsily. Doodlebug moved to the end of his leash.

'She did,' Junius added, 'organise six henchmen to stay on red alert. They're stationed on the far side of the hills.'

'No point in hanging about, then,' Marcus said miserably. 'Let's call the cavalry. Do you know the signal?'

'Inspired by *The Serving Women*,' Junius fired a venomous glance at Flavia, 'it's a fire.'

'What about the guards?' wailed Flavia. 'No one can get in or out, we're all trapped. Doomed. Destined to die.'

'Leave the guards to me,' Marcus said, selecting a stout club from the rack on the stable wall. 'I'll open that double set of gates so wide, the cavalry will be able to drive in through the front door.' Someone must be hiding the two women! They can't just disappear! 'Junius. While I'm playing with the portals, you start the fire.'

'Fire, singular? Man, I'm going to burn every fucking *building* to the ground!'

'Then make sure you search them thoroughly beforehand,' Orbilio added dryly.

But it was only while he was sprinting towards the gate, armed with his club and scimitar, that it occurred to him that he might be able to take this thing one stage further. That there was a way to destroy this commune beyond simply its physical construction.

'What I need,' he said to himself, 'is access to that big bronze tortoise.'

Chapter Thirty-five

When Claudia came to, she was surprised to find that she was not on a ferry boat on that one-way trip across the River Styx. No three-headed dog barked, no ghosts walked up to welcome her, there was no slap-slap-slap of oars on dark, grey, oily water.

She wished there was.

Because this was worse than death. This was living hell. As thunder rumbled in the background, she tried to move and found she'd been trussed up and gagged and that the harder she struggled, the deeper the bonds bit into her flesh. Her *naked* flesh. She stopped struggling at once.

You fool. You silly, bloody fool. The minute you realised what you'd walked into here, you should also have realised that he'd have heard your scream. What was he going to do? Ignore it? But so shocked had Claudia been by this whole tableau, so sickened by the discovery beneath the jackal mask that she hadn't been able to control herself.

Now she was about to pay the ultimate price.

Claudia began to shudder uncontrollably. And what of Flea? What price did that poor bitch have to pay? You led her to this. Her death is your fault, you should not have brought her to this evil valley. You should not have interfered! She flashed a glance to the girl's body with the black jackal's head.

Sixteen and thinks she knows it all. Imagines she can handle every problem life dishes out, that she is tough. But, hell, she isn't – w*asn't*. Flea was young and vulnerable, she needed protecting and you failed her. When she needed you most, you bloody failed her.

But all I wanted was to save her from a life of misery and wretchedness living off the streets.

Well, you saved her that all right. You condemned her to a terrifying death . . .

Claudia felt a tidal wave of nausea wash over her. What would Flea have felt, when the noose tightened round her neck? Did she die cursing Claudia? Claudia gulped back the sobs. Knowing Flea, she'd have died cursing herself.

Oh, Flea. What have I done? I set a sparrow among the hawks, and I deserve to suffer for your death. All I ask, oh mighty Jupiter, is that you let me see the face behind the silver mask before I die that I may return to haunt it.

She closed her eyes and tried to push back time. To forget the present, disregard the future, to go back – back – where life was full of childhood innocence, to a place of long-forgotten memories, of adolescent pranks and children laughing . . . Except time refused to budge, and the present throbbed with pain and heat and horror . . . Which bastard set this hellish table? What demon was so sick that he was beyond being wicked – perhaps, even, beyond evil? Suddenly, the nausea threatened to engulf her. The mind behind this invidious tableau was quite insane.

A man can never have too much power, she thought. Was it Min? Second in command, but nevertheless still second. Reporting to a younger brother went against nature and the grain. 'Never underestimate my power,' he'd hissed. 'Never misjudge the influence I carry.' And don't forget that lightning switch of personality. 'I never force a woman,' he had boasted. Claudia thought of her leather bonds which tightened with the slightest exertion. The same knot which she'd noticed round Flea's neck! Sweet Janus, the killer didn't force his victims. As they struggled for breath, they slowly strangled themselves.

Her shoulders began to shake involuntarily, tightening the bonds. Blood drizzled down her wrists and dripped off her fingertips. The rabbit face of Penno flashed before her. Preoccupied with rites and rituals – and with Seth in particular – he re-enacted ceremonies in the privacy of his own room. Were they *only* fantasies? Whoever planned this tableau needed to work in hurried snatches, and Claudia's stomach lurched at Penno's twig-like fingers wrapping rolls and rolls of linen over these poor brutalised bodies.

Bandages! These were Shabak's speciality, look at the way he dressed Geb's scald – tight, fast and utterly professional. And he'd know all about knots, would Friend Bluejaw. As the commune doctor, who'd be better placed to coax the trust from vulnerable young women? Women such as Berenice, who'd accept medication for her baby without suspecting it was poison. With a squad of eager helpers waiting for his commands, Shabak would not risk being absent for too long and suddenly Claudia saw the swarthy medic embalming 'patients' in his secret cave. *Whistling* while he worked.

Or was Neco's curious whistle the last sound these girls heard? Neco, who loathed himself so much that he stripped the very flesh off his own back in penance. Why do you hate yourself so much, Neco? Is it because of what you've done to these poor girls? Don't think I don't know what the bleeding and the bruising and the (holy Janus!) bites signify on Flea's young flesh. You rape them and you torture them, mentally and physically, and then you walk away and let them choke themselves to death. Is that why you whip yourself, Neco? To dull the pain inside your twisted mind?

What was it Min said of Neco? Doesn't tolerate familiarity. Of course not. Men like the killer don't. They can't. Intimacy is incomprehensible to them, they—

Claudia's heart fluttered. What was that? Footsteps. A whistle. A brisk rubbing of hands. *Sweet Jupiter, whose hands?* A light flickered in the distance. Growing nearer. Nearer . . .

Despite her gag, despite the gnawing bonds, Claudia gasped.

Of the men she had suspected, this surely was the lowest on her list and yet, dear lord, she should have guessed! Her heart began to thump. Who had access to the kitchen staff and was in charge of the commune's security? Who was so desperate to keep the guards out of the valley? Who'd be worried sick about any potential breach in the security? Only one man. The man who would not want them stumbling across a certain ancient cave.

Claudia could only stare as his broad, hairy hands pulled back the foliage from the scrambling fig across the entrance. The first night she arrived, the night she'd helped Shabak bandage the burn, Geb's hair had been damp, she remembered. It was raining that night. He'd just come in from the rain. *Just come in from killing Berenice.*

In the entrance to the cavern, the Keeper of the Central Store held up his torch, his eyes wide and manic, his skin shining with sweat. That bruise on his knuckles . . . she'd spotted it, and never thought to question its cause. Her heart was crashing wildly now, skipping several beats. Let it be quick, she prayed. Please let it be quick.

His eyes made contact with Claudia's.

Her heart stopped.

With a grunt, he lunged forward and ripped off Claudia's gag. 'What the hell—'

Fffff.

The sound was so soft, Claudia barely heard it. Like a swish of cotton, or a light exhalation of breath, the sound was soft and sensuous in the silence of the cave.

As though captured on a marble frieze, everything happened in slow motion. Geb's eyes bulged. He teetered on his feet. Then slowly – oh, so slowly – the Keeper of the Central Store pitched forward. With an arrow protruding from his back.

Her heart began to grind back into action, each beat like a blacksmith's hammer on the forge. 'Marcus! Oh, Marcus, thank the gods you found me.' She owed him one for this, she really did!

But—

In the flickering light of Geb's torch, her eyes caught a flash of silver. Her marrow turned to ice.

No one had come to save her. Geb wasn't the killer.

Perhaps attracted by the light, perhaps attracted by the unfamiliar silver mask, Geb – like Claudia – had merely stumbled on the cave. His eyes, she realised now, had been bright from drink, not from insanity, she'd caught a blast of palm wine on his breath when he ripped away her gag. Geb had been as surprised as she was!

'Always like to keep a bow handy.' The silver figure glided into the cave. 'In fact, I had to put an arrow through a dog the other day. Caught a whiff, y'see.' He indicated the figures round the table. 'After that I had to lock the buggers up. Yours with it.'

'W-why haven't you killed me?' Claudia's voice was little more than a whisper.

'Tut, tut, girl. Mustn't believe that tosh 'bout Seth being the Devourer of Souls.' The silver figure leaned over the inert form of Geb and didn't seem to notice that Claudia's gag was gone. 'Seth doesn't kill, my child. He is not a beast like Anubis there, or Bast. Even this –' Placing one foot on Geb's back, he hauled the arrow out and, outside, thunder masked the groan the big man made. He doesn't realise, Claudia thought, the silver killer doesn't realise that Geb is still alive! 'This was self-defence,' said Seth, brushing Geb's blood from his costume. 'Must apologise if you feel I'm tardy in consummating our relationship, my dear, but you will receive my holy seed, I promise. You see, I have something really special planned for you, Osiris.'

'*Osiris?*'

The silver figure misunderstood her question. 'Oh yes, Osiris must be last, because he's the only other human god present at the table. Isis over there was first, then the animals followed after – of course, their order was not important – but the ceremony must end with Osiris. Begin and end with the human gods. Begin and end with the humans.'

Silver hands picked up the gold mask and held it to the tiny light he'd brought, and while he admired it, Claudia's teeth began to chatter. This went far beyond sex and control, this was about domination of *souls.*

'Osiris thinks he's the son of Ra, y'see, but Seth is Ra's true son. He's shown me the path to eternal resurrection and soon the people will realise that Mentu is nothing but a Pharaoh over fools, the King of Clowns, a con man. Only Seth has the power over immortality, and I –' he stretched out his silver sleeves – 'am prepared to confer this immortality on you, my chosen Council. Together –' he reached for a small pot in the middle of the table – 'the eleven of us will control the destiny of mankind. Together we can rule the future.'

'And the past?'

'The past is nothing,' he said, dipping a brush in the contents. 'The future is spread across the heavens and Seth alone can read the magic written in the stars. Seth alone knows the secret spell.'

Slowly he began to stroke the paintbrush over Claudia's face, and she knew the colour would be blue.

Bright eyes glittered behind the silver mask. 'The future is my power and the future belongs to me,' he intoned quietly. 'And soon, very soon, my child, this future will be yours.'

Finishing his artwork, he stepped back to admire it, oblivious to the thunder and the white strikes of lightning.

'I have been twice blessed tonight,' he said, cheerfully touching up Claudia's cheek, one brushstroke here, another there. 'First, the jackal comes trotting like a tame dog,' he chuckled, giving Flea's mask an affectionate pat. 'Saw her, y'know, running down to the kennels. So easy to convince her I'd taken the puppy away to comfort it when it took fright during the storm, kept him safe up here in this cave. Then what do you know? Ra delivers you to my table, allowing me to advance the divine schedule.'

Slowly he placed the golden mask of Osiris, god of the underworld, over Claudia's head.

'Soon, my child, I shall return with the final member of our Holy Council and you can each watch while I implant my sacred seed inside the vulture.'

The mask was heavy. Suffocating. Heaven only knows what the others must have felt, weighted beneath the heavy animal heads. But at least Claudia's mouth was free. Who, in this storm, would hear her scream?

In the doorway, the silver figure paused. 'I've never watched before, but at the end it will be fitting, don't you think? Seth, Master of the Darkness, observing while Osiris makes his final choice.'

'Ch-choice?'

'To die, and thus follow the path to eternal resurrection. Or live and face eternal desolation in the desert of mankind.'

Under the mask, Claudia felt herself sway. Did he not realise that no one could survive these knots? She watched him disappear into the thunderstorm and prayed a bolt of lightning would strike this sicko dead.

At her feet, Geb stirred. 'Has he . . .' his voice was faint. 'Has he gone?' He'd lost a lot of blood, and the very fact that the arrow had been pulled out had signed his death warrant.

'Yes.' Claudia swallowed. She wondered if he knew how badly he was hurt. 'Geb, I know this will be agony for you, but you've got to help me. Please!'

'How?' Even to speak was excruciating for him.

'Untie my hands.'

'Can't – move.'

'I can shuffle closer.' Each lurch drove the leather thongs deeper into her naked flesh. She felt blood dribble down her arms and thighs. There was blood in her mouth, too, from biting on her lip. One more jump and the chair would be within his reach.

'Can't –' he rasped, 'can't move.'

Claudia felt panic rise in her breast. This was her only chance! Seth would be back any minute. Think, think – somehow you must get Geb to help you. 'You killed your wife,' she said.

Geb's head jerked in surprise. 'You know?'

Yes, but the next bit was a gamble. 'You joined this commune to atone for your sin, didn't you?'

'Her fault,' he whispered. 'Didn't stop me. She – made me hit her. One day – too hard. Dead. Blamed her until I found the Brothers. Know now that abstinence and – aargh! – penance will make my heart weigh light at the balance.'

Jupiter, forgive me, I have no other choice. 'You imagine that a few paltry months overseeing the domestic running of this commune constitutes penance?' Claudia forced grit into her voice. 'Dammit, Geb, you bullied and browbeat everyone to get your own way!'

'Not my way. *The* way. We – must all suffer and endure.' His voice was growing fainter. The pool of blood beneath him creeping ever larger.

'But you haven't suffered, Geb. You killed your wife and then you got this cushy job, and all you've done is try and convert others to the path.'

Kicking a man when he was down was bad. When he was on the point of death was unspeakable. Claudia screwed up her eyes and pressed on.

'If you really want your heart to weigh light – and Geb, I have to tell you, those scales will be here soon – then you must suffer pain to win atonement. You must set me free, or Seth will gobble up your soul.'

'Too late. Don't – care.'

'Then care that he'll bloody gobble mine, you selfish oaf!'

A look of utter astonishment crossed his waxy, anguished face. Then incredibly, and with superhuman effort, Geb crawled towards her, inch by inch.

'Thank you,' she wanted to whisper, but the words would not come past the lump in her throat. Every tiny movement wracked his body and every time he winced, Claudia winced with him. She shuffled the chair round towards him. Slowly he raised his body, and Claudia blanched at the raw wound in his chest, at the blood and lumps of tissue matted in his hairy chest.

She felt his bloody fingers fumbling on the knots. Please, she prayed. Please let him have the strength to undo them – It seemed to take for ever, and the pain was excruciating, because the leather bit even deeper into her skin every time she flinched, but suddenly her hands were free, and she was throwing off the golden mask and tackling the knots around her waist and ankles.

'You've saved my life,' she said. 'Geb, I—'

But he couldn't hear. Geb, the Keeper of the Central Store, lay dead, a radiant smile upon his face.

Trembling hands closed his half-open eyes and Claudia prayed his heart would indeed weigh light, wherever it was bound. She reached for her shift.

'Going somewhere, little lady?'

The silver figure in the entrance dropped the unconscious woman in his arms. Claudia recognised the white robes of a priestess.

'The killing's over, you sick bastard.'

'Sick? I am *Seth*,' the figure roared. 'Master of the Darkness, the Sorcerer, the Measurer of Time.'

'You can call yourself whatever names you damn well like, but I'm telling you, it's finished. Over. Done with.'

Flea was your last conquest. Geb, your final casualty.

'You?' The silver cloak trembled with rage, the silver plaits tinkled in his anger. '*You* can't stop me. *Nobody can!*'

'Oh, that's where you're wrong.' Claudia picked up the little light which had guided Geb here. 'I'm going to stop your evil practice right here and now.' She threw the lantern at the mummy wearing the head of the cat. The bandages caught alight at once.

'No!' The eyes behind the silver mask grew wide. '*No!*'

Sparks from Bast's fur danced in the air, and even while Seth screamed in disbelief and fury, one caught the feathers of the falcon, Horus. Two bodies began to burn. The stench was putrid.

'Bitch! I'll kill you for this,' he hissed. 'I'll kill you slowly, painfully, I'll have you die a traitor's death, roasted alive then boiled, but with you, I'll have the water heated slowly, no boiling oil for you, you bitch, you traitor, you!'

Move, dammit. He was still blocking the entrance. And the priestess still lay unconscious. Claudia had a feeling he'd kill her out of spite.

With a soft whoosh, a third mummy caught alight, and now the fumes and the smoke, trapped by the fig across the entrance, were unbearable. She began to splutter and retch. Seth, closer to the fresher air, stood confident. She had to make him move. Somehow, she had to get out of this cave before she passed out completely.

'All my work destroyed by one meddling bitch,' he snarled, kicking the unconscious priestess in the ribs. 'I'll flay you alive before I roast and boil you, I'll have you scream for mercy, but you wait – I'll show you none. No one,' he hissed, 'messes with the Dark Destroyer.'

'Except Mentu.'

'Mentu?' The silver figure leaned towards her. 'Mentu's nothing but a con man, think that weakling frightens me?'

Claudia swallowed the revolting fumes and smoke. 'Oh, yes,' she said quietly. 'He frightens you very much indeed. You've fought with him all your life, tried to prove that you're superior to him, but he's the one with all the money. He's the one who lives in luxury with his fine wines and his women, while you skulk in this cold, damp cave and move unrecognised among the people.'

'They'll know me soon enough. Or would have, before you interfered. I'll have to start all over, now, you bitch!'

Isis began to burn, pumping out more noxious fumes and foul smoke.

Claudia fought the nausea which churned in her stomach and her throat. Move, you bastard. Move away from the entrance! But the silver figure, gulping in the cleaner air, calmly stood its ground. 'You'll have to make a run for it soon,' he snarled. 'And then you're mine, you bitch. By all that's holy, you'll be mine, and I'll make you pay for this.'

'You know, don't you, that Mentu will never bend his knee to you? That no matter whether you make Osiris the first or last god at your table, he will never bow to you?'

'Oh, yes he will.' She'd touched a nerve. The silver figure clenched his fists. 'When his time comes to die, he'll know that Seth is his master and that he'll hold dominion over him for all eternity.'

The cow sprang into flames, her long horns arching outwards

through the flames. Donata, Claudia thought. That's Donata burning . . .

The smoke was choking now, she could hardly breathe. She'd have to fight him on his terms.

Picking up the high-backed chair he'd tied her to, she swished it over poor Donata's burning corpse. The dry rushes caught immediately, and with the chair on fire, she rushed at the figure in the entrance. He darted to one side, crashing into the branches of the fig. The outside air rushed in and fanned the flames.

'What's happening?' The priestess was coming round. 'What—' She began to cough and splutter.

Seth grabbed her and used her as a shield.

The rush chair was burning close to Claudia's hands. She could not attack, she'd burn the girl. Seth was laughing now. She hurled the remnants of the chair at the black jackal mask. If it was the last thing she would do, it would be to ensure Flea was cremated properly. Flames licked up the dog's long snout and pricked up ears. She could not bear to watch the rest. By her feet, Geb's long hair began to singe. The cave had become an inferno.

And shit – *Seth was going to block her in it!*

While Claudia had been concerned with cremating Flea, he'd knocked out the priestess and tossed her in the corner and was now sealing up the entrance to the cave.

The heat was intense, the smoke smothering her lungs. She pushed against the fig, but he'd used his special knots to anchor it. Another three or four and she'd be imprisoned.

Suddenly, by the mouth of the cave she saw the arrow he'd pulled out of Geb. Gripping it by its bloody shaft, she stabbed with all her might. Seth gargled as the point went in his throat. He teetered. His hands flew to the shaft, still clutched in Claudia's hand. And as he lurched forward, she pressed harder. With a spurt, the barb came out through his flesh.

Biting on her lower lip, she twisted, and with a rattle, Seth fell to his knees. He twitched and writhed, and finally fell still.

'Quick!' She grabbed the groggy priestess and pushed against the last corner of the fig. 'Hurry, before this catches fire, too.'

They scrambled through the branches, and the girl gasped when the saw the inert silver figure. 'Who's that?' she cried. 'Who the hell is he?'

'Who?' With a short laugh, Claudia jerked off the figure's silver mask. 'It's Mentu himself,' she said.

Who else could it be?

Chapter Thirty-six

Most men wrestle with their consciences. In Mentu's case, he'd spent his whole life wrestling with the dual facets of his own split personality.

At last, Claudia understood what Min meant when he'd talked about the influence he carried in this commune. He was referring to the very necessary control he'd need to have over his younger, more unstable brother. They had set up this scam between them, Min and Mentu. A means of making money, but Min soon became aware that, for his brother, the commune meant much more than a simple get-rich-quick scheme. The role of Pharaoh had taken him over, sucked him in as much as it had sucked in the cult members who contributed so generously to their Solar Fund.

Mentu would have been the one to ensnare skilled craftsmen. He would have been the one to extend the buildings, to enrol members from as far afield as Naples and Brindisi. Min would have been all for a year or two on the gravy train, then pulling out. Not so his younger, headstrong brother.

It wasn't difficult to decide which of the two should be the Pharaoh. Mentu was a born showman, Min more the backroom puller of strings, but in fairness, neither could have predicted its tragic outcome.

In a way, thought Claudia, staring at the birthmark on his face, Mentu was as much a victim as his Pyramidiots, taken over by the very showmanship he'd used to control the members' minds. Which was not to say she felt sorry for the bastard! But what had started out as a common-or-garden illusion, the faking of his own death, had grown into an obsession with resurrection and the afterlife. Reality became distorted. He believed himself the Pharaoh of his people, Osiris incarnate, son of Ra. And as Ra battled with the serpent, so Osiris battled with his antithesis. Good and evil, order and anarchy, light and dark. Even the cave symbolised this duality. Luxury swapped for sparseness. Mentu had his pick of women, Seth had to lure them. For Mentu, they'd spread their bodies on his couch, naked and compliant. For Seth, they struggled all the way. And for Seth, they died. No one died for Mentu, even as Osiris . . . that made Seth omnipotent.

At what stage did he consider setting out his grisly table? Perhaps the first body had given him the idea, and the belief in his powers had grown. Perhaps he truly believed, as any self-respecting paranoid schizophrenic would, that 'they' were after him. The Romans. The enemy. Out to get him.

And on a purely practical level (and Seth was nothing if not practical!), he would ensure that the overseers were men in his own mould. Min, of course. Callous, manipulative and ruthless. Shabak, the doctor who healed without compassion, because healing was A Good Thing and would secure him a place in the afterlife. Penno, the pernickety sneak of a temple warden, happy to report back on what the terracotta ears had heard. Neco. Probably a repressed homosexual, venting his spite on the world and himself. And Geb – Claudia could find no word to say against the man who died saving her life. The man whose corpse burned inside the cave, alongside little Flea's.

Flea, who would never cuddle Doodlebug again . . .

Claudia broke a branch off the fig tree and held it close to the fire until it caught alight. Then she held it to the silver cloak. Could Seth gobble up his own soul, when his heart clanked like a stone upon the balance? What the hell. She tossed the burning branch on to his chest. They'd made the whole religion up, picking bits of this and bits of that and tacking them together. Just like that Festival of Lamps down there.

She glanced through the trees. Lamps? She blinked, and blinked again. Those weren't lamps. Juno, Jupiter and Mars – the whole damned commune was on fire!

She skidded back down the narrow, twisty path. Screaming carried louder than the thunderclaps. As she approached the temple compound, Claudia heard a voice booming out across the commune.

'Hear me, for I am Jupiter. You have betrayed my trust, and the chariots of Mars shall charge among you and the fires of Vulcan raze this place to the ground.'

Thunder rumbled overhead, lightning bolts shot through the heavens and – incredibly – horsemen came riding through the open gates. Six of them! Is this happening? Is Jupiter really talking to us? But wait. There was something about the voice. Something cultivated. Something familiar . . .

'Your idols shall tumble.'

More screams broke out when the two alabaster sphinxes toppled sideways. In the flickering light of flames, Claudia could see the ropes. But where was the voice coming from? So loud, so deep, so . . .

'So very like a tortoise!'

'Flattery,' said Orbilio, wiping the smuts from his nose, 'will get you everywhere. Excuse me, while I crawl back into my shell.'

Claudia wriggled in alongside him, and felt the warmth from his body pressing against hers like a current in a turbulent sea.

'I won't ask,' he said, and his voice echoed in the hollow chamber, 'how you acquired a blue face, but even the Serving Women didn't set the bloody hills alight.'

'There weren't any wild fig trees locally, I had to take up mountaineering.'

'It had to be a fig?' He was studying the raw wheals on her arms.

'You know me. Stickler for authenticity.' He smelled good, she thought. Smoke and sandalwood make a heady combination, even in a dead man's clothes. 'Some investigators, I see, will go to any lengths to get their profiles raised. You took that blaze-of-glory phrase literally, I gather.'

'When a Security Policeman's under house arrest for suspicion of murder, he has to take some pretty drastic action.'

'You don't consider dressing up as a woman drastic?'

'Only at weekends,' he fired back, his eyes locked on the broad band of bruising round her throat. 'I don't suppose, while you've been idling your time up there in the hills, that you've so much as given a thought as to whose might be the body in the plaster, let alone put a name to her killer?'

'Of course I have,' she quipped, 'but if I tell you that, it'll make me cleverer than you, and men don't like that in women. Now is this a private party, or can anyone join in?'

'Oh, be my guest,' he said, wriggling to give her access to the tortoise's open mouth. Her palms were moist, her stomach was in knots. It really was a strange sensation, feeling safe . . . but there was one more thing to do before she left this evil valley.

'Hear me,' she called, 'for I am Juno, Queen of Heaven.' Hey, the acoustics are good! 'To repay your disobedience, I shall destroy your Boat of Dreams.'

Grinning broadly from ear to ear, Orbilio tugged on a rope and to Claudia's delight the whole damned barque exploded. Cedarwood, oily and fragrant, sputtered and spat and sent out a spray of red sparks. Amethysts and emeralds, pearls and lapis lazuli grew black, and slowly the gold plating on the boat's high prow began to drizzle down the side.

What a waste . . .

'I don't know what that High Priest keeps in that moleskin pouch of his,' Claudia said, and her voice sounded husky, 'but it's pretty damned effective.'

'So are you,' he rasped, and she realised that, at some stage, his arm had closed around her shoulder. 'So the hell are you.'

Inside the bronze tortoiseshell, the two of them seemed locked together, eyes on eyes, nose to nose, body pressed to body.

'Marcus?'

There was a beat of perhaps five. 'Claudia?'

She could hear his ragged breathing, even over the tumbling of buildings, the crackle of the flames, the roaring thunderbolts. 'Marcus . . .' Will you always be here for me? 'Marcus . . .'

'Claudia?'

Will you always keep me safe? 'Marcus Cornelius, will you shift that damned pommel out my bloody way?'

And in their dark, bronze, private shell she heard him chuckle. 'That,' he said, 'is not my scimitar. Behave yourself.'

Behave?

Claudia Seferius?

You must be joking!

Derry Public Library
3 4504 00184199 9